W9-BNL-894

FEAR STREET SUPER THRILLER: NIGHTMARES

Also by R. L. Stine

SERIES

Goosebumps

Fear Street

Mostly Ghostly

The Nightmare Room

Rotten School

INDIVIDUAL TITLES

It's the First Day of School . . . Forever!

A Midsummer Night's Scream

Young Scrooge

Red Rain

Eye Candy

The Sitter

R. L. STINE

FEAR STREET SUPER THRILLER: NIGHTMARES

THE DEAD BOYFRIEND
AND
GIVE ME A K-I-L-L

ST. MARTIN'S GRIFFIN
NEW YORK

FEAR STREET SUPER THRILLER: NIGHTMARES: THE DEAD BOYFRIEND. Copyright © 2016 by Parachute Publishing, LLC. GIVE ME A K-I-L-L. Copyright © 2017 by Parachute Publishing, LLC. All rights reserved. Printed in the United States of America. For information, address St. Martin's Press, 175 Fifth Avenue, New York, N.Y. 10010.

www.stmartins.com

The Library of Congress Cataloging-in-Publication Data is available upon request.

ISBN 978-1-250-13424-0 (trade paperback)

Our books may be purchased in bulk for promotional, educational, or business use. Please contact your local bookseller or the Macmillan Corporate and Premium Sales Department at 1-800-221-7945, extension 5442, or by email at MacmillanSpecialMarkets@macmillan.com.

First Edition: August 2017

10 9 8 7 6 5 4 3 2 1

THE DEAD BOYFRIEND

For Blade

Many Happy Returns

PART
ONE

1.

*H*ere I am, my dear diary, about to confide in you again. About to spill my guts, as I always do, only to you. This is the only place I can open my heart and talk about what I really feel. How many ballpoint pens have helped me share my story with you? How many late nights have I nodded off, my head drooping over your opened pages, my hand still clenching the pen, as if I could write my thoughts in my sleep?

Of course, my parents don't understand why I spend so much time bent over my desk, scratching away line after line, baring my soul when I could be doing a million things for fun. But you do, my friend. *Sigh—*

Okay. Shall we start today with some details? Since this is a new diary, I'm going to begin at the beginning. I'm Caitlyn Donnelly. I'm seventeen, a senior at Shadyside High. I'm not terrible looking. I'd say I'm a seven.

I have nice wavy blondish hair that falls nicely down my shoulders. I'm average height and weight. I have an okay smile although my two front teeth stick out a little. My friend Julie says my eyes are my best feature because they're so round and dark and serious.

I've lived in the same house on Bank Street, two blocks from the Shadyside Mall, my whole life. It's just my parents and me. Jennifer, my older sister, moved to LA to be a screenwriter.

Jen is the talented one in the family, but so far, she spends most of her time waiting tables at a taco joint in Westwood. I think I spend more time writing than she does, but I know she'll get a break one of these days. She's very sophisticated and clever, and everything comes so easy to her.

Jen and I were never that close, I guess because she's almost six years older than me. But she was someone I could talk to when I had things on my mind. Like, always. And I miss her a lot.

We FaceTime every few weeks, but it isn't the same. It's always kind of awkward, I think because Jen feels she's been out in LA for nearly a year and hasn't come close to getting anyone interested in her writing. And she's the kind of person who hates to fail.

I don't care if anyone ever sees my writing, Diary. Truth is, I don't want anyone to *ever* see it. I think I'd totally freak if someone read my true thoughts and learned what a weirdo I am. That's why I keep the book locked and wear the key on a chain around my neck.

Private. Keep Out. This Means You.

Actually, I don't think I'm a weirdo. I just don't fit in with my family. They're all so driven and ambitious and serious about life, and I mainly want to have fun. *Sigh* again.

Life is so short. I've learned that the hard way. You know all about it, Diary. You're the only one.

No one else knows the true story. No one would believe it.

Since Blade died, my life is only sadness. And fear.

I don't think I'll ever get back to the cheerful, funny, fun-loving person I was. My parents and my friends are desperate to pull me from my black mood.

But how can they? It will never happen.

Blade and I were perfect together. Perfect . . . from that first night we met.

That night . . . It wasn't a perfect night, Diary. I ran into Deena Fear that night.

I'd lived in Shadyside my whole life and never spoken to anyone from the Fear family. And now my hand is suddenly sweaty and it's hard to grip the pen, remembering . . . thinking about Deena Fear and all the darkness she brought with her.

And poor Blade. My beautiful Blade. Did I have any way of knowing he would be with me for such a short time? Any way of knowing he would die such a horrifying death?

I have to stop. My tears are smearing the page. And I'm gripping the pen so—tightly now. I want to use it to stab . . . stab . . . stab. . . .

2.

It seems like a long time ago, but it was only a few weeks, Diary. Julie and Miranda and I were squeezed into a booth at the back of Lefty's. That's the cheeseburger place across from the high school. The food at Lefty's isn't bad, but we mainly go to see who else is there. It's a hangout. That's what they'd call it in all those cornball teen movies.

It was a little after nine on a Friday night. Just about every booth was filled with kids from our high school. A few grumpy-looking adults were huddled by the front counter waiting for a table. They probably didn't appreciate the loud voices and constant laughter.

I think adults generally hate teenagers. Because they're jealous. They'd rather be teenagers than what they are.

A loud crash made us all jump. A waitress had dropped a tray of glasses. The restaurant went silent for a few seconds. Then everyone burst into applause.

I turned back to Julie and Miranda. "What was I talking about?"

"You were talking about yourself, of course," Miranda said. She's the sly one with the dry sense of humor.

"Well, it *is* my favorite subject," I replied.

"You were telling us about the little boy who dropped his popcorn," Julie said.

"Oh. Right. Well, I'm not allowed to replace it. Ricky, the manager, says no free popcorn for anyone. But I waited till Ricky stepped away from the popcorn counter, and I gave the kid another bag."

"Big whoop," Miranda said. "That's your best story for tonight?"

I grabbed her wrist. "You didn't let me finish," I said. "Then the kid dropped the second bag, too."

Julie laughed. "That's so sad."

Miranda rolled her eyes. "Caitlyn, you have an exciting life. My heart is totally pounding. Tell that story again."

"Okay, okay," I said. "So, working the popcorn counter at the Cineplex isn't a thrill a minute. What did *you* do today that was so exciting?"

Miranda sighed. "Believe it or not, this cheeseburger is the highlight of my day." She raised it to her mouth and took a small bite. The tomato slid from the bun and plopped onto her plate.

"You have to learn how to work a cheeseburger," Julie said. It wasn't that funny, but all three of us laughed.

Julie and I have been friends since ninth grade, although we're both very different. She's always sarcastic and rolling her eyes and making funny remarks. I'd say her sense of humor is kind of nasty, actually.

I'm not a rah-rah cheerleader, but I try to see the bright side of things. I get into things. I'm enthusiastic. I can't help it. I don't hold myself back. I even try to enjoy things other people might find boring, like my after-school shifts at the popcorn counter.

I'm impulsive. And emotional. I cry at movies and TV shows all the time. It doesn't embarrass me.

I don't think I've ever seen Miranda cry. Or get very excited about anything, either. She's always standing off to the side, making jokes. She's not shy. She's just all locked-up inside herself, I think.

Miranda could be really attractive if she lost a little weight and did something with her stringy brown hair. Also, her glasses have to go. The red plastic frames make them look like swim goggles.

Julie and I keep telling her she'll look so much better with contacts. But she says she doesn't want to stick sharp little things in her eyes. Stubborn.

I'm not judging her in any way, Diary. I'm just trying to describe her. She's a good friend. She'll never see what I write here. No one will. But I want to be as accurate and honest as I can.

Julie doesn't eat meat, so she had a grilled cheese sandwich, and we shared a plate of fries. She and I look like we could be sisters. Her hair is pretty much the same blonde as mine, and we both have serious, dark eyes. She likes to wear bright red lipstick, which makes her face more dramatic than mine.

We're the same age, but I think she looks older. Maybe because she's about two inches taller than I am. And, I admit it, she dresses better. Her aunt is always sending her these awesome designer tops and skirts from New York.

Julie is very practical and even-tempered. Her last name is Nello, and I call her Mellow Nello. She's always warning me not to jump into things and to be careful about different guys and to take it easy and not be so emotional.

I always accuse her of being too timid and not taking chances, of always being predictable. Of course, she thinks being predictable is a *good* quality. We may look alike, but our personalities are way different.

Miranda leaned close and gave my hair a long sniff.

I squinted at her. "Are you getting weird?"

"No. Your hair smells like popcorn," she said. "It's a great smell. Someone should make a popcorn perfume."

"A million-dollar idea," Julie said. "I'd buy it. And how about bacon perfume? We could make a fortune."

"I thought you were a vegetarian," I said.

She frowned at me. "I don't eat bacon. That doesn't mean I can't *wear* it."

I sighed. "When I get home, I shampoo my hair twice. But I can't get rid of the popcorn smell."

Julie shook more salt onto the plate of fries. "Do you ever eat any of the popcorn while you're waiting for the next customer?"

I grinned. "Ricky would like to keep count of each kernel, but he can't. I help myself to a handful or two when he isn't looking."

Miranda rolled her eyes again. "Are we going to talk about popcorn all night? Doesn't anyone have any good gossip?"

I gave her a gentle push. "Get up. I have to go to the bathroom."

She edged out of the booth and climbed to her feet. I slid out behind her. "Don't say anything interesting till I get back."

"Not a problem," Miranda said.

Lefty's has a single bathroom across from the kitchen door. I had to wait in line behind two other girls I knew from school. They were talking about a metal band concert they'd seen at the Arena in Martinsville. They thought it was awesome. They sat in the third row, and the ushers passed out ear plugs to keep everyone from going deaf.

Then the girls started talking about what the warm spring weather was doing to their hair. "Extra conditioner," was one solution. "I use half a bottle of the stuff every morning." Interesting idea.

When I came out of the bathroom, I walked right into a girl with long straight black hair, dark eyes, and black lipstick against pale skin. She was carrying a white take-out bag of cheeseburgers.

The bag slipped from her hand when I bumped her. We both bent over to pick it up, and we cracked heads.

"Sorry," she said quickly, in a tiny voice. "Sorry." Even though it was my fault.

I handed her the bag.

I knew who she was.

Deena Fear.

I didn't know that my life was about to change forever.

3.

Deena Fear wore huge round black-framed eyeglasses. Her dark eyes appeared to bulge behind them, making her look like an owl. She wore a long-sleeved black crew-neck sweater, despite the warm night, over a short straight black skirt and black tights. I noticed her earrings—small silver skulls. She had a silver skull in her nose, too.

"I'm sorry," I said awkwardly. "I wasn't watching where I was going. I—"

"That's okay, Caitlyn." I felt a quick jolt of surprise. I didn't think Deena knew my name. Her eyes went down to my wrist. "I like your bracelet." She gazed at the silver bracelet my parents had brought me from their vacation in the Bahamas.

To my surprise, she reached out and wrapped her hand around my wrist and the bracelet. Her hand was warm and dry. Her fingernails were divided down the middle, each one half-black, half-white. She held my wrist for a long moment. "Does it have powers?"

She spoke in such a soft voice, I wasn't sure I'd heard correctly. "Powers? The bracelet?"

She nodded. Her straight black hair fell over her forehead. She let go of my wrist to brush it back.

"I . . . don't think so," I said. I laughed. Was she making a joke?

She shifted the cheeseburger bag to her other hand. "I've seen you at the mall, Caitlyn," she said.

I nodded. "Yeah. I work at the Cineplex some afternoons." I turned and glimpsed Julie and Miranda watching from the back of the restaurant. "I'd better get back to my friends. See you around, Deena."

Her owl eyes locked on mine. I wanted to turn away, but they seemed to hold me there. "Sometimes I see things," she said. "Sometimes I know things about people."

I didn't know how to reply to that. A waitress carrying a tray of cheeseburgers over her head wanted to squeeze past us. I used it as an excuse to get away. I gave Deena a little wave and walked away. For some reason, my wrist felt all tingly where she had handled my bracelet.

Miranda climbed up so I could slide into the booth. I sat down in time to see Deena Fear walk out of the restaurant, her long hair sweeping behind her back.

"Since when do you know her?" Julie asked.

"I don't," I said. "I almost knocked her over. So we started talking."

"She takes Goth to a new level," Miranda said.

"She gives me the deep creeps," Julie said.

"She isn't so bad," I said.

Miranda shook her head. "Just because she's in the Fear family, does she have to wear all black clothes and have black lips and black nails and creep around like some kind of witch? Why doesn't she rebel? Wear hot colors? Be a cheerleader? Run for Prom Queen?"

Julie laughed.

"She seems really shy," I said. "She's so awkward. Think she has any friends? Ever see her hanging out with anyone at school?"

"I don't remember even *seeing* her in school," Julie said.

"She doesn't *try* to have friends," Miranda insisted. "We were at the same birthday party once. I tried talking to her. But she's obsessed with ghosts and the paranormal and the walking dead. She kept talking about these movies I never heard of. At least, I *think* they were movies."

"Maybe she doesn't have a choice," I said, not exactly sure why I was defending Deena Fear. I guess I always like to side with the underdog. Or maybe I just like to argue with Miranda. "Coming from that family—"

"She's like a total Fear Family cliché," Julie chimed in.

My bracelet still tingled, as if it had been electrified somehow. I ate a few fries. They were cold now. I turned to Miranda. "Are you having a graduation party?"

She didn't hear me. She was staring at a table near the front of the restaurant.

"Miranda has to have the party," Julie said. "I can't have it. My house is too small."

"We could have it in your backyard," I said. "My parents aren't even going to be in town. They'll be in South Africa for two weeks on a business trip. Do you believe they're missing graduation?"

"Then we should have the party at *your* house," Julie said. "No parents. A total blowout."

Miranda still had her gaze on the table at the front. She bumped my shoulder. "Who's that guy gawking at you over there? Do you know him?"

I followed her gaze. A blue-uniformed waitress began to clear a table, blocking my view. "What guy?"

"See him?" Miranda turned my head. "The guy in the red hoodie? He's been staring at you like he's hypnotized."

"Hypnotized by your beauty," Julie said. I couldn't tell if she was making a joke.

I finally spotted the guy, by himself at a small, square table, sitting sideways in his chair, ignoring his food. And yes, his eyes were on me. He was kind of cute looking. A dark shirt under the open, red hoodie. A wave of black hair falling over his forehead. "I don't recognize him," I said.

"He thinks he knows *you*," Miranda said.

I squinted harder. "No. I've never seen him. I don't think he goes to Shadyside."

"He hasn't blinked," Julie said. "Maybe he wants to have a staring contest with you."

"I'll find out," I said. "I'm not shy." I gave Miranda's chubby arm a shove. She obediently climbed to her feet so I could slide out.

Julie raised her hand to her mouth. She does that a lot. She's so easily shocked. "Are you really going over to him?"

"What's the big deal?" I muttered. I squeezed past two girls who were just sitting down at the table across from us, and I strolled over to Mr. Red Hoodie.

He had amazing gray-green eyes, and they grew wider as I stepped up to him. I placed my hands on my waist. "Hey," I said. "How's it going?"

He shrugged. "Not bad." He had a nice smile and a tiny crease of a dimple in one cheek.

"Were you looking at me?" I demanded.

He snickered. "Do you always think people are looking at you?"

"Answer the question," I said. "Were you?"

He shrugged again. "Maybe." I liked the way those incredible gray-green eyes crinkled up when he smiled.

I smiled back. "Why were you looking at me?"

"Because you have a piece of lettuce stuck on your chin." He reached up, tugged it off, and showed it to me.

Well, yes, Diary, I was expecting something a little more romantic. Of course, I was embarrassed. But I didn't want to turn and hurry away. Something about him—not just his cuteness—drew me to him.

I crossed my arms over my chest. "What's your name?"
"Blade."

"No. Really," I said.

"Really. It's Blade. My parents wanted me to be sharp."

I laughed. "Bet you said that line before."

"It's the truth," he said.

"My name is—" I started. But he raised a hand to cut me off.

"Let me guess," he said. "I'm good at guessing names. I have a talent."

I slid past him, pulled out a chair, and sat down across from him. I glimpsed Julie and Miranda in our booth in the back. They were both watching the scene intently. "Shoot," I said.

His eyes burned into mine. He studied me. "Your name is Tabitha," he said.

I nearly choked. "Tabitha?"

He nodded. "What do your friends call you? Tabby?"

I nodded. "Yes. They call me Tabby. How did you guess my name like that? That's amazing. Did somebody tell it to you?"

His cheeks turned pink. "No way. I told you. I have a talent for guessing names."

I leaned across the table and flashed him a teasing look. "And what else do you have a talent for, Blade?"

He shrugged. "What's your real name?"

"It's Caitlyn."

"I thought so. That was my second guess."

A few minutes later, after some definite first-class flirting, I said goodbye to my two friends and walked out of the restaurant with him. Where were we going? I had no idea. I only knew that after just a few minutes, I felt totally comfortable with him. More than comfortable. I was definitely attracted to him, and I wanted to spend time with him.

Is this what love at first sight is all about?

Hard to believe, but the question actually flashed through my mind as we stepped out into a warm April night, a soft, cool breeze brushing my hot cheeks, the fragrant aroma of Lefty's cheeseburgers in the air, a bright half-moon overhead in a purple sky.

I know, I know. It sounds like some kind of bad Lifetime movie. But sometimes life has to imitate that strange unreal happiness you usually see only on TV.

And this was definitely one of those times.

Blade put his hand on my back as we walked. It seemed totally natural. As if we'd been walking together for years. I found myself wondering if he felt the same way.

We strolled along Division Street, past the high school, the yellow moonlight reflected in its dark windows, and along the houses that stood across from Shadyside Park.

What did we talk about? I hardly remember, Diary. We talked about school. Blade's family moved to Shadyside last fall, and he goes to The Academy. That's the private high school across town. He talked about his old house in Shaker Heights and how he hated to leave his friends back there.

He said he plays keyboard and guitar, and he is in a jazz quartet at school. He's pretty sure he can get into Oberlin. But he was sick for a semester, so he can't graduate with the rest of his class in June.

I told him I was accepted at Middlebury College in Vermont, which is where my sister Jen went. But my parents hadn't been able to work out a student loan for me yet. I said I'd tried for a Creative Writing Scholarship, but the competition was too stiff. I didn't get it.

He turned those awesome gray-green eyes on me. "You like to write?"

I was about to answer when something across the street caught my attention. I heard blaring dance music and saw the bright lights in a large house across the street. Through the front window, I could see a crowd of dancing people. The crowd spilled out onto the broad front porch. Voices and laughter.

And I had one of my ideas. I grabbed Blade's arm. "Hey, Blade," I said. "Let's do something crazy.

4.

He narrowed his eyes at me. "How crazy?"

"Let's crash the party," I said. "You know. Hang out. Dance for a bit. Get something to drink." I motioned to the front window. "Look. It's so crowded. No one will notice two more people."

I held my breath, waiting for his answer. This was definitely a test. Would Blade pass it?

A grin spread over his face. "Love it," he said. He grabbed my hand and started to pull me across the street. "Let's *do* this thing. Party time."

That's when I knew Blade and I belonged together.

We raced up the front lawn. Two beds of tulips stood on either side of the front porch. A soft wind made the tulips bob and sway as if greeting us. We made our way past the people on the porch, nodding and saying hi, acting as if we belonged.

They seemed to be college age, maybe in their early twenties. They were casually dressed, not quite as casually as Blade and me. But we didn't really stand out. They were drinking wine from paper cups, talking in small groups, glancing at their phones as they talked.

We slipped through the screen door and stepped into the living room. It was hot in there, so many bodies jammed in. Electronic dance music was cranked up to full volume. The room buzzed and vibrated to the beat.

The lights were turned low. It took a while for my eyes to adjust. Blade held my hand and we crossed the room to the drinks table. Three or four couples were dancing. But the room was too crowded, and they kept bumping people clustered on the sides.

Blade and I grabbed bottles of beer. I don't really like beer. I guess I was trying to impress Blade. On the next table, I saw big bowls of tortilla chips and salsa and a tray of pigs in blankets.

I turned and gazed around the room, squinting into the shadowy orange light. I didn't recognize anyone. They were all definitely older than Blade and me.

I pressed my face close to Blade's ear. "I wonder whose party this is."

He gazed around. "Beats me."

We clicked beer bottles. "This is very cool," I said.

"Best party ever!" Blade joked.

A young woman with very short blonde hair, shaved on one side, and pale blue eyes, dressed in faded jeans and layers of blue and green T-shirts, bumped me, nearly spilling her wine. "Oh. Sorry," she said. "No room to move."

"No problem," I said. "Awesome party."

She nodded. "I've never seen you here before. How do you know Hannah and Marty?"

"Just from around the neighborhood," I said.

She moved on. Blade and I enjoyed a good laugh.

And that's when I saw her. Deena Fear. My breath caught in my throat. She was so unexpected, so out-of-place.

Deena sat at the bottom of the stairway that led upstairs. Dressed in black as always, she had her pale hands clasped tightly in the lap of her skirt. Her black hair fell loosely around her face.

I peered at her through the railings in the banister. Did she see me?

Yes. Her eyes flashed behind her owlish glasses. She jumped to her feet.

I nudged Blade with my elbow. "That girl who's coming over—"

Blade squinted through the crowd as Deena approached. "Do you know her? Is she a friend of yours?"

"No," I said. "I mean—"

Deena stepped through a dancing couple to get to us. Her face was even paler than usual, and her lips were covered in a neon purple lipstick. She stepped up to me, a few inches too close. I mean, she didn't give me any space at all.

"Hi, Caitlyn."

I nodded. "Hey, Deena."

She swept her long hair behind her shoulders with one hand. "Caitlyn, do you know Blade?"

"Well . . ." I hesitated. How did she know Blade's name? He didn't go to our school.

I glanced at Blade. He was studying her intently, like she was another species or something.

"How's it going, Blade?" Deena asked.

"Not bad," he said. He squinted at her. "Do I know you?"

She didn't answer him. Instead, she startled me by grabbing my wrist, wrapping her fingers around my silver bracelet, just as she had at Lefty's. I felt a shock of warmth travel up my arm.

"Great party, huh?" Her eyes peered into mine, as if searching for something. I tried to free my arm, but she held on.

She squeezed my wrist, so hard the silver bracelet cut into my skin. Then she brought her face close to mine. I felt her hot breath on my cheek.

"I saw him first," she whispered.

5.

I blinked, my mind suddenly whirring. I knew I hadn't heard correctly. The music . . . the voices . . . It all seemed to grow louder, as if I was swimming in sound. Drowning . . .

I didn't say anything. I guess I was too stunned to react. And, I just wanted to free my arm from her grip, to get away from her.

"We should get going," Blade said, his eyes on the front door.

I tried to turn, but Deena held on. She raised my hand close to her face, puckered her bright purple lips, and blew on the silver bracelet. Blew a puff of hot breath onto the bracelet and my wrist.

Her breath felt damp, almost sticky, on my wrist. I gasped and tugged my arm free. The bracelet tingled, then grew burning hot. "Hey, Deena—" I called out.

But she had already spun away from us. She bumped a few startled people out of her way and disappeared out the door, her long tangles of black hair swaying behind her.

I held my wrist, waiting for it the bracelet to cool.

Blade's face was twisted in confusion. "What was *that* about?"

"Dunno," I murmured. "Seriously. I don't have a clue."

"She is weird with a capital weird," he said.

"Her name is Deena Fear," I told him, stepping out of the way of a young man carrying a large pizza box to the food table. "She is a Fear. Do you know about the Fear family?"

He shrugged. "Not really."

"I'll tell you about them sometime. They're famous here in Shadyside." I stepped back to avoid another pizza box coming through. "Do you want to leave?"

He grinned at me. "So soon? I think our hosts would be hurt if we left this early." He put a hand on my shoulder and guided me toward the food table. "I'm hungry. I didn't get to finish my cheeseburger, thanks to you."

Blade folded a slice of pizza in his hand and started to eat it hungrily. We talked to a couple across the food table. The woman was studying to be a vet. The guy said he was working on a blog and a YouTube channel. They asked us if we knew a place to go sky-diving in Shadyside.

That's kind of a laugh, if you know Shadyside.

I caught a tall red-haired woman watching Blade and me from the kitchen door. She had a puzzled expression on her face, like she was trying to place us. I wondered if she was Hannah, one of the hosts.

The front door swung open and several more couples arrived. The red-haired woman hurried to greet them. There was a lot of hugging and cheek kissing.

Suddenly, I had another idea.

Did I want to show Blade how crazy and bold I could be? Did I want to see if he was as impulsive and crazy as me? Maybe.

He was pulling a string of pizza cheese off his fingers. I tugged him close. "Blade, I have another idea. How about this? It could be a riot," I said. "How about we stand in the middle of the living room and start kissing? You know, like we're really into it. We're all over each other. Kissing like we should get a room somewhere."

He nodded. His eyes flashed. "That could work."

"It would be a way of thanking our hosts," I said, grinning. "You know. Give them a little entertainment."

He pulled me into the center of the room. "Caitlyn, I like the way you think."

He wrapped his arms around me and pulled me to him. He was stronger than I'd imagined. He held me so tight, I struggled to breathe.

And then he lowered his face to mine, and we began kissing. A long kiss. It made me even more breathless. I wrapped my hands in his hair, then lowered them to his back. We both had our eyes wide open, watching each other, enjoying the joke. Enjoying the kiss . . . Enjoying . . .

I glimpsed people moving out of our way. Couples stopped dancing, their faces twisted in surprise.

Blade and I ground our lips against one another's, being as showy as we could. I soon realized it wasn't just a joke, not just a way to shock people. We were kissing each other for real, with real feeling.

When did the joke end and the true emotion kick in? I don't know. I only know there wasn't enough time to enjoy it. Because the pounding dance music cut off suddenly. A hush fell over the room. And then I saw the red-haired woman striding toward Blade and me, her face tight with anger.

"Who are you?" she called. "Do I know you? Who brought you here?"

Blade and I clung to each other for a few seconds more. Then we broke apart and watched her approach, her hands balled into tight fists at her sides.

"Who are you? Do you belong here?"

"Oops," I said. "Sorry." I couldn't think of anything better to say. But then I added, "Awesome party." Then Blade and I took off, barging through some startled guests. Out the front door. It slammed behind us.

We ran down the driveway, laughing, shrieking, stumbling. As giddy as I'd ever been in my life. Was it the greatest night of my life? Probably.

We held hands and ran full speed till we reached the corner. No one was coming after us. I stopped and hugged a streetlight to catch my breath.

Blade was bent over, holding his knees, gasping for breath. "Awesome party. Awesome party." He repeated my farewell line. He shook his head. "I can't believe you said that. That was classic."

"Ow." I felt a stab of pain at my wrist and realized my silver bracelet still felt hot. I backed away from the streetlight and raised my arm to the light.

"What's wrong?" Blade straightened up and walked over to me.

"It's my bracelet," I said. "This is so weird. It's burning me."

"Well, take it off," he said.

I moved the fingers of my other hand to the clasp. I'd never had any trouble snapping the bracelet off. But now I was having trouble finding the clasp.

I smoothed my thumb and pointer finger around it. The bracelet seemed solid. A solid band of metal. "This is impossible," I murmured. "I . . . I can't find the clasp."

Blade took my arm. "Let me try." He held my arm high, lowered his face, and eyed the bracelet closely.

"Turn it over," I said. "Spin it so the clasp is on top."

He tried to turn the bracelet. "Ow!" I cried out again. He tried to spin it in the other direction. Pain shot through my hand and up my arm.

Blade let go of the bracelet. He raised his eyes to me. "Caitlyn, the bracelet won't slide. I think . . . I think it's melted onto your skin."

6.

"No, Julie. The jeweler couldn't get it off. He said he didn't have the right kind of saw for silver."

I had the phone to my ear in one hand and pushed the shopping cart with my other. Whoa. I stopped just in time. I almost rear-ended a woman with a little girl riding in her cart.

"Well, what are you going to do?" Julie asked. "You can't just leave the bracelet on forever. It'll cut off all your circulation!"

"Do you think?" I said sarcastically. "Think I haven't thought of that?" I turned the cart into the produce aisle. Blade was ahead of me, halfway toward the frozen foods section. "My dad says he's going to talk to a surgeon. You know. Like a bone surgeon. Someone who can cut off the bracelet without taking my hand off with it."

"I-I . . . don't believe it," Julie stammered. "And you really think Deena Fear—"

"I don't know what to think," I said. "It's not like she

has super powers. Something happened to the silver. I don't know what. Something made it melt, I guess." I sighed. "At least it cooled down. It isn't burning hot anymore."

"Weird," Julie said.

I grabbed a head of iceberg lettuce with my free hand and dropped it into the shopping cart. "I've got to go," I said. "I'm at the Pay-Rite. With Blade."

"Excuse me? Caitlyn, you're food shopping with Blade? Are you moving in together or something?"

"Ha-ha. Very funny. I'm shopping for my parents. Blade came along because—"

"Caitlyn, here's some unwanted advice from me," Julie said, lowering her voice. "Maybe you're going too fast with Blade. Maybe you should be more careful. You know. Take it slower."

"You're right," I said. "That *was* unwanted advice. I'll talk to you later, Julie." I clicked off and tucked the phone into my bag.

Blade held up a gigantic frozen pepperoni pizza. "Is this on the list?"

"No. Maybe on *your* list, but not my parents'. Go put it back."

He turned and walked back down the aisle, twirling the pizza box on one finger. I checked the shopping list again. My parents were making some kind of stew to take over to my cousin in Martinsville.

"Celery . . ." I pushed the cart alongside the produce shelves. An old Beatles song played in the background. In the next aisle, a little boy was crying his eyes out, screaming because his mom wouldn't let him have a cookie.

Blade got there before I did. He grabbed a thick bunch of celery and tore off two sticks. He tossed a stick to me. *"En garde!"* he shouted. He came at me waving his celery stick, slapping it against mine.

I turned away from the cart and began to duel. Our celery swordfight became intense. I get aggressive with a stick of celery in my hand. Slapping at his stick, I drove Blade back. His arms flew up as he tumbled into a cereal box display, and the boxes went toppling noisily onto the floor.

I heard a few gasps. People were watching us with stern, disapproving faces. I saw a red-faced young man in a long white apron hurrying toward us, waving angrily.

Blade and I tossed our celery sticks into the cart. I brushed my hair back, took a deep breath, and prepared to face the angry store worker.

"What's going on here?" he demanded breathlessly, lowering his hands to the sides of his apron. His name tag read: CHUCK W. He had short brown hair spiked up in front. His face was very red. I could see beads of sweat on his forehead.

"We . . . had an accident," I said, motioning to the cereal boxes strewn across the aisle.

"Yeah. An accident," Blade repeated. We both put on our most sincere faces. "We're sorry."

"They just fell," I said. "Can we help you pick them up?"

He glared angrily at Blade, then me. "An accident?" He lowered his gaze to the celery sticks in the shopping cart. He stared at them a long while. He seemed to be thinking hard, considering how to handle this.

Finally, he sighed and shook his head and said, "I'll take care of it. Have a nice day." He walked off, wiping his sweaty forehead and muttering something about "teenagers."

A few minutes later, Blade and I were lifting the groceries into the trunk of my mom's Toyota. "Where did you learn those moves with a celery stick?" Blade asked.

"I took lessons after school," I said. "I wanted to be a celery fighter in the Olympics. But my parents couldn't afford the grocery bills."

He kissed me. "You sure you have to go to work?"

I nodded. "It's my duty. I don't want to deprive people of their popcorn."

We had fallen into a warm and teasing relationship. We felt so good together in such a short time. I kissed Blade again, said goodbye to him, and drove home to drop off the groceries.

On the way, I thought of Julie's warning. *Slow down with Blade.* I knew she meant well. She wasn't being jealous or mean. She's known me forever, and she knows I can go overboard sometimes.

I'm an emotional person. As I said, I cry at movies. Maybe I hug people a little too long. Maybe I get hurt more easily than some people. One cross word from someone makes me feel like I'm a total failure.

That's me. You can't help being who you are, Diary. And why not live life *large*. I mean just grab the bull by its horns. Go whole hog. Live everything to the fullest.

Well . . . listen to me go on and on. I've become a real philosopher ever since I met Blade. Ever since I fell in love with him. Face it, Caitlyn. You're in love with him. It was love at first sight.

And maybe that was making me a little crazy. A little hyper. A little more *bonkers* than I was before.

Later that night, maybe I overreacted to what happened. After my shift behind the popcorn counter . . . the most frightening minutes of my life . . . Maybe I overreacted. But that's just me. What can I do?

7.

I was daydreaming about Blade, Diary, my elbows on the popcorn counter, gazing at the nearly empty movie theater lobby. Someone had spilled a plate of cheese nachos on the floor in front of the men's restroom, and Ricky, the manager, was mopping up the mess. He was in a bad mood. But what else is new?

The popcorn machine was nearly full. It was a really slow night. I thought about helping myself to a bag of Twizzlers. I hadn't had any dinner. But with Ricky in such a foul mood, I decided it wasn't a good idea.

Ricky is twenty-four or twenty-five. He's lanky and blond with freckles around his nose and cheeks. He has these big hands that look like cartoon hands because they're too big for his skinny arms. Everything about him is bony and awkward. His jeans are too big, and the Polo shirts he wears are droopy and wrinkled.

He's almost always in a grouchy mood. I think it's because he doesn't want to be the manager here. He told me once he planned to go to Penn and be a Business major. But he didn't get accepted and now he takes courses online, and he still lives at home with his mother.

My phone vibrated. I pulled it from my pocket. A text from Blade: *C U tomorrow?*

Ricky finished mopping and walked over toward me, carrying the mop and bucket. I slid the phone back into my jeans. "Caitlyn, don't just stand there," he said.

"There's no one here," I said, motioning with one hand. "What am I supposed to do?"

"Wipe off the display case counters," he said. "Check the ice machine."

I nodded. "No problem." I'd learned not to argue with him. I wanted to keep this job. It was pretty easy, and it paid fifteen dollars an hour (and all the popcorn I could sneak).

I found a cloth in back and started to wipe down the glass countertop. My stomach growled. Those Twizzlers looked mighty tempting. I was at the far end of the counter when I saw someone enter the lobby.

It took me a few seconds to recognize Deena Fear. I stared at her as she approached the counter. She wore a dark purple sweater over a short black skirt and black tights. Her purple lips matched the sweater.

Her long black hair flowed down her back in thick tangles. She had dark mascara circling her eyes. It made me think of a raccoon.

Is she following me? Why am I suddenly seeing her everywhere?

The questions made my whole body tense up. I could feel my muscles tighten. "Hey, Deena." I tried to look casual.

She leaned her hands on the counter, her black fingernails glistening, smearing the glass I had just wiped. "I remembered you work here," she said.

I nodded. "What movie are you seeing?"

She pointed to Auditorium Four. "*Vampire High School III,*" she said.

I should have known.

"The first two were awesome," she said. "Life-changing. Seriously."

"I . . . didn't see them," I said.

"I love the books, too. I have them all. It's the *best* series."

Over her shoulder, I saw Ricky watching us from the doorway to Auditorium Two.

"How's Blade?" Deena asked. The raccoon eyes peered into mine.

"Fine," I said. Ricky didn't like for us to chat with people. We were supposed to stick to business. "Do you want some popcorn or something?"

She ignored my question. Her fingernails tapped the countertop. "Sometimes I see things," she said, lowering her voice to a whisper. "Good things and bad things."

I felt a chill. I suddenly remembered my bracelet. How

her hand wrapped around it. How it burned hot, then melted onto my skin. I lowered my arm, keeping the bracelet out of sight.

"I . . . don't understand," I said.

"I want you to be my friend," she whispered, not lowering her gaze, not blinking. "I don't want anything bad to happen to you."

"Uh . . . thanks," I murmured.

Ricky hadn't moved. He was still watching, an unhappy look on his face.

"Does Blade talk about me?" Deena asked.

My breath caught in my throat. "Talk about you? Well . . ."

"Does he? Does he talk about me?"

"Well . . . I don't know," I said. "About what exactly?"

Her eyes still hadn't blinked. She kept them locked on me. The tiny silver skull on the side of her nose appeared to gleam. "We should talk," she said finally. "We could be friends, right? We could be friends and sit down together and talk about Blade?"

I was too stunned to hide my surprise. "Talk about him? You mean?"

Her expression changed. Her eyes went dead. "I see," she murmured. Her pale hands clasped together over the countertop. "I see. You don't want to talk. I get it."

"No—wait," I said.

She slammed her hands on the glass. Behind me, the

popcorn machine suddenly started to crackle, making new popcorn. I jumped at the sound.

I turned to the machine in surprise. Beside it, both soda dispensers began pouring out soda. Sparks flew from the glass hotdog warmer. It buzzed and shorted out.

"Hey!" I shouted.

Across the lobby, I saw the alarm on Ricky's face. He came trotting toward us, shouting my name.

Deena had a triumphant grin on her purple lips. Her dark eyes flashed. "Sure you don't want to talk?"

I lunged to the back counter to shut off the soda dispensers. The soda was already puddling on the floor. My sneakers sank into the sticky, dark liquid.

I saw Deena slide her hands off the glass countertop. She edged back a step.

Popcorn began flowing over the sides of the machine like lava pouring out of a volcano. I struggled with the soda dispenser. The levers were stuck. A river of soda ran behind the counter.

"I know we'll talk," Deena said. And then she whispered, "Sorry about your bracelet."

Over the rattle of the popping popcorn and the rush of the soda pouring onto the floor, I wasn't sure I heard her right. "What did you say?"

But she turned and began to stride quickly toward Auditorium Four.

Ricky stepped breathlessly to the counter. "What's

happening? What's happening here? Why did you turn everything on?"

"I didn't!" I cried. "I didn't touch anything."

Ricky swung himself over the counter. His shoes splashed in the soda on the floor. He reached behind the dispensers and pulled the plugs. I hit the *Stop* button on the popcorn machine again and again. Finally, it slowed and the crackling and popping stopped.

Ricky and I both stood there, breathing hard, staring at the incredible mess.

"This is impossible," I muttered, shaking my head. "This can't be happening." I turned to Ricky. "I didn't touch anything. I swear. I was talking to the girl from school and . . . and . . ."

Ricky swept a bony hand back over his hair. "Must have been a power surge," he said. "Some kind of power problem. From the electric company. That's the only thing that could have caused this."

"Yes," I agreed. "A power surge."

But I didn't believe it. I believed it was a warning from Deena Fear.

Ricky walked to the supply closet to get mops. I pulled a large trash can behind the counter and began shoving the extra popcorn into it.

I had no idea the evening was going to get even worse.

8.

The soles of my sneakers were sticky from the spilled soda. My shoes made swamp noises—*thwuck thwuck thwuck*—on the concrete of the mall parking lot as I made my way to my car.

It took Ricky and me nearly an hour to clean up the counter area. We worked in silence, but every few minutes Ricky muttered, "How could this happen?"

I had a pretty good idea. But of course I couldn't share it with anyone. Who would believe it? If I said Deena Fear had power over those machines, people would lock me up as a crazed psycho, and I wouldn't blame them.

I now realized that she had a thing about Blade. I probably should have caught on earlier. But what did that mean? Did she plan to ruin my life with wild stunts like with my bracelet and the movie food machines? Was that her plan to win Blade?

That didn't make any sense at all.

I pictured her dark-circled eyes burning into mine, as

if trying to penetrate, to invade my brain. And again, I heard the creepy *click* of her long black-and-white fingernails on the counter glass.

My head was swimming with these crazy, impossible thoughts. I debated whether or not to tell Blade about Deena, about how she kept asking about him, asking if he ever talked about her.

Did he know her before I met him? He said he didn't. I should believe what he told me. He said he'd never heard of the Fear family.

Blade hadn't lived in Shadyside for long, but that was a little hard to believe. I think when people move here, they are told immediately to steer clear of the Fears and Fear Street.

I always thought it was all superstition and made-up stories about them. But with Deena around, I was no longer so sure.

With all these thoughts making my brain whir, I walked past my car. I stopped and tried to remember where I'd parked. Level C. And the sign in front of me told me I had walked all the way to D.

Get a grip, Caitlyn.

I turned and started to walk back, my sticky shoes *thwacking* on the concrete. I guess the sound kept me from hearing the footsteps behind me.

I didn't realize I was being followed until the man was only a few feet behind me. I heard the rapid scrape of shoes and wheezing breath.

I didn't have a chance to run. I didn't even have a chance to be scared. Until he grabbed me roughly and spun me around to face him.

I stared into the red eyes of a thick-stubbled face, angry, half-hidden behind the hood of a dark hoodie. I'd never seen him before.

He squeezed my shoulders and shook me hard, the red eyes glowing, his jaw clenched.

"Let me go!" I screamed. My voice rang loudly off the concrete parking garage walls. I whipped my head around. "Help me! Somebody!"

But the hooded man and I were alone.

"Give me your wallet. I can hurt you." His voice was a harsh rasp from deep in his throat. He squeezed my arms so hard, pain shot up and down my whole body.

I struggled to breathe. "Let go," I choked out in a frantic whisper. "Let me go. Please . . ."

9.

He was wheezing now, spit rolling over his lips.

"I can hurt you," he repeated. "Your wallet. Hurry."

I forced myself to breathe. My heart was thudding so hard, my chest ached. "Okay," I choked out.

Still holding my arms, he lowered his head, brought it close to mine, so close I could smell his sour breath.

I knew this was my chance, Diary.

I'm not the kind of girl to give in easily, to surrender without a fight. I knew this was the moment those self-defense classes I took last year would be useful.

I arched back a few inches, as if trying to pull away from him. Then I brought my right leg up. I snapped it up hard and fast. He uttered a startled gurgling sound as my knee smashed the middle of his face.

I heard a sick *crack*. The sound of his nose breaking.

His hands slid off my arms. He grabbed his face, as bright red blood began to spurt from his nose. With an animal howl of pain, he dropped to his knees. He covered his face with both hands. Blood flowed through his fingers, down the front of his hoodie. He howled again.

I stood there for a long moment, gasping for breath, enjoying my victory, my heart thudding in my chest . . . thudding so hard I could feel every throb of blood.

I watched him for a second or two. Then I forced my legs to move. I took off, my sneakers pounding the concrete, ran to my car, and drove away.

"Wow. Is it heavy? Can I hold it?" Julie asked.

"The handle is pretty awesome," Miranda said. "How do you open it?"

"This button here," I said, raising it to her face. "You press it with your thumb and the blade slides open." I waved it around. "It's a stainless steel blade. Careful. It's amazingly sharp. It'll cut through anything."

We were in the small den at Julie's house, and I was showing them the knife I had bought at Hunters & Company, at the mall, the knife I planned to carry in my bag from now on.

The guy at Hunters told me all about it and how to use it. It's called a Magnum Ypsilon Tan G-10 Folding Knife. The handle is black-and-tan and it feels great, heavy but not too heavy, comfortable in your hand. The blade is amazing.

I told the salesman my dad was a collector, and I was buying it for a birthday surprise. I think he believed me.

I don't think he could see on my face that I was buying it for protection, buying it for me.

"This is dangerous," Julie said, shaking her head. "I know you went through a bad thing, Caitlyn, but . . ."

"It's just for emergencies," I said. "I'm not going to walk around stabbing people."

"You're not allowed to bring it to school," Miranda said. "If you get caught . . ."

"I won't get caught," I said. "You know that big bag I always carry. I'll keep the knife at the bottom, under everything else."

They tried to argue. But they know me. Once I make up my mind, that's it. I knew I'd never use the knife. But having it with me made me feel better.

I got lucky in the parking garage with my knee kick. But what if that creep had come after me? What if he had tried to kill me?

The thought made me shudder. I still thought about it all the time, still pictured his stubbly, drooling, red-eyed face, still felt his hands squeezing my arms.

My phone beeped. I tucked the knife into my bag and pulled out the phone. "A text from Blade," I told them. "We're going out tonight." I tapped a reply. "We text each other all day long. It's awesome."

Julie and Miranda exchanged a glance. I knew what was coming. Their lecture on not getting too serious about Blade.

Well . . . it was too late for that. I couldn't be more

serious, and I knew he felt the same way, too. But for some reason, my friends thought it their duty to caution me.

"You always rush into things, Caitlyn."

"You're always so impulsive. You don't really know Blade that well. You really should be careful not to get carried away."

I rolled my eyes. "I seriously am beginning to believe that you two are jealous," I said. "I'm sorry you don't have boyfriends, but it really isn't my fault."

Julie jumped to her feet. "That's not fair. We're only thinking of you," she said.

Miranda motioned for her to sit back down. "Okay, okay, we get it, Caitlyn. You don't want us in your face. Fine. We'll stop."

Julie sighed and dropped back down.

"Blade and I are perfect," I told them. "I know we haven't known each other for long. I know it's all been so crazy and fast. But . . . we're perfect. I don't know how else to say it."

They both sank back into the couch cushions. I think I finally got through to them.

A short while later, I went home to get ready for my date with Blade. For a long while, I sat on the edge of my bed, daydreaming about him. I imagined his arms around me, holding me tightly against him. I pictured those strange gray-green eyes gazing so deeply into mine. I thought about the way we teased each other, the way we talked together so easily.

I thought about kissing him . . . kissing him till I felt lost . . . till I felt I was somewhere else in the world . . . somewhere far away from anyone and anything I knew.

When my phone beeped, it shocked me from my dazed imaginings. I grabbed my bag and fumbled the phone out.

I read the short text message on the screen—and gasped, "Oh no."

10.

The message from Blade was short: "Can't make it tonight. Got hung up."

I read it over and over, as if I could get the words to tell me more. Why didn't he explain what the problem was? Why didn't he at least say he was sorry?

He must have some emergency, I told myself. He must be as disappointed as I am.

I punched his number into the phone and raised it to my ear. My hand was trembling. I knew I was overreacting, but I was very disappointed. My daydreams had gotten me all psyched to see him.

The call went right to voicemail. I listened to his voice: "This is Blade. You know what to do." I didn't leave a message. I knew I'd talk to him later. I knew he'd explain everything. And maybe we could get together later tonight.

Dinner with my parents seemed to last forever. I hadn't told them much about Blade. I usually blurt out everything about my life to them. I'm not the kind of person who can hold anything in. But for some reason, I'd decided to keep Blade to myself.

My parents are totally great people. They're not always in my face and pretty much treat me as an adult. They put up with my enthusiasms and my wild mood swings and my general insanity. And they're not always trying to pry into my life.

I think they'd love to know what's in my diary. But trust me, that's totally off-limits to them. As I said, I keep it locked and I wear the key on a chain around my neck.

My dad is big and healthy-looking. I guess you'd call him robust. He brags that he still has all his hair at forty-three. Mom teases him that that's his biggest accomplishment.

She likes to deflate him whenever he gets too full of himself. She says it's her hobby.

He works out at a gym three days a week, and he's a cyclist. He gets up at six most mornings and rides his racing bike for ten miles along River Road to the top.

He's an administrator at Shadyside General Hospital. He says he just shuffles papers all day and deals with hospital staff problems. That's why he likes to get a lot of exercise and fresh air before work.

Mom could be really hot-looking if she paid attention to her looks. But she isn't really interested in what she wears or her hairstyle or anything. She wears a lot of baggy T-shirts and these dreadful Mom jeans.

She mostly has her blonde hair tied back in a tight ponytail, and she refuses to wear any makeup. She says she likes the fresh look. But just a little blusher and some color on her lips would make her look five years younger.

She teaches Business Ethics at the junior college in Martinsville. And she gives lectures at companies on the subject. I don't really understand what she talks about, but she reads three newspapers a day online and every book on business that comes out.

So there we were at dinner. When it's just the three of us, we eat in the little breakfast nook beside the kitchen. It's a snug little area, lots of sunshine through the windows, and a picnic table and benches where we eat most of our meals. The dining room is saved for company, so we use it mostly on holidays.

Dad had brought home take-out fried chicken and mashed potatoes with gravy. Usually my favorite, but I didn't have much appetite tonight. You know why, Diary.

I stared at the leg and thigh on my plate. Mom was talking about some kind of lawsuit against a company I'd never heard of and why it should be thrown out of court. Dad tsk-tsked and spooned more mashed potatoes onto his plate.

"Do you have a date with that boy tonight?" Mom's question stirred me from my thoughts.

"Uh . . . not tonight," I said. "I think I'm just going over to Miranda's and watch some videos or something."

Mom leaned across the table toward me. "What's his name again?"

"Blade," I said. "Blade Hampton."

"Funny name," Mom muttered. "No one has normal names these days. Do you know anyone named Jack or Joe or Bill?"

I laughed. "No. No, I don't."

"You've gone out with this guy a few times," Dad chimed in. "Why don't you invite him over sometime?"

I was pretty much keeping Blade to myself. Not exactly keeping him a secret, but not eager to share him with my parents. "Yeah. Okay," I said. Always better to agree and not start a controversy.

Dad changed the subject to how he pulled a muscle racing his bike this morning and how his leg had stiffened up. One of my parents' best qualities is that they have very short attention spans. They can never stay on a subject for more than a minute or two.

I gnawed on the chicken leg for a while and forced myself to eat some of the potatoes and coleslaw. Mainly so Mom and Dad wouldn't start asking more questions. I couldn't stop thinking about Blade. Wondering what was up with him.

After dinner, I changed into a long-sleeved top. The weather had turned cool and the sky was heavy with rainclouds. I called goodnight to my parents and hurried out to the car.

A few raindrops dotted the windshield as I drove to Miranda's house. She lives on Heather Court in North Hills, the ritzy neighborhood of Shadyside. Her house is big, with a zillion rooms, but very comfortable. Her parents collect very large old movie posters, so there are these great stars like Charlie Chaplin and Humphrey Bogart staring out at you from every wall.

Miranda is into old movies, too. If Julie and I are hanging out at Miranda's house, we usually end up watching some old black-and-white flick from the forties or fifties on Netflix. I love seeing the weird old clothes—everyone wearing hats all the time, even indoors—and the funny cars.

The rain was just a drizzle but I started the wipers. They squeaked as they scraped over the windshield. I turned onto Mission, which curved around to Miranda's street. I slowed down. There were a lot of cars on Mission. Drivers use it as a shortcut to River Road.

I pulled through a stop sign—and then let out a soft cry. "Whoa."

Was that Blade's car up ahead? I squinted through the rain-spotted glass.

Yes. It had to be.

Actually, it was his dad's car, but he drove it a lot. A '95 red Mustang. Not too many of those on the road in Shadyside. Leaning over the wheel, I read the license plate. Yes. Yes. Blade's car.

I lowered my foot on the brake. I didn't want him to see me. I didn't want to get too close.

But . . . who was that in the car beside him?

Bright white headlights beamed from an oncoming

truck swept over Blade's car and lit it up as if setting it on fire.

And I saw her. A girl. Beside Blade. A girl with short white-blonde hair. I just saw the back of her head. I didn't see her face.

His car pulled away from a stoplight and roared forward.

My hands squeezed the wheel. They were suddenly clammy and cold.

I lowered my foot to the gas. I knew what I had to do.

I had to follow them.

11.

My headlights washed over the back of the red Mustang. I slowed down, let more space separate our cars. I had a sudden urge to tromp on the gas and plow right into him. Send that blonde girl flying through the windshield.

A crazy thought, and I quickly suppressed it. What kind of person would imagine such a violent, evil thing?

The girl beside Blade had to be a cousin. Or a family member who needed a ride. Or a friend from his old school he hadn't seen in months. Or . . . Or . . .

Weird how your brain can dance around when you're upset or anxious.

The rain stopped. I shut down the scraping windshield wipers. The red Mustang made the turn onto River Road. A few seconds later, I turned, too.

The road curves along the bank of the Conononka River, a long, winding road that climbs into the hills over Shadyside. It was too dark to see the river. But I slid my passenger window down so I could hear the gentle lapping of the water against the muddy shore.

I thought the sound might calm me. But, of course, it didn't.

Again, my headlights played over the back of the Mustang. I slowed and edged to the right and let another car move between us. I didn't want Blade to see me. I didn't want him to think that I was suspicious, that I didn't trust him.

He was obviously dealing with an emergency. That's why he didn't have time to explain to me what was going on.

But . . . if it was an emergency, why was he turning into the parking lot at Fire? Fire is a dance club on River Road. It's a club for adults, but a lot of Shadyside students go there because the doorman isn't very careful about checking your ID. If you don't look twelve, you're in.

A neon sign at the street has red-and-yellow flames dancing into the air. A sign beside it reads: SHADYSIDE'S PREMIER DANCE CLUB. LADIES FREE.

The club was a long, low, red building with red and blue lights along the flat roof. A red carpet led to the awning over the entrance. The doorman stood behind a narrow wooden podium at the front of the awning. Even with the car windows closed, I could hear the drumming beat of the throbbing dance music from inside the club.

As I watched the red Mustang roll over the brightly lit gravel parking lot, a wave of nausea rolled over me. I was supposed to be with Blade tonight. He told me he got "hung up." So why was he here at a dance club with that blonde girl?

My ideas about a family emergency were quickly exploding, vanishing into air. And I fought down my dinner, which was rising to my throat. Fought down a choking feeling as I saw him pull into a parking place at the side of the club and cut his headlights.

My car rolled slowly over the gravel as I hung back, leaning over the wheel and squinting into the glare of the red, blue, and yellow lights overhead. I stopped and backed into a space between two SUVs near the club entrance.

When I looked back, Blade and the girl were out of his car. Blade wore his red hoodie over slim-leg jeans. She was tall and thin, taller than him, and the lights played over her pale face and the short white-blonde hair.

She leaned into Blade, and he slid an arm around her shoulders. They staggered sideways together, laughing.

A sob escaped my throat. I forced myself to breathe.

I told him I loved him. That night in his car up on River Ridge, the stars above us, the sparkling river down below, when we held each other, held each other as if we were the only two people on earth. We kissed . . . we kissed and . . . and . . .

I grabbed the door handle, ready to jump out of the car. I had an impulse to jump out, run across the gravel lot, grab him, grab him and spin him around, and—

—*No.*

I squeezed the steering wheel, squeezed it until my

hands ached—and watched them kiss. She turned to him and he wrapped his hands around her neck and pulled her face close. And they kissed again. The red-and-blue lights played over them, making it look like a carnival scene or some kind of glaring dream.

If only.

If only it wasn't real, Diary. But it was happening, and I was there.

I shoved open the car door. It slammed into the SUV next to me. I didn't care. I slid out and stumbled forward, away from the car. I couldn't balance. The world tilted and swayed under me.

My whole body shuddered as I forced myself forward.

Did I cut the engine? Switch off the headlights? I don't remember, Diary.

Blade and the girl stopped at the doorman's podium. He was a wide hulk of a guy, shaved head, wearing a purple sleeveless T-shirt that showed off his tight biceps and tattoos, and baggy gray sweatpants. Blade pulled something from his wallet—probably a fake ID—and the doorman waved them into the club.

"Stop!" I opened my mouth in a cry, but no sound came out. I took a deep breath. My shock quickly turned to anger.

Blade is a liar! A liar and a rat!

I couldn't erase the picture of them kissing from my mind.

Suddenly, I knew I had to confront him. I had to let him know that I was here and I saw him.

A cry of rage burst from my throat. Like an angry animal. And I roared forward, my sneakers kicking up gravel, ran full speed toward the club entrance, the red-and-blue lights flashing in my eyes, running blind, blind with my anger and hurt pushing me forward.

I had to get in there. I had to make him face me.

I was a few feet from the doorman's podium when a dark figure ran out from the side of the club. At first, I thought it was a moving shadow. It took a few seconds to realize it was someone dressed all in black.

Deena Fear.

I nearly ran right into her. She caught me with both hands before we collided. I was panting, wheezing loudly, enraged.

"Deena—what are you doing here?" I choked out, the words rasping against my dry throat.

"He betrayed us!" she cried. "Caitlyn—he betrayed us!"

12.

I gaped at her. The red–and–blue lights reflected in her glasses made her eyes look on fire.

"He betrayed us!" she screamed again, gripping my arms tightly.

"Go away!" I cried. Blade was inside the club with the blonde girl. I didn't have time for Deena Fear. I had to keep my anger burning. Or else I'd never be able to confront him.

"Get off me!" I swung my body hard and tugged free of her grip. Then I lowered my shoulder and shoved her out of my way, shoved her so hard she toppled backward over the gravel. Her glasses flew off her face and landed on the ground.

I spun away, lowered my head, and ran past the doorman. I heard him shout: "Hey—stop!" And then he uttered a string of curses as I pulled the door open and rushed inside.

Into the flashing lights and throbbing beats, deafening,

almost painful. I could see the silhouettes of dancers in the middle of the floor. Couples huddled around the sides. A crowd at the brightly lit bar against the far wall.

I took a deep shuddering breath. Then another. My eyes gazed from one wall to the other, squinting to see faces, to see Blade. The pounding beats matched my heartbeats. I stood there, gasping in the thick, humid air, inhaling the tangy aroma of alcohol and sweat.

I was so angry, so hurt, so devastated, the whole scene became a crazy blur to me. The lights pulsed with the beats of the music, pulsed with my heartbeats, until . . . until I was not myself. I was out of myself. Out of my head.

Where is he? Where?

And then my eyes stopped at the white lights of the bar. And I saw him. I saw Blade at the bar. The blonde girl was beside him. He was leaning over a tall barstool, talking to a female bartender.

I didn't hesitate. I lowered my shoulder and bolted across the dance floor like a running back. Couples dodged out of my way. I heard angry shouts:

"Look out!"

"Hey—what's your problem?"

My problem was Blade.

I let out a furious screech as I stepped up behind him. I grabbed his shoulders and spun him around.

His eyes opened wide in surprise. "Caitlyn?"

The words spilled from my throat. "What are you doing here?"

He regained his composure quickly. "Getting two beers," he said. He gave a casual shrug.

"Who *is* she?" the blonde girl asked.

"She's nobody, Vanessa," Blade said. "A friend. From school."

I felt as if I'd been cut in half, sliced right down the middle.

I stood there trembling with my mouth open.

I know I overreacted. I know I went ballistic. Totally lost it. But that's the way I am. That's me, and there's nothing I can do about it.

I am 90 percent emotion. And when Blade said those words to the girl, something inside me snapped.

"But . . . but . . ." I sputtered. "But we *love* each other!" The words tumbled out of my mouth before I could stop them.

Blade's face went entirely blank. His eyes appeared to freeze over. "In your dreams, maybe."

And there I stood, my world collapsing in a sea of flashing lights and dancing couples and pounding music.

Suddenly, Vanessa, the blonde-haired girl, moved toward me. She put a hand gently on my shoulder. "Are you okay? You're trembling. Can I get you a drink or something?"

Her dark blue eyes peered into mine. She was genuinely worried about me.

I stared back at her, unable to answer. Finally, I spun away and took off. I ran back through the dance floor, pushing my way through the dancers, startled cries all around me.

I pulled open the door and burst back into the cool darkness. The voices and music were a roar behind me. My eyes still pulsed from the crazy lights.

The doorman turned from his podium as I ran past him. "Hey, you—stop! Come here!" he bellowed angrily.

Again, I ignored him, my shoes slipping and sliding on the gravel as I turned toward my car. No sign of Deena Fear. I had a fleeting thought that she'd be there by the door waiting for me, waiting to grab me and insist that Blade had betrayed her, too.

Which one of us is crazy?

I knew the answer. I was the crazy one for caring too much. Everything I did in that club was crazy. So crazy that even the girl with Blade, a total stranger, was worried about me.

But I didn't care. Blade was so important to me. I trusted him. I believed in him. I loved him. And now . . . I didn't care. I didn't care. I didn't care.

He acted as if I was nothing. "She's nobody." That's what he told that girl Vanessa. "She's nobody."

And he was right. Now I was nobody. I thought I had something great, something wonderful to get through life. But now I was nobody.

I climbed into the car. Slammed the door. Started it up and roared out of the parking lot, sending up a tidal wave of gravel behind me.

Where was I going? I didn't know. I swung the car out of the parking lot without looking. To my left, a small van screeched to a halt. Close call. I didn't care.

I slammed my foot down on the gas pedal. The car lurched forward. The pull of speed felt good to me. I spun around the curves of River Road, sliding from one lane to the other.

I made the car squeal and scrape. The river flowed beside me. All I had to do was swing the wheel to the left, and I'd be over the side and into the water. The cold, fresh water. Was it a good night for a swim?

No. I slid the wheel to the right and followed the dark road. Was that a squirrel I almost hit? No. Maybe a rabbit. Maybe a raccoon.

I was making the big curve onto Parkview, doing at least eighty, when the oncoming headlights filled my windshield. I blinked in the blinding lights. I cursed them for having their brights on.

And too late, I realized I was in the wrong lane. I was in the left lane. Too late. Too late to swing the car. Too late to avoid them. I heard the roar of a horn, like a siren, as the lights grew even brighter, washed over me, blinded me.

I'm driving right into them. Can't stop.

13.

Sudden darkness. The long wail of the car horn ringing in my ears, bleating like an enraged animal. The
horn finally stopped as the other car swerved into the
right lane and roared past me.

Missed. The car missed. I forced myself to breathe. Silence now. The twin circles of bright white headlights
lingered in my eyes.

Breathe, Caitlyn. Breathe.

Chill after chill ran down my back. A close call. I almost
died. I didn't really want to die. I was too angry to die.

I jerked the wheel and pulled the car to the curb. I hit
the brake too hard, and the car lurched forward before it
stopped, throwing me against the wheel, then slamming
me back.

I cut off the engine. Then I sat there with my hands in
my lap, staring out into the darkness, forcing my breathing to return to normal.

Caitlyn, you're not handling this well. Caitlyn, get a grip.

Where was I?

I squinted across a narrow lawn to a square brick house with a single light on over the front stoop. A small one-car garage at the top of the driveway had its door open.

It took me a few seconds to realize I had parked in front of Blade's house. I stared at the yellow light over the stoop until the house blurred behind it.

I knew I didn't deliberately drive here. At least, I didn't *know* I was going to park in front of his house. "I should go home," I murmured out loud.

I reached for the button to start the engine. But then I lowered my hand to my lap. I needed to talk to him. No. I didn't want to see him. I didn't want to sit here for hours, till the middle of the night, waiting for him to return from his date. And then rush him, run at him, confront him crying and screaming.

No. I didn't want that.

So . . . why couldn't I start the car? Why couldn't I move? Why was I sitting here, every muscle in my body tense, my stomach rumbling and growling, wave after wave of nausea making me hold my breath and clench my jaw?

I don't know how much time passed. I glanced at the car clock when the red Mustang finally turned into the driveway. It was nearly one o'clock.

I watched the car stop in front of the garage. I watched the red taillights die. I watched the driver's door swing open. Now it all seemed to be in slow motion, like some kind of slowed-down dream.

Blade stretched his arms over his head. Then he closed the car door quietly. Quietly so he wouldn't wake his parents, I guessed.

I sat and watched, hands clasped tightly in my lap. When he started loping toward the kitchen door, I finally moved. I moved fast.

I shoved open the car door, grabbed my bag, and leaped out. I didn't bother to close it. I ran around the trunk to the driveway and began to run, gripping my bag in one hand, waving my other hand above me head. "Blade! Blade!" I shouted his name in a shrill voice I didn't recognize.

It was a warm April night, almost balmy, but the air felt cool against my burning cheeks. "Blade! Stop! Blade!"

Why did I drag my bag with me? I can't answer that question. Was I thinking clearly? Not at all.

Blade turned and I saw the surprise on his face. I kept waving my hand above my head as I ran, some kind of desperate signal.

I stopped a few feet in front of him, breathing hard, my chest heaving up and down.

He narrowed his eyes at me. "Caitlyn? What are you doing here?" No warmth in his voice. His eyes cold. Wary.

"I-I-I" I stammered. I searched for something good in

his face, just a tiny sign that he was glad to see me. No. Not even that. A sign that he *liked* me? No.

"It's late," he said, tugging the sleeves of his hoodie.

"I . . . I . . . Didn't you say you loved me?" I blurted out, my voice trembling as if underwater.

He blinked. He lowered his gaze to the ground. "We had fun," he murmured.

"Fun?" I cried. "Fun? You said you loved me. You know you did."

He raised his eyes. His mouth formed a sneer. "You didn't really think I was serious—did you?"

"Huh?" My mouth dropped open. I kept my eyes locked on him. I was straining to see the Blade I knew, the Blade I loved.

"We had fun, that's all," he said. He yawned.

I think it was the yawn that set me off. The loud, open-mouthed yawn put me over the edge.

I felt something in my brain snap. At that moment, at that second, something inside me cracked apart. I guess it was my whole life.

I really can't describe it. Something in my brain just exploded.

I saw the surprise on Blade's face. Or was it fear?

And then everything went crazy.

14.

"**F**un?" I screamed. "Fun?"

He glanced to a window at the side of the house. His parents' room? Was he afraid I might wake his parents? Is that all he cared about?

"You *creep!*" I cried. I had the handle of my bag gripped tightly in my right hand. I raised my arm and swung the bag at him, swung it with all my strength.

"Hey!" Blade uttered a startled cry and stepped back. He lowered his shoulder, and the bag swung over his head.

"Hey, stop, Caitlyn. Stop it."

"Fun?" I shrieked. "Fun?"

I swung the heavy bag again. This time it glanced off his shoulder.

"Whoa." His expression turned angry. "I'm warning you," he murmured. "Stay back. Stop it."

My next swing caught him on the chest. I couldn't stop myself. I swung again, narrowly missing his head. I swung the bag again. Doubled him over with a blow to the stomach.

"Enough!" he groaned. He made a grab for the bag. Caught it from the bottom.

"Noooo!" I struggled to pull it away from him.

"Caitlyn—chill! Stop! Calm down! Can we talk?" He gripped the bottom of my bag and jerked his hands hard.

"Give it back!" I screamed. "Give it!"

The handle snapped out of my hand. I stumbled back. Blade held onto the bottom as we both watched all the contents spill onto the ground.

"You creep! You creep!" I was shrieking without even hearing myself.

Blade tossed the bag across the driveway. He glared furiously at me. "You crazy idiot. Are you going to leave?"

In the dim light from the stoop, I saw the knife. It lay on top of a scarf I had stuffed into the bag. With a shuddering moan, I dove for it. I gripped the handle tightly and raised it in front of me.

"Hey—what's that?" Blade demanded, gazing from the knife to me.

My thumb fumbled for the button, and I released the blade. It snapped out instantly and I held it in front of me so Blade could see it clearly.

"Come on, Caitlyn. Put that down," he said, holding his arms out at his sides, as if preparing to defend himself.

"Fun? We had *fun*?" I cried.

No way he could defend himself. I lunged forward and poked the sharp tip of the blade into the front of his hoodie.

He gasped and stumbled back. "Put it away. Are you crazy? Put it away!"

I jabbed at him, just enough to make him feel it. I poked him in the chest. Then I lowered the blade and poked his stomach.

"You're crazy! You're crazy! Stop. Put it down. Let's talk."

His eyes were wide. I could see he was in a panic. He kept his arms lowered, tensed, ready to fight back. He retreated a step, then another—and backed into his car.

I had him trapped now. I moved forward and poked him again, pushing the tip of the blade against his belly.

"Give that to me!" He uttered an angry scream and swiped at the knife.

I tried to swing the blade out of his reach. But instead, I sliced through the palm of his hand. The blade cut silently. I gasped. I started to choke.

Eyes bulging in disbelief, he raised his hand in front of his face as a line of blood oozed onto the palm.

The blood trickled for a few moments. Then it started to spurt.

We both stared at the bleeding hand in silence. It was too horrifying for either of us to make a sound.

And then he began to wail, shrill high-pitched cries, waving the spurting blood in the air.

Like a fountain, I thought. *Blood spurting like a bright fountain.*

His shrieks made my ears ring. The sight of the blood made my stomach lurch. I gagged.

I had to stop that horrible sound he was making.

I swung the knife back, then plunged the blade deep into his stomach.

Again. I stabbed him again. Stabbed again.

That stopped the screaming. He made a gurgling sound and grabbed his belly with both hands. Dark blood seeped through the red hoodie and poured over his hands.

He dropped to his knees, moaning, making strange wheezing sounds. The blood ran out of his body. He raised his eyes to me, his face twisted in horror, in disbelief. He tried to speak, but blood rolled over his tongue and bubbled over his lips.

He sank on his side to the grass, hugging himself. He bled out so quickly.

I stood there watching, fighting back my nausea, gritting my teeth. So quickly. It happened so quickly. Or was I standing outside time? Did it actually take him a long time to die?

I can't tell you, Diary. I stood and watched the spreading blood. Such a big puddle of his blood, with him curled on his side inside it.

I was still gasping for breath, fighting the deep shudders that paralyzed my body, when I knew he was dead.

And as soon as I knew, I started to move, to breathe again, to think more carefully and calmly.

I wiped the blood-soaked knife on the sleeve of his hoodie. Then I folded it up and tossed it into my bag. Gathered my belongings and stuffed everything back where it belonged.

Then I drove home, sobbing all the way. Sobbing at the top of my lungs, big tears rolling down my face, burning my cheeks.

My boyfriend, my only true love, was dead. I killed him. Stabbed him and watched him bleed to death. Killed him. I killed him.

So of course I cried. Cried and sobbed and moaned all the way home. I knew my life would never be the same.

PART
TWO

15.

Thankfully, Mom and Dad were asleep in their room. I couldn't have faced them. I would've collapsed in a heap and never moved again.

How could I explain to them what I did? I couldn't explain it to myself.

I stood in the dark kitchen without turning on a light. My bag suddenly felt as if it weighed a hundred pounds. I let it fall to the floor in front of the kitchen door.

The house was so still. The only sounds were my harsh breaths and the hum of the refrigerator. I took a few steps toward the kitchen counter. My sneakers squeaked on the tile floor. I pictured them covered in blood.

I pictured Blade swimming on his side in a lake of his own blood. I never knew that blood could smell so powerful. It smelled tangy and sour, very metallic.

I pictured Blade raising his head above the blood, gazing at me. Blood flowed down his face, thickly matted his hair. But he stared at me through the layer of blood, an accusing stare. He didn't need to speak. I could read the horror and the anger on his face.

I shook my head hard, erasing the terrifying picture from my mind. I shut my eyes tight and held them closed. Could I stay in this darkness and keep all these pictures from my brain?

No. For some reason, Deena Fear appeared before my eyes. Her black hair flew about her head as if being blown by a hurricane wind. Her lips were bright red, brighter than Blade's blood.

In my imagination, my feverish imagination, she raised a red hoodie in both hands and waved it at me.

Why is she doing that? Why is she even in my thoughts now?

The frightening stories of the Fear family contained many murders. According to legend, the Fears throughout their history knew how to murder people in the most hideous and painful ways.

But I'm a Donnelly. My grandparents came from County Wicklow in Ireland. We have never been murderers . . . till now.

I made my way through the dark house, then up the stairs to my room. I leaned on the banister and stepped as lightly as I could. I didn't want to make a sound.

I closed the bedroom door carefully behind me, crossed the room in the dark, and slumped onto the edge of my bed. The window was open. The curtains drifted in and out softly in a gentle breeze. Pale light from the streetlight across the street washed over the carpet.

I sat hunched on the bed staring at the shadows of the shifting curtains. I don't know how much time passed. I didn't move. I barely breathed.

At some point, I scratched the fingernails of my left hand over the back of my right hand. Dug the nails into the skin. Just to feel something. Just to feel some pain. But I was numb. My hand was like a limp sponge. I didn't feel a thing.

I sat there staring at shadows, chilled in the breeze from the window. Images rolled through my mind. Red hoodies . . . rivers of blood . . . Blade's accusing eyes . . . I couldn't shut the pictures out.

"I have to confess," I said out loud, my voice hollow as it broke the deep silence. "I have to tell what I have done. I murdered Blade. I murdered him."

I collapsed into shoulder-heaving sobs. I lowered my head, covered my face with both hands, and cried. Cried till my face and hands were soaked from tears.

The flashing red-and-blue lights made me stop. I lowered my hands and stared at the glare of the lights outside the bedroom window.

I heard a car door slam. The sharp sound snapped me from my shock. I grabbed a wad of tissues and mopped my face. Then I stumbled to the window and gazed down at the street.

A Shadyside police patrol car had stopped at the bottom of my driveway. The flashing red-and-blue roof lights gave the front lawn an eerie, unreal carnival glow. I watched two dark-uniformed officers striding up the driveway.

My knees started to collapse. I gripped the windowsill to keep myself up. A wave of nausea made me swallow hard. Again. Again.

They were here. The police were already here. Here to arrest me for Blade's murder.

I lurched into the hall and flew down the dark stairs. So fast. The police were so fast. So quick to end my life.

16.

Gripping the banister tightly, I stopped at the foot of the stairs. The two cops stood side by side in the open front doorway. The pulsing red-and-blue lights behind them made them appear to flicker in and out of view.

They eyed me in silence as I stepped up to the doorway. They had their caps off. They both had short, black hair and dark eyes. They could have been twins, except that the one on the left was about a foot taller than his partner and had a thick black mustache.

The tall one had his right hand resting on the gun holster at his waist. They both stood erect, tense, as if expecting trouble.

I didn't plan to give them any trouble. I knew why they were there, and I knew I had no choice but to surrender to them.

I gazed from one to the other. Their faces revealed no emotion at all. I wondered if they could see how much I was trembling. "I-I . . . know why you're here," I stammered.

Their eyes grew wider as they studied me. "You do?" the shorter cop said.

His partner shifted his weight uncomfortably. "I'm Officer Rivera and he's Officer Miller. We were driving past and saw your front door open," he said. "We wanted to make sure no one had broken in."

My breath caught in my throat. I started to choke, but covered it up, made it sound like a cough.

I wanted to laugh. I wanted to do a crazy dance. I wanted to hug them both.

"Oh my God," I said, thinking fast. "My parents must have left it open. They . . . they were visiting friends. I think they just got home a little while ago."

The officers seemed as relieved as I did. Miller smiled and nodded. Rivera lifted his hand off his holster. He brushed back his short black hair.

"Or maybe it was the wind," I said, feeling braver. "I've been home all night. I didn't see the door was open."

"Check the latch," Miller said. "Make sure it works okay."

"Thanks for noticing," I said, my heart still racing. "I really appreciate it."

They started to turn away. But Rivera stopped and motioned to the sleeve of my shirt. I followed his gaze and saw the dark stain there.

My heart skipped a beat. I forced myself not to react at all.

"Is that blood?" he asked, studying it. "Did you cut yourself?"

I fingered the sleeve. Studied it, too. "It's an old stain," I said. "I don't think it's blood. I don't know what it is. It won't come out in the wash."

They both gave me two-fingered salutes, touching their foreheads. Then they turned and walked into the pulsing lights, down the front lawn to their car.

I closed the door carefully. I let out a long sigh of relief. My parents hadn't awakened. I leaned my back against the door, shut my eyes, and tried to force my heartbeats to slow.

They didn't come to arrest me for murder.

But they'd be back.

I opened my eyes and ran my fingers over the dark stain on my sleeve. Still damp.

"The knife!" Did I say those words out loud?

The bloodstain reminded me of the knife, and I realized I didn't remember what I had done with it.

The murder weapon.

In my horror, in my panic, in my insane moment of deadly rage—did I leave it beside Blade's body? Did I just toss it to the ground and run?

Or did I take it with me?

I suddenly pictured dropping it in my bag. My bag . . .

I'd left it by the kitchen door. Taking a deep breath, I pushed myself away from the front door and made my way to the kitchen. I grabbed the bag by the twin handles and carried it up to my room.

Holding the bag brought back all my panic, all the horror of that terrible scene beside Blade's house. The tug-of-war—Blade and I battling over this bag in my hands. . . . If only . . . If only I hadn't let go. If only Blade hadn't overturned the bag. . . .

The knife never would have fallen out. I never would have seen it or thought about it. . . . Or *used* it.

I heaved the bag onto my bed and bent to paw through it. Yes. There it was. It took only a few seconds to feel the knife at the bottom, to wrap my fingers around the handle, and lift it out. It trembled in my hand as if it were alive.

I held it in front of me and snapped it open. The silvery blade gleamed under the bedroom ceiling light, and tiny droplets of blood sparkled like jewels.

Blade's blood. I stared at the blade until I was nearly hypnotized by it. Stared at the glowing blood drops and the smear of blood near the handle. Stared until I wanted to scream. Until I wanted to explode.

Yes. I suddenly knew I would explode—just go to pieces in a furious burst of horrifying energy—if I didn't do something. If I didn't tell someone.

"I can't stand it." The words burst from my mouth. "I can't take it. I can't keep it all inside me."

I let the knife fall to the rug at my feet. But the spar-kling blood droplets on the blade lingered in my eyes.

Before I exploded, I had to tell someone. I had to con-fess what I had done.

Julie. I thought immediately of my friend Julie. She was so practical, so sensible. She would listen to me. She wouldn't freak out.

I grabbed my phone in my trembling hand. The key-pad came up. I stabbed at it, struggling to punch in Julie's number.

The phone rang twice before she answered.

"Julie? It's me!" I cried in a high, shrill voice. And the words just lurched from my mouth as if I were vomiting them into the phone. "I killed him! I did it. Oh, help me, Julie. Please help. I killed him. I just snapped. I lost it. I snapped. And I killed Blade!"

17.

I choked on the last words. My throat tightened and I couldn't speak. Panting, I pressed the phone to my ear.

"Who is this?" A hoarse voice on the other end, a woman's voice I didn't recognize. "Young lady, is this a prank call? If it is, it isn't funny."

Oh, wow. I glanced at my phone screen. Wrong number. I'd called a wrong number.

"S-sorry," I stammered. I clicked the call off before she could say anything else. I tossed the phone into my bag.

I dropped onto the bed and sat there hugging myself. I knew I wouldn't get to sleep that night. I wondered if I'd ever sleep again.

Blade's funeral was held in a small nondenominational chapel in North Hills. The chapel was long and narrow with dark wood-paneled walls and low wooden rafters overhead. Morning sunlight filtered in through narrow stained glass windows high on the walls.

Two huge vases of white lilies stood under spotlights in the front of a small altar. A podium stood between them. And beside the podium was Blade's coffin, made of shiny dark wood that glowed purple under the spotlights.

The coffin lid was up, and, from my seat near the back of the room, I could see that it was lined with a white satiny material. The idea that Blade was lying lifeless in that box didn't seem real to me.

Organ music played in the background. People drifted in silently. Not very many. Blade's family had moved to town so recently.

I sat between Julie and Miranda. Julie kept squeezing my hand and asking if I was okay. I nodded and wiped my tears with tissue after tissue.

I felt the whole thing was a dream. Staring at the tall flowers and the gleaming dark casket, the scene became a blur, and I knew I was about to wake up from this dream and go back to my real life. My real life with Blade.

But there were his parents in the front row, older-looking than I remembered. I'd only met them once. They huddled head to head, sobbing together, sobbing and shaking their heads as if they too didn't believe this could possibly be happening.

Miranda sneezed. The sound echoed off the low rafters. A few people turned around.

I gazed around and counted. Only nineteen or twenty people in the chapel. The pale, sad people dressed in dark colors squeezed together in the front two rows were rela-tives.

Julie, Miranda, and I were the only ones I recognized from our high school. I turned and let out a sharp breath as I saw Vanessa, the girl with white-blonde hair, the girl Blade took to the dance club. She came walking down the middle chapel aisle. She kept her eyes straight ahead on the coffin at the altar.

A few rows behind me, she turned. She saw me. She blinked. Stared for a moment, remembering. Then turned her gaze back to the front.

I felt my face start to burn as if on fire. *Did Vanessa know? She saw me go berserk at the club. Did she know?*

She walked right past my row and didn't glance my way again. She took a seat in the third row, behind the family, behind those who were sobbing and moaning and wip-ing their eyes.

I cried, too. The organ music rose, then fell. A young minister appeared, his head bowed solemnly. He had spikey dark hair and a black beard that he kept scratching as he gave his talk. He wore a brown sport jacket over dark slacks. His white shirt was open at the neck.

"Please sit down, everyone. We will begin. If you are new to this chapel, my name is Reverend Norman Prel-ler." He had a soothing voice and spoke very softly into the podium microphone. The sound echoed off all the empty seats.

"I want to confess that I never had the pleasure of meeting Blade." Preller rubbed his beard. It made a scratchy sound in the loudspeakers. "But so many people have come to tell me what a fine young man he was, that I feel the pain of this tragedy almost as much as anyone who knew him."

Yes, it was a tragedy.

Julie handed me another tissue. I wadded up the old one and stuffed it into my lap. I stared at the open coffin, at the white satin lining of the lid, and my thoughts wandered. I couldn't listen to this soft-voiced minister who had never met the boy I loved.

I thought about the night Blade and I parked up at River Ridge, high over Shadyside. The river sparkled beneath us in the light of a full moon.

We got out of my car and spread a blanket on the grass. Then we lay there on our backs, holding each other and gazing up at the stars. It was such a clear, silver, magical night.

We held each other and kissed and talked and talked. We talked together so easily. It was as if we had been close for all our lives. Blade talked about how his dream was to be an archaeologist. He wanted to live out on the prairie and dig up dinosaur bones and discover things about the distant past that no one had ever known.

Funny. I said my life's ambition was to leave Shadyside. That was my only goal.

Blade teased me. He said my goal was too easy. He said we could leave Shadyside any time we wanted. "Let's take off together," he said, his lips brushing my cheek. "We could just leave a note for our parents and head west. How about Montana? We could go to Montana."

I laughed and poked him in the ribs. "Montana? Really? Why Montana?"

He raised a finger and poked me back. "Aren't you curious about Montana?"

"Uh . . . no," I said. "I've never thought about Montana."

"That's why we should go," he said. He pulled me close. "Or maybe we should just stay here forever."

That was an awesome night, a night I'll never forget. I knew Blade wasn't serious about taking off, but I didn't care. I thought maybe someday . . .

But now here I was in this dark, stuffy chapel. Instead of gazing at the stars, I was gazing at Blade's coffin. The sermon was over. Prayers were said. And now everyone was standing, and a line was forming to walk past the coffin to give a last goodbye.

Blade's parents stood against the wall. His mother had her face buried in a handkerchief. His father kept shifting his weight nervously, his face pale and grim. The relatives were the first to march past the coffin and offer their whispered condolences to the parents.

I held back. "I don't want to," I said.

Julie and Miranda took my arms. "You have to, Caitlyn," Miranda said. "You want to say goodbye, don't you?"

I had a sudden strong urge to confess. To tell them what I had done. I bit my tongue and forced the impulse down.

I joined the line to the coffin. Julie and Miranda stayed close behind me. At the front wall, Vanessa was shaking hands with Blade's parents, nodding her head solemnly. I couldn't hear what she was saying. She turned and started up the side aisle, heading to the chapel exit. She didn't look over at me.

It all seemed unreal again. I felt as if I was floating over everything, not on the floor, not in this chapel. I wanted to be a bird, my wings spread, flying high overhead, not tied to the earth, not part of this horrible scene.

Floating . . . floating . . . My heart pattering like a hummingbird heart.

And there I was, gazing into the satiny coffin, staring at Blade's lifeless face. It was Blade and it wasn't Blade. His face was smothered behind a layer of makeup. His cheeks a bright pink. His hair matted in a clump on his head.

And the eyes . . . the blank stare . . . the glassy eyes. Open. Why did they leave his eyes open?

I sucked in a breath and pulled back. I suddenly didn't want him to see me. I didn't want to see my face reflected in those fake glass eyes.

Someone moaned. I think it was Blade's mother. Someone behind me sobbed loudly.

Julie grabbed my arm. We started to move past the coffin. But I let out a startled cry—and stopped. I stopped and stared in horror as Blade blinked those glassy green eyes.

His head slid to the right, then the left. And then it began to raise itself off the white satin pillow.

I gasped and clapped my hands over my mouth. I grabbed onto Julie with both hands as my knees started to fold. I opened my mouth to scream but no sound came out.

Was I imagining it? Was it my guilt wishing him back to life?

No. The room rang with screams and shrieks of horror, choked gasps and moans of disbelief.

"No . . . No . . . Noooo . . ." Blade's parents howled and raised their hands high in front of them, as if shielding themselves from the horror. In the middle aisle, an older woman slumped in a dead faint to the floor. No one rushed to help her. All eyes were on the coffin.

All eyes were on the corpse, as slowly . . . as if in slow motion . . . slowly . . . Blade sat up.

18.

"**H**e's moving! He's climbing out!"

"He's alive!"

"Blade—can you hear us? Blade?"

"Oh my God! This is impossible! This is crazy! Oh my God!"

Frightened voices rang out through the chapel. No one moved. Miranda and Julie had backed away from me. They huddled together at the side of the altar, their faces pale, eyes bulging.

I stood with my hands clamped to the sides of my face, frozen in front of the coffin, just a few feet from the moving corpse.

"A miracle! A miracle! My boy is alive!" his mother cried.

"A doctor. Is there a doctor here?" a woman shouted. "We need a doctor."

"He's alive! Get him out of there! He's not dead!"

Blade raised himself, his body stiff, his lips clamped tightly together, glassy eyes straight ahead. With his painted pink cheeks and lipsticked lips, he reminded me of a ventriloquist dummy. I suddenly felt like I was in one of those horror movies, the ventriloquist dummy coming to life, evil and menacing.

Of course, he was dead. I killed him. I watched him bleed out. I knew he was dead.

But here was Blade, my sweet dead Blade, sitting up in his pearly white coffin.

I watched his hand come up, so slowly, as if every inch was painful to him, as if every slight move was a challenge. Yes, Diary, his right hand slid up, and he turned his body. Twisted himself toward the horrified, paralyzed crowd of people who had come to mourn him.

The glassy eyes surveyed the crowd, moved from his parents to the middle-aged couple beside them to the older man leaning on a cane, all frozen in amazement, in disbelief.

He turned some more, a hard twist of his body. And now his eyes were on me. They had no pupils. They were solid green, the color of spring grass.

He trained his eyes on me and . . . and his lips trembled. His cheeks strained. He was trying to talk. Trying to open his mouth and talk. *But his lips were sewn together.*

He struggled and strained, mouth twisting into an ugly expression. Finally, he gave up. Eyes still on me, he raised his hand—and pointed. Pointed an accusing finger at me. The finger trembled in the air, then steadied itself, and he pointed me out to everyone.

I could almost hear his voice, almost hear him saying, "She killed me, everyone. She's the reason I'm a corpse."

"Ohhhhhhhh." A moan escaped my throat. I couldn't bear to face him. I knew I'd see those neon pink cheeks, those sewn-together red lips, the blank, blind eyes forever. Forever.

"Ohhh noooo." With another animal moan, I spun around to escape the horrifying sight. And saw a figure standing halfway up the aisle. A figure all in black.

Deena Fear.

Her straight black skirt came down nearly to the floor. She wore a black vest over a pleated, dark purple dress shirt. She stood in the aisle with her hands outstretched, curled into tight fists. And she was muttering, muttering something rapidly to herself.

Behind the owl-like glasses, her eyes were locked on the corpse.

She kept her fists tight and straight in front of her. In one fist, she carried some kind of silver ornament. An amulet, shaped like a bird with wings outstretched.

She held the amulet in front of her, tilted her head back, her lips moving rapidly. And I realized she was chanting, chanting words in a strange language, chanting under her breath, her face tight with concentration.

She raised the amulet above her head and the corpse moved. She swung her fists and the corpse swung its arm. She twisted the amulet up and down, and the corpse nodded its head.

It took me a long time to realize she was controlling him.

Chanting a little louder, she moved down the aisle toward us, her arms straight out, bird amulet gripped in front of her. She was breathing hard. Her eyes were tight slits. Her jaw was clenched in concentration.

Deena Fear brought Blade back to life.

"Deena!" I shouted her name. "Deena—what are you *doing?*"

She ignored my question and kept chanting, her lips moving rapidly, her eyes locked on the moving corpse. She took another step toward the coffin. She jerked her arms hard, and the corpse shuddered.

A hush fell over the chapel. Everyone watched Deena, watched the corpse, watched the horror show in amazed silence. The woman who had fainted was recovering in a pew at the side. Two little girls dressed in black hugged each other, crying loudly.

"Deena—" I called to her again.

"Come back, Blade," she murmured, stepping closer. "Come back now. Come back. Come back." Rivulets of sweat poured down her forehead and cheeks. The amulet trembled in her fist.

She raised her eyes to me. "Don't interrupt. This takes so much concentration . . . so much energy. I . . . I . . ."

I gasped as her eyes rolled up in her head. She uttered a short choking sound. Her knees collapsed. Her hands fell to her sides. And she collapsed onto the chapel floor.

Her head bounced hard against the wood. The amulet slid under a pew.

She didn't move.

Screams all around. I spun back to the coffin and didn't see Blade. I took a lurching step toward the alter, peered into the satiny casket lining, and saw him on his back. Eyes blankly staring up at the ceiling lights. Arms at his sides.

Dead again.

Not moving. Lifeless head sunk into the satin pillow. Not breathing. A corpse. A corpse. A corpse once again.

Blade's mother had collapsed to the floor, legs outstretched, her back against the wall. Her husband was trying to get her to take a cup of water. But his hands were shaking so hard, he spilled it on her.

People were screaming. People were crying. Julie and Miranda hid themselves behind one of the tall lily vases. They were talking rapidly, both talking at once, both making wild gestures with their hands.

A doctor trotted to the altar. He gazed frantically around the chapel, unable to decide who to help first. People sat devastated in the pews. A man slumped at a side pew, holding his hand over his heart, groaning loudly.

The doctor dropped to his knees in the aisle and leaned over Deena Fear. He raised her wrist, feeling for a pulse.

I moved over to Julie and Miranda. The three of us did a group hug, holding onto each other as if trying to hold on to reality, the real world, the world we knew where corpses didn't sit up in their coffins. Julie wiped her eyes with a damp handkerchief. Her cheeks were red from tears.

I felt a lot of things all at once. Alert and tense. Waiting for the next impossible thing to happen. Numb. And mainly frightened.

The doctor rubbed Deena's limp hand between his hands. I heard Deena groan. He reached behind her back and guided her to a sitting position.

She blinked and shook her head. Her black hair had fallen over her face. She brushed it away with both hands. "So much energy . . ." she murmured.

The doctor said something to her, bringing his face down to her ear. I couldn't hear what he said. The chapel had been silent, but now everyone was talking at once.

The doctor stood up, brushed off the knees of his dark suit pants, and moved to the man in front who was still pressing a hand over his chest.

Blade's parents were clinging to the sides of the coffin now, staring down at their dead son. His mother whispered something to him. Was she hoping he would sit up again?

I shuddered. I watched Deena climb to her feet. She grabbed the back of a pew to steady herself. Her glasses were crooked. Her face was as white as paper, and her chin and lips were trembling.

She searched until she found the silver bird amulet. Then she carefully lifted it off the floor and tucked it into her pocket.

Reverend Preller suddenly reappeared. I hadn't seen

him since the funeral ceremony began. He kept blinking rapidly, and one cheek twitched. He adjusted the sleeves of his brown jacket and kept clearing his throat nervously as he stepped up to the podium.

"Ladies and gentlemen," he began. The roar of screams and cries drowned him out. He tapped the microphone a few times. "Ladies and gentlemen, please."

The room quieted. He cleared his throat again. Played nervously with the knot on his necktie. His cheek twitched some more. "We've had an unfortunate incident," he said.

Those words caused everyone to start talking again.

An unfortunate incident?

Preller's face reddened. He cleared his throat again. "I need to make this last announcement," he pleaded. "The . . . burial will be held as scheduled. All are invited to Shadyside Oaks Cemetery. The family has requested that I tell you there will be no reception afterward. They request that they be allowed to deal with this devastating loss in privacy."

"But he isn't *dead!*" someone shouted.

This caused another roar of voices. I realized I was pressing my hands over my ears. *I have to get out of here. I can't take anymore.*

Julie and Miranda were talking heatedly to Preller, both gesturing and motioning to the coffin. I decided I would talk to them later.

I started up the side aisle toward the back of the chapel. My chest felt heavy. It was hard to breathe. I needed fresh air. I needed to go somewhere and think. I needed to escape.

I was halfway up the aisle when I realized Deena Fear was watching me. I stopped and turned toward her. She mouthed some words I couldn't understand. She seemed to be pleading with me. Her expression was intense.

She cupped her hands around her mouth and shouted. But the voices ringing off the walls and low rafters were deafening. I couldn't hear her.

I gave her a quick wave. I didn't want to talk with her. I had to escape. I turned away and trotted up the rest of the aisle. I pushed open the doors with both hands and stepped into the sunlight.

The sudden brightness made me shield my eyes with one hand. I took a deep breath of the warm air. I saw a group of children laughing and chasing each other in a playground across the street.

A sob escaped my throat. I wanted to be there playing with them. I wanted to be a child again.

I took another breath and made my way down the concrete chapel steps. A young man in blue sweats and a red-and-blue Red Sox cap jogged past me, leading a small brown dog on a leash.

The sunlight felt warm on my face. I left my car at the curb and wandered around for a while. I was dazed, Diary. In shock. Everyone at the funeral must have felt as upset and off-balance and totally weirded out as I did.

After walking in circles around North Hills, I must

have gotten back in my car. I must have driven home. I don't remember the drive at all.

The next thing I knew I was in my driveway. And then walking into the kitchen through the back door. I grabbed onto the kitchen counter. I felt dizzy and nauseous.

"Mom? Dad?" I called out. But, of course, they were at work.

I suddenly realized I hadn't eaten all day. Maybe some food in my stomach would help calm me. I was on my way to the kitchen when my phone beeped.

I picked it up and gazed at the screen. A text message. I didn't recognize the phone number. I lowered my eyes to the message and read:

It's me. Deena. They didn't bury him. It's not too late.

19.

I stared into the glare of my phone screen. I read the message again. I knew what Deena meant. I didn't have to puzzle over it.

I pictured her standing so tensely in the chapel aisle, the bird amulet raised in front of her as she chanted, chanted, and concentrated. And made the corpse move. Made Blade sit up. Made him turn and point at me. Stare at me with those terrifying glass eyes.

And I knew what she wanted now. She wanted to finish bringing Blade back to life. She wanted to finish what she started in the chapel. But why? Why did she want to bring Blade back?

To find out who killed him? Did she believe if she brought him back, he would name his murderer? Namely *me*.

The thought made me shudder. The phone slipped from my hand and dropped onto the kitchen floor. And as I fumbled to pick it up, it beeped again.

And there was another text from Deena:

It's urgent. Come to my house NOW.

And then another text:

Don't think about it. U don't have a choice.

I set the phone down on the kitchen counter. I didn't want to hold it. I didn't want to read any more messages from Deena Fear.

"She's crazy," I murmured out loud. I opened the fridge, grabbed a bottle of orange juice, tilted it to my mouth, and gulped it down. When I finished, I was breathing hard, my chest heaving.

I loved Blade. At least, I thought I loved him. But I didn't want him back. I didn't want him alive again. Alive to tell everyone that I was a murderer, that I went into an insane rage and stabbed him, stabbed him, stabbed him.

I knew if Blade came back . . . If Deena really could bring him to life again . . . my life would be over.

How could I stop her from doing this? I didn't have a clue. I didn't know how to stop her. But I definitely didn't want to *help* her.

I grabbed a container of tuna salad from the fridge and began forking it into my mouth. I was starving. I felt as if I had a vast canyon inside me. It wasn't normal. I never get ravenous like this.

Nothing was normal now. Nothing.

People would be talking about the funeral forever. The corpse who sat up in his coffin. It would be on the news. It would be all over town . . . everywhere. A major news story—and a horrifying memory for everyone who was there.

I stared at Deena's text on my phone. I wanted to take the phone and heave it as far as I could out the back door. I wanted to be by myself. I didn't want anyone to reach me.

I jumped as the phone rang. Deena. She wasn't going to leave me alone. She wasn't going to give me a chance.

I let it ring for a long while till I couldn't stand it any longer. I swung it off the counter and pressed it to my ear. "Deena—leave me alone!" I cried.

Silence at the other end. Then: "Huh? Caitlyn? Is that you?"

"Julie?" I swallowed. "Oh, hi. I . . . thought it was a wrong number."

"Caitlyn, are you okay? You left the chapel without telling us. Miranda and I—"

"Sorry," I said. "I had to get out of there. It was all so weird and—"

"It was so freaky, Caitlyn," Julie said breathlessly. "When Blade's body started to move, I . . . I thought I was in a horror movie. I've never been so scared in my life."

"Me, too," I said.

"I couldn't even scream," Julie said. "I just held on to Miranda and watched. Everyone was screaming and fainting and crying and—"

"It was too horrible," I said. "Like a bad dream."

"No one could believe it," Julie said. "That minister . . . He was a total nerd, wasn't he? He tried to explain it. He said the floor was tilted and the coffin moved—not the body. He was trying to reassure everyone, I guess."

"That's stupid," I said. My stomach growled. I opened the fridge and looked for something else to eat.

"We're not stupid. We saw what happened, Caitlyn. Right? It wasn't the coffin tilting. Blade sat up. He was dead but he sat up and he tried to talk." Her voice cracked. I heard her coughing.

He tried to talk and tell everyone that I killed him.

"Julie? Are you okay?" I asked.

"No, I'm not okay. I'll never be able to get it out of my mind. I'll always see him sitting up in the coffin, straining and struggling. I'll always see those weird green eyes. His hand slowly raising. I'll never be able to forget it. I . . . I think I'm going crazy, Caitlyn. Do you really think Deena Fear made him sit up?"

"I don't know," I said. "Maybe. She's a Fear, right? That family is supposed to know about all kinds of magic. Dark, frightening magic. You've heard the stories, too. We all have. How some of them had strange powers. I mean . . . that amulet she held . . ."

"And she was chanting something. Oh my God, Caitlyn. Do you really think she made him sit up?"

"I don't know. Maybe. Maybe she did. It's too frightening to talk about, Julie. We have to try to get past it somehow." Those words sounded phony, even as I said them.

Why didn't I tell Julie about the urgent texts from Deena, how Deena said it wasn't too late? I don't know.

Maybe I thought if I didn't tell anyone about Deena, she would go away. The whole thing would go away.

"They didn't bury him, Caitlyn," Julie said. "The body is still in the chapel. Blade's parents wouldn't let them bury him. They were totally messed up. They were screaming and crying. It was horrible."

"What do you mean? What happened?"

"They wouldn't leave the coffin. They grabbed Blade's body and began to shake it. They said it might come alive again. They said he wasn't really dead. They saw him sit up. Everyone saw him. And they wouldn't let him be buried in case he moved again."

"Oh, wow. Oh, wow."

"There was a doctor there, remember? You saw him. He revived Deena Fear when she fainted? Well . . . he managed to get Blade's parents to step aside. It wasn't easy. Finally, he examined the body.

"And what did the doctor say?" I asked.

"He said Blade was dead. Not breathing. The parents both started screaming for him to go away. And then that minister Preller started shouting for everyone to leave. He threatened to call the police if everyone didn't leave the chapel right away."

"Oh, wow. Then what happened?"

"It got way ugly. Blade's parents grabbed the sides of the coffin and said they would never leave. Preller tried to pull them away. It started to be a real fight. Miranda and I . . . we hurried out of there. I couldn't stand it anymore, and I didn't want to be there when the police arrived. It was so *horrible,* Caitlyn."

"Oh, wow." I didn't know what to say. It was so hard to imagine . . .

"Poor Miranda," Julie continued. "She threw up on the sidewalk as soon as we got outside. She just heaved up her guts. She felt totally sick. She went straight home, and I . . . well . . . I wandered around for a while. In a total daze. I mean, I still feel sick and weird, and I can't stop the shakes. I mean, it's like it all followed me home."

"Julie, I feel the same way," I said.

"Do you want to come over?"

I thought about it. "No. Sorry. I think I'm going to try to take a nap. Maybe if I sleep for a while, I can calm myself down a little."

"Oh. Okay. Call me later. When you wake up. Okay?"

"Okay," I said. I clicked off.

I knew I was lying. I knew I wasn't taking a nap. I was driving to Deena Fear's house.

Why?

That I couldn't tell you.

20.

Shadows swallowed my car as I turned off Old Mill Road onto Fear Street. Tall, ancient trees on both sides had formed an archway over the street. Sunlight struggled to get through the tangled branches.

Fear Street winds along the east side of Shadyside. Large, old houses, mostly stone and brick, line one side of the street. Most of them are far back from the street, sitting on wide front yards, hidden by tall, well-trimmed hedges.

These are the oldest houses in town. They were built by rich settlers in the late nineteenth and early twentieth century, including the notorious Fear family (who were thought to practice strange dark magic.)

The houses all face the Fear Street Woods, a thick tangle of tall, old maple, sycamore, and oak trees, deep silent woods that stretch for miles, and, some say, are always in shadow. That's one of the many legends about the street. That the sun refuses to shine on the Fear Street Woods.

So many dark stories.

Everyone in town knows about the frightening animal howls in the woods late at night. The strange, darting creatures spotted by hunters, creatures running on two legs that no one could identify. And the two Fear sisters who, many years ago, were found dead in the woods with their bones all missing. Just their skin and organs resting under a tree. No bones.

Yuck. This is what I thought about, Diary, as I drove under the tall, arching limbs over Fear Street, looking for Deena Fear's house. Fear Street looks so normal and peaceful—even pretty—as you follow its curves. But most people in town, even those who are not superstitious, avoid it if they can.

I slowed the car near the end of the street as the ruins of the Fear mansion came into view. Over a hundred years ago, the magnificent old house burned to the ground in a tragic blaze, a fire that consumed the whole house and everyone in it.

Many said it was the evil in the house that caused the fire. It was reported that the screams inside the burning house lasted for hours—and continued long after the fire had been quenched.

That was over a hundred years ago. To this day, no one has cleared away the charred wreckage of the house. There has been no one willing to clear it or to build a new house on the evil site. The black-and-burned mansion hunches on its sloping lawn like some kind of giant broken insect.

A large stone guesthouse behind the mansion, nearly hidden at the edge of the woods, is where Deena Fear lives. I parked my car on the street. The driveway curving up to the mansion was overrun by tall weeds and burned pieces of lumber.

As I made my way up the lawn past the wreckage of the mansion, a blast of wind from the woods nearly blew me over. I toppled backward, trying to keep my balance. It was almost as if I was being warned to stay back, to not come any closer.

Why *was* I there? Why had I obeyed Deena's summons and hurried here when everything told me to avoid her, to stay away. Every sign screamed *danger.* So why did I hurry to this forbidden spot to see this strange girl who wasn't even a friend? Far from a friend.

I couldn't tell you. I couldn't explain it.

I ducked my head, holding my hair down with both hands as another strong gust howled past me. I stepped around a deep pile of ashes and had to jump over a tall clump of weeds.

The house was two stories high, very long, bigger than it appeared from the street. Several windows were shuttered. The others were all dark. The walls were a gray stone. The slanting shingled roof was painted red. The door at the side of the house appeared to be the only door.

I raised my hand to knock—and the door swung open.

Deena stood in the doorway. I heard classical piano

music from the room behind her. "Come in." She stepped aside. She didn't seem at all surprised to see me.

She hadn't changed from the funeral. Same pleated purple shirt, black vest, long black skirt almost to the floor. She had tied her long hair back with a black velvet ribbon. She had a tiny silver spider in one pierced nostril.

I followed her from the narrow front hall to a large living room. The rooms were all dark. One table lamp sent a dim gray light over the leather couch. The piano music grew louder. Two large painted portraits, an old-fashioned-looking man and woman, attractive but stern, cold-faced, unsmiling, faced the fireplace.

"My famous ancestors," Deena murmured. She motioned for me to keep walking.

The hall led past a library. Sunlight filtered in through a high, narrow window. I saw floor-to-ceiling bookshelves filled with old books, a desk piled high with books, a stack of books on the floor.

I couldn't resist. "Do you like to read?" I asked.

"Yes. But those books aren't for everyone," she answered. "You have to be interested in special things to want to read those books."

"Like what?"

She didn't answer. We turned a corner. I gazed down the long hall. "Are we all alone here?"

"No. My parents are here, too."

The hallway led to a large room at the back of the

house. I blinked in the sudden light. The back wall was glass, looking out into the woods.

Outside the window, tall weeds bent from side to side close to the house. A patch of spring wildflowers caught my eye. Beyond them, I saw a thick clump of evergreen shrubs.

I heard a *squawk.*

I blinked when I saw a parrot on a perch near the center of the room. "That's Tweety," Deena said. "He's my favorite. Isn't he a pretty boy?"

The bird was beautifully plumed with red, blue, and green feathers. It hopped on the perch, as if it was excited to see us. It squawked again, making sure we were paying attention.

My eyes caught a large aquarium on a table near the parrot perch. A single bed stood against the far wall. A desk with a laptop computer. A long, cluttered worktable, test tubes, glass pipes, like a chemist's table, scattered papers, electronic equipment I didn't recognize.

"This is my room," Deena said. "We can start here."

"Start what?" I asked.

Again, she didn't answer. She strode to the worktable and picked something up. When she turned, I saw that it was the silver bird amulet she had held at the chapel.

She raised it so I could see it clearly. Then she stepped back into the circle painted on her floor. "We don't have much time, Caitlyn." Behind the owlish glasses, her dark eyes stopped on me. "If we want to do this . . ."

"Deena—I don't understand," I said. "You have to tell me what you want to do."

She rolled her eyes. "Bring Blade back, of course."

My mouth dropped open. I started to protest, but no sound came out.

Deena spun the amulet in her hand. "I came close in the chapel," she said. "You saw. You saw how close I came. But it takes so much concentration. It takes so much out of me."

I couldn't hold back. "Are you for real?" I cried. "You made the corpse sit up. But you don't really think you can bring Blade totally back to life—do you?"

"Caitlyn, you saw the books in the library. The books told me how to do it. My family—we know things. We can do things."

"This is crazy," I said. "I'm sorry. I have to go. I don't know why I came."

"I do," she said, moving to block the doorway. "You came because you want to help me."

"N-no," I stammered. "That's not true. I don't want to help you. Because it's crazy, Deena. If you're serious, you need help. If you seriously think you can bring Blade back to life . . ." My voice faded. I was trembling.

She took a few steps toward me, lowering the amulet to her side. "If I prove it to you?"

"Huh? Prove it?" My head was swimming now.

"If I prove I can do it, will you help me? I don't have

the strength to do it alone. Will you help me if I prove I can do it?"

"No. You can't prove it," I said. "I'm sorry, Deena. This is too disturbing. You have to find someone to talk to. You're not making sense. I can't help you. I'm really sorry."

I started to the door. Deena grabbed my elbow and spun me around. "Watch. I can do it. I'm not crazy, Caitlyn. I'm a Fear. I can do terrible things. I can do frightening things. You have to believe me. Watch."

"Deena, wait—"

She grabbed the parrot around its middle. The bird squawked in surprise. She squeezed her fingers around it and swung it off its perch.

"Deena—stop!" I cried. "What are you going to do?"

The parrot squawked and twisted its head, struggling to escape. Deena carried it to the aquarium—and plunged the bird down into the water. Pushed it to the bottom and held it underwater.

"Deena—no! What are you doing?"

I rushed at her. I grabbed her arm. I tried to pull the bird up from the aquarium. But Deena pushed down with all her strength, and I couldn't move it.

"What are you *doing*?" I cried. "What are you doing?"

"Drowning the parrot," she said.

21.

The bird struggled, kicking its claws, twisting its head. Deena pressed it to the aquarium bottom.

I leaped back in horror. The water tossed and splashed. A few seconds later, it was still.

The parrot slumped in Deena's hand. She pulled it up. Water dripped off the beautiful feathers. It didn't lift its head. It didn't move.

"The parrot is dead," Deena said without any emotion at all. She squeezed the bird like a sponge, and water ran off it into the aquarium.

At that moment, at that horrifying, sickening moment, I realized how dangerous Deena was. And at the same time, I realized that I could be in danger, too.

She wasn't just crazy. She could take a beautiful bird— her pet, her favorite—and drown it in her hand and *not feel anything.*

I gripped my throat. I felt sick.

"Now watch," Deena snapped angrily. "Are you

watching, Caitlyn? What's wrong with you? I'm show-ing you something."

"Sorry," I said. My eyes were on the door. I didn't want to look at the dead bird. I pictured it in her hand, at the bottom of the aquarium. Struggling. Twisting and strug-gling. Little eyes bulging. Filling its lungs with water. Taking its last breath.

Deena set the parrot down on the worktable. Water rolled off its body, forming a puddle around it. She raised the silver amulet in front of her. She pressed it against the belly of the bird.

I took a deep breath and forced myself to breathe nor-mally.

Deena was chanting now, repeating and repeating words in a language I'd never heard before. She shut her eyes and held the amulet over the parrot. And chanted, her lips moving rapidly, the words repeating so softly I couldn't hear them.

Sweat formed on Deena's forehead. Her eyeglasses ac-tually steamed up. The amulet quivered in her hands as she continued to chant. A ray of sunlight through the window made the silver bird ornament glow.

I gasped when the parrot uttered a weak cry. The bird opened its eyes. It raised its head.

Deena continued to chant. Sweat ran down the sides of her face. Her voice became brittle, raspy.

The parrot uttered another squeak. It shook its head

hard, tossing off water. It tested its wings, then climbed unsteadily to its feet.

Deena stopped chanting and opened her eyes. She mopped her perspiring face with the sleeve of her shirt. Gently, she lifted the parrot off the table and returned it to its perch.

She brushed its wing feathers tenderly with one finger. The parrot tilted its head and nibbled at her finger.

Then Deena raised her face to me with a strange, pleased smile on her face. "Back to life," she said in a whisper.

I couldn't hide my shock. My mouth hung open as I stared at the parrot, preening its still-wet feathers. I struggled to think of what to say.

"I . . . I still want to go home," I said finally. "You are scaring me, Deena. I don't need this."

Her strange, tight-lipped smile returned. "Yes, I'm scary. That's why you're going to help me, Caitlyn."

"I-I don't understand," I stammered.

"You don't have to," she snapped. "Don't try to understand. Just come with me. We don't have much time."

"To bring Blade back to life?" My voice came out tiny. Fear tightened my throat.

She nodded. "They didn't bury him. He's still in the chapel. We have to go there now." She stepped away from the parrot perch. "You saw what I can do. We have to do it before it's too late."

"But . . . why?" I said. "Why bring him back, Deena?"

The parrot suddenly spoke up: *"Why? Why? Why?"*

Deena's eyes widened behind her large, round glasses. Circles of pink appeared on her pale cheeks. "Because I saw him first."

I gasped. "Huh? What does that mean? That doesn't make any sense."

"I saw him first, Caitlyn, and now it's my turn." She started to the door. "This time he'll be mine."

"Deena, wait," I said, hurrying after her. "Wait. I'm not doing this. I can't. I don't want to bring Blade back."

She wheeled around, and her eyes bulged with anger. "Why not? I thought you loved him. I thought you were crazy about him."

"I . . . I thought so, too," I said, my voice cracking. "But no. I can't do it. I don't want him back. It can't happen because—"

I stopped. I was about to confess why I didn't want to see Blade back. I was about to tell her that I was the one who killed Blade. And if he comes back . . . if he comes back . . .

I don't know what Blade will do to me, and I'm too terrified to find out.

I was about to confess. I was about to explain. I hesitated. I stood there debating, thinking hard. I didn't want to confide in this strange, frightening girl. What would she do if she learned the truth about me, the truth about Blade's murder?

I knew I couldn't tell Deena the truth. I knew I had to get away from her.

I took a deep breath, spun to the door, and took off. I raised both hands and shoved her out of my way.

Startled, Deena uttered a cry and staggered back a few steps, off-balance just long enough for me to escape. My shoes pounded the hard floor as I burst into the hallway, glanced right, then left.

Which way? Which way had we come in?

Shouting my name, Deena came running into the hall. I spun around and bolted to the right. The dimly lit hall gave me no clue as to the right direction to run.

I passed rooms on both sides, their doors shut tight. A high window at the end of the hall let in a wash of gray evening light. It made me feel as if I was running in a fog.

A mirror to my right gave me a glimpse of myself as I ran past, disheveled and frightened. At the end of the hall, another long corridor led in both directions.

I took the right again. I remembered there was only one door to this strange, old guest house. Was I running to it—or away from it?

Deena's shouts followed me, ringing off the walls, repeating my name again and again.

A sharp pain stabbed my side. I pressed my hand against it and kept running. The hall ended in black double doors. Not the entrance. I must have run the wrong way. And now I was trapped back here. Unless . . .

I grabbed both door knobs and swung the doors open. I could see a large dark room, the darkness cut by two slender beams of light from the high ceiling.

Deena's cries in my ears, I slammed the doors behind me. I fumbled for a lock on them. But no. I couldn't find any.

Gasping for breath, I staggered into the inky shadow of the room. I gazed up at the twin beams of light. So mysterious. And then I followed the light down . . . down . . . straight down to the floor.

I opened my mouth in a choked cry.

And gaped at the twin glass display cases. Tall glass cases rising up from the floor, glowing under the lights. And inside the cases . . .

Oh my God.

Two people. A man and a woman. Dressed in black outfits, as if for a funeral. Standing very still. Eyes wide. Each one staring out of a display case, staring straight ahead, not at each other.

The man had short, black hair and dark eyes. The woman had shoulder-length brown hair and bright blue eyes. Their faces were a strange orange.

Store mannequins, I thought. *Clothing store mannequins.*

But why were they here? Why hidden in a back room? Mannequins in glass cases with spotlights on them as if they were on display?

Still struggling to catch my breath, I took a few steps closer. The man's hands were at his sides. The backs of his hands were wrinkled, like real human hands. The woman had a diamond wedding ring on her left hand.

Behind me, the doors swung open with a crash. I gasped and spun around.

Deena stood in the doorway, holding onto the sides of the doors. Her gaze went from me to the twin cases. Then she locked her eyes on me.

"I see you've met my parents," she said.

22.

I opened my mouth to speak, but no sound came out. I stared at her open-mouthed, my legs trembling so hard I started to fall.

Finally, I found my voice. "That's a joke, right? You're joking?"

She shook her head. "Not a joke. That's Mom and Dad. In the flesh."

"But how?" I uttered. "I mean, why? I mean—"

"They never should have let me take that taxidermy class," she said.

I'm in a nightmare.

That's what I thought, Diary.

I turned my back on the display cases. I couldn't bear to look at them now. I pressed a hand to my throat, struggling to keep my lunch down.

"They are mannequins, right?" I said. "I know the stories about your family, Deena. But no way. *No way* I'll believe that you stuffed your own parents."

"I don't have time to explain," she said. "They were very annoying people. I didn't really have a choice."

She grabbed my hand and pulled me back into the hall. I must have been dazed or in shock or something. I let her pull me back to her room without a fight.

The parrot bobbed up and down on his perch, excited to see us again. The tall weeds outside the wide window swayed in a shifting breeze.

"You're going to help me, Caitlyn," Deena said softly. She removed her glasses and rubbed her eyelids. Her eyes looked so much smaller without her glasses. "You don't have a choice."

I didn't reply, just glared at her. The faces of the couple in the glass cases lingered in my mind. The woman *did* look a lot like Deena.

"You're coming to the chapel with me now," Deena said, her voice low and steady. "We're going to bring Blade back."

"No. I can't," I finally found my voice. "I can't bring him back. I don't *want* to bring him back."

And then, suddenly, I told her. It just came out of me.

"Deena, I don't want to see Blade again," I said. "I *can't* see Blade again. Because . . . because I'm the one who killed him."

Deena dove forward and grabbed me by the shoulders.

She gave me a hard shake. A disgusted sneer spread over her face.

"You idiot!" she cried. "*You're* not the one who killed him. *I* did!"

23.

A shuddering cry escaped my lips. She gave me a shove, and I stumbled back a few steps. I caught my balance, but my head was spinning.

I stared at her, sucking in breath after breath.

Deena's hair was wild about her head now, as if it had come alive. Her normally pale face was red, her mouth in a tight scowl.

Was she lying? She had to be.

"You—you were there?" I choked out. "In Blade's backyard? When . . . when I stabbed him?"

"I stabbed him," she insisted. She crossed her arms in front of her black vest. "I mean, I *made* you stab him. You didn't act on your own, Caitlyn. You . . . you were too much in love with him to kill him."

She couldn't control her jealousy. She spat those last words, her face tight with fury.

"But—why?" I demanded. "Why kill him? Why did he have to be killed?"

"Because he betrayed us," Deena replied, arms still tightly crossed in front of her.

Us.

"I followed you to Blade's house that night," Deena said. She swept back her hair with both hands. "I couldn't let him get away with it. I didn't know . . . I didn't know he had a girlfriend. That girl Vanessa with the sweet smile and the mousy-soft voice. I wanted to puke, Caitlyn. Seriously. I just wanted to puke."

Behind me, Tweety the parrot chimed in again: *"Why? Why? Why?"*

"So . . . you followed me?" I said.

Deena nodded. "I waited and watched. I saw how angry you were at him. Angry and hurt. And you had every right to be, Caitlyn. I saw him first. I saw Blade first. But you had every right to be out-of-your-mind angry. And when I saw that knife fall out of your bag . . ."

Her voice trailed off. I could see Deena was picturing the whole thing in her mind as she described it to me.

"I saw my opportunity, and I took it," she said, eyes flashing behind the big eyeglasses.

"You're crazy," I blurted out. "Earth calling Deena. How about a little reality check? You didn't do anything. I picked up the knife. I held the knife. I stabbed him. I stabbed him and I killed him, Deena. Not you."

She crossed her arms again and smirked at me.

"I stabbed him! I stabbed him!" I shouted. The words came out in sobs. My whole body shuddered. I was finally confessing. Finally letting my horrible secret out. "I stabbed him and stabbed him!"

She shook her head. "Why are you such a pain? Didn't I tell you we have to hurry to bring Blade back?"

I wiped tears off my cheeks. I clenched my jaw, trying to stop the shudders that shook my body.

"Here's a quick demonstration," Deena said. "Here is how I made you stab Blade, okay? I was in charge. You weren't. I'll show you, Caitlyn."

I narrowed my eyes at her. "Another demonstration?" I shuddered and pictured her drowning the parrot again.

She pointed to the glass wall at the back of the room. Outside, I could see the late afternoon sun lowering behind the trees. Tiny white butterflies fluttered over the wildflowers at the back of the house.

Deena snapped her fingers, then worked them in some kind of code, almost like sign language. Then she pointed to the window again. "Go over there and do a cartwheel," she said.

"Okay," I said.

The parrot slid from side to side on his perch. I strode to the wall, stepped into a square of red sunlight on the floor, raised my arms above my head, and did a fairly graceful cartwheel.

I landed unsteadily and nearly stumbled into the glass. But I caught my balance and turned to Deena.

"Do another one," she said, motioning again with her fingers.

"No problem," I said. I concentrated this time and did a much more athletic cartwheel. This time I landed perfectly. "Ta-da."

"Are you catching on?" Deena said. "Are you starting to see how I can make you do whatever I want? Do you see how I used you to stab Blade?"

I felt confused. "Well . . ."

"I'll give you one more demonstration," she said. "If that's what it takes to convince you I'm telling the truth." She did that thing with her fingers again. "Caitlyn, go over there, take the parrot, and drown him again."

"Okay," I said.

24.

The parrot flapped his wings rapidly, ducked, and twisted his head. He seemed to sense what was coming. I wrapped my hand around his middle and lifted him off the perch. He squawked frantically and snapped his beak, trying to bite my hand as I carried him over to the aquarium.

I curled my hand tightly so he couldn't escape. I glimpsed six or seven goldfish in the tank, swimming slowly in a cluster. I lowered the parrot toward the water.

The bird began to squawk like crazy, squirming and twisting frantically in my hand.

"Okay, stop," Deena called. "Put Tweety back on his perch."

I turned away from the aquarium and quickly obeyed. I set the parrot down carefully on the perch. He squawked and nodded his head several times, as if telling me off.

"Tweety has had a tough day already," Deena said. "Let's give the dude a break."

I blinked. The room darkened as the sun dropped behind the trees. Somewhere far in the distance, I heard a howl. A hunting dog maybe.

Deena stood in the doorway. I could see the impatience on her face. She was waiting for me to say something.

"I understand," I said. "I get it, Deena." I let out a long sigh. "I see what you did. Mind control, right? You used me."

"It was for your own good," she replied.

My mouth dropped open. "Huh? My own good? Are you *kidding* me? You . . . you turned me into a *murderer.*"

"He betrayed us," she said. "He had it coming." She turned and headed into the hall.

"But what about my life?" I cried, hurrying after her. "My life might be over. I'm a murderer. If the police figure it out . . . If they arrest me . . ."

"It will be different this time," she said, picking up her pace, jogging to the door, her hair flying behind her.

"Slow down, Deena. You're not listening to me at all." We passed the library with all the old, dust-covered volumes from floor to ceiling, books of evil magic, I decided, witchcraft, voodoo, supernatural spells. . . . I'm sure Deena was familiar with it all.

"It will be different," she said, grabbing car keys from a basket on a table in the front entryway. "This time he'll be mine. This time he will treat me right. It's going to be awesome. Awesome, Caitlyn. You'll see."

She's totally insane, I thought. *She's in her own world.*

And here I was, going with her. Climbing into the little Honda Civic beside her. Fastening my seat belt. Preparing . . . for *what*?

"Deena, are you controlling me right now?" I demanded.

She started the car. Adjusted the mirror outside her window, shifted into reverse, and started to back down the weed-choked obstacle course of a driveway.

"Are you?" I asked. "Are you controlling me?"

"Going to be awesome," she repeated. The car bumped over something hard in the driveway. "You'll see. So different this time."

"But what are we *doing*?" I screamed. "Tell me. What are we doing right now? Where are we going?"

She backed off the driveway onto Fear Street. Across the street, the trees shivered in the woods. Long evening shadows fell over our car as she shifted into drive and sped off.

"We're going to the chapel, like I told you," she answered finally. "Blade is waiting for me. Waiting for me to bring him home."

I watched the smile spread across her face. "You're going to take him from his coffin and—"

"Bring him home and bring him back, back to life. Just like Tweety, my sweet parrot. I've already done the prep work, Caitlyn. I spent the whole night preparing. I've done everything the book said. I know I can do it. I have no doubt at all."

The houses rushed past us as she sped along Division Street. The evening rush hour traffic was mostly going the other way. I wanted to roll down the window and shout to the other cars: "Help me! Help me out of here!"

But instead, I tilted my head back against the seat and shut my eyes. I couldn't control my leaping thoughts. And I told myself I had only me to blame for this.

Why did I obey her text message and come running to her house? I could have avoided all the horrifying insanity—the drowned parrot, the dead parents under their spotlights. . . .

Perhaps she used her mind control powers to bring me to Fear Street and her house.

Perhaps I was never in control today.

From all the insanity, there was only one good thing I learned. I am not a murderer. Deena was the murderer. I wasn't in control.

Of course, the police would never buy that story. No one would. Knowing I wasn't responsible should have made me feel better. But here I was, a prisoner of this crazy girl, one more victim of the Fear family's evil, about to break into a chapel and steal a corpse from its coffin.

How could I possibly feel anything but fear and regret?

Deena pulled to the curb and parked the car near the corner. The little chapel stood in deep shadow now, the sun having completely gone down. Through the passenger window, I could see a pale sliver of moon hanging low over the trees.

A wide concrete path cut through the closely trimmed lawn. Deena made me lead the way. I guess, to make sure I didn't try to escape again.

We were halfway up the path when the front chapel door swung open.

"Quick!" Deena grabbed me and pulled me behind a wide evergreen shrub. We both ducked low and watched as Reverend Preller, still in that brown sport jacket, stepped out of the chapel. He turned and locked the door carefully. Then he raised his face to the sky. I think he was just taking a breath of the cool night air.

Deena pulled me down lower. The evergreen branches prickled my face. I couldn't see the minister now, but I heard his footsteps on the path. Growing louder. Coming closer.

My heart started to pound. If he turned in our direction, he would see us crouching there. We would be caught. And how would we explain what we were doing there?

He walked right past us. His eyes were on the sky. He walked quickly, whistling to himself, swinging his arms in a steady rhythm.

I turned and watched him reach the curb. He crossed the street and stepped up to a dark green car parked there.

Deena and I waited till he drove away. Then we straightened up and walked to the chapel entrance. "It's locked," I said. "We watched him lock it."

"Not a problem," she said softly. She motioned to the side of the building. "There's a back entrance behind the minister's office. I made sure it was unlocked before I left the funeral."

I followed her around the side. An orange light flickered dimly through the row of stained glass windows, a dim light inside. The back door was nearly hidden by tall shrubs.

Deena grabbed the door handle and tugged. The door slid open easily. We slipped inside. The air was hot in here and smelled stale.

We were in a back hallway. The door to Preller's small office was open. In the dim light, I could see a narrow desk piled high with papers, a laptop, and a stack of books.

And what were those things on top of the bookshelf? I squinted hard. *Star Wars* figures. The minister had a collection of *Star Wars* figures.

The floor creaked beneath our shoes. The sound brought me back from my wandering thoughts. I grabbed Deena's shoulder. "Do you think anyone's watching the chapel?" I whispered. "A night guard or something?"

She shrugged. "I don't know. Stay alert."

Alert? I'd never been more alert in my life. That's what fright can do to you. Every creak of the floor made me jump. Every flicker of the light made my heart skip a beat.

"It's about time for a cat to jump out at us and scare us

to death," I whispered. "Isn't that what always happens in these scary situations?"

Deena turned and glared at me. "Why are you making jokes? This isn't funny."

"I-I," I stammered. "My brain is trying to keep it light, I guess. That's one way of dealing with fear."

"Just shut up," she snapped. "Follow me."

A narrow doorway led us into the chapel. We were standing a few feet behind the altar. I let my eyes wander to the back of the long room. Electric candles along the walls sent a warm yellow glow over the empty pews, and up to the low wood-beam rafters.

The huge vases of lilies hadn't been moved. But the coffin was no longer resting between them. The sick-sweet smell of the lilies overwhelmed everything.

"There's no one here," Deena whispered. She pointed to a narrow side room in the corner. I followed her gaze and saw the dark wood coffin. Blade's coffin. The lid was down. The coffin was bathed in a deep blackness.

"They just moved it aside," Deena whispered. "Follow me. And do exactly as I say. We have to lift him out of the coffin carefully. Once he's out, we'll wrap our arms around his waist and walk him out between us."

I shivered. I'd never touched a dead person before. Blade was only the second dead person I'd ever seen. My grandmother was the first, and she was over eighty when she died.

Deena stepped up to the side of the coffin. I hung back. A wave of terror washed over me. What would the corpse feel like? Would it be all squishy and soft? Or had it hardened stiff as a board? Would it smell? Didn't all dead things smell horrible?

"What are you waiting for?" Deena motioned impatiently for me to join her.

I took a deep breath and stepped up beside her. The coffin rested on a low table. The lid was at my shoulders. I held my breath. I didn't want to smell it.

"It's . . . too dark," I whispered. "How can we see anything?"

Deena pulled out her phone. She clicked on the flashlight icon. The phone sent a bright narrow beam of white light over the coffin.

"Okay," she whispered. "Let's lift the lid together. It's probably not that heavy."

I moved my two hands to the edge of the lid. Deena held the phone light in her teeth and wrapped her hands on the lid.

"Okay. Now," she whispered.

I was shaking so hard, I didn't know if I could get my arms to move. But somehow I found the strength. We both pushed up. The lid lifted easier than I imagined.

We raised the lid high, and it clicked into place in an upright position. Then we lowered our arms, took a step back, both breathing noisily. Deena aimed the light into the coffin. It made the white satin lining glow.

We stared into the light—and both uttered sharp cries that echoed off the rafters.

The coffin was empty.

Blade was gone.

PART THREE

25.

"**C**aitlyn, can we talk to you?"

I stared at the two cops who stepped up to my car. I recognized them immediately. Rivera and Miller. They had come to my front door a short while after I had stabbed Blade.

Now here they were at the mall, studying me as I climbed out of my car. I had hoped to go to my job. My nice normal boring job behind the popcorn counter.

But . . . no way.

They motioned to their patrol car. My whole body shuddered with dread as I lowered myself into the backseat.

At the Shadyside precinct house, Rivera and Miller led me into a small square interview room. I gazed around the room, my hands clasped in front of me, my jaw clenched tightly. I was determined not to show how terrified I was.

What do they know?

In the patrol car on the way here, they told me they just had a few questions for me. They read my rights to me. Just like on *Law & Order.* They said I had the right to have my parents and a lawyer present.

That was the *last* thing I wanted.

"Are you arresting me?" I asked, my voice tiny and choked.

Rivera shook his head. "Just a few questions, that's all. A few things to clear up."

I'm guilty, I thought. *How much do you know? Do you know I'm the one who stabbed him?*

"Want us to call your parents?" Miller asked.

"No," I repeated. "It isn't necessary. I mean . . . if it's just a few questions."

The walls of the interview room were a sick pea soup green, and the paint was peeling near the ceiling. Two lights inside gray cones hung down over a long table. The tabletop was covered in names and initials carved into the wood. The windowless room was hot and smelled of stale cigarette smoke despite the NO SMOKING sign tacked to the wall.

Rivera motioned for me to sit down at one of the folding chairs that lined the table. Then the two officers disappeared, closing the door behind them.

I've seen this on TV, I thought. *They leave me here to sweat and get tense. They want to frighten me.*

About twenty minutes later, Rivera returned and took the chair opposite me. He wiped his mustache with his fingers, his dark eyes studying me. "Caitlyn, would you like some water? It's hot in here."

"That's okay," I said. "We won't be here for long, right?"

All I wanted to know was how much did they know? Did they bring me here to set a trap for me to confess? Were they going to arrest me?

"Yeah. Just a few questions," Rivera said, shifting his weight. He was too tall for the little chair.

"About Blade?" I said. I squeezed my hands together in my lap.

He nodded. He twirled a gold ring on the pinky finger of his left hand, twirled it slowly, his eyes locked on me. "We understand you were a friend of his."

"Well, we went out a few times," I said. "I didn't really know him. I think his family just moved here a few months ago."

I tried to return his stare. Somehow, I managed to keep my voice steady. I was glad there was no lie detector in the room.

A car horn honked somewhere outside. Rivera twisted the ring on his finger and kept his eyes on me. "Where were you Saturday night, Caitlyn? The night Blade was killed."

"Saturday night? I . . . uh . . . I was home," I said. "Remember? You and your partner came to my door? I told you then I hadn't gone out."

He let go of the ring and lowered both hands to the

edge of the table. Did he believe me? I couldn't tell anything by his blank expression.

"Try to remember," he said. "When was the last time you saw Blade?"

I hesitated. "I don't really remember. Maybe Thursday or Friday at Lefty's."

Rivera sighed again. He leaned across the table toward me. He rubbed the black stubble on one side of his face. "Caitlyn," he said, "why are you lying to me?"

26.

My whole body went cold. A choking sound escaped my throat. I struggled to breathe normally. "Wh-what do you mean?" I stammered.

Don't lose it, Caitlyn, I warned myself. *Don't let him mess you up. You can play this out.*

I tried to reassure myself. But my heart was going crazy like it was doing a drum solo, and Rivera's hard stare was sending chill after chill down my back.

"We have a witness," Rivera said, speaking softly, slowly.

Oh my God! Someone saw me kill Blade?

"We have a witness who told us you were one of the last people to see him alive."

I swallowed. I didn't say a word. I waited for him to continue.

He brushed a fly off his forehead. He rubbed his cheek again. "Caitlyn, is the witness telling the truth?"

"Yes," I said. "I guess. I'm sorry. I'm just so . . . so

upset. My brain isn't functioning. I mean, I've never had a friend die before."

I wiped sweat off my forehead. It had to be two hundred degrees in the tiny room.

"Well, do you want to tell me the truth now?" Rivera asked. "You were at the dance club called Fire Saturday night?"

"Yes. Yes, I was," I confessed, lowering my eyes. Then I snapped, "Who told you that?"

"Blade's girlfriend. Vanessa Blum," he replied.

Girlfriend? She said she was his girlfriend?

A sharp pain exploded in my chest. As if I had been stabbed.

Blade had a girlfriend. He was just playing with me.

"Okay. Yes," I said. "I went to the club." I crossed my arms tightly in front of me, trying to stop the pain, trying to shield myself from his questions.

But there was no escape. I had to tell the whole story. Or at least *part* of the story of Saturday night.

"I was supposed to go out with Blade," I said. "We had a date. But he stood me up at the last minute. So . . . I went to my friend Miranda's house for a while, and then I was bored. So I went to the dance club. You know. To see if any of my other friends were there." I took a breath.

"And you saw Blade?" Rivera urged me on.

I nodded. "Yes. I saw him there. And I was . . . well . . . shocked. I mean, we did have a date, and he told me he got hung up and couldn't make it. And then there he was, at Fire with another girl."

"And that made you angry?" Rivera demanded.

"Well . . ."

"You had a screaming fight with him at the bar?"

I felt totally trapped. How could I get out of this? Not by telling the truth. Could I get away with half-truths?

If only I knew how much Rivera knew.

"Yeah, sure. I was angry," I said. "He lied to me and there he was with this girl. Vanessa. So yes, I was angry. But . . . we didn't have a screaming fight."

Rivera's eyes widened. "You didn't?"

"No. No way," I said. "I told him off, and then I left the club."

This was all true. I was telling him the truth.

Rivera shifted his weight on the little folding chair again. His expression remained blank. "Then what?"

"Then I went home," I told him. "I was upset. I went up to my room. You came to my house, remember?"

"And found the front door open," he said. "Caitlyn, did you leave the door open? Were you so upset and angry that you left the front door open?"

"Maybe it was me," I admitted. "I don't know."

He toyed with the ring on his pinky finger again as he studied me. "So you went straight home from the club, and you didn't leave the house again Saturday night?"

I nodded. "I tried to go to sleep, but I couldn't."

Rivera took a long pause, as if he was trying to think of what to ask next. "You didn't go to his house and wait for him after you left the dance club?"

"No," I said. "I went home. I . . . I told you, we weren't that close. I was only at his house once. I'm not even sure I could find it."

Did Rivera believe me?

"Well, Caitlyn, how angry were you Saturday night? Would you say you were angry enough to get violent?"

"Of course not," I said. "I . . . I'm not a violent person. I've never had a real fight with anyone. I . . . think I was more hurt than angry. Just because he lied to me. You know."

Rivera nodded. He studied me for a long moment. Then he scooted his chair back till it hit the wall. He climbed to his feet. "I'm sorry if this was hard for you," he said. "I know—"

"Yes. Yes, it was hard," I said. I reached into my bag for a tissue and wiped my eyes. "I liked him. I really liked him. And now I'm totally freaked out knowing I was one of the last people to ever see him. And I'll never have a chance to make up with him. Never. I . . . can't stop thinking about it. I really can't." I wiped my eyes some more.

He opened the door and motioned for me to follow him out. "I appreciate your cooperation," he said. "Officer Miller will drive you back to the mall."

He waved to Miller, who had a desk against the wall

in the front room. I strode quickly toward the exit, eager to get away from there.

Rivera's voice followed me to the door: "Caitlyn, stick around, okay? I may want to talk to you again. "

27.

I hurried to the Cineplex, Diary. I was late but I didn't care. I needed to get back to a normal life, or at least go through the motions. I knew my life would never be normal again, never be like before.

I was edgy, alert to everything, so tense my skin prickled. I knew the police would be back. I knew they'd be coming to arrest me any day. Arrest me for murdering Blade, and I had no way to prove I wasn't responsible. No way to prove that I was being controlled by Deena Fear.

Maybe, I could plead insanity.

Which was quite possible. I mean, my being insane.

Yes, I was insane for getting involved with Deena Fear. Insane for falling into her trap. Insane for going along with her scheme to bring poor dead Blade back.

Insane.

Was there any other word for it?

I hadn't heard from Deena since we had fled from the North Hills chapel. We had stared disbelieving into the empty coffin. Then we ran out the back door without saying a word to one another.

Deena ran to her car, expecting me to follow. But I took off down the street, running full-speed, the cool wind brushing my hot cheeks, the ground solid and real beneath my pounding shoes. I needed something real.

I needed to get away from her, away from the horror. My brain was exploding with questions. Had someone moved Blade's body earlier from its coffin? Perhaps refrigerated it or something to keep it in good shape? Had he been buried after all? Or had Deena brought him back to life the night before without realizing it?

That was truly crazy. But she said she'd been up all night preparing, doing whatever magic she did.

No. No. I refused to believe it.

For two days, I kept checking the local news websites. Waiting for the story of the missing body, the corpse stolen right out of the chapel. Every morning, I grabbed my dad's copy of the Shadyside *Citizen-Gazette* at breakfast and pawed through it, searching for the story.

But it wasn't there. It wasn't anywhere. And no one wrote about his funeral, either.

Dad looked up from his toaster waffles. "Since when are you interested in the news?"

"Uh . . . I thought my friend might be in it," I said.

He took the paper back and folded it to the sports section. He didn't ask why my friend might be in the news.

Dad doesn't like to talk in the morning until his second cup of coffee.

I didn't see Deena in school. I felt too distracted to be there. I couldn't listen to any of my teachers, and then Ms. Ryan, the gym teacher, called me away from our volleyball game and asked if I was feeling well.

I avoided Julie and Miranda. They wanted to be sympathetic and fawn over me and tell me they knew how bad I felt and how tragic the whole Blade thing was (if they only knew!) and ask what they could do to cheer me up.

Nothing. Nothing could cheer me up.

They were my best friends, and they meant well. I mean, they really did care about me. But I couldn't bear to eat lunch with them. While everyone marched to the lunchroom, I slipped outside.

A warm April day, more like summer than spring. I took a long walk behind the school, past the student parking lot, and the stadium.

Shadyside Park stretches behind the school. I sprawled on a bench, tilted my head into the sun, shut my eyes, and tried not to think. I thought of how you erase a whiteboard. Just wipe it clean, wipe everything away.

Start all over . . .

Of course, I couldn't do that. How could I wipe away all the horror that had come into my life?

I sat there in the sun, in the quiet park, daffodils popping through the ground, tiny new leaves unfurling on the still-wintry trees, half in a daze. I think I would have sat there all day. Except two women pushing baby strollers came ambling by, and one of the babies was crying.

The shrill sound snapped me out of my hazy daydreams. I jumped to my feet, shook myself like a dog, turned, and made my way back to school.

I searched for Deena Fear in the halls and waited for her by her locker after school. But she didn't appear.

I didn't really want to see her. I hoped I'd never have to see her again. But I needed to talk to her. I needed to find out if she knew anything. If she'd heard anything. If she knew why Blade's body wasn't in its coffin and why no one was reporting it missing and . . . and . . . ? My brain was spinning with so many questions. "Deena? Where *are* you?" I shouted to the empty hallway.

And now here I was. Making my way through the movie theater lobby. Back at work for the first time.

Of course, Ricky came running over as I stepped into the lobby. His face was filled with concern, his eyes wide, his mouth twisted in a pout of sympathy.

He grabbed both my hands in his. "Oh, Caitlyn, I'm so sorry. So sorry to hear about your friend."

"Thank you, Ricky," I muttered. I was waiting for him to let go of my hands.

"I know how you must feel," he said. "Losing someone you were close to so suddenly." He shook his head sadly. I thought he might start to cry.

I slid my hands out from his. "Thank you," I repeated. "I just thought . . . it would be better to get back to work."

He nodded. He had to squeeze my hands one more time. Then he turned and strode out of the lobby. *He was just being nice,* I thought. *But that was way icky.*

I washed my hands, then stepped behind the concession counter. The popcorn machine was getting low, so I added some oil and started it up. It was a busy afternoon. The theater had a special *Star Trek* double feature starting at five, and it drew a pretty big crowd.

I was wiping the counter down after the last customer had gone into the auditorium when my phone rang. I glanced at the screen. My friend Miranda.

I raised the phone to my ear. "Hey. How are you? I'm at work."

"I think you've been avoiding me," Miranda said. "I haven't talked to you in days."

"I . . . I've been weird," I admitted. "Sorry. It's been tough, Miranda. You know."

"Well, if you want to talk about it, I'm here," she replied. "I mean, if it would help at all."

"I don't know," I said. "I'm pretty messed up. I—"

"Julie and I want you to come to the basketball game at school tonight," she said. "Maybe it will help take your mind off things."

"I don't know. I think—"

"We could go to Alfonso's and share a pizza afterward," Miranda said. "Or maybe two. Like we used to."

I thought about it. I thought about how nice it was to have such considerate friends. Friends who were eager to help me.

"Well . . . maybe . . ." I said.

"It's going to be a good game," Miranda said. "We're playing Green Valley. I know you're not into basketball, but you should come, Caitlyn. We'll have fun."

"Well . . . okay," I said. "Okay. Thanks, Miranda. I'll meet you in the gym at seven thirty."

I clicked off. *Why not try to have some fun?* I thought. *It's just a basketball game.*

What could happen?

28.

There had been a tenth-grade dance in the gym on Saturday night, and some of the red-and-blue streamers were still hanging overhead. A few stray balloons lingered in one corner near the coach's office.

I was early. The game didn't start till eight. A few kids were already in the bleachers. They sat staring at their phones or talking with their friends.

I recognized some guys from my class up in the top row of seats, passing around bags of tortilla chips. I saw Michael Frost, a guy I went out with a couple of times last year. He was sitting with Lizzy Walker, a new girl in school.

Lizzy was a mystery girl. She arrived in the middle of senior year. No one knew anything about her. But the guys were interested in her because she was blonde and pretty and spoke with a sexy soft voice.

She was sitting with her leg pressed against Michael's, tossing her hair from side to side as she talked, her face close to his cheek. Even from this distance, I could see that Michael was entranced.

I was still staring at them when Julie and Miranda arrived. They both wore maroon-and-white Shadyside Tigers T-shirts pulled down over straight-legged jeans. They spotted me right away, hurried over, and we hugged.

"We're so glad," Julie said. "We didn't think you'd come."

"Sorry I've been such a downer," I said. "I just—"

Miranda clamped a hand over my mouth. "Don't talk about it. Seriously. Tonight is a fun night. Go, Tigers."

"Go, Tigers," I repeated, trying to show some enthusiasm.

Miranda sniffed my hair. "Mmmmm. Popcorn."

I rolled my eyes. "Tell me about it."

Julie guided me toward the bleachers. "Let's sit up high so we can see everything. Hey, maybe those guys will share their chips with us."

We started up the bleacher stairs. "No, wait." Miranda tugged me back. "You know I have a thing about heights. How about here? Right in the middle?"

We squeezed past Michael and Lizzy who sat pressed together on the aisle and dropped down on the bench in the middle of the row. On the court, both teams were practicing, taking jump shots from all over the floor, the balls bouncing everywhere, pounding the floor like drumbeats.

Green Valley is nearly fifty miles from Shadyside, so the

guest team bleachers across the floor were only about a third filled. Over the thunder of the balls, I could hear some kids from the other school chanting, "Giants! Giants! Giants! Go, Big Green!"

The team brought cheerleaders in their shiny, short green pleated skirts. And their mascot, a very tall, costumed character called the Jolly Green Giant. He did cartwheels along the front of the bleachers, and got a few of the Giants fans clapping and cheering.

I'm not into basketball. Actually, tennis is my sport. But it was great to be kidding around with Julie and Miranda and to be in the middle of a happy, cheering crowd.

The game started and the Giants quickly took an early lead. They had a couple of players who *had* to be eight feet tall. Well, maybe not. But they were a lot taller and *wider* than our players.

The Giants played a very aggressive game. A lot of shoving and elbows and charging into players. They had several fouls called against them, but they also bullied their way under the basket to score a lot of points.

Shadyside's shooting was off. They have two awesome three-point shooters. But tonight, the ball wasn't dropping for them.

Our team was down by twelve points, and I found myself really getting into the game. I was cheering and screaming, waving my fists, urging them on. Julie and Miranda kept glancing at me. I could see they were happy that I was enjoying myself.

And then the fun stopped.

I saw the two men in dark uniforms enter the gym.

I didn't recognize them until they strode closer, edging their way toward the bleachers along the sideline. The police officers. Rivera and Miller.

They walked slowly, stiffly, arms tensed at their sides. At their waists, I could see their holstered guns. They weren't paying any attention to the game. Their eyes were on the bleachers.

I knew why they were here. They had come for me. This was it. This was the end of my fun normal night. They had come to take me away.

I read it on their faces as they scanned the crowd. Row by row.

"Here I am." I had the urge to shout.

No way I could hide. No way they wouldn't see me.

Rivera's eyes stopped on me. A soft moan escaped my throat.

"Here I am. Here I am. The murderer. Here I am. Come and arrest me. Take me away."

29.

My whole body tensed as I watched the two cops at the bottom of the bleachers. The cheers of the crowd faded from my ears. All sounds faded away until I heard only the pulsing of my racing heartbeats.

Rivera turned and said something to his partner. Miller nodded. The two of them began to climb up the aisle.

They've seen me. They're coming for me.

I had a strong urge to open my mouth and scream, to let out all my horror, all my fear, and just scream and scream until I had no voice or breath left.

Somehow I held it in. I leaned forward on the bench, every muscle tensed, as I watched Rivera lead the way up the side of the bleachers.

He stopped three rows below me and pointed. Miller nodded. The two of them squeezed into the row and took seats about a third of the way across.

"Huh?" A startled gasp escaped my throat. I watched

the two cops settle themselves and turn to focus on the game.

Miranda turned to me. "What's wrong?"

"Uh . . . nothing. I . . . can't believe that last whistle. Johnson didn't foul that guy."

"Of course he did," Miranda said. "He practically took his head off."

Julie laughed. "Hey, you're really into this, Caitlyn."

I glanced at the backs of the two cops. "Yeah," I said. *Now that I can breathe again.*

I realized that I had to take my happy moments when I could. I knew it was only a matter of time before the police *did* come after me.

I gazed at the scoreboard. Only a minute left in the first half. Shadyside had pulled to within four points of the Giants. Kids were standing now, jumping up and down and cheering. Deafening excitement. The bleachers were actually rocking.

Julie, Miranda, and I jumped to our feet. A steal and a fast-break layup brought the Tigers within one basket. Someone called time out. I watched the players trot to their benches on the sidelines.

A flash of color caught my eyes. I peered across the gym to the visitors' bleachers.

I nearly fell over. I grabbed onto Julie and Miranda to catch my balance. A guy in a red hoodie hunched in the second row. He stood out among the green jackets and shirts of the visitors.

Of course, I thought of Blade. *No way* I could see a red hoodie and not think of him. I squinted into the glare of the bright gym lights, trying to see the guy more clearly. He had his head down and the hood pulled over his hair. I could see only the top of the red hood and his chest and arms.

My two friends didn't notice my alarm. They stood on both sides of me arguing about what kind of pizza to get after the game. Miranda liked to plan ahead. And she doesn't like pepperoni. We have this conversation nearly every time we go for pizza at Alfonso's.

I didn't join in. I was watching the boy in the red hoodie, waiting for him to raise his head. The buzzer rang, indicating the time-out was over.

The guy raised his head, and the hood fell back to his shoulders. I leaned forward, studying his face, his dark hair.

"Oh no."

Blade.

It *was* Blade!

He raised his eyes to the Shadyside bleachers. He was gazing right at me. The game started up. He didn't look away. He stared at me intensely from across the gym.

Before I could even think, I had shoved my way past Miranda and I was rushing to the aisle, stepping on feet, brushing kids back, everyone a blur, just a blur because I had the red hoodie in my eyes.

"Caitlyn? Hey—Caitlyn?"

"What's wrong? Where are you going?"

I heard my friends calling after me in alarm. I didn't turn back. I stumbled into the aisle, hurtled into a few kids blocking my way, and dove past some others.

I made it to the gym floor just as the half-time buzzer rang out. A groan went up from both bleachers. No one wanted the game to stop. My shoes slipped on a wet spot on the gym floor, and I nearly fell onto the team bench.

I took a deep breath and ran along the sidelines.

Blade is back.

I didn't ask any of the obvious questions. Had Deena Fear brought him back? Did he come back to haunt me? To accuse me? To let everyone know that I was his murderer?

I ran past the team bench where the players were grabbing towels and water bottles and heading to the locker room. I darted between two striped-shirt referees who were mopping their faces with towels, heatedly discussing some penalty call.

I ran against the crowd of kids coming down off the visitors' bleachers, making their way to buy hotdogs and drinks at the stand outside the gym.

"Blade! Hey, Blade!" I breathlessly shouted his name, my chest about to burst from running, from my shock. "Blade!"

My eyes ran along the bleachers. To the second row. Empty now. Empty.

No red hoodie. No Blade. He was gone.

I spun around, my eyes searching every face.

I'm not crazy. I didn't hallucinate him. He was here.

I felt a hard bump from behind. "Blade?"

I turned to see a big red-headed kid in a green-and-yellow Green Valley jersey. "Hey, sorry," he said. He had a large cup of Coke in each hand. "Didn't see you. Sorry."

"No worries," I said.

Then Julie and Miranda appeared beside me. "Caitlyn? What are you doing over here?" Julie demanded.

"You got up before halftime," Miranda said. "What's wrong?"

"I-I saw him," I stammered. "I saw Blade."

They both gasped. Julie wrapped an arm around my shoulders. "You mean someone who looks like Blade?"

"No." I stepped away from her. "Blade. I saw him. He was sitting right there." I pointed to the middle of the second row, now empty. "He . . . was staring at me. Staring across the gym right at me."

Miranda and Julie exchanged glances. They weren't prepared to deal with an insane person. They brought me here to snap me out of my depression, and now here I was, ruining everything.

Miranda shook her head, her face tight with concern. "Caitlyn, you know it couldn't be Blade. What made you think—"

"He was wearing the red hoodie," I said. "That's what made me look at him. The hood slipped off and . . . and . . ."

"Do you want to go home?" Julie asked. "Where's your car? I could drive you—"

"No!" I cried. "I have to find Blade. He's here. I'm not making it up, Julie."

I pictured Deena Fear. Pictured Blade's empty coffin once again. He was here. I knew he was here.

I broke away from them and ran toward the gym doors. I pushed through the double doors into the hall. Nearly knocked a girl over. "Sorry. Didn't see you."

My eyes searched up and down the hall. Several kids were lined up at the concession table. No. No sign of him. Their faces all blurred in front of me. No red hoodie. No Blade.

Back into the gym, the roar of voices ringing in my ears. The scoreboard buzzed. Almost time for the game to resume. The visitors' bleachers were filled, but no sign of Blade.

I waved to Julie and Miranda who were starting up the aisle of the home team bleachers. I cupped my hands around my mouth and shouted: "Hey, I have to go!"

No way I could stay. No way I could watch the game knowing that Blade was back, knowing that he saw me, stared at me from across the gym.

My two friends rushed back over to me. "You're going home?" Julie asked.

I nodded. "My car is in the student lot."

"I really think you should let us drive you," Julie said,

her eyes searching mine, as if trying to decide if I'd gone crazy or not.

"No. I'm fine," I said. "It's such a short drive. Really. I'm fine."

Miranda gave me a hug. She couldn't hide her distress. "We'll talk later," she said.

They turned to go back to their seats. I hurried from the gym, into the hall. Only a few stragglers out here. I heard the game start up, the drumbeat of the basketball on the floor, the roar of voices. The sounds followed me as I pushed open the back doors to the school and stepped into the night.

The air had turned cooler. The moon was hidden behind low clouds. I felt a few cold droplets of rain on my hair and forehead.

I turned toward the student parking lot, jammed with cars. The halogen lamps along the tall iron fence made the lot nearly as bright as day. Someone with a blue Toyota RAV4 had left the headlights on.

I saw my car halfway down the back row, facing out. And I saw the red hoodie.

Blade, leaning casually, his back against the driver's door of my car, waiting for me.

30.

I stopped and stared into the harsh halogen glare. Stared until the hoodie became a red glow in my eyes, and the rest of Blade vanished ghostlike behind the ray of red.

He pushed himself away from the car, standing up, his eyes on me. He didn't move toward me. Just waited there, still casual. Did he expect me to go running to him? To throw my arms around him and tell him how thrilled I was that he was back?

I forced my legs to move. Took a few steps toward him. And then the words tore from my mouth: "You can't be here. You're dead! You're dead, Blade. Why are you here?"

He gave a slow shrug. His greenish eyes glowed under the lights. He didn't say anything.

"Blade? What do you want? Why are you here? You know you can't be here." I couldn't stop myself. I knew I wasn't making any sense. I was talking to a dead person.

But he was there, leaning one hand on the side of my car. He was there. I wasn't imagining him.

"Blade—say something." My voice trembled on the air. Raindrops pattered the parking lot, the cars. "Did you come back to hurt me? What do you want? *Tell* me."

The wind ruffled his red hood. He didn't reply. He didn't move. He stood there. Waiting. Waiting for me to come closer.

And then what?

I had to get to my car. I had to get away from him. I didn't want to talk to a dead person. I didn't want to know why he waited for me there so silently, so patiently.

I wanted him to go away. And stay away.

Fear choked my throat. I brushed raindrops off my forehead.

I was only a few feet from him now. "Blade? What do you want?" I asked in a tiny voice. "Blade—please."

He didn't answer. He grabbed my wrist.

"Hey—let go!"

He pulled me close. He gripped both of my wrists and pulled me against him. His hands were hard and cold as ice.

"Let go! What are you doing? Let go!"

The blank green eyes glowed. He grabbed my face with both frozen hands. Spread his hands over the sides of my head and drew me to him.

He pressed his lips against mine in a hard kiss. An angry kiss. He held me there, held my face against his, pressed his lips, so hard and cold, against mine, grinding them against my lips until my mouth ached.

I finally pulled my head back, gasping for breath, the taste of his icy lips still on mine. And then I uttered a horrified gasp.

His lips were still sewn together.

I started to gag. I forced myself not to vomit. I rubbed my mouth but I couldn't get the cold of his lips off them.

He held my shoulders, breathing heavily into my face. His breath was rotten. It smelled like spoiled meat. Like death.

A twisted smile spread on the stitched-together lips. I could see the black thread clearly. Some of the stitches at one end had popped.

I struggled to back away, but he was too strong for me.

He slid both hands around my head and pulled me forward for another kiss. Choking, I struggled to breathe normally as he moved the cold dead lips over mine, caressing my cheeks with his thumbs as he held my head.

Held me in a kiss with a corpse. I thought it would never end.

The stitches scraped against my lips until I cried out in pain.

I stuck one leg behind his—and gave him a two-handed shove in the chest. He toppled backward and fell to the pavement. His eyes flashed with surprise.

I grabbed my car door and swung it open. I had the ignition key in my bag. I only had to push the *start* button to start the car. I dropped behind the wheel, tugged hard to close the door.

But Blade was on his feet. He grabbed the door by the handle and held it open. Grunting like an animal, his glassy green eyes gleaming, he reached for me with his other hand. Slapping at my shoulder, trying to get a grip on me.

He was grunting like a dog through his stitched-up lips, grunting and growling and grabbing at me. I struggled to shove him back. Then I grabbed the door handle with both hands and jerked it hard, pulled it with all my strength.

The door slammed on Blade's hand. He didn't even scream. Could he feel it?

One more hard pull and the door clicked shut. I pushed Start. The car revved up quickly. The chest of the red hoodie was pressed against my window. I ignored it. Slammed the car into Drive. Shot my foot down on the gas, and took off with a squealing roar.

I saw Blade tumble back. He sprawled over the hood of the car in the next space.

My car roared into the aisle. Too fast. Too fast. I had to brake hard to avoid crashing into the wire fence.

I was crazed. Heart beating like crazy. My head throbbing. My lips ached from those horrifying, sick kisses. I swung the car toward the exit. Nearly scraped the Rav4 with its headlights on at the end of the row.

And then I bumped out of the short driveway, onto Division Street. Made a wide right turn, forgetting to look for traffic. A horn honked angrily close behind me. I sped away. Sped through a stoplight. More horns honking.

I just had to move, had to get as far away from the living corpse as I could. Rain spattered the window, but I didn't turn on the wipers. I stared out through the shiny droplets, little diamonds sparkling against the dark night. Like driving through a dream.

Only this was a nightmare.

Somehow I made it home. I slammed on the brake in front of our garage. An inch or two from the garage door. The glare of the headlights off the wide white door filled the windshield with eerie white light.

I sat there staring into the light with my hands gripping the wheel. Sat there as if I didn't want to open the door and step back out into the world. My throat still tight. My lips scraped and burning.

I'm home.

Safe . . . for a while.

I cut the engine and started to reach for the headlights switch. But my hand stopped in midair.

What was that in my lap? Something sitting in my lap.

What was it?

I reached down and picked it up. I raised it to my face to see what it was.

Blade's hand.

Blade's cold, dead hand. I'd sliced it off when I slammed the door.

I opened my mouth and started to scream.

PART
FOUR

31.

I tossed the hand into the alley behind my house. It made a sick soft *thud* as it bounced off a fence and hit the gravel.

Should I hide it under something? Should I bury it? I couldn't think straight. "No one ever goes back there," I told myself.

I couldn't breathe. My stomach churned. The hand felt hard and cold, curled into a fist. Sliced cleanly at the wrist, it didn't bleed at all.

It didn't bleed because Blade was *dead*.

I trembled in the light from the house that swept over the backyard. My eyes darted back and forth. Had Blade followed me? Had he come to take his hand back?

He won't leave me alone now. He'll want his hand and he'll want revenge.

I slipped into the house through the kitchen door. My parents had gone to bed, but they left a few lights on for me. I tiptoed silently up the stairs and to the bathroom across from my room.

I felt sick. My throat tightened. I leaned over the toilet and tried to throw up. But the waves of nausea faded.

I washed my face. I washed my lips. I could still taste those dead, hard lips on mine. I washed my hands three times.

I darted into my room and closed the door carefully behind me. I dropped onto the edge of my bed, clasping my hands together tensely in my lap.

I needed help, and there was only one person who could help me.

Deena Fear.

I wished I didn't need to see Deena again. I *never* wanted to see her. I pictured the man and woman in the glass cases. Were those really her parents? Did she really stuff them and put them on display there?

It couldn't be true. It *couldn't*. But I saw them there in that frightening room. And Deena actually bragged about it. Joked about using her taxidermy lessons on them.

I hugged myself to stop shivering. I suddenly realized I was *terrified* of Deena. Was she totally psycho? A crazed killer? I didn't want to go near her again.

But did I have a choice?

Even in my terror, I knew she was the only one who could help me.

Deena brought Blade back to life. She made me kill him. Then she brought him back.

Deena wanted him to be hers this time. But where was she? She was the only one who could control him. The only one who could protect me. My only hope was that she could stop him from coming after me.

"Deena." I whispered her name as I grabbed my phone. I pushed her number and raised the phone to my ear. It rang three times . . . four times. . . .

And then I heard a series of beeps. And a recorded woman's voice, much too loud, so loud I jerked the phone away from my ear, announced, "You have reached a number that has been disconnected. Please check the number and dial again."

Disconnected? No. No.

Why would Deena disconnect her phone?

I tried it again and got the same announcement. Then I clicked the phone off and tossed it in frustration, in anger, in fear, across my bed.

I'll find her in school tomorrow. She will know what to do about Blade. She will help me.

I tore off my clothes and tossed them in a heap in the middle of the floor. I pulled on a flannel nightshirt. It was a warm spring night, but I couldn't stop trembling.

The rain had picked up. It drummed against the window. My bed is right under the window. Normally, I love lying in bed, looking out at my backyard below.

But tonight, I pulled the covers up over my head. I shut my eyes tight and listened to the patter of the rain on the window glass.

Maybe the sound will soothe me to sleep, I told myself.

But, of course, that was crazy. I lay there curled under the covers until it got too warm to breathe. Then I tossed the covers off and tried sleeping on my side. I kept changing position, hoping to get the horrifying events of the night to fade to the background so I could catch some sleep.

But no. It all played over and over in my mind.

I suddenly remembered I had an oral report to give to the class tomorrow. "The History of the Stradivarius Violin." My grandfather was a classical violinist. He played with the Detroit Symphony and many other orchestras. He owned one of the priceless Stradivarius violins. He showed it to me when I was a little girl and explained why it was so valuable and perfect.

Shortly before my grandfather died, the violin was stolen. From all those years ago, I remember my grandmother saying that he died a few weeks later of a broken heart.

I was too young to fully understand then. But her words lingered in my mind. I wanted to add that personal story to my essay about Stradivarius violins. I knew Mr. Lovett, my English teacher, would appreciate it.

I'm a good writer, Diary. I love to write and tell stories. The essay was kind of special to me since my grandfather died when I was seven. I had started to write it. Actually, I had almost finished it.

What time was it? Two in the morning? Should I get up and work on it now? Maybe it would take my mind off Blade?

I yawned. No. No way I could concentrate. I didn't feel sleepy but I felt worn-out. Wrecked. Maybe if I tried to clear my mind. . . . Maybe count slowly down from one hundred to one. . . .

I was only down to ninety-three when I heard the rattling from outside my window. I sat up, alert.

The rain had stopped but the window glass was covered in raindrops. A bright half-moon floated high in the gray sky.

I listened. I heard another sound. Like a low cry. Maybe a cat?

I leaned forward and pressed my face to the glass and gazed down at the yard. "Oh no. Oh no."

I sucked in a breath as I saw Blade in his red hoodie.

He stood in the cone of yellow light that washed over the grass. The hood was down and I saw his green eyes gazing up at my window.

"No. Please." I shut my eyes and tried to erase him, tried to banish him, send him away. I wanted to plead with him, to beg him. *Disappear, Blade. You're dead. Please disappear.*

But when I opened my eyes, he hadn't moved. He stood in the light, red hoodie gleaming, and I saw the hand. The hand my car door had sliced off. He had it tucked in his hoodie pocket.

He found the hand. He had it.

I started to back away from the window, but he had already seen me. I watched him raise his good hand above his head.

What was he holding? What did he have clenched in his fist?

I squinted through the rain-smeared glass, struggling to focus. The light from the house caught the object in his fist. A knife. The blade flashed.

"Oh my God."

Blade held the knife above his head. Held it high so I could see it. His head tilted back. His eyes locked on mine.

I screamed as he plunged the knife down.

He sank the blade into his head and killed himself again.

32.

I swung my gaze to the bedroom door. Had Mom and Dad heard my scream?

Silence out in the hall.

I didn't want to look down into the yard again. I didn't want to see Blade sprawled on the grass with the knife buried in him.

But I had no choice. I had to know if he really was dead again. I had to know if—

Oh my God. No.

He didn't kill himself. He dug the knife into his mouth—and sliced the blade between his lips. He was using it to cut away the stitches, to free his mouth.

In the bright light, I could see the heavy black thread pop, see the stitches fall away until there were just a few scraps of black thread stuck to the sides of Blade's mouth.

Gripped in cold horror, my burning face against the cool window glass, I watched him test his mouth. Move his jaw up and down. His lips twitched. He slowly pulled them open. He slid his mouth up and down several times. He tugged bits of thread from his lips and worked his mouth some more.

Then he raised his eyes to me and shouted in a hoarse, ugly animal groan: "I'm back for you, Caitlyn. I'm back. I'll never leave you. Never!"

With a gasp, I slammed the shade down, stumbled back to my bed, and pulled the covers over my head.

I didn't want to go to school the next morning. How could I sit through classes with all this horror whirling in my brain? I started thinking up excuses to give my parents. But then I remembered I couldn't stay home. I had to go to school and find Deena Fear.

Deena was my only hope. From those old books in her family library, she had learned the secret, learned the power to bring Blade back to life.

She *had* to know a way to send him back to his coffin.

As I parked my car in the student lot, I thought once again about the two people frozen in glass cases at the back of Deena's house. I shuddered, my hands squeezing the steering wheel. A sensible person would stay as far away from Deena as she could.

But I wasn't a sensible person. I was a crazed, terrified person. Every sound, every fast movement of color or light, made me jump. Every burst of red made me want to scream. I knew I'd see that red hoodie forever in my nightmares.

Did Blade really say he would stay with me forever? I had to take his words seriously. I had to believe he meant it. Even though just thinking about it made my stomach churn and my heart start to do flip-flops in my chest.

Deena, where are you?

I waited in the front hall until it was almost time for the bell to ring. She didn't show.

I asked some kids if they knew which homeroom Deena was in. No one seemed to know. With her strange, dark looks, her wild tangles of black hair all the way down her back, and her black outfits and her general weirdness, kids stayed away from her.

She was a total loner. I don't know if she had any friends at all in school. She wasn't in any of my classes. I never saw her with anyone.

The bell rang. The hall had emptied out. Everyone was in homeroom. I peeked into a few rooms on my way to Ms. Chow's room. I didn't see her.

Ms. Chow looked up from her laptop as I walked in. "Please close the door, Caitlyn," she said. "Try to be a little more prompt, okay?"

I closed the door behind me. "Ms. Chow, do you know what homeroom Deena Fear is in?" I asked.

She squinted at me. She scratched her straight black hair, which she wears very short with straight bangs across her forehead. "Deena Fear? I'm sorry. I don't know her, Caitlyn. Is there a problem?"

"Well . . ." I hesitated. I saw Julie at the end of the front row, watching me, her face tight with concern. "It's kind of an emergency," I said. "I really need to find her."

Ms. Chow nodded. "Why don't you go to the office? Mrs. Vail can tell you where to find her."

"Thanks." I dropped my backpack onto my desk. "I'll be right back. I really appreciate it, Ms. Chow."

"Hey, Caitlyn," Julie called to me from across the classroom.

But I was already out the door and into the hall. Silent and empty out here. The two gym teachers were having some kind of conference in front of the trophy display case. They nodded at me as I jogged past them.

The principal's office is near the front entrance. I stepped inside. A couple of solemn-looking boys sat hunched on the bench in front of the main desk. Sophomores, I think. Must have been in some kind of trouble.

Mrs. Vail, the office secretary, had a phone pressed to her ear. She stood at the desk, sifting through papers as she talked. I stepped up to the desk and rested my arms on the desktop in front of her.

She nodded and kept on talking. It seemed to be something about the hot-lunch program. She kept saying, "I have no control over that. The state tells us what to serve."

I was practically bursting, silently begging her to get off the phone. If she talked much longer, homeroom would be over and I'd be late for Advanced English and my violin report.

I let out a long whoosh of air when she finally hung up. "Caitlyn, what can I do for you?"

"I need to find Deena Fear," I said. "It's kind of important. Can you tell me her homeroom?"

"That's an easy one," she said, smiling at me. "I like the easy requests."

She moved to the desktop computer at the edge of the counter and began to type rapidly on the keyboard. "I'll just pull up her schedule. What was her name again?"

I told her.

Mrs. Vail turned her gaze on me. "A Fear? From the famous Fear family? Really? How come I don't know her?"

I shrugged.

She returned to the computer, squinting at the screen. "That's strange," she murmured. She typed some more. "D-e-e-n-a, right?" She spelled the name.

"Right," I said. I leaned over the counter, trying to read the screen over her shoulder.

Mrs. Vail rubbed her chin. "Let me bring up the student directory. Is she a senior like you?"

"Yes. I'm pretty sure she's a senior."

"Okay. No problem." She typed some more. Then she studied the screen. She scrolled up and down the list of students.

"Is she new?"

"No. I don't think so. I don't really know."

She typed some more. Gazed at the screen intently.

Then she turned to me. "Caitlyn, there must be some mistake. There *is* no student named Deena Fear enrolled at our school."

33.

I tried to hide my shock, but I guess I didn't do a very good job. Mrs. Vail squeezed my hand. "Caitlyn? Are you okay?"

No. I'm not okay. I'm losing my mind. I'm inventing imaginary people.

I swallowed hard. My throat suddenly felt dry as sand. It took me a few seconds to assure myself that I didn't invent Deena Fear.

She was definitely real. Julie and Miranda had both seen her and talked about her that night when I bumped into her at Lefty's.

"She's real," I murmured. I didn't realize I was talking out loud.

"Maybe she goes to Collegiate," Mrs. Vail offered. That's the private girls' school in North Hills. "Have you seen her here in school?"

I wanted to get away from Mrs. Vail. She was gazing at me so suspiciously, like maybe there was something wrong with me. She is a nice person, but you don't want to confide in her. Anything you tell her she goes and tells to Mr. Hernandez, the principal.

"Actually . . ." I said. I tilted my head, thinking hard. "I guess I've only seen her out of school." I forced a smile. "Thanks, Mrs. Vail."

I didn't give her a chance to reply. I spun away and bolted from the office, nearly knocking over the two gym teachers, who were walking in.

The hall was bustling now, crowded and noisy. Home-room had ended and everyone was heading to their first period class.

I moved slowly to my English class. Some kids called out to me, but I ignored them. I kept rubbing my forehead, massaging my temples as I walked. My head felt about to explode.

This was an Advanced English course, mainly for creative writing students. We all sit around a big, round table and share our stories and essays and critique them.

Normally, this is my favorite class. But now, I just wanted to hide in a corner, shut my eyes, and try to think. Of course, that was impossible. There's nowhere to hide at a round table.

And naturally, Mr. Lovett tapped me on the shoulder as I walked to my seat and said, "You'll go first this morning, Caitlyn."

As the other kids settled in, I pulled my essay from my bag. I don't get nervous reading in front of the whole class.

I'm pretty confident as a writer, and, everyone knows I'm not shy.

But today, my hands were shaking as I glanced through the pages I had written. The essay wasn't quite finished, and I wished I had time to polish it. My head was still throbbing. I hoped maybe reading the essay to everyone would give me a chance to calm down and stop puzzling over Deena Fear.

That didn't happen.

When Mr. Lovett gave the signal, I stood up and introduced my essay. "It's about the Stradivarius violin," I said. "I wrote it because this priceless instrument has special meaning to my family."

Mr. Lovett leaned forward and crossed his hands on the table. "Interesting," he murmured. "Go ahead, Caitlyn."

I started to read. "Stradivarius musical instruments were made in the seventeenth and eighteenth century by an Italian family named Stradivari. Today, they are valuable beyond belief, not just because of the quality of the workmanship, but because only 650 of them survive in the entire world."

I raised my eyes from the paper to see if everyone was listening. And uttered a gasp when I saw Blade. He stood in the open doorway.

He wore his red hoodie. One sleeve was pulled down low, covering the stump where his hand was missing. His hair was disheveled, falling around his pale white face.

He gave a thin smile as our eyes met. His eyes flashed.

Then he raised the back of his hand to his lips. He puckered his dead lips and, eyes locked on me, began to make loud kissing noises against his hand.

I lowered the essay and pointed to the door. "Don't you hear that?" I cried. "Don't you hear what he's doing? Look! See him? Do you see him there? It's Blade!"

Chairs scraped as everyone turned to the door.

But Blade was gone. The doorway was empty.

They quickly turned back to gape at me. I heard whispers and some muffled laughter.

"Caitlyn, I don't see anyone."

"What are you talking about?"

"Blade? You mean the kid who was killed?"

I tossed my essay onto the table, shoved my chair out of the way, and ran. I hurtled out of the classroom. Mr. Lovett's startled shouts followed me down the hall.

I lowered my shoulder and pushed open the side door to the school. I burst outside, breathing hard, my temples throbbing.

"I can't go back there," I told myself. "I can't go anywhere. Not till Blade is gone. But . . . how do I get rid of him?"

34.

I knew Deena Fear was the only one who could answer that question. I jogged into the student parking lot. I glanced in all directions.

Every nerve in my body was tense. My skin prickled. I felt sure that Blade would come leaping out at me.

The parking lot was deserted. Everyone was in class. Across the street, I saw a woman pushing a baby stroller. A tall white poodle followed after them. Normal life.

I wanted my life to be normal, too.

I climbed into my car. The steering wheel was hot from the sun burning through the windshield. I pulled out of the narrow parking place.

I glimpsed someone watching me from the school entrance. Was it Mr. Lovett? I didn't care. How could I care about school? How could I care about anything with a living corpse following me, haunting me?

The drive to Deena's house was a blur of flashing lights and streams of sunlight, shade then sun, houses sliding past, trees and cars and everything . . . everything just a jumble, a pulsing wave of motion and color. I didn't even realize I had turned onto Fear Street until the street became dark under the archway of tangled old trees.

As I reached the cul-de-sac where the street ends and the woods begin, Deena's house came into view. No car parked in front.

A black cat sat watching me from the front yard, very still, green eyes glowing, half-hidden in the tall weeds that led up to the house. The green eyes reminded me of Blade. And once again, I saw those glassy blank eyes green as emeralds, pictured them watching me as he stood in the classroom doorway making those obnoxious sounds. Enjoying himself. Having fun as he haunted me and drove me crazy.

I pulled to the curb and climbed out of the car, my eyes on the house. Sunlight reflected off the windows along the front. I couldn't see inside them.

The cat didn't move. It sat up straight as if ready to defend its territory. Its eyes followed me as I made my way past it to the door at the side of the house.

I pushed the doorbell. I didn't hear it ring inside. I waited a short while. The cat lost interest and wandered toward the burned-out remains of the Fear Mansion.

I could feel my heartbeats start to race. I rang the bell again. Then I knocked on the door. "Deena? Are you home? Deena?"

Silence.

The morning sun, now high in the sky, beamed down hard, but it didn't warm me. A chill covered my body, as if I'd just stepped from a cold bath.

"Deena? Where are you?"

I pulled out my phone. I studied her number again. I'd called it before today, and it had worked. Maybe if I tried it again . . .

I punched it and waited. *Please be there. Please answer.*

No. I got the same message telling me the number had been disconnected. With a sigh, I dropped the phone into my bag. I turned and pounded the door with both fists. Pounded until my knuckles throbbed.

"Deena? Deena?" I was about to totally lose it. I could feel myself about to snap, about to explode into a million pieces. "Deena?"

A window slid open at the side of the house. A head poked out. I squinted into the glare of the sun and recognized Deena. "You're home?" I said in a tiny, choked voice.

"Caitlyn, it's you," she said. "I've been expecting you." *Expecting me?*

The window slid shut. A few seconds later, I heard footsteps inside the house, the front door swung open. "I rang and knocked," I said breathlessly. "I've been shouting your name and—"

She motioned for me to step inside. "I was in the back. Getting ready," she said. "Getting ready for you."

I edged past her into the small front entryway. The

house smelled strange, as if something was burning. "Do you have something on the stove?"

She shook her head. "No. But I *am* cooking something up."

I didn't like the sound of that. I tried to interpret the thin smile that spread on her black lipsticked lips, but I couldn't figure it out. Was she making a joke?

She had her long hair tied back with a wide purple ribbon, but strands had come loose and fell about her owlish face. She wore a satiny purple top over black straight-legged jeans.

She took a few steps toward me. I instinctively stepped back.

"I . . . looked for you in school," I blurted out.

"But, Caitlyn, I don't go to your school."

"I didn't realize," I said. "Where do you go?"

"Actually, I'm homeschooled." For some reason, that made her laugh. A scornful laugh.

"By your parents? You said your parents are dead," I said.

She laughed again. "I homeschool myself."

I nodded. My fists were clenched. Every muscle in my body was tensed. *Was I crazy to come here?*

No. Just desperate.

She studied me. She seemed very amused. "Why are you stalling? We don't have to chat like we're best friends. I know why you came."

"Okay," I said. "Can you . . . can you help me?"

Her smile faded. "I think I can. I'm very prepared. I have what we need."

I shook my head. "Deena, you're talking in mysteries. What are you saying?"

She reached under the oversized purple blouse. She pulled something out from beneath her shirt, something round, a little smaller than a softball.

A hand. Coiled into a fist.

Blade's hand.

I stared at it. The thumb poking over the curled fingers. The hand had turned a light purple color. "H-How . . . did you get that?" I stammered.

"Never mind," Deena said. "It doesn't matter." She tossed the hand up, then caught it in her palm. Tossed it again and caught it. Then she motioned me toward the hall. "Caitlyn, are you ready to rock and roll?"

35.

Deena led me down the long, shadowy hall to her room. The burning smell grew stronger as we walked. And as I followed her into the room, I saw that it came from dozens of burning candles, black candles that she had placed on every surface.

Eleven tall black candles formed a pentagram on the floor. The candles were scented and filled the air with a tangy incense aroma, kind of cinnamon.

The parrot made a chirping cry as I came near and flapped its wings as if it wanted to escape its perch. Three or four silvery fish floated through the aquarium on the table to the right of the parrot's perch.

Deena didn't speak, silently tossed Blade's hand up and down as we walked to the center of the room. Red morning sunlight filled the glass wall looking out on the Fear Street Woods.

She motioned to two black, square cushions she had set down in the middle of the tall, burning candles on the floor. "You sit there, Caitlyn," she said, breaking the silence.

I hesitated. "Wh-what are we going to do?"

"You'll see. We have a lot of work to do."

She walked to the table and picked something up from beside the aquarium. I recognized it as she draped the chain around her neck. The silver bird amulet. She arranged it over her purple blouse and returned to the pentagram.

She carefully stepped between the flames and, without warning, tossed the hand to me.

I fumbled it. Caught it before it hit the floor. "You hold it," Deena said, taking her seat across from me, so close our knees almost touched.

I gripped Blade's hand in both hands, afraid I would drop it. The hand had hardened. It felt like grainy plaster. The thumb and fingers were locked tight. At the stub end where the wrist had been, I could see dark spots where there once were veins.

I shuddered. How did I get involved with this terrifying girl?

"Deena, tell me," I insisted. "What are we doing here?"

She squinted at me through her big, round glasses. "Bringing Blade here, of course." She raised the amulet off her chest with one hand and smoothed the front of it with two fingers.

"Bringing him here?"

She nodded. Candlelight flickered off her pale face, reflected in her glasses. "He betrayed us again," she murmured. "Well . . . actually, he betrayed *me*."

Blade's hand felt heavy between mine. I didn't want to hold it. I lowered it to my side to get it out of sight. A wave of nausea rolled up from the pit of my stomach.

"Betrayed you? He's been haunting *me*," I said. "He said he would never leave me."

Her black lips tightened into an angry scowl. "That's exactly my point, Caitlyn. It was supposed to be *my* turn. I worked all that night to bring him back . . . to bring him back to *me*, not to you."

She tossed the loose strands of hair off her face. "He betrayed me again. I cannot allow it."

Suddenly, without thinking, my most frightening thought burst from my lips. I never should have said it. But it was there in my mind, terrifying me as I sat cross-legged across from her. As I sat there, such an easy victim.

"Deena, if you killed me . . . Blade might be yours. Is that your plan? To get me out of the way?"

Her eyes widened in shock and she uttered a short gasp. "Kill you? Of *course* not. What are you *thinking*? You're my best friend in the world."

She's crazy. Totally insanely psycho.

I swallowed, trying to force down my nausea. "So you're going to bring Blade here and—?"

"Explain to him," she said. She leaned over a black candle, lowering her face to the flame. She raised the amulet in front of her. "Caitlyn, pick up Blade's hand. Hold it in front of you. We want him to know we have it."

Obediently, I cupped the hard purple hand between my trembling hands. I raised it high.

"He will come," Deena said, lowering her voice to a whisper. "He will know we have it, and he will come for it. And then . . ." She raised her eyes to me. ". . . We will have him."

She dropped her gaze to the amulet and lowered it to the candle flame. Shutting her eyes, she began to chant. Words in a strange language I'd never heard.

Her lips moved quickly, her tongue clicking against her teeth, her eyes shut, the sound of her voice just a murmur against the flickering light, a whisper so light, I wasn't sure I was hearing it.

She didn't move a muscle. Kept the amulet in place over the flame and whispered her strange words, her back straight, her legs spread out from the cushion.

I held the hand in front of me. My arms started to ache, and my back stiffened. I shifted my weight but it didn't help. I took deep breaths and wondered how long Deena would chant, how long it would take before Blade came knocking on the door.

And then what? Then what? Deena was being so mysterious. She didn't want me to know her entire plan.

Was she keeping it a secret because it would end badly for me, too?

I didn't buy that BFF nonsense. I knew I was in danger, too.

But I couldn't just jump up and run. If she really wanted to help me get rid of Blade . . . If she really wanted to use her powers to send Blade back to his coffin . . . I had to stay. I had to do what she asked.

I shifted my weight again. My arms throbbed. My back ached. I stared straight ahead at Deena and listened to her drone on . . . and on.

My eyelids suddenly felt heavy. The soft rush of her whispered words were lulling me to sleep. I struggled to stay alert—and gasped when something moved between my hands.

I gazed down and saw the fingers on Blade's hand start to move.

I let out a horrified cry and dropped the hand to the floor in front of me. It made a squishy *thud,* bounced once, and stopped at Deena's ankles. And I stared in horror as the dead fingers slowly unfurled. The thumb slid out stiffly, and the fingers curled and uncurled, as if testing themselves.

Deena opened her eyes for only a second. She glimpsed the moving hand, like a fat purple insect trying to get off its back. Her expression didn't change. She closed her eyes again. She chanted softly.

Gripped in horror, I watched the hand flop onto its other side. Like a crab, it began to crawl over the floor.

"Deena—" I shouted. "It's moving. It's crawling away." I couldn't hold in my terror.

"That means Blade is near," she said, still whispering. "That means he is coming. Listen. Listen for his knock, Caitlyn."

Fingers scrabbling steadily across the floor, the hand crawled toward the table. The parrot squawked and shuffled its wings, its eye on the approaching creature.

"Blade is near," Deena whispered. "Listen carefully. Listen for his knock."

I realized I'd been holding my breath. I let it out in a long *whoosh*.

I froze again when I heard a sound. A soft *thump*.

Where was it coming from?

Deena stopped her chant and tilted her head, listening.

Thump . . . Thump . . .

Someone knocking softly on the glass wall.

"He's here," Deena whispered.

Thump . . . Thump . . .

36.

I froze as chill after chill rolled down my back. I couldn't breathe. I couldn't move. Finally, I forced myself to turn to the glass wall.

Thump . . . Thump . . .

I shielded my eyes with one hand against the harsh sunlight. Then I uttered an astonished cry and jumped to my feet.

Deena and I both stared at the black cat up on its haunches. It peered into the room from the other side of the glass and tapped the wall with one paw.

Thump . . . Thump.

Not Blade. Not Blade.

Deena let out a long sigh. Her breath blew out one of the candles. It sizzled and sent up a thin column of black smoke.

Her shoulders drooped. She tossed the amulet onto one of the cushions. "It didn't work, Caitlyn," she murmured, avoiding my eyes. "Blade is out of my power."

Thump. The cat tried one more knock. Then it lowered itself to all fours and took off, its tail raised high, sprinting through the tall weeds of the backyard.

Once again, I felt cold all over. Strange how fear can control your body temperature. Fear and shock. I really expected to see Blade in the glass. Now that he wasn't there, I didn't know what to say or what to do next.

Deena picked up the hand, which was halfway to the aquarium table. The fingers curled as she lifted the hand off the floor. She tossed it into the aquarium. The water splashed violently and the fish inside scattered. The hand sank to the bottom and didn't move.

I stood there with my mouth open, trying to clear my head. I was surprised to see that Deena had tears running down her face. "All my energy," she murmured. "I used it all. I'm drained, see. The dead take so much energy. To bring them . . . and to send them back again. I . . . I don't have it, Caitlyn. I'm drained."

"But, Deena—" I started.

She wiped her tears with her fingers. Her eyes were narrow slits. Her cheeks were pale and puffy. The color had faded from her lips. "Drained. The amulet is empty. My words have no power."

She grabbed my shoulder. Her hand was ice cold. "I can't help you, Caitlyn. Blade is out there and he's on his own." She sighed. "I guess I took on too much. I thought I knew how to bring him here, how to control him. My family has always had such strong powers. But . . . I wasn't ready."

"Deena, that doesn't help me," I cried, backing away from her grip on my shoulder. "He's following me everywhere. He's haunting me and he says he'll never leave."

She shook her head wearily. "What can I say? I tried."

"But I can't live like this!" I screamed. "I can't live with a dead boy following me everywhere, grabbing me, kissing me with his dead lips, fighting, haunting me. How can I live with that?"

"Caitlyn, listen to me. I'm telling you the truth. I can't do anything," she said. She leaned against the wall. Her face grew even paler. In the harsh sunlight through the glass wall, she nearly disappeared. "You have to deal with Blade on your own."

"Huh?" I gasped. "On my own? What on earth do you mean, Deena? What can I do?"

"Isn't the answer obvious?" she said. "You have to kill him again."

37.

At my shift behind the popcorn counter that afternoon, I must have looked dazed or distracted. Ricky kept coming over and asking if I was okay. "If you'd like, you can take a ten-minute break," he said after I'd been on duty for only an hour. What a guy.

The theater was pretty crowded. I kept my eyes on the lobby entrance. Anyone wearing red made my breath stop. I knew Blade would show up. I knew he'd come to haunt me, to terrify me.

By the end of my shift, the tension from waiting and watching for him made me feel exhausted. Ruined. I almost forgot I'd made a plan to meet Julie after work.

I met her at Fresh Chopped, the salad restaurant in the mall near the Cineplex. We meet there a lot since Julie is a vegetarian. "How's it going?" she asked, her eyes studying me.

I shrugged. "Not bad. Do I smell like popcorn?"

She nodded.

We made our salads. I didn't pay much attention to what I put in mine. My stomach felt too tight to be hungry.

We slid across from each other in a booth away from the open double doors. In the next booth, two little kids were whining and complaining to their mother.

"But I *hate* salad."

"The lettuce gets stuck in my teeth. I *hate* this. It's yuck."

"We want McDonald's!"

"It's delicious," the mother argued. "Eat some of it and I'll buy you some ice cream."

"With sprinkles?"

"Okay. With sprinkles."

That seemed to quiet them down. Bribery almost always works with little kids.

Julie mixed the dressing into her salad with a fork. Her dark eyes were still on me. Her straw-blonde hair fell loosely to the shoulders of her striped tank top.

I noticed a bandage over her right earlobe. I pointed. "What happened to your ear?"

She rolled her eyes. "A piercing accident."

"You got your ears pierced again? That's very bold of you." As I've said, Diary, Julie is usually timid about things. She says she's "old-school."

"Yes. I wanted two holes. But the guy messed up or something. It got infected."

I tsk-tsked.

Julie stirred her salad some more. "Let's not talk about me," she said. "You left school this morning. What's up with that?"

I set my fork down. "Why? Were people talking about me?"

"Caitlyn, I *saw* you leave. You ran out the door like you were being chased. Were you sick or something?"

I opened my mouth to answer, then stopped, my brain spinning. And in that instant, with Julie peering across the table at me with such concern, I decided to tell her the truth.

I had to confide in someone. Deena Fear admitted she could be no help. But I couldn't face this entirely on my own.

"Julie," I started. "I know this is going to sound totally crazy, but I'm going to tell you the truth. Please listen to me. Please believe me, no matter how nuts it sounds."

She squeezed my hand. "Are you in trouble, Caitlyn?"

"No," I said. "I mean . . . yes. I mean . . ."

"Take a breath, okay. You're scaring me," she said. "Take a breath and start at the beginning. You know you can trust me, right?"

I nodded. I leaned over the table so I could whisper. I didn't want my story to scare the little kids in the booth behind me.

"Blade is back," I whispered. "Remember? They didn't bury him? Deena Fear brought him back from the dead. She—"

"You've been hanging out with Deena Fear?" Julie said, narrowing her eyes at me.

"Not hanging out exactly," I replied. "But she has powers. You know her family's story. They're all weird and they . . . can do things. And she brought Blade back to life. And . . ."

"Caitlyn, you're hyperventilating," Julie interrupted. "You're scaring me. Try to calm down."

Behind me, the two kids were arguing about where to go for ice cream. They both wanted Dairy Queen. Their mother was insisting on Tastee-Freez.

A wave of sadness washed over me. I wished I could talk about normal happy things like ice cream.

"Blade is back from the dead, Julie," I whispered. "And he came back to haunt me, to torture me, to terrify me."

Julie shook her head hard. She swept her blonde hair back. "Why, Caitlyn? Why you?"

I hesitated. *Should I tell her the whole story?*

Yes, I decided. It was all spilling out of me. I couldn't hold it in any longer.

"He's haunting me because I killed him, Julie. I'm the one. I'm the one who stabbed him. And now . . . now he's come back for revenge."

I grabbed both of her hands on the tabletop. "Do you believe me? *Please* say that you believe me. Please, Julie."

She stared at me for a long moment. I could practically see the gears of her brain spinning. She didn't move. She didn't blink.

Finally, she nodded. "I believe you, Caitlyn. I believe you."

I squeezed her hands. I wanted to jump up and hug her. "Oh, thank you!" I cried. "I can't tell you how much that means to me, Julie. I can't tell you how much better I feel that you know the truth now."

"You must be so frightened, Caitlyn," she said. "Blade back from the dead? It's like a horror movie. What are you going to do about him? What *can* you do? You have to get rid of him. You have to—"

"Deena Fear tried to help, but she couldn't," I said, my voice breaking. "I-I don't know what to do next. I'm so scared. I'm scared all the time." I held my breath, trying to hold back my tears. "I'm just so glad to have someone who believes me."

"We've been friends since sixth grade," Julie said. "I want to help you. Maybe I can help you."

"Help? How?" I asked. I watched a group of guys from our school walk into the restaurant. One of them was wearing a red sweatshirt. It made me gasp. Then I realized it was actually a maroon-and-white Shadyside High sweatshirt.

"Come to my house," Julie said. She slid out of the booth. "In half an hour, okay? Come in half an hour. Maybe I'll be able to help you. I mean, maybe."

"Okay," I said. "Okay. Half an hour. I'll kill some time here in the mall. I'll be there. Thanks, Julie. I mean, really. Thanks."

I watched her hurry away. Neither one of us had touched our salads. But I felt so much better, knowing that I had a true friend who believed me, believed my story no matter how insane it sounded.

How did she think she could help me? I didn't have a clue. But I was no longer alone.

I made my way to the exit. One of the guys from school called to me. I waved, but I didn't go over to them.

I wandered around the mall, just gazing into windows, not really seeing anything. The place was nearly empty. A lot of tables were filled at the food court in the basement. But bored salespeople stood around in empty stores, leaning on counters, their eyes on the clock, waiting for nine so they could close.

I remembered I had to buy a birthday present for my dad. I saw a Brooks Brothers store across the aisle. I took a few steps toward it, then stopped. I was in no mood to shop for anything.

I glanced at my phone. Time to head to Julie's house. My car was in the lot at the other end, near the Cineplex. I walked quickly past the stores, not seeing anything now but a blur of color and light.

My car stood all by itself in Row B. I felt a chill tighten the back of my neck. Parking garages give me the creeps. I thought about the guy who tried to rob me after work that night. You're just so totally vulnerable in a deserted parking garage.

My car squealed around a turn as I followed the circling aisle down toward the exit.

Julie lives on Bank Street, a short drive from the mall. She has two younger sisters, so there are five in her family. Their house is small, almost like a cottage. The kitchen, dining room, and living room are all one open room. Julie's sisters share a bedroom.

Julie says she doesn't mind being a little cramped. Her main complaint about the house is that it has only one bathroom. When her sisters go in to do their hair, it can take hours!

She says she loves her family because they're all pretty mellow. Bathroom time is the only thing they fight about. I know they were thinking of moving to a bigger house before Mr. Nello hurt his back. He was an assistant manager at a Walmart warehouse, but he had a bad accident unloading a truck. Now he gets some kind of disability.

I had all these thoughts about them as I drove. I guess I was trying to think about normal things, trying to keep my mind off my terrifying troubles. A few minutes later, I parked my car at the curb and walked up their small, square front yard. Her sister's scooters leaned against the front stoop. A jump rope was tangled around a low evergreen shrub at the foot of the steps.

I took a long breath of the cool night air and held it for just a second. Then I climbed onto the narrow stoop and rang the doorbell.

The door swung open almost instantly. Julie greeted me with a solemn face. "Hi, Caitlyn. Come in."

I stepped into the small front room. Saw the people standing there, standing there so stiffly. And I let out a cry: "What are *you* doing here?"

38.

Diary, I was trapped.

My mom stood behind Julie, her eyes moist, her chin trembling the way it always does when she's upset. Dad stood beside her, one hand on her trembling shoulder. He squinted at me as if he didn't recognize me.

"Come in," Mom said. "Come sit down, Caitlyn." She spoke slowly, softly as if she was speaking to a sick person.

I saw Julie's parents huddled together behind the couch at the back of the room. Julie's cheeks were bright pink. She could see the anger on my face, the betrayal I felt.

"I had to call them, Caitlyn," she said, clasping her hands tensely in front of her. "I had no choice."

"Why?" I said coldly. My jaw was clenched. "Why did you think you had to ambush me?"

"No one is ambushing anyone," Mom said.

"What was I supposed to do?" Julie asked, near tears. "What you were saying . . . What you were telling me at that restaurant was so crazy . . . ? I was worried about you.

I mean, really worried. You need help, Caitlyn. I mean . . ." Her voice trailed off.

Mom took my hand and squeezed it between both of hers. "We came as soon as we could. Julie said you were having a breakdown."

A breakdown?

She wouldn't let go of my hands. Her watery eyes peered into mine. Dad took my arm and pulled me to the couch. "Sit down. Come sit down. You're not well. I can tell by your eyes."

"Thanks, Doctor," I said sarcastically.

"Can I get anyone any coffee or tea?" Mrs. Nello chimed in.

No one answered her.

I could hear Julie's sisters talking upstairs in their room. I had a strong impulse to break away from my parents, run up there and join them.

"We're so sorry to intrude," my mom told Julie's mom.

"You're not intruding. I completely understand. If there's anything I can do. . . ."

"Caitlyn, I'm sorry." Julie was still apologizing. She stood by the front door, as if she was afraid to come near me. "You're my friend," she said. "I couldn't bear to see you in trouble. Please—forgive me."

"Nothing to forgive," My dad answered for me. He sat down next to me on the couch. He kept some distance between us, like I was contagious or maybe a wild animal that might attack him if he got too close.

Mom stood over me, her arms crossed in front of her. "Tell us what you told Julie. Okay, Caitlyn? Tell us the story so we can help you. Don't be afraid."

"You don't understand!" I screamed. "You don't understand! It isn't a story. I didn't tell Julie a *story*! You don't understand!"

I was shrieking at the top of my lungs. I realized I truly *did* sound like a crazy person.

"Screaming won't help," Dad said softly.

"This isn't going to help, either," I said sharply.

"Let's have a talk," Mom said. She motioned for me to slide over so she could sit on my other side. "That's what families do, Caitlyn. They help each other."

She and Dad were talking to me like I was a mental patient, and they both had these wet-eyed stares that made me nauseous.

"*You* talk about it!" I shouted. I jumped to my feet. I pushed my mother out of the way, dodged past Julie, who uttered a startled cry, and bolted to the front door.

I leaped out onto the front stoop and slammed the door hard behind me, shutting out their cries and pleas to come back. I took a deep breath of the fresh, warm spring air, dove off the stoop, and started to run.

I hesitated, seeing my car at the curb. No. I needed to run. I needed to run off my anger. I needed to feel the air against my face and let the silence clear my mind.

I lowered my head and picked up speed, my bag bouncing on my shoulder, swinging my arms as I ran through the night. Past mostly dark houses and small front yards, an empty lot with a FOR SALE sign near the curb, a narrow playground with a swing set and slide.

They think I'm crazy.

Julie thinks I'm crazy.

Some friend.

I knew this would happen if I confided in someone. And now here I was, running full speed, running like an animal at night, running who knows where. On my own.

Deena Fear couldn't help. Julie couldn't help. God knows, my parents couldn't help. They looked ready to have me locked up.

So here I was running along the street, running two blocks, then three, in and out of the dim spotlights of yellow light from the streetlights. Light, then shadow.

Would the rest of my life be spent in shadow?

I couldn't run forever. Even in my crazed state, I knew I'd have to go home. And then what?

My shoes pounded the soft grass. Somewhere in the distance a car horn honked three short beeps. The only other sound was the thudding of my shoes on the dew-wet ground.

When I neared the bus shelter on the corner, I stumbled to a stop. Had to catch my balance. My breaths came so hard, my chest ached.

I caught myself, my arms flailing, the bag suddenly heavy on my shoulder. Stopped, struggling to breathe, and stared at the glass bus shelter, lighted by a tall streetlight.

Stared at the stain of bright red through the glass. Squinted hard, focusing . . . until I saw that the blotch of red was a red hoodie. Through the shelter glass, I saw the red hoodie. And the boy wearing it. Hood pulled over his head. The boy hunched on the edge of the shelter bench, tapping one leg up and down.

Blade. He didn't see me. His back was turned, as if he was watching for the bus. But I knew. I knew he was waiting for me.

How did he know I would be here? It didn't matter. He was haunting me. I knew he would show up everywhere I went. I knew he would always be there.

I watched him, tapping his foot so casually, rubbing the knees of his jeans. I stood there, fists clenched, letting my anger grow until I saw red spots before my eyes, as red as his hoodie. And now I was seething, boiling over, swept up in a tidal wave of fury.

He can't do this to me!

Deena Fear's words came back to me then. I could hear her as if she were standing beside me. *"You have to kill him again."*

And I already had the knife from my bag. Already had the handle gripped tightly in my fist. The blade still blood-smeared from before.

I had never cleaned it. I had never tossed it away or hid it. I kept it . . . kept it because maybe I knew all along that I would have to use it again.

I wanted to shout. I wanted to scream out my fury. But

I held it in. I held it in, not breathing, no longer thinking like a human. I held it all in and raised the knife in front of me.

I slipped into the bus shelter before he could turn around—and I stabbed him in the back. Sank the blade into the middle of the red hoodie, sank it deep and pushed, pushed it deeper, pushed it with all my anger.

I slashed it to the right. Then pulled back and sliced it to the left. Dug it in and stabbed and sliced.

His arms flew up weakly. He uttered a long low groan of pain. Then sank forward. Just collapsed on himself.

Panting like a dog, wheezing loudly, I raised my eyes—and started to choke. I started to gag and choke because I saw Blade watching me. Blade, in his red hoodie, watching me from under a streetlight across the street.

39.

The knife fell from my hand and bounced into the curb. A cold grin spread over Blade's face, and he flashed me a thumbs-up.

A low howl escaped my throat. My knees started to fold. I grabbed the back of the shelter bench to keep myself up.

I sucked in a deep breath and held it. Then I reached over the back of the bench and grabbed the boy in front of me by the shoulders of his hoodie. I turned him around.

The hood fell back and I saw his lifeless face. Wide dark eyes staring blankly up at me. Mouth frozen open in a startled cry of pain. Curly brown hair matted to his forehead. A silver ring in one ear.

I've never seen him before.

Oh my God. Oh my God. I killed a stranger. I killed the wrong boy.

Over the throbbing pulses of blood at my temples, I

heard Blade's laughter. High, giddy laughter, as if he had just heard a funny joke.

I gazed across the street. But he had vanished into the deep shadows. His laughter faded slowly.

I realized I was still gripping the dead boy's shoulders. I had the sudden impulse to pull him to his feet. To tell him he was okay. To make him walk away.

His head fell back, smacking the bench loudly. The sound sent a shattering chill down my body. I let go of his shoulders. I stumbled back.

I'm a murderer.

"Deena! Did you make me do this?" I shouted, surprising myself. "Did you make me kill this boy, too?"

Silence.

Of course I heard only silence.

Deena was nowhere near.

I killed this one. I killed this boy. Not Deena.

I jumped as pale light spread over the grass. I turned to see a light go on in the front window of the house on the corner. Squinting up the lawn, I could see two people staring out the window at me.

I'm a murderer. I'm going to be caught.

I moved to the curb. I bent and picked up the knife. My hands trembled as I folded it and let it drop back into my bag.

Blade's cold laughter rang in my ears. I couldn't see him. But I could hear his gleeful, scornful laugh.

Covering my ears with both hands, I took off running again.

Running across the street and along the curb of the next block. Running. Holding my ears, shutting out the cold laughter of a dead boy.

Running into a blur of gray and purple and black night. Running. But, where?

I thought of Miranda. My only other friend. No. No way. Miranda wouldn't believe me, either. Why should she? I was sure Julie had already been on the phone with her, already shared what I had confided, already described the meeting with my parents. The ambush.

I was sure they had already discussed my *breakdown*. Crazy Caitlyn and her delusions of her dead boyfriend returning to haunt her. I was sure my two friends were very sympathetic. They wished there was something . . . anything . . . they could do to help me recover my sanity.

Yikes.

I couldn't run to Miranda's house. No way. Miranda wouldn't help me.

So where could I go? Where could I go with a blood-stained knife in my bag and chilling laughter in my ears? And the picture of me stabbing that boy, slashing and slicing him, stabbing him again and again, a stranger . . . the picture lingering in my eyes, replaying itself with every footstep.

Where could I go?

I had no choice. I had to go home. I had to surrender, to give up, to turn myself in, to confess my guilt, to prepare to face the consequences and pay for what I did.

Okay. Maybe I wasn't thinking clearly, Diary. Maybe my thoughts were a jumble. But that's what I was thinking as I ran down the dark, empty streets.

Back to Julie's house. My car parked at the curb. All the lights off in her house. The car bathed in darkness.

I fumbled for the key. Drove home in a frenzied blur of lights and passing houses and trees. Drove home without stopping, without seeing stop signs or traffic lights.

And when my house came into view, the world finally came back into focus. I actually felt relieved. I could stop running. Maybe I could find some safety inside.

My parents would be horrified when I confessed everything to them. They wouldn't understand. And it would be hard to make them believe me. But they would try to help me. I knew I could count on that.

My shoes slipped on the wet grass as I started to the kitchen door. I stopped short when a figure jumped out from the darkness at the side of the house.

Blade. Eyes glowing. He grabbed my arm with his remaining hand. "Time for you to join me, Caitlyn," he rasped through his ragged, torn lips.

I tried to tug free, but he was too strong. He pulled me toward him. Slipped a hand behind my head. And forced his lips against mine. His cold, dead lips, grinding against mine.

My stomach churned. I couldn't end the kiss. His mouth scraped against mine. I could feel the bump of stitches that he had missed.

Sick. I'm going to be sick.

The horrifying kiss seemed to last forever. Finally, Blade pulled his head back. He stared into my eyes. His glowing green eyes had no pupils. They were solid glass.

"It's time, Caitlyn," he repeated. "Time for you to come with me."

I gasped. "Come? Come where?"

He slid his face close to my ear and whispered: "*To the grave.*"

40.

"**N**ooooo!"

The scream burst from deep in my chest.

"Nooooo!" I tossed my head back and shrieked. Gathering all my strength, I shot my arms out and broke his hold on me.

He stumbled back. I struggled to breathe, the cold, sour taste of his lips still on mine.

With a desperate cry, I spun away and searched the ground for my bag. It had fallen into a flower bed at the side of the driveway. I took a step toward it, and Blade came at me. Arms outstretched, he roared as he prepared to tackle me.

I swung to the right and wriggled out of his reach as he dove. He shot past me and plunged to the ground, uttering a cry of surprise.

I made a grab for the bag. But he wrapped a hand around it before I could get there. He tossed it in the air. I watched it come down on the roof of my car.

As he climbed to his feet, grunting and growling like an angry animal, I raced to the car. I pulled the bag off the roof, gripping the handle in both hands.

Blade slashed a fist at me. I ducked, and the punch sailed over my head.

"You're coming with me," he growled. "You're dead, too, Caitlyn. You and I, we're dead together."

"No way!" I cried. I shot my hand into the bag, frantically pushing everything out of the way, fumbling, as I watched him prepare to lunge at me again.

There!

I had it. The knife at the bottom of the bag. The knife that had already killed him once. I wrapped my trembling fingers around the handle.

As he dove for me, I slid the blade out and swiped the knife at him.

Missed.

He slammed into the car, so hard it shook on its tires. He uttered a muffled gasp. Bounced off.

I spun and tried to drive the blade into his back.

"Kill him again." Those were Deena's instructions. That was her only solution. The only way to get rid of a dead boyfriend. *"Kill him again."*

He twisted his body to the side. The knife blade cut only air.

Green eyes glowing angrily, he raised both hands toward me.

I swung the knife again, off-balance this time. He

lurched forward and grabbed my arm. Grabbed my hand and struggled to pull the knife free.

I opened my mouth to protest, but I was breathing too hard, wheezing noisily. No sound escaped my mouth.

I tried to pull my arms away, to twist my body away from him. But he wrapped his hand around mine. And grabbed the knife from me.

A wide-eyed look of triumph spread for only an instant over his dead, pale face. And then he moved toward me, holding the knife blade high, aimed at my heart. He swung it down fast.

I stumbled and fell. Fell flat on my back. And before I could scramble to my feet, Blade was on top of me. He straddled my body, his knees digging into my sides.

I shoved him with both hands. Desperate to squirm out from under him. But he had me pinned down. Helpless.

The blank eyes bulging in his head, he raised the knife high, and I watched the blade, the gleaming blade, come plunging down.

41.

A scream escaped my throat. With a burst of strength, I grabbed his hand before he could bury the knife in me. Straining, groaning, I pushed the hand away.

We fought, a desperate wrestling match, me on my back, Blade straddling me, bent over me, using all his strength against me to push the blade down.

I gasped as the blade point came within an inch of my neck. With a superhuman heave, I shoved it back up. Blade uttered a cry of anger, frustrated that he could not stab me.

I twisted my body, struggling to squirm out from under him. Twisted hard—and saw Deena Fear running up the driveway.

"Deena—" I gasped her name.

Blade raised his head, turned to the driveway. He stopped his attempts to force the blade down. Just for a second, he loosened up.

And I took advantage to swipe the knife from his hand. He was still gazing at Deena as I steadied the knife, raised the blade, and plunged it up, straight up, into his stomach.

He uttered a breathy gasp. His hands flew up.

I stabbed him again. Stabbed the top of his stomach. Sliced through the red hoodie. Cut and sliced. Stabbed his chest between his ribs. Again. Again.

No blood this time. How could there be blood? He was dead. And now he was dead again, only he didn't seem to realize it.

I couldn't see Deena's face. Her hair blew wild about her head, covering her face. She stood with her arms crossed at the edge of the driveway, stood very still, made no attempt to interfere. As if she wasn't surprised. As if this was what she expected to find.

Finally, Blade uttered a final groan. His body started to slump to the right. I reached up, grabbed his side, and gave a hard push. He fell off me, his head bouncing on the grass.

I slid away from him. Gave him another push. He was stretched out on his side on the ground now. Eyes wide open but not moving. Not moving. Still as death.

Deena rushed forward and helped pull me to my feet. I stood there, my face wet with tears, my arms aching from the battle, blood pulsing at my temples.

My knees buckled and I started to fall. Deena held onto me, kept me standing up. I leaned against her. I couldn't catch my breath. I felt like I was choking.

"Wh–what are we going to do?" I stammered, my voice a choked rasp.

"Easy. Take it easy," Deena said softly, holding onto me. "I'll take care of it."

I blinked. Wiped the cold sweat off my forehead with the back of my hand. "Take care of it? How do you mean?"

She didn't answer. I started to feel a little more normal. My arms ached from my struggle with Blade. My neck felt stiff and sore. I glimpsed Blade, sprawled lifelessly on his side, head tilted at a strange angle, mouth hanging open.

"What do you mean take care of it?" I repeated.

Deena tugged her wild hair off her face with both hands. "I'll take him back to the chapel. Return him to his coffin."

I studied her eyes, trying to determine if she was telling the truth. Did she mean it? Would she leave him dead this time? Not bring him back to torture me some more? Not bring him back in hopes that he would be *hers* next time?

"His family will want to bury him right away," Deena murmured. She motioned to the body. "Help me get him in my car."

I started to follow her across the grass. "I'll come with you," I said. "I want to make sure—"

"No. You're totally messed up," Deena said. "He nearly killed you, Caitlyn. Go inside. Take a long hot bath. Get some rest."

"But I should—" I tried to protest.

She waved me back. "No. Just help me lift him into my backseat. I can do this myself. Really." I grabbed his legs. She started to lift him from under the shoulders. "It's my fault, after all," she said. "I never should have brought him back. I . . . I'm sorry."

I didn't reply to that. I felt too weary. I could barely hold my head up. Blade weighed more than I thought. Or maybe it's just that dead bodies are really heavy.

We dragged him to her car at the bottom of the drive-way. We lifted him off the ground and heaved him face-down onto the backseat. His legs stuck stiffly out of the car. Deena carefully tucked him in and slammed the door.

She walked to the driver's door. "I can handle this. Seriously," she said. "Go inside, Caitlyn. Get some rest."

I won't be able to rest. How can I rest after what I did tonight?

I stared into her headlights as she backed down the drive. My mind was spinning. My whole body ached. I decided I had to follow her.

She had aroused my suspicions. Why did she insist on returning Blade to the chapel on her own. I didn't think she was just being considerate of me. I didn't think she was that worried about me.

What did she really plan to do? Was she telling the truth, or did she have another plan for Blade's body?

The lights were on in the den at the far side of my house. I knew my parents were waiting there. I slipped into the car and, as silently, as I could, backed slowly down the driveway with the headlights off.

I could see Deena's car a block or so ahead of me. I kept the lights off. I didn't want her to see me following. I slowed down as she stopped for a light. She made a right turn and I waited, even though the light was green.

There was no traffic on the road, so I let her get a three-block lead. Was this the way to the chapel? I'd been concentrating so hard on the back of her car that I hadn't looked to see where we were.

Deena's twin red brake lights floated in front of my eyes. I saw her make another right turn. I kept thinking about Blade, back in his coffin. Blade finally buried deep in the ground where he couldn't come after me, where he couldn't try to pull me with him.

I was nearly to the right turn when I heard the rise and fall of the siren and saw the flashing lights in my rearview mirror.

As the patrol car came into focus in the mirror, I let out a groan and swung the car to the right. The cop car edged past me, and I saw a dark-uniformed officer in the passenger seat wave me to the curb.

I hope Deena really is returning Blade's body to the chapel.

That was my first thought. My second thought was more frightening: *Are the police stopping me because they know I killed Blade? Have they finally solved the case? Are they arresting me for murder?*

I gripped the wheel with both hands and clenched my jaw, trying to stop the chills that ran down my body.

I stared straight ahead until I heard the hard tap on my window. I turned and saw Officer Rivera peering in at me. "Caitlyn? Is that you? Step out of the car, please."

42.

grabbed the door handle, then hesitated. I spun around and saw my bag on the seat. Was the knife inside it? Or had I left it on the ground near my driveway where it had fallen?

Rivera tapped impatiently on the window. "Please step out of the car." He raised a flashlight and sent a white beam of halogen light over my face.

I shut my eyes and climbed out of the car. I stood there stiffly, blinking in the bright light. "Wh-what's wrong?" I stammered softly. I tensed myself for the bad news.

I turned away from the light and glimpsed his partner still behind the wheel of the patrol car. Rivera studied me intently. He had one hand on his holster.

Ready to arrest me for murder.

He lowered the light from my face. "Caitlyn, were you aware that you were driving without headlights?"

"Huh? Excuse me?"

"Didn't you notice your headlights were off? Didn't it seem a little dark to you?"

"Well . . ." My throat tightened. I couldn't speak. I wanted to burst out laughing. I was expecting to be hand-cuffed and dragged off to prison for murder. And these guys pulled me over because of my headlights.

I pressed my hand over my mouth so he wouldn't see my grin.

"Caitlyn, have you been drinking?" Rivera brought his face close to mine, I guess, to smell my breath.

"I don't drink," I said.

"It's pretty late," he said, his eyes glancing around the dark street. "Where are you going this time of night?"

"I'm just . . . coming from a friend's house," I said. "My friend Julie."

"And where does Julie live?"

"On Bank Street. A couple of blocks from the mall."

He nodded. He took off his cap and swept back his black hair. "Well, I'll let you go," he said. "Is everything okay? Did you just forget about the headlights?"

I nodded. "Yeah. I was thinking about school. I just forgot."

He pushed down his cap. "Well, be careful, okay? Put on your lights."

"Will do," I said. I watched him walk back to the patrol car. He slid into the passenger seat and closed the door. He and his partner didn't pull out. I guess they were waiting for me to go first.

I clicked on the headlights. Then I shifted into drive and drove away. Too late to try to catch up with Deena. I turned at the next block and made my way toward home.

A heavy wave of dread rolled over me. My stomach began to ache. I knew my parents were waiting up for me. How would I explain tonight to them? What was I going to say?

I'm sure they were mortified to have that emotional confrontation with me in front of Julie's parents. And how could I explain it? As I pulled up the driveway, my brain was doing jumping jacks in my head, leaping from thought to thought until I felt like my head was about to blow apart.

Sure enough, the front door swung open before I even climbed out of the car, and Mom and Dad came rushing at me. "Are you okay? Where did you go? How do you feel?"

I had the car door open only a few inches. "At least, let me out of the car," I said.

They obediently stepped back. I climbed out, straightening my top over my jeans. They put their arms around my shoulders and we walked into the house in a line.

"Can you explain to me what's going on?" Dad demanded after we had settled on facing couches in the den.

"I'm perfectly fine," I said. "I'm just tired, that's all. Way tired. But I'm okay. Seriously." *Especially since Blade is dead again and won't be coming to haunt me.*

"Do you expect us to believe that?" Mom said, arms

crossed tightly in front of her. She's the tough one. I knew I'd have trouble getting past her.

"Well . . . yes," I said. "I do expect you to believe me. I'm not a liar, Mom. I think you know that."

She ignored that. "Where did you go?" she demanded, eyes piercing mine. I could practically feel the heat from them. "Where did you go after you ran out of Julie's?"

I shrugged. "Just drove around."

"Caitlyn, you have to explain what's going on," Dad said, his fingers tapping the couch arm. "What did you tell Julie? What did you say to get your friend so upset?"

"You have to tell us," Mom insisted. "You can't just shrug it off and not say anything."

"Look, it was a joke," I said. "I made up a story about Blade Hampton and—"

"That boy who died?" Mom interrupted. She shook her head. "That was so sad."

"Yes, Blade Hampton," I said. I shut my eyes and rubbed my temples. "It was a joke. I told Julie a story about him and . . . I forgot she doesn't have a sense of humor. I guess she thought I was serious."

They both stared at me in silence. Were they buying my lame story?

No. Not at all.

Too late to make up a new one.

A hush fell over the room. Dad tapped the couch arm rhythmically. Mom didn't move. She finally broke the silence. "Well, Caitlyn . . . your joke must not have been too funny. Whatever you said to her got her so upset, she called us and said you were having a breakdown."

I forced a laugh. "Breakdown? What's a breakdown? You mean like a car?"

"Don't be glib," Dad said sharply. "Your friend was really upset and worried about you."

"Sorry," I muttered. "But you've got to believe me. It was all a joke. I guess Julie took it the wrong way. I'm perfectly okay. I'm not a wacko. I haven't gone berserk or anything."

I started to stand up. Maybe I could make it to the stairs and escape to my room. I could see from their faces that they were unsatisfied.

My parents aren't dumb. In fact, they're really smart. And they knew they weren't getting a very good explanation from me. They knew they weren't getting any explanation at all.

"You'd better go to bed," Dad said, motioning to the stairs. His expression was suddenly sad, his eyes weary, as if I had disappointed him.

"But we're not finished," Mom said, jumping up and leaning over me. "We're not finished, Caitlyn. We'll come back to this, hear me. We'll talk when you're not so exhausted."

"Good," I said. I didn't know what else to say. I stopped at the den doorway and turned back to them. "Sorry," I murmured. "Sorry you got that phone call from Julie and had to run over there. Sorry. Seriously. Sorry if you were

worried about me . . ." My voice trailed off. "Goodnight."
I grabbed the banister and pulled myself up the stairs.

I paused at the top of the stairs. I could still hear Mom
and Dad, both talking heatedly in the den. I heard Dad
say, "Teenagers all have secrets. But she'll be okay."

Secrets? He didn't know the half of it.

I picked up a stray sock that someone must have dropped
in the hall and carried it to my room. I closed the bedroom door carefully behind me. The window was closed
and the air was stuffy, but I didn't bother to open it. I began to pace tensely back and forth. My room is small.
Not much room to pace. I felt like a caged animal.

How would I ever get to sleep?

If Blade was safely back in his coffin, maybe I could begin to rest again. I'd be in even better shape if I knew his
coffin was deep in the ground.

But I had no way of knowing Deena's real intentions.
I didn't trust her. I knew she was insane about Blade.
But . . . insane enough to awake him again? To try her
magic on him one more time?

"No. No way," I muttered to myself.

I had no way to get in touch with her. She wasn't re-
sponding to texts or phone calls. It was too late to sneak
out and drive to her house. I just had to pray that she returned Blade's body as she said she would.

I changed into a nightshirt, clicked off the light, and
climbed into bed. My hands felt clammy. My heart was

still racing. My mind skipped from thought to thought, from ugly picture to ugly picture.

I killed someone. I killed someone tonight. . . .

I knew it would take a long time to fall asleep, Diary, and it did. I lay staring at the shadows on the window for at least an hour. Somehow, I finally felt myself fading into unconsciousness.

I fell into a deep, dreamless sleep. I must have slept a long time.

When I opened my eyes, red morning sunlight filled the window and poured onto the foot of my bed. I blinked, and slowly realized I'd been awakened by a sound. I started to pull myself up, listening hard.

Yes. A tapping sound. *Tap tap tap.* Soft but insistent.

Tapping on the window. I raised my eyes. A shadow appeared in the red sunlight.

I held my breath. Terror made me grip the bed sheet with both hands.

Tap tap tap.

Someone tapping on my bedroom window. Just inches away from me.

Blade!

43.

The tapping repeated, but the shadow vanished from the window glass. I forced myself to sit up.

Oh, please, no. Go away, Blade. Please go away.

Another drumbeat of soft taps.

Shielding my eyes from the bright sun with one hand, I peered out.

"Blade?"

I uttered a long sigh of relief.

Not Blade.

A woodpecker perched on the siding beside the window, pecked away, tapping its steady rhythm.

If I was in a normal state of mind, I would have remembered. This wasn't the first morning that woodpecker decided to have breakfast right outside my room.

But I wasn't in a normal state of mind. And as I got dressed for school, I wondered sadly if I'd *ever* be in a normal state again.

★ ★ ★

I avoided Julie and Miranda at school. I saw them watching me from across the hall before homeroom. They were whispering, their faces close together, peering at me as if I were crazy or some strange new animal species.

Julie started toward me. Maybe she wanted to apologize again for getting my parents on my case. But I wasn't ready to tell her everything was hunky-dory again. I felt betrayed. I knew I'd probably get over that. But not yet.

I slammed my locker door and hurried off in the other direction, leaving them both open-mouthed behind me. I stepped into the classroom and searched up and down for Blade. Can you blame me?

He'd surprised me in school before, the day I tried to read my violin essay. I had no guarantee he wouldn't be back to haunt me. No guarantee he wouldn't be waiting for me, waiting to grab me in English class, or my Advanced Math class, or in the library where I had my fourth-period study hall.

I knew I had to stay alert all day, Diary. It wasn't easy. It was a horrible way to spend the day, always frightened, never able to relax or let my guard down for a second.

At lunch period, I grabbed a tuna fish sandwich in the lunchroom and carried it outside to the parking lot. I didn't want to run into Julie and Miranda. We always sat together at a table on the far side, and I figured it would be less awkward for all three of us if I ate outside by myself.

It was a warm day, with strong sunlight making it feel

more like summer than spring. The daffodils behind the school, bright as sunshine, fluttered in a soft breeze. Two squirrels scampered together along the edge of the parking lot.

I leaned against the trunk of my car and tried to eat the sandwich. But my throat was dry and I didn't bring anything to drink. I wasn't hungry anyway. My stomach was knotted tight.

Suddenly, I knew what I had to do. The rest of the school day would be a nightmare if I continued to expect seeing Blade. I couldn't go back inside.

I climbed into my car and tossed the uneaten sandwich on the passenger seat. I fumbled the key from my bag and started the engine.

The North Hills Chapel was a short drive from school. My plan was to drive to the chapel and make sure that Blade had been returned. Once I knew that for sure, I could return to school and maybe . . . just maybe . . . my life would start to return to normal.

When I arrived at the chapel, I found the front doors open. Blue-uniformed workers were setting up ladders on one wall, preparing to clean the stained glass windows that ran along the ceiling.

I started to the front, searching for someone who could help me. And nearly got tangled in a wide canvas tarp two men were spreading over the aisle.

"Is anyone here?" My voice came out louder than I'd planned. Several of the workers turned to look at me.

A gray-haired woman in a maid's uniform had been hidden behind the podium on the altar. She poked her head up, a dust cloth in her hand. "Can I help you?"

I nodded. "Yes. I'm trying to get some information."

Before she could answer, the minister appeared from the back hall. Reverend Preller was wearing the same brown sport jacket he had worn at Blade's funeral. He carried a clipboard in one hand and had a pen tucked behind one ear.

He narrowed his eyes at me. "Yes?"

A crash behind me made me jump. I turned to see that one of the workers had dropped a bucket. The soapy water flowed over the carpeted aisle.

The minister scratched the back of his hair. "As you can see, we're closed today. But if you need information—?"

I suddenly realized I didn't know how to ask my question. I couldn't just blurt out "Is Blade Hampton in his coffin?" I stood there with my mouth hanging open, thinking hard.

"I . . . I came to ask about Blade Hampton," I finally managed to say.

His eyes flashed. His features tightened. I'd definitely grabbed his attention.

"The funeral was last Saturday. Are you a relative?" he asked, studying me intently.

"Yes," I lied. "He . . . he was my cousin." My heart began to thud. Did he believe me?

"Well, I can't really tell you—" he started.

"I just need to know where he's buried," I said. "I . . . My family got to Shadyside late. And we need to know . . ."

He scratched the back of his hair again. "Buried?"

I nodded, biting my bottom lip.

Please answer. Please tell me that he has been buried.

"Miss, have you talked to Blade's parents? If so, you know they are in shock. You know they are beyond themselves with grief."

"W-We . . . we just got here," I stammered. "We haven't had a chance—"

"Blade hasn't been buried," Preller said. "Because his body has been stolen."

44.

"Oh, wow." I couldn't hide my horror and disappointment. I could feel the blood rushing to my face. My knees started to fold. Deena didn't return him to his coffin.

I don't know what Reverend Preller thought. I really didn't care. Blade was out there somewhere. And I knew he wouldn't rest till he dragged me with him, dragged me to my death.

"Sorry for the shock," he said. But I had already spun away from him and was running full speed, running past the startled workers.

To my car. I slammed the door. Started it up. Pounded my foot on the gas until the engine roared. I wanted to roar along with it. I wanted to roar and scream and howl like a wild animal.

I don't want to die, Blade. I don't want to join you.

But I knew he was waiting somewhere for me. Deena Fear was a liar. Not just a liar, she was evil. She couldn't give up her desperate hope that Blade would decide he wanted her instead of me.

She couldn't give up. . . .

I pounded the steering wheel with both fists. Pounded till both hands ached. One of the chapel workers stopped to peer in at me. I turned my head away, and he kept walking.

I didn't know if I was more frightened or angry. I only knew I was about to go insane, totally berserk.

It was time to tell my parents. I had no choice. It was time to tell them the whole story. I knew it would be impossible for them to believe what had happened in the last few weeks.

But I had to try. . . .

I knew they were both home. Mom thought she might be coming down with the flu, and Dad took a personal day so he could stay home and take care of her.

I burst into the house, my head spinning. *Where do I start? How do I start to tell them what has happened?*

I didn't want to burst into tears and be unable to talk. But as I ran through the house, I wasn't sure I could hold myself together.

"Mom? Dad?" I found them sitting side by side on the couch in the den. I roared into the room. Opened my mouth to try to start my story. Stopped when I saw what they had on their laps.

And let out a horrified scream: "What are you *doing* with that?"

45.

I stood there, my finger trembling as I pointed at my diary. My diary sitting open in front of them.

"How did you get that? What are you doing with that?" I screamed.

Dad went pale. Mom was the first to speak. "Cathy-Ann, I know we shouldn't have read it. I know we invaded your privacy. But it was open on your desk and . . . and . . ."

"We were so worried about you." Dad finished her sentence.

"B-B-But—" I sputtered.

"We had to find out what has been troubling you," Mom said. "Cathy-Ann, we had no idea. Reading your diary . . . So much violence. And killing. And crazy things happening."

"Your diary reads like a horror story," Dad said. His eyes were wet. His chin trembled. He was as pale as the sofa cushion.

"It *is* a horror story!" I cried, rushing over to them, standing above them."

"Why did you change your name?" Mom demanded. "Why did you call yourself Caitlyn?"

I let out a long sigh. "Because it's just a story, Mom. It isn't my diary. It isn't a diary at all."

Mom blinked. "But Cathy-Ann . . . all your friends are in it. Julie and Miranda. They're real people. And your teachers are in it. And—"

"I used them in my story, Mom. I used them as characters because I knew them. I knew how to describe them. But it isn't true. It's not a diary. It's a novel I've been writing. None of it is true. I swear. None of it."

Dad swallowed hard. He kept blinking, as if he was having trouble focusing. "It's a novel? It's fiction?"

"Yes, I've been writing a novel," I said. I rolled my eyes. I let out a bitter laugh. "Did you two honestly believe that I killed a boy? Seriously? You believed I stabbed a boy to death—*twice*? Did you?"

Mom hesitated. "Well . . . no. Of course not, dear. But that boy Blade *did* die. He drowned, didn't he? On vacation with his parents?"

I nodded. "It was very upsetting. He was a friend of mine. So I used him in the story. But—"

"It says you killed a stranger," Mom said, biting her bottom lip. "You wrote that you stabbed an innocent boy in a bus shelter. Cathy-Ann—?"

"It isn't true. It's all made up," I insisted. "It's fiction, Mom. Can't you understand?"

"Well, who is this Deena Fear?" Dad demanded. "I never heard you mention her before."

I rolled my eyes again. "That's because she doesn't exist, Dad. There *is* no Deena Fear. I made her up. You know all those crazy stories people tell about Fear Street. I made up a new one."

He nodded, exchanging a glance with Mom. She ran her hand over a handwritten page in her lap. "Well, Cathy-Ann, this is quite a piece of writing. But . . . I'm sorry to say this, but it's the work of a very troubled person."

"Maybe you need to see someone," Dad said. "These thoughts you have here—"

"You two are ridiculous," I said. "I'm not troubled at all. You know I love to write. I decided to write a horror novel. That's all. I used my imagination. I dreamed up a frightening story."

I tugged at both sides of my hair. "But that doesn't mean I'm troubled. That doesn't mean I have horrifying abnormal thoughts. I made up characters and I wrote a story. Can't you two understand that?"

They shook their heads. They couldn't get over the fact that my writing was filled with violence and blood and murder and a boy coming back from the dead. I guess they thought I should write about kittens and lollipops.

I reached out both hands and Mom handed me the book. "You should be proud of me," I said. "Look how creative I am. I do my schoolwork. I have a B-plus average. And I've written almost an entire novel."

I shook my head, frowning at them. "Instead of sitting there with those disapproving expressions on your faces, you should be telling me what a cool thing I've done."

I turned and started from the den. But Dad called me back. "You're right. You're totally right," he said. "We *are* proud of you, Cathy-Ann. We just didn't understand. . . ." He shook his head. "You took us by surprise. You completely fooled us. The writing is so good, we believed it all."

"Your dad is right," Mom said. She pointed to the book in my hands. "You know what? It really is a good story. Maybe you should try to get it published.

ONE YEAR LATER

46.

Cathy-Ann straightened her skirt over her tights, then swept back her hair with both hands. She shielded her eyes from the bright afternoon sunlight and peered across the parking lot to the bookstore.

"Look, dear, there's already a line," her mother said. "Isn't it exciting? They're waiting for *you*."

Exciting isn't the word, Cathy-Ann thought, feeling her heart begin to flutter in her chest. *It's unreal!*

Her dad took her arm and she walked between her parents toward the bookstore. She counted at least twenty people lined up outside the entrance. Most of them were high school girls. She recognized a few from Shadyside High. But she saw a sprinkling of adults there, too.

She stopped in front of the big window at the side of the entrance and peered through the sun glare at the poster—her photo, smiling and holding the book. Below it, the words in bold type: **APPEARING TODAY. SIGNING AT 3:00**.

Dad pulled out his phone and snapped a few photos of the display. A few people in the line recognized her and called out to her.

The door opened. A pleasant-looking young woman in jeans and a red-and-white striped t-shirt stepped out to greet her. "Hi, Cathy-Ann. I'm Mandy Wade, the store manager. Welcome to Books & Things."

"Thank you." Cathy-Ann felt her throat tighten. *Was this really happening?*

What a crazy year it had been. It had taken weeks to type up what she had written in the diary. Then she sent the manuscript to her cousin Barry in New York, whose girlfriend worked in publishing. What a shock when, two weeks later, Cathy-Ann received an offer for the book. It was going to be published!

Now here she was, about to do her very first book-signing at the only bookstore in Shadyside. The book had been out for only a week and had already received some good reviews.

Cathy-Ann had to laugh. Here was Mom beaming proudly as they walked through the bookstore. She had been so appalled and upset the first time she read the story. Now she kept a Pinterest page of photos and reviews and everything about the book.

"Sit behind the table here," Mandy Wade said, pulling out the chair for Cathy-Ann. "I have a lot of different pens and markers. I didn't know which you prefer."

"I don't really know, either," Cathy-Ann replied, sitting down next to the tall stack of her books. This is my first signing."

Mandy patted her hand. "The main thing is to relax and enjoy it. These people came all the way here to see you. So there's no reason to be nervous." She turned to the front. "I'm going to let people in now. You have a great crowd for a first-time author."

Cathy-Ann's dad was busy taking photos of her. Her mom stood at the side, arms crossed, a proud grin stuck on her face.

Cathy-Ann cleared her throat, opened the water bottle in front of her, and took a long sip. Then she picked up a pen and watched as people began to stream toward the table.

The first two in line were Rachel Martin and Amy O'Brien, two girls from her senior class at Shadyside High. They chatted about how exciting this was. "I've already read it," Amy said as Cathy-Ann thanked her and signed their books.

A middle-aged woman set a book down in front of Cathy-Ann and opened it to the title page. "Could you sign this to my daughter Coral? She likes to write, too. Could you write something encouraging to her?"

Cathy-Ann signed the book to Coral. She didn't really know what to say, so she wrote: "Keep reading and keep writing!"

The next woman had bought three books she wanted signed. "No message. Just sign your name. They're going to be birthday gifts," she said.

Cathy-Ann leaned over the books and signed them. "Are you working on another book?" the woman asked, gathering them up.

"Not yet," Cathy-Ann said.

Next in line was a tall young man with wavy black hair and silvery sunglasses that caught the light from the ceiling. He set a book down in front of her. Then he slowly removed the sunglasses.

She stared into his strange gray-green eyes—and recognized him.

He shoved the book toward her. "Just sign it to The Dead Boyfriend," he said.

"Blade? Blade?"

Cathy-Ann dropped her pen and started to scream.

GIVE ME A
K-I-L-L

PART
ONE

1.

Gretchen Page stroked a brush through her straight blonde hair as she pressed the phone to her ear with her free hand. She tried parting her hair in the middle and letting the sides fall to her shoulders. Then she brushed some forward to see what a row of bangs might look like.

Gretchen couldn't look into a mirror without knowing her hair was her best feature. If only her olive-colored eyes were spaced a little farther apart, not so close to her nose, which she considered short and too cute and not at all elegant. And then there was that tragic tiny cleft in her chin.

She ranked herself a seven, which was good enough to be the prettiest cheerleader at Savanna Mills High. But now she was starting at Shadyside High, ten times the size of her old school, and how could she compete? There wasn't even a Sephora in Savanna Mills!

"I miss you, too, Polly," she said, fumbling the phone against her ear. She set down the hairbrush, turned away from the mirror with a sigh, crossed the bedroom, and perched on the edge of her bed. "Starting a new school junior year is the pits."

Gretchen leaned back against the big, plush Hello Kitty pillow her Grandma Hannah had given her when she was eight. A lot of the stuffing had oozed out, but she couldn't bear to part with it. Grandma Hannah was the only relative she liked.

"I always call you when the nightmares start," she told Polly. "Talking to you always makes me feel better. Yes, I had one last night. It's so sad. It was so real, so totally vivid . . . I couldn't tell if I was dreaming or not."

Gretchen sighed. "I woke up drenched in sweat. And my jaw hurt from gritting my teeth. Thank goodness I can always call you."

She shifted the phone to her other ear. "No, I haven't made any friends here," she said.

Gretchen and Polly Brown had been inseparable—like sisters—back in Savanna Mills. Their friendship went well beyond being cocaptains of the Hawks cheer-leading squad.

"How could I make friends in only two weeks? The kids here aren't unfriendly. But they've all known each other for *ages*. I'm the only outsider."

She tugged at a string on the bedspread, listening to Polly's purr of a voice. She pictured Polly—round-faced with freckles and curly copper-colored hair. Polly looked about twelve—but she had a deep, sexy voice that seemed to come from deep in her throat.

"So your new school is really big?" Polly asked.

"The first few days, I couldn't even find my homeroom," Gretchen told her friend. "That's how big the school is. I mean, it's on three floors and it stretches on forever. It's like as big as the mall back home. Some kids drive from class to class!"

She listened to Polly's low chuckle. Gretchen wasn't known for her sense of humor. In fact, she was earnest and serious most of the time. But she always knew how to make Polly laugh.

"I guess it's nice to have a fresh start," Gretchen said, shifting the phone to her other ear. "And I understand why Mom had to move. I mean, after Dad left, she had to do *something*."

"True," Polly murmured. Polly never liked talking about serious, real-world troubles. She really *was* like a twelve-year-old in more than just looks.

"She got a really good deal on this house," Gretchen continued. "The real estate woman said because it's on Fear Street. I don't really get it. It's a perfectly nice street, with awesome old houses and lots of trees and big front yards."

She shifted the phone again. She realized she was squeezing it so hard, her hand ached. "My room is huge," Gretchen continued. "I even have my own bathroom, believe that? No more sharing. But I guess Fear Street is a big deal here in Shadyside. I haven't had a chance to Google it."

A cool breeze fluttered the curtains at the open bedroom window. The air chilled Gretchen's skin, an early sign of fall. Clouds covered the sun, and a gray shadow swept across the bedroom floor.

"Of course, I'm dying to make the cheerleading squad," Gretchen told Polly. "But I'm totally tense about it. Everything is so big and serious here. The high school has a real stadium behind the parking lot. Not what we had—bleachers set up on the grass."

Gretchen snickered. "No, everyone isn't rich here. It's a normal place. But they take their football seriously. The Shadyside Tigers were All-State last season. And the cheerleaders went to the state tournament and got an Honorable Mention."

"With you on the squad, they'll do better than that," Polly replied.

Gretchen sighed. "I'm not so sure about that. I've been so tense about it, I've been practicing after school all week in my backyard, believe that?"

Before Polly could answer, Gretchen's mom strode into the room, her eyes on the phone in Gretchen's hand. "Who are you talking to?"

Mrs. Page was tall and trim and athletic-looking. Back in Savanna Mills, she played tennis at her club almost every afternoon and spent at least an hour in the gym six or seven days a week.

She had short blonde hair, darker than Gretchen's, with stylish white streaks back through the sides, a broad tanned forehead, high cheekbones like a fashion model, and dark green eyes.

She was young-looking for forty-three, but Gretchen saw that the divorce and all the trouble back home had aged her. She had dark circles under her eyes, a tiny network of wrinkles on both cheeks, and even her eyes had lost some of their sparkle.

Mrs. Page made up for the change with too much makeup and too much bright orange lipstick. At least, that was Gretchen's harsh opinion.

Her mother strode quickly up to Gretchen. She wore a turquoise crewneck T-shirt over white tennis shorts that showed off her thin legs. "Gretchen, who are you talking to?" she repeated.

"None of your business," Gretchen snapped. The words came out louder than Gretchen had intended. She ended the call.

Mrs. Page let out a short gasp. "Oops. Sorry."

"Go away," Gretchen said, making a shooing motion with her free hand.

"I was just asking a simple question, Gretchen."

"Mom, what don't you understand about the words *go away*? Stop hovering over me like a drone!"

"Gretchen, think you might be overreacting a bit?"

"You can't treat me like an infant, Mom. I'm a person. I'm entitled to a little privacy. You can't barge into my room and—"

"I just want you to get off to a good start here," Mrs. Page said, suddenly breathless. She tugged the turquoise T-shirt down over her shorts. Then she ran both hands back through her short hair. "I don't think asking who you are talking to on the phone is a very big invasion of your privacy. Seriously."

Gretchen softened her glare. She nodded. "Okay. Maybe I overreacted a little." She shrugged. "Whatever."

She and her mother had always had what her mother called a *difficult* relationship. The simple fact was they hadn't gotten along since Gretchen was two and learned the word *no*.

Mrs. Page tried to show how much she cared about her daughter by involving herself in everything Gretchen did. Gretchen felt constantly smothered. The more she tried to push her away, the more Mrs. Page clung to her.

At least, that was Gretchen's side of the story.

And now that her dad had flown the coop, it was much worse.

Mrs. Page softened her expression, too. "Would you like to talk about why you overreacted?"

"Would you like to get out of my way?" Gretchen snapped. She pushed past her mother and crossed the room to her closet. She pulled out a silky maroon hoodie and swung it over her shoulder.

"Where are you going?" Mrs. Page asked.

"To school," Gretchen said, checking herself one more time in the dresser mirror.

Her mother followed her to the bedroom door. "But it's Saturday, dear."

Gretchen sighed. "I know, Mom. I have an appointment. With the cheerleading coach."

"Gretchen, just wait a minute," her mother insisted. "Just give me a minute, okay?"

Gretchen spun around in the hall. "Mom—I'll be late."

"Are you sure you want to be a cheerleader right away?"

"Excuse me? You know how important this is to me, right?"

"I'm just saying . . ." Mrs. Page hesitated. "Don't you think you should settle in first?"

"*Settle in?*" Gretchen's words burst out high and shrill. "You're joking, right? You can't be serious, Mom. Settle in? That had to be a joke."

Mrs. Page took a few steps back, as if retreating. "I'm only thinking of what's best for you, dear." She shook her head. "That's all I ever do. I just want things to go right for you. I'm not your enemy. We have to be friends. With your father gone, we have to try harder, don't you agree?"

Gretchen sighed again. "You're right, Mom. Bye."

She pounded down the stairs, taking them two at a time, and out the front door.

As she climbed behind the wheel of her mother's blue Camry, the nightmare lingered in her mind. The knife . . . the blood . . . the screams . . .

She clenched her jaw tightly. Pounded the wheel with both fists.

"Got to get past this," she said out loud. "Got to put it all behind me. Time for my fresh start."

2.

retchen drove to the high school. It wasn't a long drive, but she was still unfamiliar with the streets. There were probably shortcuts, but she stayed on Park Drive, which she knew cut straight through the middle of town and led to the high school at the corner of Division Street.

She could feel her heart start to beat faster as she pulled the car into the student parking lot behind the school. She didn't have a parking permit yet. But it was Saturday, so she figured no one would be checking.

As she climbed out of the car, she could hear the shouts and cries of the football team, having their afternoon practice in the stadium. She was tempted to go watch them, but she was already five minutes late for her appointment.

She trotted to the back doors of the school. It still looked immense to her. With its brick walls, faded from the sun, ivy climbing up one side, rows of tall windows, and sloping red tile roof, it looked unreal to her. Like a movie high school. Somehow high schools always looked too perfect in movies, and this one did, too.

She stepped into the back hallway. The lights had been dimmed. Silence. A ringing silence that made her stop and squint down the long, empty hallway. Gray metal lockers down both sides. Perfect. Too perfect.

Her footsteps thudded noisily as she hurried toward the front. She turned a corner and could hear the Shadyside cheerleaders practicing in the gym all the way down the hall.

She stepped under a hand-painted maroon-and-white banner that had been hung from the ceiling: TIGERS ROAR. It reminded her that the first football game was only a week away. That thought made her heartbeats race even faster.

The chanting voices from the gym grew louder as she approached. Gretchen was only a few doors away from the gym when a tall boy in faded jeans and a denim jacket burst into the hall in front of her.

She let out a startled gasp. Nearly walked right into him. "What are you doing here?" she blurted out.

"Shhhh." He raised a finger to his lips. "I'm stealing some laptops. Want to help?

3.

Gretchen stared at the laptop tucked under his arm. She raised her gaze to his dark eyes. Serious eyes that crinkled up as he started to laugh. "I'm messing with you," he said. "Did you believe me?"

"I-I don't know," Gretchen stammered. She quickly got herself together. "You *do* look a lot like a thief," she joked.

He had a great smile, very warm. She liked the way his eyes crinkled up. He had short brown hair, buzzed close at the sides. The only thing that kept him from being totally awesome-looking were his ears, which stuck out like small cabbages.

"Sid Viviano," he said, introducing himself. He actually shook hands with her, and as he did his dark eyes seemed to study her face. "I'm the equipment manager for the cheerleaders."

She blinked. "Equipment manager?" They didn't have an equipment manager back in Savanna Mills.

He grinned. "I just like hanging out with a bunch of hot girls in short skirts."

"Well, at least you're honest," Gretchen said, grinning back at him.

He's very cute, and he seems to know it.

Sid raised the laptop. "I took this from the AV room. We need it for music for the practice."

"I'm late," Gretchen said, glancing at the time on her phone. "Can you tell me where Coach Walker's office is?"

"It's in the gym," he said. "This way." He motioned for her to follow him. "You're new, right? I think I saw you in Sawyer's Government class. What's your name?" He put a hand on her shoulder. "No. Wait. Let me guess. I'm good at guessing names."

He studied her for a long moment, his hand resting on her shoulder. He brought his face so close to hers, Gretchen thought he might kiss her.

Would she like that? Well . . . it was a little soon.

"I've got it. Heather," he said. "Your name is Heather, right?"

"Right," Gretchen said. "Wow. How did you do that?"

He laughed. "I just read your mind."

"Actually, my name is Gretchen. Gretchen Page."

He shook his head. "No way. *No way* do you look like a Gretchen."

"What does a Gretchen look like?"

He grinned but didn't answer.

"I'm really late," Gretchen said.

He brought his face close to hers again. His dark eyes burned into hers. "Would you like to hang out some-time?" he asked, just above a whisper.

Gretchen was about to answer when she saw the cheer-leader at the gym doors. She was short and blonde and very pretty, and even from this distance, Gretchen could see that she was glaring at them angrily.

"Oh." The word slipped from Gretchen's mouth.

The girl strode up behind Sid, her face set in a scowl. She wore a maroon-and-white cheerleader uniform, a short skirt over maroon tights and a long-sleeved top with a large tiger head across the front.

Sid didn't see her until she was next to him. He was still grinning at Gretchen. His eyes widened in surprise as the girl wrapped herself around him. She draped one arm around his shoulders and pressed her face against his cheek.

As if she owns him, Gretchen thought.

"Are you Gretchen Page?" she asked, eyeing Gretchen up and down.

Gretchen nodded. "Yes. Sorry I'm late. I—"

"I'm Stacy Grande. I'm the cheerleading captain." She laughed. Her blue eyes flashed. "Did you think you could get a spot on the squad by flirting with my boyfriend?"

Gretchen could feel her face grow hot and knew she was blushing. She was one of those people who blushed easily, blushed all the time, often for no big reason at all, and she hated that about herself. It embarrassed her so that she blushed even darker.

"I-I wasn't flirting," she stammered. "I'm . . . late." She brushed past Sid and Stacy and vanished into the gym.

"Well . . . *that* went well," she muttered.

Not a good start. But she had no way of knowing her troubles had just begun.

4.

Coach Walker's office stood at the far end of a row of small glass-windowed offices along one side of the gym. The cheerleaders, Gretchen saw, had taken a break from their practice. They were perched in the bleachers, water bottles in one hand, phones in the other.

Through the glass window, Gretchen could see that two girls were already in Walker's office, seated in front of the cluttered desk, both talking animatedly. Gretchen hesitated outside the door, unsure whether to go in or wait.

Coach Walker was a tall, lean black woman. She was dressed in purple sweats and had a blue-and-white Yankees cap over her short hair. She saw Gretchen through the glass, stood up, and opened the office door. "Are you Gretchen? I'm Coach Walker."

Gretchen nodded. "Sorry I'm late."

"No worries. I'll be right back." Walker was at least a foot taller than Gretchen. She turned and jogged to the gym doors.

The two girls in the office both stared intently at Gretchen. She swept her hair back with both hands and entered the office to introduce herself.

"I'm Devra Dalby," said one of the girls. She had beautiful, wavy red hair and creamy white skin, unreal skin, Gretchen noticed immediately. Her blue eyes were large and round and icy cold. And she had an amused little grin on her face even though Gretchen didn't see anything to be amused about. "And this is my friend Courtney Shaw."

Courtney was in a cheerleader uniform. She had very short black hair, shaved close on one side. She had a slender face, gray eyes surrounded by a lot of dark eye makeup, a short turned-up nose, a silver ring in one nostril.

Courtney had the same amused look on her face as Devra. As if the two of them shared a joke.

Am I the joke? Gretchen wondered.

"I like your outfit," Devra said. "Nice hoodie."

The girls exchanged glances. Gretchen caught their vibe. They were laughing at her for some reason.

"Coach Walker said you were from Savanna Mills," Devra said. "Is that really a place? It sounds made up."

She and Courtney laughed, as if that was a great joke.

"It's a real place," Gretchen said. "But if you blink, you miss it."

"Small towns are the best," Courtney said to Devra, her eyes flashing.

"If you're a small town person. . . ." Devra added. She

changed to a funny voice and did a short dialogue. " 'Want to hang out at the 7-Eleven tonight?' 'Huh? The 7-Eleven? That's too exciting. How about the DQ?' "

Gretchen watched them laugh. *How do I win them over? They're both so snotty.*

Devra's smile faded. Her blue eyes turned icy. She had a red-and-yellow bandanna tied tightly over her forehead. She untied it, then tied it again. "Listen, Gretch," she said, peering out to see if Coach Walker was returning. "If you've come for the cheerleader position, it's already taken—by *me*."

The two girls didn't wait for Gretchen to reply. They both jumped up and hurried out of the office. Gretchen could feel that her face was still hot. Without realizing it, she had balled her hands into fists. She watched the two girls as they crossed the gym to the bleachers.

But her eyes wandered to the wall at the side of the bleachers. She saw Sid and Stacy. Sid had his arms around Stacy's waist, and they were locked in a long kiss.

To Gretchen's surprise, Devra stopped halfway across the gym floor. Her mouth dropped open as she watched Sid and Stacy against the wall.

Why does Devra suddenly look so angry? Gretchen wondered. *She looks as if she wants to kill them both.*

5.

A few minutes later, Coach Walker returned to her office. She dropped behind her desk and slid her phone onto the desktop. She adjusted the Yankees cap over her hair. Gretchen saw that she had tiny diamond studs on both sides of her nose.

"Sorry to keep you waiting. Did you meet Devra and Courtney?"

Gretchen nodded. "Yes. We . . . uh . . . talked for a bit." She clasped her hands tightly in her lap, surprised to find them damp and ice cold.

"Your family just moved to Shadyside?"

Gretchen nodded again. "My mom and me. A few weeks ago."

Coach Walker toyed with the silver whistle that dangled from her neck. "How are you finding it?"

"Big," Gretchen said.

That made the coach smile for the first time. But the

smile faded quickly. "I'm afraid your timing is bad. We had only one position to fill, and I just gave it to Devra."

Gretchen couldn't hide her disappointment. She let out a long sigh.

"Devra was the alternate last year," Coach Walker said. "So I thought she should move onto the squad for this year."

"But . . ." Gretchen fumbled in her bag and pulled out the disc she had brought. "I have a highlight reel," she said, raising it to the coach. "Maybe if you have time, you can watch. . . ."

Coach Walker took the disk from her. "Is this video from your old school?"

"Yes. I was cocaptain. The school was smaller, but we had six girls on the squad, just like here."

Coach Walker studied the disc for a moment. She smiled again. "Why don't we watch it now?"

She pulled a disc drive from a bottom desk drawer and plugged it into her laptop. Then she motioned for Gretchen to slide her chair around to her side of the desk so they could watch it together.

As the video started and Gretchen watched the Savanna Mills cheerleaders run onto the floor to start their routines, she felt a pang of sadness. She watched Polly do a series of cartwheels across the floor. She liked all these girls. They had so much fun together. They were a real *team*.

The girls suddenly looked so young to Gretchen. She

had the weird feeling she was watching an old movie. Something that happened far away in a different time.

Can't let the sadness take over. . . .

She raised her gaze to Coach Walker, who was watching the routines intently. "Good. Very good," she murmured. She turned to Gretchen. "Very good L Stand to a Shoulder Sit. That's so basic, but you made it look fresh."

"Thanks," Gretchen said. "I think the Thigh Stand is next."

Coach Walker turned her attention back to the laptop screen. "Yes. That's impressive," she said, nodding her head. "Both Thigh Stands are perfect. And I like your smile, Gretchen. I like the way you make it look as if you are enjoying yourself."

"Well . . . actually, I *was*," Gretchen said.

Coach Walker stopped the video. "I'm impressed."

Gretchen felt her heartbeat start to race again. "Thank you. I do a Flying Somersault at the end. It's kind of my specialty."

"I'm going to watch the whole thing later," the coach said. "Have you met Stacy? She's our captain. I want her to watch it, too."

"I met her. Out in the hall," Gretchen said. Then she thought: *And Stacy thought I was flirting with her boyfriend.*

"Tell you what, Gretchen," Coach Walker said, twirling the silver whistle. "Devra isn't going to like this, but I'm going to let you try out. I think this team has a chance of going to the state tournament. And I want it to have only the best cheerleaders we have in school. I think you're really good, and it's only fair to give you a chance to make the squad."

Gretchen's heart skipped a beat. She wanted to jump up and hug Coach Walker. "Oh . . . thank you," she managed to say.

Walker jumped to her feet. "I have to tell Devra right away." She saw Devra sitting beside Courtney at the far end of the bleachers. She cupped her hands around her mouth and shouted for Devra to come to the office.

Devra entered the office with her arms crossed in front of her, a suspicious look on her face. Coach Walker motioned for her to take the chair next to Gretchen. "Change of plans," the coach said.

Devra's blue eyes grew wider. She adjusted her red-and-yellow bandanna and flipped back her wavy, red hair with a toss of her head.

Coach Walker hesitated. She took a breath. "I've decided to give Gretchen a chance to try out for the position on the squad," she said. Both of her hands gripped the edge of her desktop, as if she expected a torrent of protest.

Devra yawned.

She squinted at Coach Walker. "What did you just say?"

"I said we want the best talent we can get on the squad," the coach replied. "So I've given Gretchen a chance to try out."

Devra's eyes flashed. She glared at Gretchen, a hard, angry stare.

But then she said in a voice just above a whisper, "No worries. No worries at all."

A few minutes later, Gretchen was driving home, singing along to the radio, the music cranked way up. She roared up Park Drive, made a squealing turn into a street she didn't know, singing and laughing, and feeling the joy of being a winner.

She sailed through several blocks, the houses and cars a colorful blur sweeping past the windshield. Stopping for a light, she cut off the music and pulled out her phone. She pushed Polly's number to tell her the good news.

"I know I can beat Devra Dalby," she told her old friend. "I know I can make this squad. You should have seen the coach's face. She was definitely impressed. And I'm impressed with her. I think it took courage to give this girl Devra the news. Devra seems to be some kind of tiger."

Gretchen turned back onto Park Drive. "Hard to believe, Polly, but I made *two* enemies in one day. Stacy and Devra. But they'll get over it. I'm sure they will."

Gretchen let out a shocked scream as a gunshot—a deafening *crack* of sound—rang out right behind her. Her hands flew up, the phone fell to the floor, and the car squealed out of control.

6.

Gretchen's foot slammed the brake. She grabbed the wheel and twisted it as the car slid toward a light pole at the curb. A low moan escaped her throat as the car bumped onto the curb, jolting her whole body, and came to a stop an inch from the pole.

A shrill wail rose up around her. It took her a few seconds to realize she was leaning on the horn. Struggling to catch her breath, Gretchen gripped the wheel again and pressed her back against the car seat.

A close one.

Her hand trembled as she pushed open the door. She leaned over and saw the flat tire even before she climbed out. The front tire on the driver's side. It spread flat on the pavement.

A blowout. Not a gunshot. A tire blowout.

She stared at it until it blurred in front of her eyes.

You're just tense because the nightmares have returned, she told herself. *You have got to get your imagination under control.*

A few miles away in North Hills, the expensive neighborhood of Shadyside, Devra Dalby leaned forward on the leather desk chair in her bedroom and gazed at her father on her laptop screen. "Dad, the only way I see you these days is on FaceTime," she said.

He frowned. "I know. Inventory time is always crazy. And we've had board meetings all week to make matters worse." He rubbed his eyes wearily.

He's looking older, Devra realized. Why hadn't she noticed the gray that had crept into the sides of his hair and the dark lines under his eyes? Was it because he was never home?

Her dad had always prided himself on being the energetic, dynamic, handsome Dalby. His two brothers were no match for him. They helped him run the department store chain, but they were just helpers, and everyone knew it.

As CEO of the Dalby stores, he wore $2,000 suits and wore them well. He had a collection of Rolex watches and a hundred Ferragamo neckties. Everything he wore had to be the best. He said it was important since he represented the image of the stores.

He kept himself in excellent shape. He had two personal trainers who came to the house. The gym in the basement was state-of-the-art.

But here he was looking tired, and it wasn't just the bad lighting on the laptop screen. Devra had always thought of him as a young George Clooney. The resemblance was definitely there. But leaning forward with her elbows on her desk, studying him now as he sat behind the wide glass desk in his office, his cheeks were puffy and his eyes were bloodshot.

"Gretchen, what's up?" he said, unable to hide his impatience. He never liked a conversation to last more than five minutes.

"A little problem at school," Devra told him. She pushed back her hair with both hands. "I told you how I was being promoted to cheerleader, remember? Coach Walker said I could have the position? Well . . . this new girl marched in and is messing everything up."

Mr. Dalby turned away from the screen for a moment and called something to someone who had entered his office. Then he turned back to the camera. "Messed everything up?"

Devra nodded. "Yeah. Now Walker changed her mind and is letting this new girl try out."

Mr. Dalby rubbed his chin. "That doesn't seem right."

"Of *course* it isn't right," Devra snapped. "She promised me the position on the squad. I was an alternate all last year, right? I earned it, Dad."

"Okay, okay. Don't shout, Devra."

"Sorry. But I'm so steamed. This new girl . . . Gretchen Something-Or-Other . . . with her blonde hair

29

and big olive eyes . . . AAARRRGH. You know I need this, Dad. I need the extra-curricular points to get into Princeton."

"I know, I know," Mr. Dalby said softly. He let out a long whoosh of air. "Try to calm down. . . ."

"Calm down?" Devra cried. "What if she's really good? What if she's better than me? Does that mean I spend another year as an alternate? That's unacceptable. Seriously. That's unacceptable, Dad."

"Devra, you're shouting," Mr. Dalby said. He drummed his fingers on the glass desktop. "Listen. Maybe I can make a call to the principal. Mr. Hernandez. You know I donate a lot of money to the school development fund every year. That has to count for something, don't you think?"

"It better," Devra muttered.

"Well . . . I can't promise anything. But—"

"Call him, Dad. We can't let this new girl do this to me. It just isn't fair."

"Okay. I'll see what I can do."

"I really miss you. When are you coming home?"

Mr. Dalby shrugged. "I'm in Chicago tomorrow. Then Toronto. Then there's a meeting of all the buyers." He adjusted his tie with both hands. "Did Courtney move in with you? To keep you company?"

Devra nodded. "Yes. She's here. I put her in the blue guestroom across from my room."

"Good. That's good. What are you two up to?"

Devra leaned toward the camera on top of the laptop. "We're already plotting ways to kill this new girl. Gretchen."

Mr. Dalby laughed. "Well, don't kill her yet. Let me make a friendly call to Mr. Hernandez first."

7.

Gretchen groaned as she started her stretching exercises in the backyard. She thought she might do some jogging around the neighborhood. She had never been a runner, but she really needed to work off some nervous energy.

Her leg muscles felt tight. She knew that thinking about the cheerleader tryout was making her tense. She had a stupid fight with her mother that morning. She couldn't even remember what it was about. Something about too much milk making her breakfast cereal soggy?

It was warm, the sun high in the afternoon sky, a summer day lingering into September. She exercised on the small square patio outside the kitchen door. Weeds poked up through the cracks, and many of the flagstones were cracked and broken.

Gretchen's new backyard was wide but not very deep. At the side of the two-car garage, a long, bare dirt patch stretched where there obviously had been a flower garden.

The back of the yard was marked by a low wooden fence with several missing slats and badly in need of a paint job.

Mrs. Page said she didn't want to deal with the yard at all, not until spring, not until they'd made the house livable. Gretchen didn't really care. But her yard sure looked shabby next to the neighbor's yard, which was mowed smooth and low without a single protruding weed, and had a long row of late-blooming red pansies running the length of an evergreen hedge at the far side of the property.

Gazing at the neighbor's yard, Gretchen suddenly heard violin music. Running scales followed by a short melody. It wasn't the first time she had heard it. She turned to the house next door and, squinting against the sunlight off a side window, saw a girl in the house, a violin on her shoulder.

The girl swung her head and shoulders as she played. She appeared to be staring out at Gretchen. When she flashed a smile, Gretchen stood up, pulled down her sweatshirt, and trotted toward the girl's kitchen door.

The girl met Gretchen at the door. She smiled, holding the violin and bow at her side. "Hey, you're the new neighbor," she said. "I've seen you in school."

Gretchen introduced herself. "I've heard you playing before."

"Hope it isn't too loud. I usually keep the window closed. But it's such a beautiful warm day. . . . I'm

Madison, by the way. Madison Grossman. I'm in another eleventh-grade homeroom. Mr. Bartleby. I saw that you're across the hall. Do you drive? We could drive to school together."

"I drive sometimes. My mom usually needs the car," Gretchen said.

Madison spoke rapidly, very precisely, without seeming to take a breath. She was very thin, birdlike, with very curly black hair down to her shoulders, dark, close-together eyes over a sharp, almost pointed nose. Her skin was pale, almost colorless, as if she never went outside.

She wore an orange crewneck T-shirt over a short black skirt over black tights.

She stepped aside and motioned with the violin bow for Gretchen to come inside. "I'm in the school orchestra. Did you know Shadyside High had a symphony orchestra? We're pretty good, actually. Mr. Colon—he's the advisor—used to be with the Detroit Symphony. We give two full concerts a year. Last year we did a concert at the Vets Memorial Theater in Martinsville, and we sold the place out."

"That's awesome," Gretchen said. She followed Madison into a small den of dark green walls and brown leather armchairs and a couch.

A large oil painting stood over the green marble fireplace. It showed a nine- or ten-year-old girl with black curly hair, holding a violin to her neck. "That's me," Madison said. "My mom paints a little. Well, more than a little. She has a studio down in the basement. She's down there all the time. She isn't a name or anything yet. But she's actually sold some of her paintings."

Gretchen gazed at the painting and laughed. "You haven't changed very much."

Madison laughed, too. Pink circles formed on her pale cheeks. "Ha. I guess you're right. I have kind of a baby face."

"And you were playing violin when you were little?"

Madison nodded. "My parents started me on a Suzuki kids' violin program when I was three. I thought I'd hate it, but I was some kind of prodigy, you know. I mean, I loved it right away."

"You must practice a lot," Gretchen said, her eyes still on the girl in the painting.

"I've seen you practicing, too," Madison said. "Cheerleader stuff." She blushed again. "I wasn't spying or anything. It's just that our backyards connect and—"

"I'm trying out for the cheerleader squad," Gretchen interrupted. "Coach Walker is giving me a chance. Since I just started at school."

"You were a cheerleader before?"

Gretchen nodded. "I was cocaptain at my old school. We were really good. I'm not just bragging. We got a lot of attention. They have cheerleading scholarships at some colleges I'm interested in. It's really important for me to make the squad."

Gretchen realized she was chattering as much as Madison. But Madison seemed so easy to talk to. It didn't happen to Gretchen often, but once in a while, she found someone she clicked with, someone like Polly, on her wavelength, someone she felt immediately comfortable with.

Madison brought some bottles of iced tea from the kitchen, and they sat across from each other in the den, talking and getting to know one another. After about half an hour, Madison glanced at the old-fashioned-looking wooden clock on the corner of the mantel.

She jumped to her feet. "Wow. I almost forgot. I have to go try on a dress I bought. It's for my cousin's bar mitzvah, and I promised my Mom I'd go try it on today."

Gretchen followed her toward the front door. "Well . . . nice to meet you. I'll see you in school and—"

"Hey, want to come along?" Madison asked.

Gretchen stopped walking. "Where are you going?"

"To the department store. It will only take ten minutes."

"Well, actually, I need to buy some things," Gretchen said. "I need tights. And some new workout clothes." She tugged at the top of her shorts. "Look at this. The elastic is all stretched."

Madison picked up a set of car keys from the table in the front entryway. "So you're coming?"

"Let me get changed into some jeans, and I'll be right back."

Gretchen ran full speed back to her house. *Madison is really nice,* she thought. *Maybe I've made a new friend.*

She felt happy for the first time since arriving in Shadyside. She had no idea how much trouble a visit to a department store could cause.

8.

Madison played a classical music Pandora station as they drove to the Division Street Mall. "I like new music, too," she said. "But this perfect for driving. It's so quiet and calm."

Gretchen nodded. Her family didn't listen to classical music. Gretchen seldom ventured from the top hits stations.

At the far end of the mall, the department store loomed high over the other buildings. Madison parked and they entered from a side entrance, into the bargain basement department.

Gretchen followed Madison onto an Up escalator, and they traveled to the first floor. Gretchen took a deep breath. The heavy perfumed air washed over her. The cosmetics department stretched as far as she could see, the floor brighter than daylight. Glass counters reflected the light. Videos played on big flatscreens. Women leaned on the counters or arranged the products, or chatted among each other, or sprayed passersby with perfumes and cologne scents.

"We had a Sears and a Kmart," Gretchen told Madison. "But nothing as big as this. Or as modern. Or as crowded."

Then she stopped and grabbed Madison's arm when she recognized a girl behind a makeup counter. "Hey—!" A cry escaped her throat. She stared at Devra Dalby.

"Madison, what's *she* doing here?" Gretchen asked.

Madison followed her gaze. "You mean Devra? What's she doing here? You're joking, right? This is *her* store. Her family owns all the Dalby stores."

Gretchen's head was suddenly spinning. "I-I didn't see the name when we came in," she stammered.

"Devra's grandfather opened this store," Madison continued. "Now there are like dozens of them all over. Devra is richer than anyone in Shadyside—and she acts it!"

Devra didn't see them. They both watched her disappear around the back of the counter. Gretchen breathed a long sigh. She knew Devra hated her, or at least, resented her. She didn't want to have an encounter with her here in front of Madison.

"I took her spot on the squad away," Gretchen tried to explain to Madison. "I mean, Coach Walker gave it to her, then changed her mind. She's letting us both try out, and only one of us will get the spot."

Madison did an exaggerated shudder. "Trouble," she murmured. "I wouldn't mess with Devra."

"You mean—"

"I got into a fight with her on the playground in second grade," Madison said. "She was a beast. She grabbed my hair and wouldn't let go. The teacher couldn't even pry her hands off me. She's relentless. I mean, she's psycho. And you know what? She hasn't spoken to me since. Do you believe that? The fight was in second grade, and she still holds a grudge."

"Wow." Gretchen shook her head. "Wow." A thousand frightening thoughts flashed through her mind. "Madison, you don't really think she's *dangerous,* do you?"

Madison shrugged. Gretchen couldn't read her expression. Madison suddenly seemed to be far away. "I'll meet you downstairs where we came in," she said, starting down the aisle. "Half an hour?"

Gretchen nodded. She watched her new friend walk past the cosmetics counters toward the back of the store. Then she gazed around quickly, looking for Devra, glad she wasn't there.

A few minutes later, she was checking out workout tights in a large athletic-wear department on the second floor. The shelves of running shoes and sneakers covered one wall from floor to ceiling. An old Rolling Stones song blared from hidden ceiling speakers. People in the crowded aisle seemed to move in rhythm with the music.

Beat. Beat. Beat.

Gretchen spotted another display of tights near the far wall. She squeezed past a young couple with a baby stroller, turned toward the display—and bumped hard into a boy.

They both stumbled, off-balance. He grabbed her by the arms and steadied her. And she recognized Sid Viviano. Stacy's boyfriend. Sid from school. Sid the cheerleader equipment manager. Holding her by the arms, a broad smile on his handsome face.

Did he bump into me deliberately?

"Hey," he said. "That was like a head–on collision. Are you okay?"

Gretchen felt her face growing hot. She eased her arms free of his grip. "Yeah. Fine. Hi. How's it going?"

"Not bad." His grin didn't fade. His eyes locked on hers. He appeared to be studying her intently, like trying to dig into her brain.

"What are you doing here?" Gretchen blurted out.

"Ha. Stalking you."

"No. Really."

He pointed. "There were these awesome new Air Jordans. I thought I'd check them out. But . . . you have to be a millionaire. No way I could afford them."

"I . . . I'm just getting some workout stuff," Gretchen said. "This store is so big. Back home, we—" She stopped. His stare was starting to make her feel uncomfortable. "Sid, why are you staring at me like that?"

His smile finally faded. His eyes flashed. "That day I met you . . ." he started. "In the hall outside the gym, remember? I . . . I kind of felt there was something between us." He grabbed her arms again. "Did you feel it, too?"

Gretchen tried to back away. *This is too intense.* But there was something so attractive about him. A kind of power. An aura that drew her to him like an invisible magnet.

And now he was pushing her against the display table, tightening his arms around her.

"Sid—no. I don't think—"

She started to protest. But now she was kissing him back. He was holding her, pressing her against the table . . . kissing her, his lips hard against hers.

And as they kissed, her eyes traveled to the mirror on the floor. She gazed into the reflection—and saw Devra Dalby watching . . . watching them . . . her features twisted in an ugly scowl.

9.

Lefty's, the Home of the Two-Dollar Double
Cheeseburger, was conveniently located across from
Shadyside High and instantly became a popular hangout. Madison had a seven o'clock violin lesson on Tues-
day nights, so Gretchen met her there a little before six
for an early dinner.

Madison slid into the red vinyl booth at the back wall
of the restaurant and carefully tucked her violin case beside her. She gave her head a hard shake, sending her curly
hair into place around her head.

Gretchen shivered and tugged down the sleeves of her
sweater. The weather had turned cool but, for some reason, Lefty's still had its air conditioner going.

The waitress said hello and set down the yellow-
and-red menus. The menus were short. There were few
choices other than cheeseburgers.

"How's it going, Rachel?" Madison asked the waitress.
"Gretchen, do you know Rachel Martin? She's a senior."

Gretchen and Rachel exchanged hellos.

"Tuesdays are quiet," Rachel told Madison, motioning around the restaurant. "That's good and bad. I don't have to work so hard, but the tips are really lame."

Madison tsk-tsked. "What's the special tonight?"

"Cheeseburgers."

All three of the girls laughed. *Rachel seems nice,* Gretchen thought, turning back to Madison. She had a question she was eager to ask her.

But Madison started talking first, chattering on in her rapid-fire way. "I'm totally tense. I didn't sleep last night."

"What's wrong?"

"I don't think I mentioned it, but my mom is on the school board. She arranged for a very famous string quartet to come play for an assembly at school."

"Nice," Gretchen said.

Madison frowned. "Let me finish. Mom also arranged for them to let *me* sit in with them onstage for one of the pieces. That would make me nervous enough. But it's a Bach piece I just started to learn." Madison shook her shoulders. "I'm shaking just talking about it now. Seriously."

Gretchen patted Madison's hand. "No worries. You'll be great."

"How do you know that?" Madison snapped.

"I don't," Gretchen replied. "I didn't know what else to say. I was trying to be nice. Maybe you'll suck in front of the whole school."

That made Madison laugh. "You're funny." She shifted the violin case beside her. "My violin teacher is going to give me some hints on how to learn the piece. But I need more than hints. I need faster fingers and a faster brain."

"I was at my cousin Marty's house a few years ago," Gretchen said, "and he made me watch this horror movie about a violin player. The musician had his hand chopped off, and the hand continued to play the violin on its own."

Madison narrowed her eyes at Gretchen. "And you're suggesting . . . ?"

They both laughed.

Rachel Martin returned and set down the cheeseburgers and fries they had ordered. "Do you need mustard or mayo or anything?"

Both girls said no.

Rachel lingered, her eyes on Gretchen. "I hear you made a new friend your first week in school."

Gretchen squinted at her. "Excuse me?"

A thin smile crossed Rachel's face. "Devra Dalby?"

"You're being sarcastic?" Gretchen said.

Rachel nodded. "Yes. I'm being sarcastic. Devra was talking about you at lunch yesterday. I don't think she's a fan." She leaned toward Gretchen. "What did you do to tick her off?"

"Showed up," Gretchen said.

Lefty rang the bell at the kitchen window. Rachel hurried away. She had more cheeseburgers to deliver.

Gretchen lifted the top half of the bun and dabbed some ketchup on her cheeseburger. "I want to ask you something about Devra," she told Madison.

Madison snickered. "I'm not exactly a Devra expert, you know. I told you, we don't speak to one another." She cut her cheeseburger in half and lifted one of the halves in both hands.

"Did Devra ever go out with Sid?" Gretchen asked.

Madison lowered the cheeseburger to the plate. "Huh?"

"Did she ever have a thing about Sid? Do you know if they ever went out together?"

"It's possible." Madison took a bite of the cheeseburger and chewed for a while, looking thoughtful. "Sid has had a lot of girlfriends. He's a definite chick magnet." She giggled. "I read that phrase in a really bad romance novel."

"But before Stacy—?" Gretchen started.

"I don't think he and Devra were ever a thing. And now he and Stacy are like the perfect couple. At least, *they* seem to think so."

Both girls concentrated on their food for a while. Then Madison asked, "Why did you ask me about Devra and Sid?"

Gretchen wiped grease off her chin with a napkin. "I saw her a couple of times, and when Sid was around, she got this unhappy look on her face. I mean, he was kissing Stacy in the gym, and Devra just stopped and scowled at them."

"Weird," Madison murmured. She glanced at her phone. "Oh, wow. I'm going to be late." She grabbed the violin case and started to slide out of the booth. "Can you get this?"

"Sure, I'll pay," Gretchen said.

"My treat next time."

"Talk to you later?"

"If I survive Bach!" Madison called. Then she was out the door.

Gretchen gazed after her. The restaurant became a bright blur. Loud voices and clinking plates and shouts from the kitchen and the slam of the door. She couldn't get Devra out of her mind. She kept seeing all these vague images of Devra's cold, unhappy face. Like a swirling nightmare, only Gretchen was awake.

And when Devra actually slid into the booth across from her, Gretchen nearly screamed.

10.

O h. Sorry," Devra said. "Did I scare you?"

"No. I . . . uh . . . was daydreaming," Gretchen managed to say.

Gretchen stared at the necklace that swung down from Devra's throat, large jewel-like blue beads, a little darker than the blue designer top she wore. Her red hair was pulled back in a single braid. Gretchen couldn't help but notice how creamy and perfect her skin was under the harsh ceiling lights.

Devra's thin smile revealed that startling Gretchen had pleased her.

Gretchen lowered her eyes to Devra's hand. Two of her fingers were heavily wrapped in bandages. "What happened to your hand?" she asked.

Devra held it up. "Acid burns. Believe it?"

Gretchen blinked. "Excuse me? Acid? How—?"

Devra lowered the hand to her lap. She rolled her eyes. "I don't know where I get these crazy ideas. There's an antique cabinet my dad loves. It was painted badly, and the paint is cracking. I decided to refinish it for him. For his birthday. I'm going to surprise him with it."

"And the acid?" Gretchen said.

"I'm using this kind of acid to remove the old paint. They showed me how to use it at the home crafts store. But I had trouble opening the bottle and . . ." She raised the hand again. "It burned so bad. Do you believe our housekeeper had to drive me to the emergency room?"

"Whoa. That's horrible," Gretchen said.

Devra rolled her eyes again. "Dad will love the cabinet . . . . If he ever sees it. He's away a lot."

What does she want? Gretchen wondered. *She didn't sit down to discuss her cabinet. Or her father. Is she going to ask me about kissing Sid in the department store?*

"I want to talk to you," Devra said, burying the bandaged hand in her lap. "You're just a junior, right?"

Gretchen nodded. "Yeah." She gazed down at her half-uneaten cheeseburger. Her stomach was twisted in knots now. She knew she'd never finish it.

"Well, I'm a senior," Devra said. "This is my last chance, you know?"

Gretchen squinted at her. "What do you mean?"

"I mean, this is my last chance to make the cheerleading squad. Because I'll be gone next year."

Gretchen nodded. She realized she had her suddenly icy hands clasped tightly in her lap. "So?"

Devra leaned across the table. "So maybe we can

make a deal." When Gretchen didn't respond to that, Devra continued. "I don't know if you're any good or not. I guess Coach Walker thought you were good enough to compete with me. But—"

"Can I get you anything else?" Rachel Martin reappeared at the table.

"You could try not interrupting people," Devra snapped.

Rachel blushed. "Sorry. I—"

"Just the check, please," Gretchen said.

Devra waited for Rachel to leave. "All I'm saying is, let me win the tryout tomorrow. You'll be an alternate. Chances are, you'll get to fill in for somebody. You'll be with the squad the whole year. Then I'll graduate and go happily away. And it'll be all yours."

Gretchen suddenly realized that her mouth had dropped open. She was staring at Devra in disbelief. Devra's words kept repeating in Gretchen's mind. She just couldn't get her head around what Devra was asking her.

Deliberately blow the tryout?

"I . . . don't . . . think . . . so," she managed to say.

Devra let out a whoosh of air. She couldn't hide her frustration. Gretchen saw that she wasn't used to people saying no to her.

"Devra, I can't fail on purpose tomorrow," she said softly, clasping her hands together even more tightly. "Coach Walker saw my highlight reel. She saw what I can do. If I suddenly turned into a klutz . . ."

Devra's eyes flashed angrily. "What would it take to change your mind? How about a five-hundred-dollar credit at Dalby's?"

Gretchen gasped. "Are you actually bribing me?"

"Think of the outfits you could buy, Gretchen. You could upgrade your whole wardrobe. You wouldn't have to wear those Old Navy rejects."

"That's disgusting!" Gretchen cried. "Do you really think you can get anything you want by paying people? By using your family's store to—"

"How about a thousand-dollar store credit?" Devra interrupted. "Just stop and think about it."

"No way." Gretchen realized her whole body was trembling, trembling in anger. "I can't believe this is happening," she said. "I can't believe you would stoop so low. How can it be so important to you, Devra?"

"I need it for college," Devra replied through gritted teeth. Her cheeks were bright pink. Her features were tight with anger. "Listen to me—"

"No. I'm going to try my hardest at the tryout," Gretchen insisted. "And if I'm better than you—"

Devra leaned close and practically spit her next words in Gretchen's ear. "You wouldn't want Stacy to know about that little love scene you had at the store with her boyfriend—would you?"

Gretchen pulled her head back. She crossed her arms in front of her, as if shielding herself. "No way. No way.

No way. I won't do it." Her heart was pounding so hard, she felt dizzy.

Devra didn't reply. She just nodded. She slid out of the booth and glared down at Gretchen. "You'll regret this. I promise."

"Good luck at the tryout," Gretchen said.

Devra sneered at her. "Break a leg."

11.

*H*ome alone. Gretchen slumped back on the soft leather of the living room couch and listened to the rattle of a tree branch against the front window. Her mom knew the front yard trees had to be cut back. The limbs had grown dangerously close to the house. But that problem wasn't at the top of her list.

Gretchen pressed her hands into the cushion and listened to the *tap-tap-tap*. It sounded like someone knocking on the window, trying to get in.

Don't freak yourself out, she scolded herself. She'd felt tense, totally on edge since her confrontation with Devra an hour earlier. She kept playing the conversation over again in her mind.

Each time it made her angrier—and more anxious about how desperate Devra was to win the cheerleader spot this year.

"Spoiled brat," Gretchen murmured out loud. Obviously, Devra was used to getting whatever she wanted.

Gretchen sighed. Didn't Devra realize how lucky she was? Her father owned department stores. He and Devra lived in North Hills. Madison had explained to her that was the fanciest section of Shadyside, with enormous mansions, gated to keep the rest of the world out.

Gretchen's father had moved to Milwaukee with his new girlfriend. He didn't care if he heard from Gretchen or not. He never tried to call her or even email. Not a word from him on her last birthday.

She shifted tensely on the couch, listening to the insistent *tap-tap-tap* at the window. The house was silent. So silent she heard the *click* of the fridge rumbling on in the kitchen.

With a sigh, she raised her phone. Maybe Madison was back from her violin lesson. She wanted to tell her about Devra's attempt to bribe her. She listened to the ring until Madison's voicemail came on. Then she clicked it off.

Gretchen realized her hands were shaking.

Why am I so upset?

I'm too old to be scared of being home alone.

She knew it wasn't that. She had looked forward to a new start here in Shadyside. A house on Fear Street sounded intriguing, even exciting. Why would someone give a street that name?

It wasn't being home alone in a new house on a windy night that disturbed her. It was Devra Dalby. Once again, she pictured Devra's head toss, sending her red hair back over her shoulders . . . her icy blue eyes. . . .

Devra's harsh whisper: *"How about a thousand-dollar store credit?"*

Gretchen squeezed the phone in her hand. *Maybe I'll call Polly. Talking to Polly always helps me get my head together.*

Just as Gretchen started to push Polly's number, the doorbell rang.

A loud *clang clang.*

Gretchen jumped, startled. She hadn't heard the doorbell before. No one had visited yet.

She set down the phone and earphones and strode to the front entryway. She frowned at the framed color print her mother had hung on the entry wall—six dogs wearing human clothes, sitting around a card table playing poker.

"Just a joke," Mrs. Page had explained. "Until our real art arrives from Savanna Mills."

Gretchen thought it embarrassing that her mother had even *bought* something so atrocious.

The bell clanged again. "Who is it?" Gretchen called, her throat clogged from not talking to anyone for an hour.

No answer.

"Who's there?"

Gretchen pulled the door. It stuck. The wood had swollen, making it too tight against the frame. Another fix-it project on her mother's list. She gave it a hard tug with both hands, and it swung open.

Gretchen stared into the triangle of yellow light from the porchlight.

No one there.

"Hello?" she called. "Hey—are you there?"

The wind made the trees shake. Dead leaves rained to the ground. The lawn was already covered in a blanket of fallen leaves. Gusts of wind made a whispering sound all around.

Gretchen squinted to the street. No cars. No one there. A quick glance at the front of Madison's house next-door. No one.

With a shiver, she shoved the door closed. She stood in the entryway, staring at the hideous dog print on the wall. *The wind couldn't have rung the doorbell.*

A hard tap on the front window made Gretchen spin around. It seemed louder than the gentle tapping of the tree branch.

Another hard knock. Another. Was someone pounding on the window?

Gretchen lurched back into the living room. She tripped over the edge of the carpet that hadn't been tacked down yet. Caught her balance. Eyes on the window. Only darkness beyond the pale curtain of light from the front porch.

She pushed her nose against the cold glass and peered out.

No one there.

Is this a joke? Or am I going crazy?

The hard, repeated knock on the kitchen door made her cry out. The sound rang down the back hallway. Definitely a fist pounding on the glass section of the back door.

"Who is it?" Gretchen shouted. Sudden fear tightened her throat as she ran through the hall, shoes thudding loudly on the bare floorboards. "Who's there?"

Into the kitchen. A single ceiling light on dim. Neat and clean. No one had eaten at home tonight.

A drumlike pounding on the door. Gretchen saw only darkness in the glass square that formed the top half of the door.

She grabbed the knob. Breathless. Heartbeats racing now. Grabbed the knob with both hands and yanked the door open.

A whoosh of cold air greeted her. "Who's there? Who is doing this?"

A lawn rake on its side against the back stoop. The wooden lawn chairs and table glowing dully under the light of a half-moon.

No one there. And no footsteps. No one running to the side of the house.

A ghost.

Gretchen allowed herself a stupid thought. *Yes, a ghost. That must be why they call this Fear Street.*

She still held the knob to the kitchen door in her hand when she heard the *clang* of the front doorbell.

Someone is playing a mean joke.

Someone is trying to scare me. And it's working.

She slammed the kitchen door and carefully locked it. She checked the kitchen window. Locked.

The doorbell rang again.

Gretchen stopped halfway down the back hall. *I'm not going into the living room. I'm not going to answer it.*

Her whole body shuddered. Did someone plan to break in? Or were they just trying to terrorize her? Such a mean, babyish stunt. But she had no way of knowing if it was just a joke, a trick, a harmless prank.

Or if . . .

Someone pressed the front doorbell and kept it clanging.

Gretchen sucked in a deep shuddering breath and held it. Fighting back her panic, she forced her trembling legs forward. To the door. The bell deafening now.

She grabbed the knob in both hands and pulled with all her strength. The door shot open, sending her tumbling back, off-balance. She stared wide-eyed at the face in the doorway—and screamed. "Mom? It was *you*?"

Mrs. Page shifted the hooded cloak she wore. "Sorry. I forgot my keys." She stepped into the house. "What took you so long, Gretchen?"

"I . . ." Gretchen gaped at her, her whole body still tense and trembling. "Mom, you tapped at the window? You went around back?"

"Of course not," Mrs. Page said, letting the cloak fall off her shoulders, wrapping it in her arms, and carrying it to the coat closet. "Marci from work dropped me off and I rang the front bell."

"But, Mom—" Gretchen started.

Someone banged on the window. And pounded on the back door.

"Close the door," Mrs. Page said. "You're letting the cold air in."

Gretchen stepped back to the door and started to push it shut. But she stopped when something caught her eyes. She squinted into the yellow porchlight.

Something on the evergreen shrub at the side of the front stoop. She stepped out of the house. The wind ruffled her T-shirt and tossed back her hair.

She tugged the object off the bush. And raised it into the light.

A bandanna. A red-and-yellow bandanna. It had become caught in the pine needles.

Gretchen stared at the bandanna, wrapping it around her hand. Where had she seen it before?

On Devra Dalby?

12.

On Saturday, tryout day, Gretchen awoke at five thirty in the morning and couldn't get back to sleep. Her mind was spinning. She kept going through routines she already knew by heart, routines she had done a thousand times.

I don't want to overthink. My moves should all flow easily from muscle memory.

But images of Devra kept interrupting, breaking her early morning concentration. Devra's face turning pink, then red as Gretchen refused to cooperate. Her features going so tight on her face. Her words spit through gritted teeth.

Gretchen couldn't remember ever seeing that kind of anger on another person.

Maybe Coach Walker showed Devra my highlight reel. Maybe Devra saw that she isn't as good as me. Maybe she realizes she can't compete.

Gretchen waited till seven thirty to call Polly. "I've

never been so crazy tense in my life," she told her old friend. "I tried to eat a bowl of cornflakes for breakfast, and I couldn't choke them down."

She took a deep breath. "I'm tense, Polly, but I'm also totally psyched. Devra didn't ruin my confidence. I know I'm an outstanding cheerleader, and I know I can contribute to this squad. It's not like I want to prove anything to Devra. I only want to win this for myself. You understand, don't you?"

Gretchen did some stretching exercises in the backyard. It was a cool, gray morning with tiny raindrops in the air. Low overhead, a black storm cloud rolled closer, darkening the sky to near nighttime.

She turned and gazed at Madison's house next door, somehow expecting to see Madison practicing her violin in the window. But the house was dark.

Gretchen wanted to practice a few running cartwheels. But the rain started to come down harder, blown into her face by gusting winds. She trotted back into the house.

In her room, she pulled on a tank top and yoga pants. Swept her blonde hair straight and tied it tight with a plastic barrette. She checked herself out one last time in the mirror. "You can do this," she told her reflection.

She found the keys to her mother's Camry on the table in the front entryway, and was nearly to the front door when her mother appeared. "What's up, Gretchen?"

Gretchen frowned at her. "You know perfectly well what's up. I'm going to my cheerleader tryout. Are you going to wish me good luck?"

"Of course," her mother replied, apparently startled by Gretchen's sharpness. "Can I give you a hug?" She opened her arms.

Gretchen had no choice. She stepped forward, and they had a brief, awkward hug. Her mom wasn't the touchy-feely kind of person, and that was okay with Gretchen. At least, she had grown used to few hugs or kisses or almost no physical signs of affection from her mother.

"My mom isn't cold. She's just not very approachable," she'd told Polly once a year or so ago.

"Is that why your parents got divorced?" Polly had asked.

Gretchen shuddered. "Eww. I don't want to think about that."

The hug ended quickly, and Gretchen started to the door.

"I just want to say one thing," Mrs. Page said, blocking her path. "I know you have high hopes, dear. But if you don't get the position, you have to remember it isn't the end of the world."

Gretchen's mouth dropped open. "Excuse me?"

"I mean you're new in this school, and it might be nice to settle in. You know, get used to things and make new friends and get comfortable in your classes. If you don't make the team—"

"Mom, I don't *believe* you!" Gretchen snapped. "Why do you do this to me? Why are you always trying to discourage me and pull me down?"

Mrs. Page took a step back. She pressed a hand against her throat and gaped at Gretchen, as if hurt and surprised. "Pull you down? I would *never* do that, dear. I just don't want you to be crushed if you fail today."

"Fail? *Fail?*" Gretchen could feel herself losing it. She suddenly pictured a huge, red bomb about to explode.

"I never want to discourage you," her mother said. "But I don't think it's wise to get your hopes up. That's all."

Gretchen could feel the good energy flowing out of her. Her mother always knew exactly how to bring her down. With a cry of disgust, she bumped past her mother, burst out the door, and slammed it hard behind her.

I can nail this tryout, she told herself. *I know I can nail it.*

13.

Devra was already in the gym when Gretchen arrived. She was doing stretching exercises near the far wall. She wore a maroon-and-white Shadyside jersey over white Spandex shorts. Her red hair fell loosely around her face as she stretched.

Courtney, in her cheerleader uniform, stood with Devra, leaning against the wall. The two girls chatted easily. Neither one of them turned to greet Gretchen.

Stacy and the other cheerleaders were all in uniform—Ana, perky-looking with green cat eyes and short, straight black hair, bangs across her forehead; Becka, crinkly brown hair falling around a slender serious face, at least a head taller than Ana; and Shannon, tall and athletic, with cocoa-brown skin, round, dark eyes, her black hair pulled to one side in a tight ponytail.

They clustered around the doorway to Coach Walker's office. Through the glass office wall, Gretchen could see Walker talking on the phone.

One person sat in the bleachers at the back of the gym. As Gretchen crossed the floor, she recognized Sid. He waved to her, a can of Coke in his other hand.

Stacy turned to greet her. "Hey, Gretchen. This is exciting. Are you psyched?"

Gretchen swallowed, her mouth suddenly dry. "Well . . . that's *one* way to put it. Actually, I'm terrified."

"I get nervous, too," Stacy said. "I think it helps me perform better. You know. Gets the adrenaline going."

Coach Walker hung up the phone and stepped into the office doorway. She glanced around. "Are we all here?"

"Yes, we are," Stacy replied. "Ready to rock and roll."

Normally, Gretchen would hate Stacy's kind of rah–rah enthusiasm. But Stacy was the only cheerleader acting warm and welcoming to her. So she decided she had to like Stacy's bright personality.

I wish I could be more like her.

"Gretchen, did you bring any music or anything?" Coach Walker asked.

"No. I'm just going to do a basic routine and show some jumps and moves."

"Stacy and Ana will help you if you want to include any Thigh Stands or High Jumps," Coach Walker said. She motioned with her head toward Ana, who smiled at Gretchen.

"I think we'll let Devra go first," Walker said. She

turned and shouted: "Devra? Courtney? Would you like to join us? Are you ready to begin?"

Devra did a few more leg stretches, then followed Courtney toward the others. Her eyes were on Gretchen as she approached. She nodded but didn't say hello.

Devra took a towel from the shelf in the coach's office and mopped her forehead. "I think I'm warmed up." She picked up a bag that leaned against the wall, pulled out a water bottle, and took a long drink.

"Follow me, everyone," Coach Walker said, motioning with one hand. She led the way across the gym to the bleachers. Sid raised his Coke can in greeting as the cheerleaders took seats on the bottom benches. Gretchen was too nervous to sit down. She stood at the side of the bleachers, gripping the railing tightly.

"Devra, you're up," Coach Walker said. "Show us something, okay?"

Devra nodded, wiping water off her chin. She set down her water bottle. Then she brushed back her red hair and stepped to the middle of the floor. As she stepped into place, the sky outside brightened, the storm clouds parted, and yellow sunlight washed through the high windows of the gym.

"Great special effects, Devra," Coach Walker called. "You brought your own spotlight."

The cheerleaders leaned forward on the bleacher benches and grew silent, preparing to watch. Gretchen crossed her arms in front of her. She took a deep breath and held it. If only her heartbeats would stop fluttering like a hummingbird's wings.

She turned in time to see Sid flash her a thumbs-up.

"Go, Devra!" Courtney shouted.

Stacy scooted close to Gretchen. "Courtney and Devra have been friends forever," she whispered. "But don't worry. Courtney isn't going to vote. The other cheerleaders don't vote. Only Coach Walker and I will decide who wins."

Gretchen started to reply, but Devra had begun her tryout.

"I'm going to do a few new cheers that I wrote," she announced. "I've been practicing different jumps, and I'll show them to you. It's hard to stand here and do this alone. I think you all know that I'm a *team* player, and I do my best work when you others are with me. I think I need your support—"

"Can we skip the acceptance speech?" Coach Walker interrupted, raising one hand to signal for Devra to stop.

A few girls laughed. Ana whispered something to Shannon beside her.

"This isn't a joke, Coach Walker," Devra said, scowling. "You know I'm trying out under protest. Everyone knows I worked hard all last year and I deserve this spot on the squad."

Walker shook her head. "Devra, please. We all know how you feel. You're not exactly shy about telling people.

But we want what's best for the squad. We have a good chance of going to the state tournament this year. You know that. So we have to put the best team we can out there. You want that, too, don't you?"

Devra rolled her eyes and didn't answer.

An awkward silence fell over the gym. Devra gazed at Gretchen for a long moment, as if challenging her. Then she stepped into position and delivered one of the new cheers she had written.

"Do you dig it?
That Tiger beat!
Have you got it?
Stomp your feet!
Go, Tigers!"

Gretchen watched, still standing tensely with her arms crossed tightly over her chest, and felt some of her anxiety fade. *Devra isn't very good,* she realized. *Her Toe Touch Jumps were okay. But those are the simplest jumps in the world. Her Spread Eagle Jump at the end looked awkward, off-balance.*

Everyone watched in silence as Devra did a short and simple floor routine with some basic tumbling tricks. The sunlight washed down on her, making the floor shine and sending her shadow in all directions.

She isn't bad, Gretchen thought. *But she has no spark. And she keeps forgetting to smile. She's going through the routine, but she isn't selling it.*

"Here's another cheer I wrote," Devra announced.

She picked up a pair of red pom-poms from beside some water bottles beneath the lowest bench. Then she trotted back to her spot, turned, and performed her cheer.

"Do you dig it?
That Tiger beat?
Tigers roar!
More! We want more!
Tigers roar! Tigers SCORE!
GO, TIGERS! YAAAY!"

Devra punctuated each line with a tuck jump, raising both arms in a High V, then tucking her knees to her chest as she jumped. She finished with a series of Pike Jumps. Each time she jumped, she brought her legs up to meet her hands. She had good height on the pike, but her landing on the toe touch was off, and she struggled to keep her balance.

The girls clapped as Devra came running off the floor. A grin on her face, she shook the pom-poms above her head, as if in triumph.

She isn't terrible, Gretchen thought. *But she isn't very good, either. Especially if she had all last year to practice with the squad.*

Gretchen knew she was a better cheerleader. She knew this fact should help her lose her nervousness. But the heavy feeling in her stomach didn't fade, and her hands remained ice cold and sweaty.

Coach Walker looked up from her clipboard, where she had been rapidly scribbling notes about Devra's performance. "Good job, Devra," she said.

"I can do the Pike Jumps a lot better," Devra said. "I usually get my legs up higher at practice."

"It's not an easy jump," Walker said, writing some more on the clipboard pad. "I liked the cheers you wrote. The second one needs a little work on the cadence. But . . . very good."

"Thanks," Devra said. "I think they'll work for basketball, too."

"And air hockey!" Sid chimed in.

That made some of the girls laugh. Devra just glared at him.

Coach Walker shook her head. "Thanks for sharing that, Sid."

"Just trying to keep it light," Sid replied.

Devra took a seat next to Courtney. The two girls whispered together. Stacy leaned close to Gretchen and murmured, "Go out there and nail it!"

Gretchen stepped into the bright rectangle of sunlight on the gym floor. She took a deep breath and held it. To her surprise, she suddenly didn't feel so tense. She raised her arms in a V and practiced a straight Cheer Leader Jump. A grin spread over her face. She felt light and strong.

I can do this.

"Tigers roar!

Roar Tigers Roar!

Tigers roar!

Tigers SCORE!

She knew her Toe Touch Jumps were perfect. She performed the cheer again, this time with Spread Eagles. She showed off with a Double Hook Jump, kicking her legs out to the side, hooking her feet.

Time to REALLY show off!

Her running cartwheels made some of the girls gasp. Her Power Jumps were perfect. The double cartwheel into a Hook Jump made them burst into applause.

Gretchen ran off the floor, screaming, "Go, Tigers!" Cheering herself.

Coach Walker had her head down, writing on the clipboard pad. "Excellent job," she told Gretchen. "Very smooth and confident."

Stacy moved next to Coach Walker and said something in her ear. The coach nodded. Stacy gestured toward Gretchen and said some more to the coach.

Gretchen watched them intently. *Stacy and Coach Walker are the only two voting on who makes the team,* she thought. *What are they saying?*

Two rows up, Courtney was patting Devra's shoulder. Devra kept shaking her head, her eyes down. Courtney was obviously reassuring her.

Gretchen's heart was pounding. Sweat rolled down

her forehead. She grabbed a water bottle from under the bleachers and raised it to Devra. "Is this yours?"

Devra motioned with one hand. "Go ahead. Take it."

Gretchen mopped her forehead with her arm. Then she uncapped the bottle, tilted it to her mouth, and drank it nearly to the bottom.

Devra suddenly jumped to her feet. "Coach Walker, can I do some more? I didn't really show off my floor tumbling routine."

Coach Walker lowered her clipboard. "No. I think that should be enough," she told Devra. "You both did five minutes and showed us your best moves and—"

"No. I didn't show you my best moves," Devra insisted. "I thought you'd want to see my basic jumps. But I do much harder stuff." She frowned at Gretchen. "I don't do all those cartwheels. I mean, I'm not a circus clown. I don't see what they have to do with leading a crowd in cheers."

Coach Walker jumped to her feet, too. "That's enough, Devra. Let's keep this nice and civilized, okay?"

Devra didn't reply. She sat back down, shaking her head. Courtney leaned closer to commiserate with her.

Gretchen stood at the side of the bleachers. Stacy and the coach were gazing at Coach Walker's notes, going over them line by line. Gretchen saw Ana slide next to Sid. He put his arm around her shoulders and whispered something in her ear. Ana giggled and shoved his arm away.

Gretchen's stomach rumbled. She suddenly felt strange. A wave of nausea rolled up from her belly, tightened her throat. She tried to swallow, but her throat had tightened.

Another wave of nausea made her stomach churn. She tried to force the feeling down. She felt really sick. Felt her stomach rumble and tighten.

"Ohhhh." A moan escaped her throat. She tried to fight back the feeling, struggled to keep her lunch down. But her stomach gave a sharp, violent lurch.

She grabbed her sides, shut her eyes, leaned over—and spewed a tidal wave of green-yellow vomit onto the gym floor at her feet.

An ugly groan burst from deep inside her. And another gusher of vomit poured onto the floor.

Holding her stomach, Gretchen bent over grunting and groaning as violent spasms shook her body, and her stomach continued to heave up everything it held.

Over her groans, Gretchen heard the startled cries of the other girls. She held her breath, trying to stop the sick upheavals.

Raising her head, she saw Coach Walker pick up the nearly empty water bottle at Gretchen's feet. The coach raised the bottle and sniffed it. "Hey," she said. "This doesn't smell right. Someone put something in this water bottle."

Gretchen spit the last glob of vomit onto the floor. Stacy handed her a towel. She wiped her face with it. Her whole body shook. She swallowed, swallowed again and again, her mouth bitter and sour.

Coach Walker put an arm around Gretchen's shoulders. "Are you all right? Do you feel better?"

Gretchen nodded. Then raised her eyes to the bleachers—and caught the pleased smile on Devra's face.

14.

S he poisoned me, Polly. I know she did." Gretchen adjusted the phone on her ear.

She had driven home, still fighting down her nausea. Her head pounded, throbbed in pain. She ran into the house, to her bathroom, brushed her teeth for five minutes, struggling to scrub the sour taste from her mouth.

Her mother wasn't home. She left a note saying she was having dinner with a new friend she had met at the hairdresser's.

Gretchen couldn't wait to call Polly and tell her about the tryout.

Polly was speechless with shock. "Devra put something in the water," Gretchen told her. "Coach Walker sniffed it. She said it smelled like cleaning fluid or something."

Gretchen felt her stomach churn. She took a deep breath, then let it out slowly.

"I saw the smile on Devra's face," Gretchen continued.

"She was so proud of herself. But guess what? She loses. She loses, Polly, because I won the tryout. She wasn't in the same league, and everyone saw it. Even her friend Courtney knew that I was better."

Gretchen rubbed her forehead. *If only this headache would give me a break and go away.* It felt like some creature was trying to burst out of her skull. She shut her eyes, but it didn't help.

"If I tell Mom that Devra tried to poison me, she'll call the police," Gretchen said. "But Devra will only deny she did it. Look, they're going to announce the winner of the tryout in a few days. Devra's going to be an alternate all year, and she'll have to stand on the sidelines and watch me perform. That's punishment enough, don't you agree?"

Before Polly could reply, the doorbell rang. Gretchen said goodbye, tossed the phone onto her bed, and hurried to the front door.

Through the peephole, she saw a boy standing on the front stoop, his face hidden behind a gray hoodie. "Who's there?"

"It's me."

Me?

She pulled the door open. "Sid? Hi. I didn't expect—"

"Gretchen, are you okay?" He pulled back his hood. His eyes searched hers. "I was worried. I—"

"I feel a lot better," she said.

She stepped aside for him to come into the house. But

instead he wrapped his arms around her waist, lowered his face to hers, and kissed her. The kiss lasted a long time. She gave herself to it. Let all other thoughts leave her mind.

Kissed him. Kissed him . . . then pushed him away. *Stacy.* The name flashed into her thoughts.

Her face felt hot. On fire. She could still taste his lips on hers. She grabbed his hand and pulled him into the living room. Most of their furniture hadn't arrived yet from Savanna Mills. She tugged him to the couch facing the fireplace. He pulled her down on top of him and they kissed again, another long, lingering kiss.

Again, she broke the kiss and pushed him away. Her heart fluttered in her chest. She felt a rush of emotion, suddenly realized how attracted she was to him.

Stacy. Stacy is his girlfriend. This isn't right.

But it feels right.

Sid tugged down his hoodie and sprawled back on the couch, tilting his head back, gazing up at the bronze ceiling fixture. "Wow," he murmured. "Wow."

She slid to the couch arm. "Did you really come to see if I was okay?"

He nodded. "Whoa. Devra. I don't *believe* her."

"Do we have to talk about her?" Gretchen said, playing with the end his hoodie sleeve.

"You should have heard her ranting after you left," Sid said. "She's really psycho."

"Huh? You really think she's crazy?"

"No. I just think she's a spoiled brat. No one has ever said no to her. Devra always gets what she wants."

"Not this time," Gretchen said. "This time, Devra loses and I win."

Sid smiled. Gretchen saw that he had two tiny dimples in his cheeks when he smiled. He reached for her and started to pull her to him.

But she resisted. "Can we talk about something?" she asked.

He frowned. "You want to *talk*?" He ran a finger tenderly along her cheek.

"What about Stacy?" Gretchen asked.

Sid let out a long sigh. He pulled himself up straight. "Stacy? Stacy is a long story."

"Well . . . aren't you two going together?"

"Forever," he said. "We've been together forever. Our parents were all best friends. When I was little Stacy's family lived right across the street from us. Stacy and I played together when we were two years old."

"Whoa," Gretchen murmured.

"Yeah. Whoa." He rolled his eyes. "It's like we've been together forever. We're even going to college together. We're going to Wisconsin. Our parents expect us to get married. *Everyone* in our families expect us to get married. It's like this great romantic story, only . . . only . . ."

"Only what?" Gretchen demanded.

Sid took a breath. He shrugged. "I like her a lot. Seriously. But I don't want to marry her. I've tried to break up with her."

"Really?" Gretchen studied his face, trying to determine if he was telling the truth.

"Yes, really. I've tried to explain a dozen times. Tried to say we should just be friends. But I can't get through to her. She doesn't think I'm serious. I mean, I guess she doesn't want to believe the truth, that I want to break up with her."

"Everyone thinks you're the perfect couple," Gretchen said.

"Everyone is wrong," Sid said, lowering his eyes. "Stacy keeps acting like everything is perfect between us. You know how gung-ho she is. She's a cheerleader even when she isn't being a cheerleader. But . . ." He shook his head sadly.

Gretchen leaned forward. She placed her hands on Sid's cheeks and pulled him close. She shut her eyes and kissed him.

The tryout . . . Sid . . . things are finally going my way.

He left about ten minutes later. He had to do some shopping for his mom.

Gretchen leaned back on the couch, waiting for her heartbeats to slow. The image of him kissing her, kissing her lingered in her mind.

She felt as if she were floating on air as she picked

herself up and made her way upstairs to her room. As she entered, a bell *ding* on her phone startled her out of her dreamy thoughts.

She picked her phone up from where she had tossed it on the bed. She gazed at a text message on the screen:

YOU COULD BREAK YOUR NECK

All in capital letters. From Devra?

A chill tightened the back of Gretchen's neck as she read the words again.

The phone *dinged* again. Another message appeared beneath the first one:

SOMETIMES CHEERLEADERS DIE

Gretchen stared at the words until they blurred. She squeezed the phone so hard, her hand ached.

Is Devra serious? Am I really in danger?

15.

Madison set her violin down on the coffee table. She rubbed her neck as she crossed her living room and took the phone from Gretchen. "You got these messages right after the tryout?"

Gretchen nodded. "Do you believe it? How *crazy* is this?"

Madison studied the screen. "Well . . . they are definitely from Devra. There's her name under the phone number at the top. Devra Dalby. She didn't try to disguise it or anything."

Gretchen shook her head. "I guess she wanted me to know the texts came from her."

"Wow." Madison handed the phone back to Gretchen. "She doesn't care what she does. She thinks she's just above us all. It's like the rules of decency don't apply to her."

Gretchen blinked. "Rules of decency? This is just plain psycho, Madison. What do I do?"

Madison rubbed the soreness from her neck. Gretchen saw that her hands were covered in rosin. "I've been practicing for two hours," she said. "I don't want to look like a jerk in front of the string quartet."

Gretchen tucked the phone into her bag. "You won't look like a jerk. You play beautifully."

"What if I break a string or something?" Madison's eyes grew wide. "Oh, I'm sorry. We were talking about you. Sorry to be so self-obsessed."

"It's okay," Gretchen said, perching on the edge of a brown leather armchair and swinging her bag onto her lap. "I just don't know whether I should ignore these threats. I mean, how serious could they be?"

Madison pressed her hands against the waist of her jeans. "You can't ignore them, Gretchen. You have to report them."

"No way. I can't go to the police."

Madison shook her head. "No, not the police. You have to show them to Coach Walker. She needs to know what Devra is doing to you."

Inside Gretchen's bag, a bell rang. The phone.

Gretchen fumbled in the bag until she found the phone. She raised it to her face and read it. "Another message," she told Madison. "From Devra."

GIVE ME A K-I-L-L

Madison squinted at it. Her mouth dropped open. "Oh my God. Gretchen, that's a *death threat*. You have to show it to Coach Walker. You don't have a choice."

Coach Walker stared at the messages on Gretchen's phone. She kept blinking as if trying to blink them away. Her face at first had shown surprise. but now she stared blankly, all the emotion drained from her features.

She blew out a breathy whistle. "Wheeew."

"I had to show it to you," Gretchen said, her voice just above a whisper.

They were in Walker's office. The door was closed. Walker sat stiffly in her desk chair, the glare off the phone reflecting her troubled face. She wore a long-sleeved Shadyside High T-shirt over white gym shorts. Gretchen stood close beside her.

Outside the window, Gretchen could see the cheerleaders practicing a cheer in the center of the gym floor. Their shouts were muffled by the window glass.

"I think Principal Hernandez has to see this," Coach Walker said. She set the phone down on her desktop. "This is not a small thing, Gretchen. This is very bad."

Gretchen nodded. She didn't know what to say.

Walker started to rise from her desk chair. "Maybe we should talk to Devra first," she said. She didn't wait for a reply from Gretchen. She pulled open the office door and shouted for Devra to come.

Courtney and Becka were helping Devra practice a Thigh Stand. Devra perched high on their thighs, caught her balance, and raised her arms above her head. Hearing the coach's call, she leaped to the floor and came running to the office, her red hair bouncing behind her.

Coach Walker ushered her inside and carefully closed the door.

Devra brushed back her hair with both hands. She tugged her white sleeveless T-shirt down over her black tights. She gave Gretchen a quick glance, then turned to the coach. "You wanted to see me?"

Coach Walker motioned for Devra to take the wooden chair against the wall. "Devra I want to ask you about some text messages," she said.

Devra wrinkled her face, as if confused. "Text messages?" She glanced at Gretchen again.

Gretchen stood with her arms crossed beside the coach's desk. She held herself tightly, trying to stop her whole body from trembling. She gritted her teeth and tried not to show any emotion at all.

Coach Walker lifted the phone off the desktop and pushed the screen into Devra's face. "Did you send these threatening messages to Gretchen?"

Devra squinted at them, moving her lips silently as she read the messages. She raised her eyes to Coach Walker. "No way. I didn't send those."

The coach held the phone in front of Devra, held it steadily in front of Devra's face. "Look at the top of the screen, Devra," she said in a whisper. "That's your phone number at the top."

"I swear I didn't send those messages," Devra said, her

face bright pink. "Someone took my phone. My phone has been missing."

Gretchen felt a chill run down her back. *What a good liar she is. Look at that innocent, wide-eyed expression on her face. If she didn't send the texts, why is she blushing?*

"After the tryout," Devra said. "The phone wasn't in my backpack. I think someone stole it."

"Someone on the squad?" Coach Walker demanded.

Devra shrugged. "I don't know. I just know my phone was gone. Ask Courtney. She'll tell you I'm telling the truth. She helped me look for the phone, but we never found it."

Devra turned her gaze on Gretchen and her features tightened in anger. "You can't accuse me. I didn't do it. Do you think I'm crazy? Do you really think I'd send you a death threat? That's sick."

Gretchen opened her mouth to speak, but no words came out.

"You're sick," Devra said. "Did you send those texts to yourself? Did you send them to make me look bad? To get me in trouble and out of your way?" Devra was red-faced, screaming now. "It won't work, sicko. Because I didn't send them. I didn't! I didn't!"

Gretchen glared back at her without speaking.

She's lying. It's obvious. She's totally lying.

16.

The next day, Stacy met Coach Walker at her office in the gym. "I think this is going to be a very short meeting," Stacy said. "We both know which girl is the better cheerleader. It isn't a real puzzler, is it?"

Stacy was surprised by the grim expression on the coach's face. "I'm afraid it isn't that easy, Stacy," she said, avoiding Stacy's gaze. "If it was just up to you and me . . ." Her voice trailed off.

Stacy turned when she heard footsteps thudding across the gym floor. She saw Sid striding quickly toward them. Sid gave her a quick wave as he poked his head into the office. "Is there practice today, Coach Walker? Should I get out any equipment?"

"I made the announcement yesterday, Sid. No practice today." Coach Walker couldn't hide her impatience. "Stacy and I are meeting about the tryout and who will make the squad."

Sid grinned. "Do I get a vote?"

Coach Walker made a shooing motion with one hand. "Go away."

"I can take a hint," Sid said.

Stacy grabbed his arm as he turned to leave. "See you later?"

"Sure." He shoved his hands into his jeans pockets and jogged out of the gym.

"Where were we?" Walker said. She checked her watch. "We have to go to Mr. Hernandez' office."

Stacy blinked. "Excuse me? He's meeting with us? About the tryout?"

Coach Walker nodded. "He instructed me not to make a decision about the cheerleader position until he had a chance to speak to me." She hesitated. "Actually, he didn't want you at the meeting. He said it wasn't anything for a student to hear."

Stacy blinked. "Really?"

"But I reminded him that you are the captain of the squad," Walker said, "and you have a vote. I insisted that you be there. He finally said okay, if you promise to keep it all confidential."

"Wow." Stacy didn't know what else to say.

"Maybe I shouldn't have told you all this," Walker said. "But I think it's important for the captain of the squad to know what's what."

Stacy swept her hand back through her hair. "This is totally weird."

"I know," Walker said. She clicked off her desk lamp

and stood up. "Come on. Hernandez gets cranky if you keep him waiting."

Principal Hernandez was a big man with a big rectangular head, topped with close-cropped salt-and-pepper hair. He wore thick black-framed glasses that made his gray eyes appear to bulge like frog eyes. A short goatee, more gray than black, framed his square chin.

Hernandez had been a football lineman in college, and he kept in shape, his gray suits tight, almost unable to contain his bulging shoulders. He looked like a hulking giant of a man, and with his bulging eyes, his expression always appeared menacing, sour. But Shadyside High students knew him to be gentle and soft-spoken. No one ever saw him raise his voice or shout in anger.

He greeted Stacy and Coach Walker at the door, a coffee mug in one hand. "Come in." His expression was solemn as he led them through the front reception area to his office in back.

Hernandez pushed the door closed and motioned for them to take the leather guest chairs that faced his desk, cluttered with papers and files. "How are you, Stacy?" he asked, dropping heavily into his desk chair. "I saw your parents at the Fall Carnival at Shadyside General last week."

Stacy spread her hands over the soft leather arms of the chair. "Yes. My mom is on the board of the hospital," she said.

"We had a nice talk, mostly about you," Hernandez said, shoving a stack of files to the edge of the desk.

"That's nice," Stacy said awkwardly.

All through the conversation, Hernandez hadn't smiled. His eyes went from Stacy to Coach Walker. He tilted back in his chair and raised a hand to scratch the top of his head.

"I'm afraid you may not like what I have to say," he told the coach

"About the cheerleading tryouts?" Coach Walker asked, shifting her weight in the chair.

Hernandez nodded.

"Is there a problem?" the coach asked.

Hernandez nodded again. He remained silent for a long moment. He appeared to be thinking of how to begin.

"I just got off the phone with Daniel Dalby," he said finally. "Devra's father." He paused, watching for Stacy or the coach to react.

But they both sat still, their faces expressionless.

Hernandez cleared his throat and leaned forward, his arms crossed on the desktop. "Perhaps you're not aware of this, but Daniel Dalby is the biggest contributor to the school's development fund every year. The Dalby family donates more than a third of our budget."

"Whew." Coach Walker blew out a whoosh of air. "Very generous."

"Very generous and very needed by us," Hernandez said. Behind his glasses, his eyes were wary. As if he expected trouble.

"Mr. Dalby has been on the phone with me more than once in the past week," he continued. "He wanted to tell me how important being on the cheerleader squad is to Devra's college plans."

Hernandez cleared his throat again. "Seems Devra is desperate to go to Princeton and thinks extra-curricular points from cheerleading will help sway the university to accept her."

"But Mr. Hernandez—" Coach Walker started to protest.

He raised a hand to silence her.

"I know you held a tryout last week between Devra and the new girl, Gretchen Page. Can you tell me your feelings about the tryout?"

"Gretchen was a lot better," Stacy said, her hands clasped tightly in her lap.

"I think Stacy and I agree that Gretchen is a far better performer and a much more skilled athlete than Devra," Coach Walker said.

Hernandez frowned. "I'm sorry to hear that," he said. He lowered his eyes to the desk, as if avoiding their stares. "Because I'm afraid I have to step in here. I promised Daniel Dalby that Devra will be chosen for the squad."

Stacy gasped. Coach Walker's mouth tightened in anger. "That isn't right," she said. "Gretchen is a hard worker and a talented cheerleader."

"She's really awesome," Stacy chimed in. "Gretchen could take us to the state finals. She really could."

Again, Hernandez raised his hand. "I'm really sorry. But I don't care if she's an Olympic gymnast. We have to give the spot to Devra. I hope you'll understand. The school cannot afford to lose one-third of our development money. We just can't."

Stacy's mouth hung open. She suddenly felt as if she couldn't breathe. This was so unfair . . . so wrong.

Coach Walker pulled herself more erect. She appeared to stiffen in her chair, her jaw clenched. She tugged at one ear. "Am I really hearing this correctly?" she said finally, her voice just above a whisper. "We're going to give this spot to Devra because her family is rich?"

"I hope you won't make a fuss about this, Violet," Hernandez said. "Don't think I feel good about it. Because I don't. But I have to do what's right for the school. Some-times reality means you have to make a hard decision. And my decision stands."

He gazed from the coach to Stacy. "You've promised not to discuss this with anyone, am I right?"

Stacy nodded. "Yes."

Walker opened her mouth to say something—but stopped. Her eyes were on the office doorway. Stacy and Hernandez followed her gaze.

And saw the door open a little more than a crack— and Gretchen Page standing with her face poking through the opening.

"Gretchen!" Coach Walker cried. "How long have you been standing there?

17.

It's so unfair," Gretchen complained to Madison. "I just can't believe they did it to me."

"I can't, either," Madison replied, taking Gretchen's arm. "Do you want to drown your troubles with a Cinnabon? Or with some cheesecake from the Cheesecake Factory?"

They were wandering through the Division Street Mall because Madison thought it might help Gretchen if she got out of the house. Gretchen had been locked in her room, pouting and pacing the floor, muttering to herself and shaking her fists at the mirror.

"I didn't cry," she told Madison. "I was too angry to cry."

"No one would blame you if you cried," Madison said. "You were robbed, Gretchen. It was worse than robbery. It wasn't fair in any way."

"I-I don't know how I'm going to get over this," Gretchen stammered. "I-I worked so hard. It meant so much to me. I know I could take this squad to the state tournament. I just know it. And now . . ."

"And now, Cinnabon or cheesecake?" Madison said.

Gretchen chose cheesecake. They made their way into the restaurant. The hostess led them to a booth against the back wall and dropped enormous menus on the table.

"We don't need menus," Madison told her. "We just want to bury ourselves in tall mountains of cheesecake."

"Your server will be with you in a second," the hostess said. She poured ice water into the two glasses on the table.

Gretchen tilted the glass to her mouth and took a long drink. She brushed a strand of blonde hair off her forehead. "I promise I'm going to stop talking about this soon. Seriously."

"Go ahead and vent," Madison said. "What are friends for?"

"Everyone saw that I'm a better cheerleader than Devra," Gretchen said, spinning the water glass between her hands. "Everyone knows it."

"Well," Madison said, "won't she feel like a total fake performing with the other cheerleaders, knowing she had to buy the spot?"

Gretchen shrugged. "Who knows what Devra feels?"

Madison patted the back of Gretchen's hand. "At least, you'll practice with the squad. If someone gets hurt or can't make a game, you'll have your chance."

Gretchen didn't seem to hear Madison. Her eyes had a faraway look. "Devra was so mean . . . so vicious," she said. "Those horrible texts she sent. . . . Putting something awful in my water bottle so I'd throw up in front of everyone. What kind of person does that to someone?"

"A bad person?" Madison said. "I'm just guessing here."

Gretchen didn't laugh.

"Hey, I'm trying to get you to smile," Madison said. "What Hernandez did was horrible. But you'll still be with the squad. And look on the bright side. Maybe now that she has the spot on the squad, Devra will stop playing all those dirty tricks on you."

Gretchen had that faraway look again. She remained silent and still for a long moment. And then she murmured in a soft whisper: "I still have the knife."

Madison blinked. She leaned closer to Gretchen across the table. "Excuse me? What did you just say?"

"I still have the knife," Gretchen whispered. And then her eyes appeared to come back into focus. She stared uncertainly at Madison.

"What knife?" Madison demanded.

Gretchen shook her head. "Knife? Did I say something about a knife?"

"Are you okay?"

Gretchen forced a smile. "I was daydreaming. Really. I don't know why I said that. Just crazy, that's all. I don't have a knife. Only in my dreams. I guess I was remembering the dreams."

"Y-you . . . scared me," Madison stammered. "Your face got all weird and—"

Gretchen sighed. "Let's change the subject. How are you doing with your practice for the string quartet assembly?"

The two chatted through tall slices of cherry cheesecake and Rocky Road cheesecake. At times, their talk was awkward with long silences. Gretchen tried, but she just couldn't pull herself out of her thoughts about Devra and the cheerleaders.

As Madison talked about fall term exams, Gretchen found herself thinking about Sid. Aside from her new friendship with Madison, Sid was one of the few bright spots in her new life in Shadyside.

She thought about how he wrapped her in his arms on the couch in her living room . . . how understanding he was . . . how thoughtful, and how he kissed her with such feeling . . . long, urgent kisses.

Gretchen didn't blame Stacy for wanting to hold onto him. But Sid assured Gretchen he was trying to get through to Stacy, trying to convince her that he was serious about ending things.

And then it will be Sid and me.

Gretchen knew if she could just keep her thoughts on Sid, she would feel a lot better . . . concentrate on the positive. But it was so difficult.

And then there he was.

"Oh, wow." Gretchen gazed to the front of the restaurant and saw the hostess leading a tall boy in a denim jacket and black straight-legged jeans to a table. The boy had his hand on the waist of a girl with long black curls down past the shoulders of her blue sleeveless top.

It took only a few seconds to recognize Sid.

Gretchen stared at the hand he had on the girl's waist, guiding her to the table.

Madison caught Gretchen's stare. "Hey, what's wrong?"

"It's Sid," Gretchen said. "And he's with another girl." She slid to the edge of the seat and jumped up from the booth.

"Gretchen?" Madison called. "Hey, Gretchen. Where are you going? Come back here. What are you doing?"

18.

*G*retchen heard her friend shouting after her, but she didn't turn around. Her heart pounding, the cheesecake suddenly making her stomach feel heavy as lead, she stomped through the narrow aisle toward the table. Sid was just sitting down. The girl already had her menu raised in front of her.

Too much bad news, Gretchen found herself thinking. *First I'm cheated out of my cheerleader spot. Then . . .*

She took a deep breath. She wanted to act calm, nonchalant in front of Sid and this girl. She didn't want to act like a crazy person. After all, she and Sid didn't really have any kind of understanding.

He had indicated in every way that he was dumping Stacy for her. Gretchen hadn't imagined that. She wasn't jumping to conclusions. The way he kissed her that day . . .

She strode up to the table and gripped the back of the

empty chair with both hands. "Hey, Sid—" She felt pleased that her voice didn't tremble.

The girl had big, dark blue eyes. They grew wide as she returned Gretchen's gaze. Her hair was beautiful, Gretchen thought. Long strands of of shiny black curls that caught the light from overhead and glistened like starlight.

Sid didn't show any surprise. "Gretchen, hi. How's it going? Are you feeling any better about the cheerleader thing?"

"Not really," she replied. He didn't seem eager to introduce her to this new girl. She motioned with her eyes, thinking maybe he'd take the hint.

"Oh, yeah," he said, setting down the tall menu. "This is my cousin Maya."

His cousin?

They *did* have the same dark hair. They were both tall and thin.

"Maya lives in Martinsville," Sid explained. "We don't get to hang out that often."

His cousin.

Gretchen suddenly felt a lot lighter. "Nice to meet you," she said, forcing a smile.

Sid motioned to the empty chair. "Want to join us?"

"Oh. No. I can't," Gretchen said. "I'm here with Madison." She pointed.

"Well, okay. See you," Sid said.

"Nice to meet you," Gretchen said to Maya. Had she already said that? She turned and made her way back to Madison.

Behind her, she heard Maya ask Sid, "Who was that?"

A baby started crying at the table beside her and drowned out Sid's reply.

"It's his cousin," she told Madison, sliding back into the booth.

"Really?"

"I think so," Gretchen said. "I don't think he'd lie to me."

"Don't get ahead of yourself with Sid," Madison said.

"Excuse me? What does *that* mean?"

"It means don't get ahead of yourself with Sid."

The text message came after school the next afternoon. Gretchen wondered why no one had mentioned a special meeting to her during the day.

She read the message twice to make sure she had it right:

Hey, it's me Stacy
Important squad meeting.
Cheerleaders & alternate.
8 2night in the gym.
Don't be late.
Go, Tigers

At dinner, her mother argued with her. "Do you

really think you should give up your homework time for a meeting so late at night? Shouldn't you be using your time better? You're not even on the squad."

Gretchen set down her fork. "How many times are you going to remind me, Mom?"

"I'm just saying . . ." Mrs. Page hesitated. "I'm just saying don't let the cheerleading thing take over your life. They didn't want you on the squad and—"

Gretchen raised her hand. "Stop. Just stop. You're just going to start a screaming fight, Mom. Between the two of us. I showed you the message. Stacy said cheerleaders and alternate. That's me. So I'm going tonight. That's it."

Her mother opened her mouth to reply, but thought better of it. "Whatever," she muttered and returned to her tuna and macaroni casserole.

Gretchen pulled her mother's car into the student parking lot a little before eight. Two other cars were parked near the teachers' lot. Two spaces down, a squirrel sat straight up, rolling an acorn between its paws. It turned and scampered away as Gretchen opened her car door to climb out.

Her sneakers thudded loudly in the long, empty hall. Someone had left their locker door open, and papers and notebooks had spilled out onto the floor. Gretchen hummed to herself, and her voice rang hollow against the tile walls.

Stepping through the double doors, she blinked against the bright light of the gym. All of the lights had been turned on, and the gym floor glowed like a yellow sun, reflecting the lights.

"Anyone here?" Her eyes swept from the bleachers against the far wall, across the empty floor, to the glass-windowed offices at the side. "Hey? Anyone?" Her shout echoed all around her.

She pulled out her phone and glanced at the time. 8:05. She checked to see if she had received any other texts. No.

"Where is everybody?" she asked out loud.

Gretchen moved to Coach Walker's office and leaned back against the closed door. She checked her Snapchat and her email, but kept raising her eyes to the gym entrance, expecting to see the others arrive.

At 8:15, she began to suspect that something was wrong. Pacing back and forth along the wall now, she retrieved Stacy's text message. She read it again. Then she tried to reply:

I'm at the gym.

Where is everybody?

Did I get the night wrong?

She pushed *send*, but the message wouldn't go. She pressed *send* again.

And gasped when all the lights went off.

"Hey—!" The deep darkness hit her like an ocean wave. She actually stumbled back against the wall. "Hey—!" She frantically tried to blink away her blindness. But it had been so bright, and now . . .

"Hey, somebody! Who turned off the lights?" Her voice revealed her surprise.

The narrow windows along the top of the walls were solid black. Gretchen turned toward the doors. The windows in the gym doors were black, too. Someone had turned off the hall lights.

Gretchen took a deep breath and fought back her fear. *Are the school lights on a timer? Or did someone deliberately turn them off?*

"Hey, anyone?" she shouted again. "I'm in here. Turn the lights back on."

No reply.

Silence.

Then she heard a loud *click*. From the entrance doors?

"Hey—is someone there? *Answer* me!"

Silence.

And then a soft footstep. And a cough. And another soft scrape of a shoe against the floor.

"Who is it?" Her voice suddenly tiny, trembling. "Who's there? I hear you."

I've got to get out of here.

Her back against the wall, Gretchen began edging toward the doors. The blackness pulsed before her eyes. She couldn't see anything.

But she knew she wasn't alone.

More scraping footsteps. And then Gretchen heard the shallow breathing of someone close by.

She sucked in another breath. And the scent invaded

her nose. A sweet citrus scent. It took a few seconds to recognize it. The citrus scent Devra used.

"Oh, wow," she murmured. "Devra? Is that you?"

She didn't wait for an answer. She grabbed the bar on the gym door and shoved it hard.

It didn't budge.

She pushed the door. Leaned into the next door and pushed it.

No. Locked.

That was the clicking sound. Devra had locked it. Turned off the lights and locked the doors. Locked her in. And now was moving slowly toward her.

If only she could see in this thick blackness. . . .

"Devra, I know it's you. Devra, you're not scaring me. SAY something!"

Silence.

"Devra—you've already WON! Why are you doing this to me?"

Another muffled cough in reply. And then . . . running footsteps.

Gretchen squinted into the darkness. She froze. She didn't know which way to run. Panic paralyzed her as her pursuer came at her hard, footsteps thudding loudly in the dark, empty gym.

And then Gretchen opened her mouth in a scream as a body crashed into her, bone-hard shoulder diving into her middle, taking her breath away, slamming her to the floor.

19.

Unable to breathe, pain like a fire in her stomach, Gretchen hit the floor hard. She rolled onto her side and curled up to protect herself. Choking, struggling to get her breath back. It felt as if heavy black waves were rolling over her, pressing her down.

Was Devra going to keep fighting? Was she done hurting her?

Still gasping, Gretchen looked up when she heard the gym doors open and then slam shut. She heard the footsteps of her attacker out in the hall.

Forcing herself to breathe, she sat up. She gazed into the swirling darkness, waiting for the pain to fade, waiting for her chest to stop burning, for her head to clear.

Devra, I know it was you.

You shouldn't have worn that perfume, Devra.

She knew her attacker. But what good did that do? If she accused her, Devra would just deny it. Gretchen had no proof. In the thick darkness, she hadn't even seen Devra.

I have to wait. I have to stay on guard and wait my turn.

I'll find a way to stop her from terrorizing me.

I know my turn will come.

"We have to talk about fire batons," Stacy said.

After school on Wednesday found them heading to the gym for practice. With the first Tigers football game Friday night, the practices were becoming more intense. Gretchen was pleased that Coach Walker allowed her to practice some of the routines, even though she wouldn't be cheering with the squad Friday night.

Gretchen put a hand on Stacy's arm to stop her. "Can I ask you a question first?"

Stacy nodded. "Sure."

Gretchen pulled out her phone. "Did you send me this text message?" She showed her the message that brought her to the gym.

Stacy's eyes went wide. "No way," she said. "Someone used my name? There *was* no practice last night, Gretchen."

Gretchen tucked the phone back into her bag. "That's what I thought."

"Well, what happened?" Stacy demanded. "You didn't go to the gym, did you?"

"Of course not," Gretchen lied. "I knew it was a phony."

"What a dumb joke," Stacy said, shaking her head.

"Yeah. Dumb," Gretchen said. "So . . . tell me about fire batons. We didn't have fire batons at my old school."

"Well, we do a fire baton routine at halftime," Stacy said. "Lighting them is a little tricky. And since it's your job as the alternate to light them, I thought I should give you a lesson."

"I light them?" This assignment caught Gretchen by surprise. "I light them and hand them to a cheerleader?"

Stacy nodded. "Yes. Didn't Coach Walker talk to you? She probably forgot. No problem. I'll show you."

Coach Walker greeted them both. "I'm going to give Gretchen a fire baton tutorial," Stacy said.

The coach called Sid over. He had been sitting on the bottom bleacher, sharing a sandwich with Ana. "Sid, set up the kerosene bucket and bring out a couple of fire batons. Stacy and Gretchen are going to practice outside."

"No problem," Sid said, giving the coach a two-fingered salute. He grinned at Gretchen. "Lesson Number One. Don't burn down the school if you can help it."

"That's very helpful, Sid," Coach Walker said. "But we really don't want to hear Lesson Number Two. Just go get the equipment."

A few minutes later, Stacy and Gretchen stood in the grassy area behind the gym. It was a warm fall day. High clouds floated over the yellow and red leaves of the trees. A fat crow peered down at them from the low roof of the building, cawing angrily as if telling them to go away.

Sid set two blue plastic buckets in front of them. One was half-filled with kerosene, the other with water. He handed two fire batons to Stacy. And he pulled a couple of heavy rags from his jeans pocket.

Stacy stepped forward and gave him a quick kiss. "See you later?"

Sid's face reddened. He glanced at Gretchen. "Yeah. Maybe." He started back into the gym, but turned at the door. "Hey. Almost forgot." He pulled something from his shirt pocket and tossed it to Gretchen. A large candle lighter. "Have fun." He disappeared into the gym.

"It's very simple. Watch," Stacy said. She demonstrated as she talked. "They look like normal batons, but they have these big bulbs on the end that catch fire. Here's all you do. You dip one end of the baton into the kerosene. Then you dip the other end. Then you use the rag and wipe it off carefully to make sure no kerosene dripped onto the baton part. We don't want flaming cheerleaders, do we?"

Gretchen laughed. "That could be an awesome finale."

Why am I making jokes? Gretchen thought. *This is more dangerous than I thought.*

"Then you hold the baton sideways like this and light one end, then the other." She clicked the lighter. It flamed and Stacy held the flame over each end of the baton. "You hand one to Devra, then light another one and hand it to me," she instructed. "Easy?"

"Ha," Gretchen said. "Not so easy. But I think I can do it. Let me try one."

Stacy handed her the other baton. Gretchen twirled it in one hand, let it fly high in the sky, and caught it as it dropped. "Can you believe I took twirling lessons in third grade?"

"You are so talented," Stacy said, her voice light. She doused her fire baton in the water bucket Sid had brought out. She leaned close to Gretchen. "Listen, I feel bad about what happened. You know. You really are talented. What they did wasn't right."

"Thanks for saying that," Gretchen said. She turned and dipped one end of her baton into the kerosene bucket. She suddenly felt confused. She liked Stacy. Stacy was a nice person. But she didn't want to get too friendly with her. After all, she was stealing Stacy's boyfriend.

How could they possibly be friends?

"Dip it quickly," Stacy instructed. "You don't want to soak it."

Gretchen flipped the baton and dipped the other end. Then she grabbed a rag from Stacy and carefully wiped the middle of the baton. When she was sure it was dry, she lighted both ends. "Should I try to twirl it?"

"Better not. It takes a lot of practice. You have to hold it pretty far away from you."

"I want to try," Gretchen said. "If I catch fire—"

She didn't finish her sentence. The gym door swung open and Coach Walker stuck her head out. "What are

117

you doing? Are you roasting marshmallows out here?" she called.

"Just teaching Gretchen the basics for Friday night," Stacy said.

"Come in," the coach said, waving them in. "I have a surprise for everyone."

Gretchen doused her baton in the water bucket. Then she tossed it on the ground and followed Stacy back into the gym.

She saw Sid standing in the center floor beside a pile of boxes.

"The new uniforms have arrived," Coach Walker announced. "Sid, hand them out. Come on, everyone. Go try them on."

A lot of excitement, cheers, and eager talk. Sid raised the boxes and called out the names. "Devra . . . Courtney . . . Shannon . . . Becka . . . Ana. Gretchen held her breath. Would there be a new uniform for the alternate?

Yes. Her box was at the bottom of the stack. Sid handed it to her, and she trotted to the locker room to try it on. The girls had strewn the boxes all over the locker room floor. Gretchen pulled hers from the box. A short, pleated maroon skirt with a long-sleeve maroon sweater top, a large white S on the front, a growling full-color tiger on the right shoulder.

Sweet.

The skirt fit perfectly. She kept turning it, trying to

find the front. It didn't seem to matter. She pulled on the top and adjusted it over the skirt. Tugged down the sleeves.

Sweeping back her hair with both hands, Gretchen turned to Ana at the locker across from her. "What do you think?"

"Lookin' good," Ana said. "These new uniforms are a lot hotter than the old ones." She bounced off to look at herself in the mirror beside the shower room door.

Arms around each other's shoulders, Courtney and Devra were performing a cheer together between the lockers. Gretchen adjusted the sleeves again. The sweater felt a little tight. No. Not tight. A little stiff. She stretched her arms out.

Her back started to itch. She tried to scratch it but couldn't reach. The uncomfortable feeling spread to her shoulders. Her stomach began to itch.

What's happening?

She rubbed her arms, scratched her shoulders. Her whole body prickled.

Something was wrong. Gretchen stumbled to the mirror. The backs of her hands itched now. Her chest felt aflame.

"What on earth—" she murmured, scratching her itching neck.

She stepped up close to the mirror, squinted hard, studying herself—and opened her mouth in a horrified scream.

20.

ourtney and Devra stopped their cheer. The locker
room grew silent.

A hand gripped Gretchen's shoulder. She spun around
to see Stacy holding onto her, her eyes wide with surprise. "Gretchen? What's wrong?"

"Look! Look!" Gretchen cried. "Look at them. Cockroaches. Don't you see them? My uniform. It's *crawling*
with cockroaches."

Stacy stepped back, her dark eyes bulged in horror. "I
see them. Oh, yuck. Hundreds."

"They—they're crawling on my skin!" Gretchen
cried. "Crawling all over me. Like little pinpricks. Oh,
help." She started slapping at herself, slapping her sides,
her chest. "Help. Get me out of this!"

The other girls clustered around her, eyes wide in
shock. Stacy stared at her, helpless, open-mouthed. "The
other uniforms are perfectly fine."

Two orange-brown cockroaches slithered up Gretchen's

neck. A few had climbed into her hair. She scraped both hands over her head, twisting, squirming. She rubbed her back against the wall. Cockroaches fell at her feet and scampered across the concrete floor.

Becka and Ana screamed and backed away. Shannon covered her mouth with both hands.

"Ohhhhhh." A sick groan escaped Gretchen's throat. Then, suddenly, her expression changed. Her face reddened and she clenched her jaw, narrowing her eyes, as if she was pondering a new idea.

Then, with an angry cry, she hurtled forward and grabbed Devra by the shoulders and spun her around. "YOU did this!" she screamed. "YOU did it! I know you did it!"

Devra pulled out of Gretchen's grip and stepped away from her, eyes wide with surprise. "Let *go* of me. Are you crazy? What are you talking about?"

"Look! Look what Devra did!" Gretchen cried, turning to confront everyone. She tugged the front of her sweater. Eight or ten cockroaches tumbled to the floor.

Gretchen pulled a cockroach off her neck and tossed it at Devra. It slid off Devra's sleeve and dropped to her feet.

"How could you *do* this to me?" Gretchen screeched in a high voice she had never heard before. "You won. You won, okay? I lost. So why are you torturing me?"

Coach Walker burst into the locker room. She stepped

into the circle of cheerleaders and took Gretchen by the shoulders. "Take a breath, Gretchen. Take a deep breath. Let's take this uniform off you. Then you can take a nice long shower."

"Why does she always blame me?" Devra cried. "Why does she blame me for everything?"

"Because you did it?" Gretchen said in a trembling voice. She moved toward Devra as if to fight her.

"You're totally psycho," Devra said. "Seriously. You're crazy. Why would I do that? Where would I get all those cockroaches?"

Gretchen brushed cockroaches off her legs and frantically tried to stomp on them. "Everyone knows you've declared war on me," Gretchen said through gritted teeth. "Everyone."

Devra crossed her arms over her chest. Her blue eyes were cold as ice as she returned Gretchen's stare. "I don't care about you," she said. "I never even *think* about you. So why should I go to the trouble of filling your uniform with bugs?"

"Because you know I'm better than you!" Gretchen shrieked. "You know I'm a better cheerleader. You're a *fraud*, a fake, and you know it."

Devra rolled her eyes and frowned. She turned to Coach Walker. "She's crazy. Look at her. She's practically frothing at the mouth."

"Gretchen, we have to get you out of that uniform,"

Coach Walker said softly. "Let's get you into the shower. We're going to have to call an exterminator for the locker room now."

But Gretchen didn't move. "You don't believe me? You all think I'm crazy?"

No one said a word. Devra kept her cold stare on Gretchen.

"I know how to prove it," Gretchen said. "I know how to show you that Devra did this." She shook her head hard. Three or four cockroaches came tumbling out.

Coach Walker tugged her arm. "Come on, Gretchen. Let's—"

"No!" Gretchen cried. "Where did these uniforms come from, Coach Walker? Where did you order them from?"

Coach Walker shrugged. "I don't remember. I think . . ." Her voice trailed off.

"Let's check one of the boxes," Gretchen said.

Coach Walker bent down and picked up a box.

"Where did it come from?" Gretchen repeated. "Where do the uniforms come from?"

The coach pulled off the box lid. She pulled out a slip of paper. She slowly raised her eyes to Gretchen. "They come from Dalby's Department Store."

21.

Gretchen took a shower in the locker room, then took another long, hot shower as soon as she got home. But she couldn't stop her skin and her hair from itching. Thinking about the cockroaches crawling all over her head and body sent chill after chill down her back.

How could she stop thinking about it?

The uniforms came from Dalby's. That proved that Devra had to be the culprit. But Coach Walker wasn't about to accuse Devra or investigate in any way. And Gretchen knew that Principal Hernandez wouldn't do anything, either.

The Dalbys' money was too important to Shadyside High. Devra could do whatever she wanted and no one would ever make a move to stop her or punish her.

And, of course, the question that kept preying on Gretchen's mind was: *Just how far will Devra go? How dangerous is she?*

Gretchen paced back and forth in her room. She

rubbed her arms. She could still feel the cockroaches prickling her skin. She had her wet hair wrapped in a towel, and her hair at least had stopped itching.

Maybe I should wrap my whole body in towels. Make a nice cocoon to hide in.

Finally, she decided she needed to talk to Polly back in Savanna Mills. That might distract her, take her mind off her itching skin. She decided not to tell Polly about the cockroaches. It would only worry her and gross her out, and she would feel sorry for Gretchen.

Gretchen felt sorry for herself, but she didn't want anyone else to feel that way.

She'd always been a winner back in Savanna Mills— at least until the trouble started. She wanted everyone back home to think of her as a winner now.

Gretchen stretched out on her bedspread and rested her head on the headboard. It felt good to lie down. She could feel the anger and the anxiety floating off her. She shut her eyes and just breathed for a while, taking slow, steady breaths.

Then she punched Polly's number into the phone. Polly answered after the first ring. Somehow, she always answered after only one ring.

"How's cheerleading?" Gretchen asked after they greeted one another. "Do they miss me?"

"No way. They have *me*," Polly joked.

Polly had always been the only one who could compete with Gretchen. She was tiny, at least a head shorter than Gretchen, and energetic as if she had a powerful electrical current running through her. She was so light, she could jump higher than anyone. Her jumps and moves were so effortless, Gretchen accused her of being weight-less.

"I miss you *so much*," Gretchen blurted out without intending. And to Gretchen's surprise, she had tears in her eyes. "Hold on a minute, Polly," she said. She lowered the phone and took a few deep breaths to get herself together.

All of the disappointment, anxiety, and anger in her new school had obviously gotten to Gretchen. She was more tense than she knew, and she felt as if her emotions were all tingling just beneath her skin.

"I'm totally psyched for the first game of the season on Friday," she told Polly. It wasn't entirely a lie. "You won't guess what my assignment is."

"Sit on the bench and watch the other girls perform?" Polly said.

"Ha-ha. You're so funny. Remind me to laugh."

"Sorry. I couldn't resist. I can't believe you're an alternate, Gretchen. You were the *best*."

"Anyway, my job is to light the fire batons. We never had fire batons. I think everyone thought they were too dangerous. Or maybe the school was just too cheap to buy them."

"We were lucky to have pom-poms," Polly said. "Remember? They were shedding all over the place?"

"I'm a little freaked about the fire batons," Gretchen confessed. "I mean the kerosene really flames up when you light it. I have to be really careful. I mean, what if I mess up and . . ." She didn't finish her sentence.

Her mother burst into the room.

Gretchen said a quick goodbye and ended the call.

"Hey, Mom—" Gretchen started. She sat up and fiddled with the towel around her hair.

Her mother picked up a T-shirt from the floor and started to fold it. "You took a shower?"

"Yeah. I . . . uh . . . felt grimy from practice," Gretchen said.

"Did you use my bath gel? It's almost out."

"No. I used soap. Why do you always accuse me of using your stuff?"

"Because you do?" She set down the T-shirt on top of the dresser and began to straighten some books on Gretchen's bookshelf. "Practice was so hard, you had to lie down in bed?"

"I'm just relaxing, Mom. At least, I was until *you* came in."

"Can't you ever be civil to me? I'm not allowed to spend any time with you?"

"Sorry." Gretchen stood up and removed the towel. She walked to the dresser mirror to brush out her hair, which was still damp. She turned. "Mom, please don't rearrange my room."

Mrs. Page shrugged. "Just trying to be helpful."

"It isn't helpful," Gretchen snapped. "It's annoying. You wouldn't like it if I went into your bedroom and started pawing over everything."

Her mother's cheeks reddened. "I wasn't pawing." She sighed. "Can't we have one conversation without snapping at each other's throats?"

Gretchen rolled her eyes. "Very dramatic, Mom." She gave her head a shake and her blonde hair fell into place. She set down the hairbrush and adjusted her top over her jeans. "I'm going out."

Her mother studied her. She brushed a strand of hair back from Gretchen's forehead. "Where?"

"A cheerleader meeting," Gretchen lied. She didn't care where she went. She didn't want to stay here with her mother. It wasn't just anger at her mother's attitude. Gretchen was afraid she might break down and tell the horrible things that were happening to her because of Devra.

Gretchen knew if she started to tell everything to her mother, the tears would start to flow. And Gretchen *never* wanted to cry in front of her.

When Gretchen cried, Mrs. Page was seldom sympathetic. She would freeze up. Clamp her teeth shut in a hard expression. Like putting up a wall in front of her face.

Gretchen's tears brought out a coldness in her mother that Gretchen never wanted to see. Better to keep things inside. Her relationship with her mother was hard enough without adding more emotion.

"You know, I've been thinking," Mrs. Page said, following Gretchen out the bedroom door and down the hall.

Uh oh, Gretchen thought.

"I think maybe being an alternate is a good thing for you, dear. It will give you time to adjust."

Gretchen exploded in a roar of curses.

"Language, dear," her mother said softly. "Please—watch your language."

Gretchen sucked in a deep breath. She waited for some of her anger to cool. "Mom, why do you say those things? You knew that would make me furious. You knew how disappointed I was. Why do you want to bring it up now and make it worse?"

Mrs. Page's eyes widened in shock. She placed an open hand at her chest, as if she had been punched. "I didn't mean—"

Gretchen stormed out the door. She could feel the blood pulsing angrily at her temples. *Why do I let her get to me like that? Why can't I ever just ignore the horrible things she says?*

She realized she had left the house without any idea of where she was going.

Maybe I'll take a long, aimless walk. Maybe I should get the car keys . . . .

She heard violin music from Madison's open window next door. Without thinking about it, she turned, walked across the lawn, and rang the bell at Madison's front door.

Madison greeted her warmly. "Hi. Come in. I needed an excuse to take a break." She led Gretchen into her bedroom and picked up the violin. "Listen to this. This is the most difficult section. I think I've almost got it."

Gretchen perched on the edge of Madison's pale blue bedspread and listened. The notes came fast and furious. Gretchen stared at Madison's fingers on the fingerboard, sliding so rapidly, Gretchen could barely see the movement.

"Awesome!" she declared when Madison finished. "It's . . . beautiful."

Madison laughed. "Aw, shucks. It was nothing." Then she added, "Just three days of practicing that one part."

Madison carefully slid the violin into its case. "What's up?"

Gretchen sighed. "More of the same. You really won't believe this."

Madison's expression grew serious. "Try me."

She told Madison about the cockroaches in the new cheerleader uniform.

"You're right. I don't believe it," Madison said, shaking her head. "It doesn't make sense, Gretchen. Devra knows she's won. She has the spot on the squad."

"I know," Gretchen agreed. "There's no reason for her to keep torturing me." She frowned. "Okay, okay. I know Devra doesn't like me. But there's no reason why—"

"I know some things about Devra," Madison interrupted. She lowered her voice to a whisper. "Seriously. I know some things about her."

"Like what?" Gretchen demanded.

Madison smiled, but she didn't answer.

22.

"Go, Tigers
Down the field!
Go, Tigers
We never yield!

Go, Tigers
We want more!
Go, Tigers
Score, score, SCORE!"

Gretchen tried hard to enjoy the game. But she couldn't hold back her feelings of frustration as she watched the other girls perform their cheers from the end of the bench on the sidelines.

She tried not to concentrate on Devra, who was the klutziest of all the girls and nearly dropped Becka during a simple Thigh Stand. But she couldn't help catching the smirk on Devra's face when she glimpsed Gretchen slumped on the bench by herself.

It had rained during the day. The field was wet and a heavy dampness clung in the chilly night air. The stands in the Tigers' stadium were nearly full, and the shouts and cheers were enthusiastic, partly because it was the first game of the season, and partly because the Tigers were mauling the visiting Yellow Jackets from Pleasant Springs. It was nearing halftime, and the Tigers were up 17–3 and threatening to score another touchdown.

"Tigers roar
More more more!
Tigers Roar
More more MORE!"

Gretchen mouthed the words along with the cheerleaders. She had to fight down the urge to leap up from her lonely spot on the sideline and perform the cheers on her own.

A renegade cheerleader. The thought made her smile.

A tap on her shoulder made her jump. She turned to see Sid, motioning to her eagerly. "See the clock?" he pointed. "Two minutes till halftime. I set up the kerosene and the batons over here."

She let him pull her to her feet. She thought he was about to kiss her, but he turned his face away quickly.

Stacy might be watching.

Had he told her the truth about breaking up with Stacy?

No time to think about that.

A roar went up from the stands as Cory Wagner, the Tigers' tailback, crushed through the Yellow Jackets' line into the end zone. Gretchen didn't see the touchdown. She was inspecting the kerosene bucket, then unfolding a rag to keep handy for wiping the baton down.

Her heartbeats began to race. She felt happy to be off the bench and contributing to the squad. Actually *doing* something. She picked up one of the batons and twirled it in front of her.

"Devra, then Stacy," she murmured to herself.

The plan was for Devra to take the first fire baton, Stacy the second. Then the two of them would run in front of the stands together and do their fiery routine side by side.

Gretchen's throat tightened as the teams ran off the field for halftime. The Tigers band began to play. Gretchen glanced up at the crowd. Many were standing and stretching. The aisles were filled with people heading down to the hotdog booth in the student parking lot.

As soon as the band finished its two numbers, it was time for the cheerleaders' halftime routines. Gretchen silently went over her instructions one more time. She held the first fire baton tightly, preparing to dip one end, then the other into the kerosene bucket.

Maybe I should test the lighter, she thought. But then she saw Coach Walker waving to her from the cheerleaders' bench. Gretchen set the baton down on the grass and trotted over to her.

"Is anything wrong?"

Coach Walker shook her head. "I just wondered if you are ready, Gretchen. Are you sure you're okay with this? Do you need Sid or anyone to help?" She had to shout over the blare of the band.

Gretchen shook her head. "I'm fine, Coach Walker. I'm on it!"

Coach Walker flashed her a thumbs-up. Gretchen turned and trotted back to the fire batons.

A light cheer went up as the band finished its second song. The stands rang with laughter and shouts, people talking to friends, standing in small groups, gulping hotdogs and sodas.

"Show time," Gretchen murmured. "Here we go."

She lowered the baton into the kerosene. Dip one end. Swipe the rag across the middle. Dip the other end. *Okay. Okay.* Now hold it carefully. Click the lighter. The flame rolls out. One end catches. The other end flames up. *Yes. Yes.*

Now hand it to Devra.

She shoved the flaming baton to Devra. But to her surprise, Devra took a step back. She grabbed her stomach. "Ohhhh." Devra groaned.

What's happening?

Devra's eyes rolled up. She waved the baton away. "I . . . feel sick," Devra said. "Ohh, my stomach. Something wrong." She waved frantically at Gretchen. "Give it to Stacy. I don't feel well."

Holding the baton out in front of her, Gretchen turned to Stacy. The smell of the burning kerosene invaded her nose, strong enough to make her eyes water. Everything suddenly became a blur.

She shoved the baton into Stacy's hand. Stacy flashed her a smile. Stacy spun around and, twirling the baton slowly, ran in front of the stands.

The drummers of the band began a roaring drumroll. Stacy turned to the onlookers in the stands and began to twirl faster. The bright orange-yellow flames danced and darted.

Gretchen began to dip the second baton into the kerosene. She glanced over at Stacy—just as the flames began to roll up Stacy's sleeve. One arm. Then both arms.

The flames shot up her sleeves and over the front of her sweater. They dipped and swirled, sunlight yellow against the purple night sky.

Stacy screamed, a shrill cry of panic, a hoarse, inhuman wail.

She dropped to her knees and the flames shot higher. A jagged, shimmering outline around her writhing body.

Stacy's head was tilted back, her mouth locked open

in wail after wail of horror. Her cries were muffled by the roar and crackle of the flames.

And then Courtney's scream drowned out Stacy's wails. "Somebody help! Stacy's on fire! Help her! Somebody! Stacy's on fire!"

PART
TWO

23.

We just want to talk about it," Hernandez said. He motioned for Gretchen to take the leather chair opposite his desk and next to Coach Walker. He carefully closed the door to his inner office.

Gretchen lowered herself into the chair and rubbed her cold, wet hands on the legs of her jeans. Coach Walker kept her eyes on the wall behind the principal's desk. She appeared to be avoiding Gretchen's gaze.

Gretchen cleared her throat. Her mouth suddenly felt so dry. She followed Hernandez as he brushed aside a stack of papers on his desktop, then dropped heavily into his big desk chair.

"Cold in here," Gretchen murmured, rubbing her hands on her legs again.

Coach Walker nodded but didn't reply.

Gretchen noticed a stain on the lapel of the principal's gray suit jacket. Ketchup, maybe? He removed his glasses and wiped the lenses with a red handkerchief. With his glasses off, his eyes looked tiny, she thought, too tiny for his large square face.

The three of them remained silent as Hernandez wiped his glasses. Gretchen heard some girls laughing out in the hall. She wished she could be out there with them.

It was the Monday after the Friday night football game. A weekend of sadness and tension had somehow passed. Gretchen spent most of the time alone in her room with the door closed and music cranked up really loud— to help keep her mother from intruding, and to help drown out her guilt-ridden thoughts.

She wished Sid would come over. Sid could comfort her. Sid could assure her it wasn't entirely her fault, whether that was true or not. Sid could hold her and maybe stop the chills that shook her body, the coldness that gripped her and wouldn't let go.

But he texted that he was at Shadyside General with Stacy and her family. He texted on Saturday that Stacy was in the ICU, that doctors couldn't say how badly she had been hurt. And then on Sunday afternoon, Sid texted that Stacy was "stable," whatever that meant. He said she was being moved to a private room.

Gretchen couldn't breathe any sighs of relief. She had set someone on fire. She didn't really know how it happened. But she had set Stacy on fire, maybe ruined her life forever—if she lived.

If she lived.

That thought made Gretchen's stomach heave, and she had to force her lunch back down.

And then the principal had called her house and asked her to come for a meeting after school on Monday. Thank goodness her mother wasn't home. The call filled Gretchen with troubled questions. Was she going to be suspended from school? Expelled? No. They'd want her mother to be there if that was true.

Would there be police at the meeting? Were Stacy's parents pressing charges?

Attempted murder?

Was Hernandez going to accuse her? Did someone think the whole thing was deliberate?

Gretchen realized she was scaring herself. Hernandez said he was investigating. He didn't say he was accusing her of anything.

And now, here she was facing him, sitting hunched in the chair across from him, her cold hands clasped tightly in her lap, so tightly her fingers ached.

He forced a smile. "Don't look so frightened, Gretchen," he said softly. "We're not here to assign guilt. We just need to know exactly what happened." He scratched one side of his face. "Stacy's parents are going to want to know, too."

"H-how is she?" Gretchen stammered. "Have you heard anything?"

"She's stable, according to the last report I heard," Hernandez said.

"Thank God," Coach Walker murmured.

"She has serious burns over her arms and chest," Hernandez continued, his eyes probing Gretchen's. "The most serious question is if Stacy will regain the use of her right arm again. It's the most badly damaged."

A sob burst from Gretchen's throat. "How awful. I mean—"

"The burn unit at Shadyside General is supposed to be top-notch," Coach Walker said, her gaze on Hernandez. "My cousin was in a car fire, and they performed miracles with him."

"That's good to hear," Hernandez said softly. He picked up a pencil and began rolling it in his fingers. He narrowed his eyes at Gretchen.

Sudden dread tightened her throat. She felt as if she couldn't breathe.

"Any idea how the accident happened?" the principal asked her.

She swallowed. "Uh . . . no. Not really. I mean . . ." Her voice was quivering. Did it make her sound as if she wasn't telling the truth?

"I mean . . . I can't understand it at all. I was so careful. It was my first time doing it, and I wanted to do a perfect job." Gretchen took a breath. Beside her, Coach Walker was now staring at her intently.

"I went over it, step by step," Gretchen continued. "I concentrated on doing it right. I . . . I can't understand. . . ." Her voice cracked.

"Did you see anyone else go near the batons or the kerosene bucket?" Coach Walker asked.

Gretchen thought hard. She shook her head. "No. I don't remember anyone. I . . . I was there the whole time. Well . . ." She suddenly remembered something. "You called me over to the bench, Coach Walker. Remember? You asked if I needed help, and I said no. But that only took a few seconds. I hurried right back."

Coach Walker nodded. She rubbed her chin, swept a hand back through her hair, her face knotted in a frown.

"Gretchen, did you notice anything strange at all? Before or after the accident?"

Gretchen concentrated again. "Well . . . one thing was strange." She hesitated.

Hernandez let go of the pencil. He leaned closer over his desktop. "What was that?"

"Maybe I shouldn't say. . . ." Gretchen murmured.

"Gretchen, anything you think of can be helpful," Coach Walker said. "Don't hold back to protect someone. And don't feel you have to be one-hundred percent positive about something you think you saw. A terrible thing has happened. We need to know why it happened."

Gretchen swallowed again. Her mouth was dry as sandpaper. "Well . . . I'm a little confused about Devra."

"Devra Dalby?" Hernandez sat up straight. He squinted at Gretchen through his glasses. "What about Devra?"

"Devra was supposed to take the first fire baton," Gretchen said. "But when I started to hand it to her, she backed away. She said she didn't feel well. She told me to give it to Stacy."

"I noticed that," Coach Walker said. "I noticed that Devra held back and Stacy ran in front of the stands to perform without her."

"I . . . uh . . . I-I don't want to accuse Devra of anything," Gretchen stammered. "But . . . it was like she *knew* there was something wrong with the baton. I mean, how did she know not to take it?"

A hush fell over the room. Gretchen's words seemed to linger heavily in the air.

Coach Walker rubbed her chin some more, her eyes on the bulletin board behind the principal's desk. Hernandez tapped the pencil against the desktop. He appeared to be faraway, deep in thought.

I had to say it, Gretchen thought. *It was just so strange how Devra wouldn't take the baton. It couldn't be a coincidence.*

"We'll talk to Devra later," Hernandez said, finally breaking the silence. He pointed the pencil at Gretchen. "We know that you and Devra have been feuding. We know—"

"Feuding?" Gretchen interrupted.

"Well, you're not exactly best friends," Coach Walker chimed in. "You've accused Devra before. . . ."

Hernandez raised a hand to silence her. "Let me finish. I hate to ask this, Gretchen, but I have to. Coach Walker has told me how eager you were to be on the squad. And we all know that Devra probably doesn't belong there. So tell me this . . ." He hesitated.

Gretchen felt her heart skip a beat. She gripped the leather arms of the chair.

"You didn't try to hand Devra a dangerous baton, hoping to get her off the squad—did you?"

Gretchen gasped. Without thinking, she jumped to her feet. "Of *course* not! That's *horrible!*" she shrieked. "Is that what you think? You think I'm a *killer*?"

A sob escaped Gretchen's throat, and then she couldn't hold back. A flood of tears rolled down her cheeks. She folded herself back into the chair and cried, sobbing hard, her shoulders heaving up and down.

Coach Walker tried to pat her comfortingly on the back. But Gretchen brushed her hand away.

Hernandez sat helplessly, biting his lips, shaking his head. "I'm sorry. It was a question I felt I had to ask."

Gretchen could barely hear him over her sobs. She sucked in breath after breath and finally managed to stop crying. Her cheeks were tear-soaked and burning hot. She wiped her eyes with the palms of her hands.

"I'll never forgive myself," she finally managed to

choke out, not looking at either of them. "I'll never forgive myself for what happened to Stacy. Never."

Gretchen's heavy footsteps echoed down the long, empty hall as she made her way to the exit. She held her breath, struggling not to start crying again. She fumbled in her bag for her car keys, and dropped the bag. She stood watching everything tumble out onto the floor.

"At least the day can't get *worse*," she muttered. She bent down and swept everything back into the bag.

"Hey—!" Gretchen called out, surprised to find Sid waiting for her in the student parking lot. She rushed forward and he wrapped her in his arms.

"I don't need to ask how it went," he said. "I can see your face is a total wreck."

"Thanks a bunch," she muttered. But she pressed her cheek against his chest. She could hear his steady heartbeat. She wondered if hers would ever beat so slow and normal again.

"They think I'm a murderer," she said, raising her eyes to his.

"No way," Sid replied. "You're not serious. They don't think that."

Gretchen sighed. "I don't know what they think. It's all a horrible mystery."

"I just came from the hospital," Sid said.

Gretchen took a step back. "And?"

He shrugged. "Third-degree burns over both arms. It's horrible. She's bandaged up like a mummy."

"Did you talk to her?"

Sid shook his head. "No. She wasn't awake."

Gretchen couldn't help it. The tears began pouring from her eyes again.

Sid stepped forward and wrapped her in a close hug.

And she heard a harsh voice from behind them. "Well! It didn't take *you* long to steal Stacy's boyfriend!"

24.

Gretchen spun away from Sid and stared at Devra's friend Courtney Shaw. Courtney wore a black-and-white-striped T-shirt over white tennis shorts. She had a tennis racket raised in one hand. Her short black hair glistened from sweat. Her silver nose ring flashed in the light of the afternoon sun.

"Courtney, I—" Gretchen couldn't figure out what to say.

"How's it going?" Sid asked casually. As if she hadn't made an accusation. "You have a good game?"

Courtney ignored Sid and glared at Gretchen. "I saw you from the tennis courts." She motioned to the courts at the back of the parking lot. "I just wanted to tell you something."

Gretchen squinted at her. "Tell me something?"

"You're on the cheerleader squad now, right? Because poor Stacy got burned to a crisp?"

Gretchen gasped. "Are you accusing me?"

"Not at all," Courtney said. "I'm just saying."

Gretchen stuck her chin out, ready to defend herself. "Saying what?"

"You're on the squad now, so you and Devra will be together a lot. You probably know that Devra is my good friend."

"So?" Gretchen demanded impatiently.

"So I wanted to warn you. Devra has had enough."

"Are you kidding me?" Gretchen exploded. "Are you out of your mind? Devra has had enough?"

"Listen to me, Gretchen—"

"Devra has been torturing me!" Gretchen shouted. "She has been ruining my life."

"Not true!" Courtney said, slamming her tennis racket against a pole. "Not true! Not true!"

"Can't you both dial it down?" Sid shouted. "I've got sensitive ears."

"Devra doesn't care a thing about you!" Courtney screamed, ignoring Sid. "She isn't interested in you at all. She just wants you to stop blaming her for everything. It's crazy."

"Sending threatening texts isn't crazy?" Gretchen cried. "Cleaning fluid in my water bottle? Jamming my uniform full of cockroaches? And *I'm* the one who's crazy?" She took an angry step toward Courtney. "*You're* the one who's crazy."

Courtney stepped back until she bumped into a car fender. "You've got it all wrong, Gretchen. Devra isn't doing anything to you. I'm telling the truth." She smacked the head of the racket against the ground. "Listen to me. Do you know about the cheerleader retreat?"

"Of course I know about it," Gretchen snapped. "We're all going to stay in these cabins in the woods for a weekend."

"Devra says when we're there, just keep away from her and everything will be okay."

Gretchen pressed her hands against her waist. "She's threatening me?"

"No way. She just wants peace, Gretchen. A truce. Know what I mean? She hasn't done anything to you. She swears it. So just leave her alone." Courtney finished her speech, breathing hard, sweat glistening her short black hair.

Gretchen let out a long breath. "She's a total liar, Courtney. Do you really believe her?"

Courtney didn't answer. She flashed a look of disgust at Sid, swung her racket in the air as if batting him away, turned, and strode off.

Gretchen watched her until she disappeared behind the tennis courts. Suddenly, she felt more confused than ever. Her thoughts whirred through her mind.

If Devra isn't behind all these horrible things . . . then, who? Courtney is lying. She has to be. I know she and Devra are friends. But why would Courtney lie for Devra?

25.

Gretchen and her mother ate dinner in near silence. Mrs. Page was not a good cook, and parts of the roast chicken were nearly raw and the baked potatoes were hard.

Gretchen didn't have much of an appetite, anyway. She hadn't eaten much since the football game. Her stomach was so tightly knotted, she never felt hungry.

The house was so quiet, Gretchen could hear the ticking of the mantelpiece clock in the next room. *I don't know which is worse,* she thought. *Forcing a conversation with my mom, or this horrible silence.*

"I don't know what to say," Mrs. Page said, as if reading Gretchen's thoughts. She set her fork down on the table. "Sorry about the chicken. I knew I should have left it in the oven longer. I get distracted."

"It's . . . okay," Gretchen murmured.

"You can't blame yourself," her mother said, abruptly

changing the subject. "It was a horrible accident, dear. But it *was* an accident."

Gretchen sighed. "That doesn't really help, Mom."

"There's nothing I can say. You tried to be as careful as you could. I know you did."

Gretchen clenched her jaw. "I wasn't careful *enough*." She shoved her plate away. "You're right, Mom. We can't talk about it. It's too awful to talk about."

"You have to put it behind you," Mrs. Page said, licking her lips.

Gretchen hated the way her mother was always licking her lips. Why didn't she wear lip gloss or ChapStick if her lips were so dry? And what was this *put it behind you* nonsense? How stupid was that? What a useless a thing to say.

Gretchen opened her mouth to tell her mother to just stop talking. But her phone rang before she could get a word out. She had the phone on the table in front of her. She picked it up and squinted at the screen. Madison was calling.

Gretchen jumped up. "Mom, I have to take this."

Mrs. Page frowned. "I made dessert. I mean, I bought a pound cake."

"Later." Gretchen gave her a wave and hurried upstairs to her room.

She dropped onto the edge of her bed and pressed the phone to her ear. "Madison—where've you been? I tried calling you all weekend."

"My cousin Emma had a baby," Madison said. "She's the one that lives out on that farm beyond Grove City? My mom wanted to help out, so we spent the weekend there. My phone wouldn't work there. No cells, I guess. And Emma doesn't have WiFi. I've been totally out of touch."

"Oh, wow. I really wanted to talk to you. I—"

"And I need to talk to you," Madison interrupted. "I have to tell you something, Gretchen. Something really horrible."

Gretchen heard her mother coming up the stairs. Was she spying on her?

"Something horrible? Oh my God. Madison, what *is* it?"

"I-I'm supposed to be practicing my violin," Madison stammered. "For the assembly tomorrow morning. But . . . I can't concentrate. I can barely think straight. I . . . I'm so upset."

"Madison—what *is* it?" Gretchen repeated.

"You have to come over. Hurry. I don't want to tell you over the phone."

The bedroom suddenly began to spin. Gretchen shut her eyes to stop her dizziness. *What could be so horrible?*

"Is it about Stacy?" Gretchen demanded, her voice quivering. "Is it?"

"Just hurry over here," Madison insisted.

Gretchen ended the call, tucked the phone into her pocket, and hurried down the stairs, taking them two at a time. Her mother appeared at the front door just as Gretchen was about to pull it open.

How does she do that? Gretchen wondered. *Appear at the door from out of nowhere every time I'm about to leave? She is so annoying!*

"Just going next door." She tried to squeeze past her mother.

"What for?" Mrs. Page demanded, not budging.

"Madison wants to tell me something."

"Sorry." Mrs. Page, hands on hips, shook her head. "You're forgetting your promise."

Gretchen blinked. "Promise?"

"You promised you'd help me with the photo albums tonight. Don't pretend you didn't."

"But, Mom—" Gretchen had her eyes on the door knob. So close yet so far.

"The albums are a mess. In total disarray. You promised you'd help, Gretchen. Tonight's the night. No excuses."

"No, I can't. Really," Gretchen replied, trying to keep her voice low and calm. But she knew she was about to lose it. "Madison—"

"You know I've been obsessing about the albums ever since we moved, Gretchen. It's the next thing on my list, and I want to check it off tonight."

Gretchen let out an exasperated groan. "Mom, you're being really annoying. Madison has something she wants to tell me. We can do the stupid albums tomorrow night!" she screamed.

"Don't you scream at me. Do you think you can convince me by acting like an infant? No way. You're not going out. Whatever your friend has to say can wait, I'm sure. You're staying home and helping me. Keep your promises, Gretchen."

Mrs. Page stood stiffly, whole body tensed, arms crossed tightly in front of her, blocking the door.

"Mom, I swear—"

But Gretchen saw that she had lost.

Do I have the most annoying mother in the world? She's impossible. Impossible!

Her shoulders slumped. She rolled her eyes. "Okay, Mom. Photo albums. If it will make you happy."

Maybe we can get through the albums early, Gretchen thought. *And I can run over to Madison's. Or else I'll have to talk to her after the assembly tomorrow.*

And then questions flashed one after another in her mind.

What is Madison so desperate to tell me?

Is it about Devra?

What could be so horrible?

26.

Gretchen took a seat in the third row of the auditorium next to Ana. She turned to gaze down the rows of seats as kids filed in for the morning assembly. She looked for Sid. He had said something about sitting with her. But he was nowhere to be seen.

Ana held her phone in her lap and was busily texting someone with both thumbs. She held the phone low behind the seatback in front of her because students weren't allowed to use their phones during school hours.

Gretchen glimpsed at Devra at the far end of the row. Devra saw her, too, but quickly glanced away. She and Courtney began talking animatedly, their faces close together.

Ana finished her text and slid the phone into her bag. She shook her head hard, straightening her bangs. "How's it going?"

"A little better," Gretchen said. "I don't know if I'll ever stop thinking about Friday night."

Ana nodded solemnly. "I still hear Stacy's screams in my ears. Last night, I dreamed my house was on fire and I was trapped in my room."

Gretchen shook her head. "Oh, wow. That's terrible."

The auditorium lights dimmed. Principal Hernandez, in his gray suit, strode up the stairs at the side of the stage.

"Did Coach Walker tell you?" Ana asked. "Hernandez banned fire batons. We can't perform with them anymore."

"I guess he's right," Gretchen murmured.

It's all my fault, she thought.

She realized Ana was staring at her intently, studying her. She wondered what Ana was really thinking. Did she think Gretchen was a careless idiot who should be punished for what happened to Stacy? Is that what everyone in school thought?

Or was Gretchen being paranoid?

Stacy was so pretty and lively and funny and energetic. Everyone likes Stacy. And now I'm going to be remembered for the rest of my time here as the idiot girl who set Stacy on fire.

"Have you been to the hospital?" Ana asked. "Did you go see Stacy?"

"Well . . . no," Gretchen answered, avoiding Ana's gaze. "But Sid gives me reports about her."

Ana's eyes widened in surprise. "You talk to Sid? You've been hanging out with him?"

"Kind of."

Gretchen swallowed. Did she just say something

wrong? Ana seemed more than surprised. Her questions sounded like an accusation.

Ana appeared to be studying her even more intently. Gretchen was glad that the auditorium had gone dark, and Hernandez was stepping up behind a podium at the side of the stage.

Four musicians, two men and two women, wearing black suits and white shirts, had taken their seats, facing each other on folding chairs in the center of the stage. The woman holding a tall cello was busily tuning it. The two men sat casually, chatting, violins perched in their laps.

It took Hernandez a while to get everyone quiet. Some guys in the back row were loudly doing a rap song that Gretchen had heard on the radio, pounding the seats in rhythm with their beats, and others were laughing and cheering them on.

"We're going to enjoy a *different* kind of music this morning," Hernandez told them, bringing his mouth too close to the microphone so that his words made popping sounds as he spoke.

"But that's a classic!" a guy in the back row shouted. Laughter spread down the rows of seats.

Hernandez raised both hands above his head and kept them there until everyone was silent. "We have a special treat this morning," he announced. "The four members of the Chicagoland Arts String Quartet have graciously come to our school to perform for us."

A mild burst of applause greeted his announcement. Onstage, the four musicians sat upright, readying their instruments.

"And to make this concert really special," Hernandez continued, "one of the eleventh-graders from our orchestra will be joining the quartet."

Gretchen suddenly felt tense. This was Madison's big moment. She must be so nervous now, Gretchen knew. *Maybe that's why Madison wanted me to come over last night. Just to help her get over her nerves.*

Gretchen was suddenly feeling it, too. "Go, Madison! Go, Madison!" she chanted to herself.

"Let's bring Madison Grossman out to join the quartet," Hernandez said. He motioned with both hands, and everyone applauded.

Madison strode onto the stage. She wore a white blouse, pleated in the front like a tuxedo shirt, and a long black skirt. She had put her hair up high on her head. She took a funny, exaggerated bow, reacting to the applause, and everyone laughed. The laughter seemed to relax her, and she smiled for the first time.

"Madison is going to join the quartet to play . . ." Hernandez raised a sheet of paper to his face and read, ". . . the first two movements of the Mozart Viennese String Quartet Number Eight."

A pleased smile crossed his face. He gestured to the musicians, turned, and walked off the stage.

Madison sat down on the empty chair facing the cello

player. Her violin case stood beside the chair. She bent and raised the case to her lap. One of the women said something to her, and Madison laughed.

She opened the case and lifted out the violin and the bow. Then she snapped the case shut and returned it to the floor beside her chair.

The cello player said something to her. From her seat in the third row in the audience, Gretchen couldn't hear what they were saying. Some kids shifted in their seats impatiently.

The musicians raised their instruments. The male violinist tapped his bow twice on his instrument. They began to play.

Gretchen watched Madison. Madison's face was tight, intense, her eyes narrowed on the music stand in front of her. Sitting up straight and stiff, she counted off several measures. Then she raised the violin to her chin.

Gretchen relaxed a little. *Madison is doing it. She's going to be great.*

The melodic flow of the strings floated over the auditorium. Gretchen slid down in her seat and raised her knees to the seatback in front of her.

The music was sweet, gentle, very rhythmic and precise.

It lasted only thirty seconds. Then a hideous, high animal scream, a shrill bleat of shock and pain, shot over the auditorium and rang off the walls.

It took Gretchen a few seconds to realize that Madison was the one shrieking and crying.

Madison leaped to her feet and tossed her violin across the stage. She grabbed her neck and dropped to her knees. Cry after cry burst from her throat.

The four musicians jumped up, too. They stumbled back, eyes wide with shock, staring down at Madison as she held her neck and screamed.

"I'm burning! It's *burning*! Somebody! Help me! Help! I'm burning!"

Screams rang out across the auditorium. Teachers ran toward the stage.

Gretchen jumped to her feet. She could see that Madison's neck was a flaming red. Madison gave out one last shriek and, gripping her neck, fell sideways, collapsed to the floor. Bright red blood gushed up from her neck like a fountain. The blood shot up in a wave of scarlet and then splashed down on the stage floor, splashed all around her. Madison didn't move.

Principal Hernandez was running across the stage now, his necktie flying over his shoulder. He pushed one of the shocked musicians aside and dropped to the stage floor beside Madison.

A horrified hush fell over the auditorium. It was as if someone had taken the volume knob and turned it all the way down to silent. Students stood, gaping wide-eyed, pressing their hands over the seatbacks in front of them.

It was so quiet, Gretchen could hear Hernandez's

imploring pleas as he leaned over Madison, his face close to hers. "Madison? Madison? Please answer me. Can you hear me? Madison?"

Gretchen realized she'd been holding her breath. Her hands were clenched into tight fists. Her stomach had knotted in dread.

"Call a doctor!" a teacher shouted from the edge of the stage.

"Somebody—call 911!" someone else cried.

Leaning over Madison, Hernandez raised a hand. "It may be too late," he said. "She's not breathing."

27.

Sid wrapped his arm around Gretchen. She slid against him and pressed her head against his shoulder.

I want to disappear, she thought. *I want Sid to wrap his arms around me, shut out the light, and I'll disappear forever.*

The real world was too hard to face, Gretchen decided. Too horrifying and cruel.

"How could someone murder Madison?" Her words came out in a choked whisper. She hadn't been able to think of anything else since yesterday morning in the auditorium. Just kept asking herself the same question again and again.

And what a cold-blooded, horrifying murder it was. Someone had doused acid over the chin rest of Madison's violin. Enough acid to burn right through Madison's neck. It had burned through Madison's aorta, and Madison had bled to death before anything could be done.

About as cold and cruel as a murder can get. And Gretchen knew she had no proof. But the only person she knew who had acid was Devra Dalby. Acid powerful enough to burn paint off furniture.

She snuggled against Sid's chest. His warmth wasn't enough to stop her chills.

"The school building is completely closed off," Sid said, shaking his head. "The Shadyside police are everywhere, and they are talking to everyone."

"They haven't talked to *me* yet," Gretchen said, her voice muffled against his chest. "I . . . I need to talk with them."

Sid's body went tense. "Why? What do you know?"

Gretchen pulled away from him. She sat up, arranging her hair behind her shoulders. She knew she looked a mess. She hadn't even brushed her hair this morning. And her eyes were red and puffy from crying, her cheeks tear-stained and pale.

She wore the jeans, torn at the knees, she'd been wearing all week. And a sweatshirt with orange food stains on the front that she'd pulled out of her laundry bag. She didn't care how she looked. Her friend was dead. DEAD. Murdered.

She couldn't stop picturing the gusher of bright blood shooting up from Madison's open throat, spouting over Madison and splashing onto the stage floor. She couldn't stop hearing again and again the screams and horrified shrieks of everyone in the auditorium as they looked helplessly on.

Sid waited patiently for her to explain.

Gretchen took a deep, shuddering breath. "Madison called me the night before the music assembly," she began. "She sounded kind of frantic. She said she had something important to tell me, something she didn't want to tell me over the phone."

Sid frowned at her. "What was it?"

"I-I don't know," Gretchen stammered. "I started over to her house, and my mother stopped me. She wouldn't let me go over there." She uttered a low growl. "So typical. She's just always in my way."

Sid patted her hand. "Let's leave your mother out of this," he said softly. "You have no clue as to what Madison wanted to tell you?"

"No clue." Gretchen lowered her eyes to the floor and stifled a sob. She'd already cried so much. She was desperate not to start again.

Sid swept a hand back through his dark hair. "Do you think Madison was killed because of what she wanted to tell you? Do you think someone killed her to shut her up?"

"Wait. I have to tell you this. A while ago, Devra told me she had a powerful acid," Gretchen blurted out. She had been holding that information in for too long. Just knowing it felt as if it was burning a hole in her.

Sid's mouth dropped open. "Excuse me? Say that again."

"I was at Lefty's. Devra sat down at my table. She wanted to bribe me not to win the cheerleader tryout.

And she said she was working on a cabinet to surprise her dad. She told me she was using acid to remove the paint."

Sid stared blankly at her, as if her words didn't make sense to him.

"Don't you see?" Gretchen urged impatiently. "Don't you see?" She tugged his sleeve. "A while ago, Madison told me she knew some things about Devra."

"Some *things*? Like what?"

"She never told me," Gretchen said. "Maybe she wanted to tell me the night before she was killed. And—"

"And Devra doused Madison's violin with acid to keep her from telling?"

"It sounds crazy. . . ." Gretchen said softly.

"Yeah. Crazy," Sid murmured. "Devra is a crazed killer? Crazy."

"Hernandez and Coach Walker questioned me about Stacy," Gretchen said, squeezing her fingers around his arm, as if holding on to a life raft. "I told them my suspicions about Devra. I mean, why Devra backed away and didn't take the fire baton, so Stacy had to take it."

"And what did they say?"

"They said they'd talk to Devra. But nothing came of it. They probably thought I was just trying to get Devra in trouble. You know. Because of the competition, because of the troubles between us."

Sid shook his head. "It's hard to believe. Devra burned Stacy and murdered Madison? That's like . . . impossible." He turned to her. "But you do have to tell the police what

172

you suspect. I mean, lots of people could buy acid. Just because Devra was using acid doesn't mean . . ." His voice trailed off. "But what if you're right? What if Devra really is crazy? What if she really did those things?"

Gretchen could see his mind spinning. She could tell he didn't want to believe that Devra was a cold-blooded murderer. The whole idea that someone they knew could deliberately kill . . .

"Shouldn't you be at the hospital? What about Stacy?" Gretchen asked suddenly.

Sid didn't answer. Instead, he wrapped her in a tight hug. They kissed.

"Stacy and I . . . I told you, it's over," he said when the kiss ended. "It's over but she refuses to accept it. I told you. And as long as she's in the hospital, I can't really fight with her or argue or try to make her see the truth."

He sighed. "I have to be there with her. I can't upset her. She's . . . she's really messed up."

They held onto each other. They kissed again.

Sid stood up to leave. "I'm sorry. I have to go check in on Stacy."

Gretchen's mind was still on what they had talked about. "What if Devra really is a murderer? And we're the only ones who know it? What does that mean? What does it mean, Sid?"

He stared at her. "That she'll come after *us* next."

28.

"Polly—I wish you were here." Gretchen gazed into her laptop screen.

"But FaceTime is almost as good," Polly said.

"Did you add highlights to your hair?"

Polly grinned. "Think it works?"

"Definitely."

Gretchen studied her friend on the screen. Polly was so light and small. With her flood of auburn curls bouncing on her round face, pale creamy cheeks, and those huge brown eyes, she looked like a little doll. Everything about her said energy and dynamo and electricity and pep.

She was the best cheerleader at Savanna Mills. So light and springy and a total daredevil. Gretchen sometimes felt like an elephant beside her, although Polly never stopped talking about how much she admired Gretchen's skill and athleticism and mature good looks.

A perfect team.

"So tell me what's happening," Polly said, her expression turning serious. "This must have been a total nightmare for you, Gretchen."

Gretchen nodded and once again stifled a sob. "Madison was my friend, the only friend I've made in Shadyside."

Polly brushed a strand of curls off her forehead. "Have they caught the murderer?"

Gretchen shook her head. "It's Devra Dalby. I told you on the phone last night, I know it's Devra. I'm so terrified. I'm the only one who knows."

Gretchen raised her eyes to the clock over the sink. "I have to go to a cheerleader meeting in a little while. I . . . I'm dreading it, Polly. I'm afraid to be in the same room with Devra."

"And what about the retreat?" Polly asked." You said there was a cheerleader retreat . . . ?"

Gretchen nodded. "Can you imagine? We're all going to be staying in cabins in the woods. In the woods with a crazed killer? A crazed killer who *hates* me. I'm so scared, Polly, I can't even think about it."

"Did you talk to the cheerleader coach?" Polly asked. "Did you talk to the police?"

"I finally talked to two officers last night," Gretchen said. "I told them everything. About the acid Devra was using on a cabinet. Everything."

"And?"

"They said they were following all leads." Gretchen

sighed. "They were very nice. I told them what good friends Madison and I were. I think they were being careful not to upset me. But they didn't seem terribly interested in what I had to say."

"Weird," Polly muttered. "And are they opening your school again?"

Gretchen nodded. "Tomorrow. It's been closed for two days. But it's opening tomorrow, and guess what? The principal decided to go ahead with the football game Friday night."

Polly's eyes widened in surprise. "Really?"

"Really. He said it would be good for school morale."

Polly twisted a corner of her mouth up as she thought about that. A tiny dimple formed in her cheek. *She really does look like a toy doll,* Gretchen thought, even when she's being totally serious and thoughtful.

She's so sweet. The best friend I could ever have.

"I have to go to the cheerleader meeting," Gretchen said. "I'm so glad we had a chance to talk. It really helps, Polly. It really does."

Gretchen clicked off the connection. She had to drive to school now. She had to see what Coach Walker had to say to the cheerleaders. She had to stand in the same space as Devra Dalby.

Was she in total danger? She never dreamed she'd be in the same room as a murderer.

And one chilling question kept repeating in her mind: Would Devra kill again?

29.

Gretchen drove through a gray afternoon, rain clouds low in the sky. A few raindrops drizzled onto the windshield. Gusts of wind sent dead brown leaves toppling from the trees, dancing in the air as they fell.

The high school was dark, she noticed, as she slowed and pulled the car around the side of the building to the student parking lot. Only two other cars parked back here. And a single black-and-white police cruiser parked at an angle at the back entrance.

Why are the police still here? It's three days later. What could they possibly find?

She tried to shake her thoughts from her mind as she entered the empty building. The hallway was dimly lit and cold, as if they had turned off the heat while everyone was away.

The gym was even colder. Coach Walker was scurrying along the wall, turning on lights. Basketballs, normally stacked in the equipment room, were scattered across the gym floor as if they'd escaped their prison.

Gretchen spotted Courtney doing stretching exercises on the floor in front of the coach's office. Ana and Devra were against the far wall, chatting quietly. Becka and Shannon sat cross-legged on the floor, backs against the wall, studying their phones.

Gretchen looked for Sid, but then remembered he hadn't been invited to this meeting. She swung her bag off her shoulder and tossed it against the wall. She rubbed her hands together, trying to warm them. "You can almost see your breath in here," she told Coach Walker.

Walker nodded. "I think the school was trying to save money while no one was here. I don't think they ran the furnace at all." She stopped and studied Gretchen. "How are you doing? I mean, seriously."

"Seriously, not so great," Gretchen said. "It's kind of weird being back in this building."

"Did you see one of the counselors the school made available?" the coach asked.

Gretchen stared at her. *What could a counselor tell me? Not to be upset even though a good friend was murdered in front of my eyes?*

"No," Gretchen answered simply.

She glanced to the far wall and saw that Devra had turned away from Ana. Devra was watching Gretchen now. Staring hard. Her face a blank.

Why is she looking at me?

"I think getting back to a normal schedule is the best thing we can do," Walker said. She rearranged the baseball cap on her head. "I mean, no way we can forget what happened. But we have to get past it."

She didn't wait for Gretchen to reply. She motioned with both hands for the other cheerleaders to gather around.

"We're not going to practice today," the coach announced. "I think we're prepared for the game against the Bisons tomorrow night. I know nothing feels normal, and we all have a million questions, and we're all troubled and tense because of the horrible thing that happened in our school. But I think we have an important job to do, all of us. And I asked Courtney to say a few words."

Courtney swept a hand back over her short hair. She stepped into the center of the circle of girls, adjusting the sleeves of her Shadyside High jersey.

"I agree with Coach Walker," she started. "We cheerleaders have an important job to do. We can help get our school back on track. I mean, this week has been the pits, and I think everyone in school feels terrible. There've been a lot of tears and a lot of nightmares and a lot of sadness."

Her voice cracked. She took a breath. "First Stacy has a horrible accident. Then Madison is murdered onstage. How can we ever recover from that? How can our school return to just a little bit of normal?"

Her eyes swept the circle of girls. "I think that's where *we* come in. I mean, we're cheerleaders. That means we're the spirit leaders of the school. I thought about this a lot when Coach Walker asked me to speak. Everyone talks about school spirit. But what is it really?

"It isn't just a slogan. It means the feeling of the school. How the students here feel about themselves and about our high school. And I think if we do a good job at the game Friday night . . . if we get everyone really yelling and screaming and cheering . . . we will do our part in lifting everyone's spirits."

Courtney glanced around the circle again, as if checking if everyone was with her. "That's what cheerleaders can do," she continued. "A lot of people think cheerleading is old-fashioned or sexist or dumb. But I think we can show that they are wrong. We have a real purpose. Maybe we can call it a goal. And that's to get everyone here out of the dumps and get them cheering again."

Courtney let out a relieved sigh. She stepped back. She had an uncertain expression on her face. *Maybe she was expecting us all to burst into applause,* Gretchen thought.

The girls remained silent. Finally, Ana spoke up. "I agree with Courtney. Good job, Courtney. You made me feel better already." The others murmured agreement. A smile slowly spread over Courtney's face.

"Yes, good job, Courtney," Coach Walker chimed in. "I think you described our mission perfectly. I'd say you were even eloquent."

Courtney's cheeks turned pink. "Thank you. I gave it a lot of thought."

"And you had another thought," Walker said. "About Gretchen."

Gretchen stiffened at the sound of her name. Why was Courtney thinking about Gretchen? She knew Courtney wasn't her friend. Courtney was Devra's friend. She and Gretchen had never said a kind word to one another.

Courtney cleared her throat, her eyes on Gretchen. "Well, I just thought we should do something different for the crowd Friday night, something special. I mean, if we do something totally awesome, we can really get them shouting."

"Tell them your idea," Coach Walker said.

"Coach Walker and I were watching your highlight video," Courtney said, turning to Gretchen. "From your old school. And we both totally couldn't believe your Double Flying Somersault. Has anyone else here seen it?"

To Gretchen's surprise, Devra raised her hand.

Why was Devra watching my highlight reel?

"Well . . ." Courtney continued, "You flew up so high, it was totally amazing, Gretchen."

"You have to jump pretty high to do a double," Gretchen said.

"Well, Coach and I thought you could do it Friday at the game and . . . just blow everyone away. I mean, it could be so awesome."

Gretchen glimpsed a look of disgust on Devra's face.

"What do you think?" Coach Walker asked Gretchen.

Gretchen felt her face turning red. She hated the fact that she blushed so easily. But having all eyes suddenly on her got her heart pumping. "I have a better idea," she said. "Why don't I teach it to someone else, and we can *both* do it Friday night? That would be even more spectacular, right?"

Walker shook her head. "Nice thought, but I don't think we have time. The only time we have to practice it is after eighth period tomorrow."

Gretchen hesitated. "Well . . ."

"You'll have time to teach it to the others before the state tournament," Walker suggested. "We could really wow the judges."

"I guess I can do it Friday night," Gretchen said, still thinking hard about it. "But I need a really strong catcher. I come down really fast, and the timing has to be perfect."

Courtney shook her head. "Too bad. That's a problem. Stacy was our best catcher."

Silence.

Then: "Devra, do you think *you* could catch Gretchen?" Coach Walker asked.

Gretchen gasped. *Coach Walker—what are you trying to do? KILL me?*

30.

Where are we going?" Gretchen fiddled with the cigarette lighter on the dashboard. Sid's Pontiac was so old, it had a cigarette lighter. And a cassette player.

"Just driving around," Sid answered, slowing for a stop sign. He had one hand on the wheel, one hand on her thigh.

"Let go of me," Gretchen said, gently removing his hand. "Watch where you're going."

Sid turned onto Park Drive. He had waited for her after the cheerleader meeting and suggested they take a drive.

The late afternoon sun was slipping behind the trees, sending rays of shimmering red through the nearly bare branches. "Finish your story," he demanded. "Walker asked Devra to catch you. And what did Devra say?"

Gretchen snickered. "She said no. You could have knocked me over. She had this perfect opportunity to drop me on my head, and she turned it down."

"Weird," Sid murmured.

"She said she hurt her shoulder at her tennis lesson, and she didn't think she could do it," Gretchen told him. She slumped in the seat, the scratchy seat cover rubbing her back, and lifted her knees to the dashboard.

"Weird," Sid repeated. He made a whistling sound through his lips. "Maybe she has something worse planned for you."

"Worse than dropping me on my head?"

"Maybe she's waiting for the cheerleader retreat."

"Maybe," Gretchen said in a whisper.

He followed the sloping curve of the road, picking up speed, passing a slow-moving SUV filled with little kids.

"So you're not going to do your famous Double Somersault?"

"No, I'm doing it. Shannon said she'd catch me. She's been working out, working on her upper body strength for gymnastics."

"Shannon is awesome," Sid murmured, eyes crinkling as a smile crossed his face.

"Shut up," Gretchen said, giving him a slap on the arm. "She seems nice. I don't really know her. She and Becka sort of hang by themselves."

Gretchen gasped as Sid swerved hard. She saw the dog running in the road, a large German shepherd. Sid had swerved to miss it.

"That dog is lost," she said. "Look. It doesn't have a collar."

"Almost hit it," Sid said. "It's as big as a deer."

"Where are we going?" Gretchen asked, still breathless.

"I thought we'd park up at River Ridge." He grinned at her, moving his eyebrows up and down.

"I don't think so," she said. "Mom is expecting me for dinner. And I have homework since school is starting up again. Did you forget homework?"

"What's for dinner?" Sid asked. "Maybe I'll join you."

"You're not invited." She hit him again. "Hey, how come we never go to your house?"

His grin faded instantly. "We can't," he said softly, eyes narrowing on the curving road ahead of them. "My dad is always there, and he's a beast most of the time."

Gretchen laughed. "He's a beast?"

"Not funny." Sid's hard expression didn't change. "Ever since he lost his job, he takes it out on me and Mom."

"When did he lose his job?" Gretchen asked. "What does he do?"

"Don't go there," Sid said, his jaw tight. "I don't want to talk about it."

"No. Really."

"I don't want to talk about it." He slammed his shoe on the gas pedal, and the old Pontiac roared and lurched, and then shot forward, up the River Road.

Confused, Gretchen turned away from him. She gazed out the window, at the darkening waters of the

Conononka River below as the sun disappeared behind the tall pine trees.

Okay. He doesn't want to talk about it. Fine.

But he doesn't have to bite my head off.

Their first angry words. And she had no idea why he was angry.

"My mom is kind of a beast, too," she said, still turned to the window. "I mean, I'd invite you to dinner, but you wouldn't like her at all."

Sid didn't reply.

"She's totally negative." Gretchen continued anyway. "A total downer. All the time. She never says anything cheerful or encouraging. Always just puts me down and tries to make me feel small."

"Bad news," Sid murmured.

"I really have to get home," Gretchen said, turning back to him. "I'm sorry if I said something to get you angry, but—"

"No worries," he said. He forced a smile. "It's just my dad is kind of a bad subject right now. I'm . . . uh . . . well, I'm trying to work things out, you know?"

"Okay."

The River Road widened to two lanes. Sid waited for a truck to rumble past. Then he made a wide U-turn and started back the way they had come.

Gretchen squeezed his hand, eager to pull him out of his sudden black mood. "One good thing about the halftime show," she said. "No fire batons. You won't have to worry about a kerosene bucket and all that."

He nodded. "Yeah. Guess my job is easier now." He turned his eyes to her. "That reminds me. I was at the hospital. Some good news. Stacy has the use of her right hand back."

Gretchen swallowed. "You mean—"

"They thought maybe she'd never be able to use it," Sid said, turning back to the winding road in front of them. "But she can move her fingers now. It should be okay."

"I didn't know—"

"You should go visit her," Sid said. "You're the only girl on the squad who hasn't been to the hospital."

"I'm the only girl who set her on fire," Gretchen said, her stomach suddenly heavy with dread. "No way she wants to see me. I'm sure she blames me. I couldn't go there, Sid. I couldn't—"

"She knows it was an accident," he said.

Gretchen shook her head. "No. I can't do it. I can't visit her. First I set her on fire. Then I stole her boyfriend." She leaned forward in the seat. "Have you told Stacy about us?"

"Not yet," Sid answered quickly. "It isn't the right time. She's concentrating so hard on getting better. I don't want to do anything to spoil it."

I'll bet Courtney told her, Gretchen thought.

Sid turned the car onto Fear Street. The old trees arching over the road made it suddenly seem dark as night. High on their wide lawns, the big houses rolled past. The shrill screech of a cat somewhere nearby sounded over the rumble of the car engine.

Sid pulled to the curb in front of Gretchen's house. He turned in his seat and squeezed her hand. "I was serious about Devra planning something for you at the cheerleader retreat," he said, dark eyes exploring her face. "Maybe you shouldn't go to the retreat."

Gretchen shook her head. "I *have* to go," she said. "I really don't have a choice."

"But if she's killed once . . ." Sid started.

Gretchen raised a hand to silence him. "First I have to survive my Double Somersault," she said.

31.

Gretchen tugged down the sleeves of her maroon-and-white uniform sweater as she trotted after the other girls into the stadium. The lights cut through the thin layer of fog that had washed in earlier that evening. *The stadium appears as bright as a dream,* she thought.

The two teams were warming up at opposite ends of the field. A Tigers player let a long pass sail over his head, and the ball bounced in front of Gretchen. Without breaking stride, she kicked it back onto the field.

That brought her a few cheers from the stands. She turned and saw that the home seats were only about two-thirds filled, a smaller crowd than usual.

"Some of the parents were protesting," a voice said in her ear. Gretchen turned to see Coach Walker trotting beside her. Their shoes crunched on the gravel of the running track that circled the field. "A few parents believed it was too soon after Madison's death. They wanted us to cancel the game."

Gretchen's eyes swept the empty seats. "I guess some people stayed away."

"Maybe the weather kept them away," Walker said. "This fog. And it's cold for October."

The cheerleaders formed a line in front of the stands and began to perform a warm-up cheer.

> *"Give me a T*
> *Give me an I*
> *Give m a G*
> *Give me an E*
> *Give me an R!*
> *What does that spell?*
> *What does that spell?*
> *It spells ROOOOOAAAAAAR!*
> *Go, Tigers!"*

Mild applause. A few shouts. People were still arriving. In the bleachers to the right, the Shadyside High band started to play a march that Gretchen didn't recognize. The sound was muffled by the fog. The stadium lights appeared to flicker, but Gretchen saw that was caused by shadows from the fog.

Everything seems unreal tonight. Everything is just a little bit weird.

A hand grabbed her shoulder. Coach Walker pulled her aside. "Tell me about your practice this afternoon." She shouted over the tinny blare of the band. "Do you think you're ready to do the Double Somersault?"

"Ready as I'll ever be," Gretchen joked.

"Seriously," Walker said. "Do you think Becka and Shannon can handle it? Be honest, Gretchen. Are you confident? If you're not up to it, we can postpone it. Do it later in the year."

Gretchen nodded. "We practiced for an hour. They're both pretty strong. They give me a good hard boost to send me up, and Shannon didn't have any trouble catching me as I landed."

The band ended the march and began a brassy version of "Beat It," the Michael Jackson song. Gretchen watched Sid handing out maroon-and-white pom-poms to the other girls.

"You landed on your feet every time?" Coach Walker demanded.

Gretchen nodded again. "Shannon had to straighten me out a few times. She was very good."

"Okay." Walker patted Gretchen's shoulder. "Do it. It will be a big boost for everyone, I think. But, listen . . ." She brought her face close to Gretchen's. "If you feel anything is wrong at all, don't try for the double. Just do a single. That will be spectacular enough. Okay?"

"Okay," Gretchen agreed. She could see the concern

on Walker's face. Two tragedies in the school this fall were more than enough. The coach obviously didn't want Gretchen to become another.

The cheerleaders were doing another welcome cheer. Gretchen ran to Sid to get her pom-poms. He flashed her a thumbs-up. "Everything good?"

"So far," she said. "Practice was good. I feel good."

He looked around. "Do you believe this fog? Where did it come from?"

Gretchen turned and saw Devra watching her, pom-poms pressed to her waist, eyes narrowed, her expression hard. Devra's red hair had come loose and was blowing wildly around her head. She pushed it down and, with a final glance at Gretchen, turned back to the stands.

Gretchen hurried to join the line of cheerleaders. The game was about to begin, but the stands were still about a third empty. The lights overhead suddenly appeared brighter. Everything snapped into focus. She realized the fog had lifted.

Right in time for the game.

Whistles blew. The two teams broke their huddles on the field and began to line up.

"We're the Tigers and we like to roar!
We're the Tigers and we like to score!
What do we want? More!
What do we do? SCORE!
Go, Tigers!"

The first half flew by. Gretchen concentrated on the cheers and sideline routines. She concentrated on being a teammate. She forced thoughts of her Double Somersault from her mind.

Leaping high with the other girls, shouting, urging the crowd to cheer—it gave her a strong feeling of confidence she didn't normally feel. That was one reason she loved cheerleading. She became someone else. Her doubts and negative feelings and worries disappeared.

She was an athlete. A performer. A member of a team.

Her good feeling lasted until halftime.

32.

A light drizzle had started to fall. Ponchos and rain gear appeared in the stands. A few people headed for the parking lot, but the score was tied 14–14, so most people stayed.

The Tigers marching band took the field with their *Star Wars* halftime show. Gretchen had heard them practicing and wished she could watch the show. She loved the music from *Star Wars*. Two white-helmeted stormtroopers led the band into its formations.

Gretchen turned away to huddle with the other cheerleaders. Their tradition was to form a circle and hold hands before their halftime routine. Beside Gretchen, Ana was trembling. "So cold," she murmured, brushing raindrops off her forehead.

"We'll warm up once we start our routines," Gretchen told her.

"Showtime, everyone," Coach Walker called, as the

band marched off the field, following the stormtroopers back to the bleachers.

The cheerleaders ran in front of the stands, cheering and shouting. Gretchen took her place in the center of the line. She could feel excitement making her blood pulse. A surge of energy shot through her body.

This is what I love.

She was halfway through the first cheer when she spotted Shannon at the far end of the line. *Whoa. Wait a minute.*

Becka stood at Gretchen's left, doing her arm motions as she shouted the cheer. Shannon was supposed to be at Gretchen's right. Had she forgotten her role in Gretchen's Double Somersault?

They began the new rap cheer that they had practiced earlier in the week. The crowd quieted for this one. Maybe because it was new.

Gretchen nearly lost her place when she saw who stood at her right. Devra? Why was Devra in Shannon's spot?

The rap cheer ended and applause echoed down the rows of benches. Despite the cold drizzle, the crowd was warming up.

Gretchen turned to Devra. "I have to do my somersault now," she said. She meant for Devra to move away so Shannon could take the spot.

But Devra nodded. "Okay."

Gretchen started to protest. "Shannon—"

"Hurt her ankle," Devra interrupted. "I said I could catch you. No problem."

No problem?

Gretchen shuddered. She saw Shannon jumping up and down at the end of the line. Her ankle didn't appear to be hurt.

"Ready, Gretchen?" Coach Walker shouted from the sidelines.

"Ready, Gretchen?" Devra repeated, a cold smile on her face.

Gretchen felt a wave of panic rise up her body. Her muscles tightened. She knew what Devra planned. Devra planned to drop her on her head.

What had Devra said to Shannon? Had she threatened her? Bribed her? A gift certificate at Dalby's Department Store? How had she persuaded Shannon to step aside so that Devra could injure Gretchen?

She'll make it look like a terrible accident. No one will believe she dropped me deliberately.

I can't do this. I have to say no.

But she saw Coach Walker staring at her. The crowd had lost interest. People had turned away from the field, talking and laughing, slapping their hands together to keep warm.

Gretchen flashed a questioning look at Becka. Becka shrugged in reply.

I guess I have to do this. I promised Coach Walker.

But will Devra catch me?

Gretchen shut her eyes and took a deep breath. She nodded to the other cheerleaders. She decided she had no choice. They began the cheer.

Tigers ROAR
Bisons WEEP!
Tigers SOAR
*TIGERS **LEAP**!*

At the shouted word *leap,* Becka and Devra gave Gretchen a high boost. Arms straight up, she jumped off their hands and went flying into the air. No thinking now. No time to think. Her muscles did the thinking. Her muscles knew the routine.

And now she appeared to float for a few seconds. High above them. And then she was leaning forward. Head down. One somersault. Two. Two breathless somersaults. With no thinking. No time. No time. Flashes of color. A pounding heartbeat. No time to breathe or think.

Defying gravity, her body flipped once. Twice.

And then she came down, screaming all the way.

33.

Devra caught Gretchen, wrapping her arms around her waist. Gretchen landed hard, her knees bending as her shoes hit the ground. It took a few seconds to gain her balance. Then she ran to the sidelines, following the other girls. Her heart was pumping in her ears, too loud to hear the shouts and applause of the crowd.

Coach Walker slapped Gretchen on the back as she ran past. "Perfect!" she cried. "A perfect ten!"

A wave of nausea rolled over Gretchen. She held her breath, forcing it down. The stadium lights flashed in her eyes. Her blood pulsed in her ears, refused to fade.

I did it.

"Why did you scream like that?" Devra demanded, one hand on Gretchen's shoulder. "What was *that* about?"

You know what it was about. You attacked me in the gym that night in the dark—and you deliberately tried to terrify me tonight.

That's what Gretchen wanted to say.

Instead, she shrugged. "Just wanted to make it more exciting," she said.

Devra's eyes burned into hers. Devra had a strange smile on her face. A smile of triumph, Gretchen guessed.

She scared me without hurting me. That smile says this won't be the end of it. She has something planned for me. She's waiting for the retreat.

"So you can't come over?" Gretchen pressed the phone to her ear. "I know it's late, Sid. But I can't get to sleep. The adrenaline rush from the game. You know."

She glimpsed the old-fashioned-looking wooden clock on the bookshelf. Twelve-fifteen. She curled her bare feet under her, sitting sideways on the big leather armchair in the den.

Sid's voice sounded tired, hoarse. "Is your mom home?"

Gretchen snickered. "Why do you care?" She didn't give him time to answer. "Actually, Mom is out on a date. Some guy she met at the Pick-N-Pay. Seriously. I think she picked him up."

"Is your mom hot?" Sid asked.

Gretchen's mouth dropped open. "Never thought about it. I guess she's okay. She's got a good body, for forty-five. I mean, she's thin, you know. And she's got great hair. But her expression is always so droopy. Her face is like, Keep Away from Me or You'll Be Sorry."

"Maybe you know her too well," Sid said.

That didn't make a lot of sense to Gretchen. "Yeah. Maybe. Maybe they're hooking up and she won't even be home tonight. Ha. That's a laugh."

"My dad is yelling at me to get off the phone," Sid said. "Can you hear him? He keeps shouting at me, 'Don't you know what time it is?'"

"Well, okay. Bye." Gretchen started to end the call. Then she remembered. "But you're coming over to help me tomorrow, right?"

A brief silence. Then: "Oh. Right. Clean your garage. Did I really say yes to that? Yeah. Okay."

"Well, don't sound so enthusiastic," Gretchen said. "You *said* you'd come over and help."

"Did I promise, or did I just say?" Sid replied.

"Shut up."

He laughed. "I'll be there. Do I get to meet your mom? I hear she's hot."

"Shut up again, Sid. You're getting annoying."

Sid showed up at Gretchen's house a little after one thirty on Saturday afternoon, dressed in faded jeans torn at both knees and an oversized gray sweatshirt, ready for garage cleanup duty.

Mrs. Page behaved very well. She didn't embarrass Gretchen as she usually did in front of her friends. Gretchen chalked it up to her mom's being tired after her date.

Mrs. Page did make a comment about how dumb you have to be to buy jeans that are already ripped. And she did tell Sid, "I'm glad you're helping with the cleanup because Gretchen is a total slob. Maybe she won't be so lazy with you around."

That was pretty good behavior for her, Gretchen thought.

"Mr. Simkin left us a mess in there," Mrs. Page said. "He was supposed to clean the garage out before we moved in, but he didn't. Feel free to throw everything out." She pointed out the kitchen window. "See? I rented a dumpster for all the junk. Just toss everything that's not worth keeping in there."

"Think there's anything valuable in there?" Sid asked.

She rolled her eyes. "Mr. Simkin showed us his collection of bottle caps. I think that was the most valuable thing he had."

She squinted at Sid over her coffee cup, as if seeing him for the first time. "What are *your* favorite subjects in school?"

Sid shrugged. "The usual."

"Are you going to college?"

"Probably," Sid replied.

She tapped a fingernail against the coffee cup. "Like one-word answers?"

"Yes," he said.

Mrs. Page didn't laugh. She made a shooing motion with her free hand. "There's stacks of old rusted tools in there. Try not to injure yourselves. No open wounds. I don't have insurance yet."

"That's cheery, Mom," Gretchen said. She led the way out the back door to the garage.

Sid banged a rhythm on the side of the big metal dumpster in the driveway. "Your mom is funny," he said.

"Ha-ha."

They stopped in the open doorway of the garage and peered inside. It was a two-car garage, concrete walls, a small dust-covered window on one side letting a square of pale afternoon sunlight wash in.

Gretchen's eyes swept over a long, coiled garden hose, rakes and brooms, a hand lawn mower, a big unopened bag of fertilizer, and boxes of gardening equipment against the wall to her left. A bike with both tires missing hung on the back wall next to some kind of rubber raft and a torn kite with no string.

Gretchen pointed to a tall stack of cartons against the other wall. "Let's start with those boxes. You pull them down, and I'll go through them."

"We'll *both* go through them," Sid said, squeezing her shoulder. "That's the fun part."

Gretchen pinched her nose. "What's that sour smell?"

Sid sniffed a few times. "Maybe a dead mouse behind the cartons. Or a dead raccoon or something."

"Oh, yuck."

Sid snickered. "This is Fear Street, remember? Could be a rotting corpse!"

"You're not funny," Gretchen said, trying not to inhale. "What's the big fuss about Fear Street, anyway?"

Sid hoisted a large cardboard carton down from the top of the stack. "Hasn't anyone told you about this street? About the Fear family? All the twisted, freaky things that happen here?"

Gretchen shook her head. "You mean for real?"

"For real. I can tell you some of it later." He grinned. "But I don't want to scare you away."

"Oooh, I'm shaking!" Gretchen said sarcastically.

Working together, they pulled open the first carton. It was filled with rusted ice skates, several pairs. Sid picked up the box, carried it to the driveway, and heaved it into the dumpster with a loud crash.

The kitchen window slid open. Mrs. Page stuck her head out. "Keep it down, okay?"

"Sorry." Sid turned and trotted back to the garage.

The second carton contained ragged bath towels, many of them with large brown stains. They were neatly folded and smelled of mildew. That carton went into the dumpster. The next carton held a tall stack of *Popular Mechanics* magazines. The magazine on top was dated June, 1986.

"Too bad he didn't save comic books," Sid said. "Those could be valuable."

Gretchen wiped a smudge of dirt off her forehead with the back of one hand. Despite the coolness of the late October afternoon, it was becoming hot in the garage.

They worked steadily, pulling down cartons from

several stacks lined against the wall. It became obvious that Mr. Simkin hadn't left anything of value behind. So far, everything they looked at had ended up in the dumpster.

Gretchen checked her phone. "We've been working an hour and a half," she said. "Want to take a break?"

Sid wiped his hands on the front of his sweatshirt. "Let's just deal with this bookshelf over here." He stepped up to a wide wooden bookshelf. All the shelves were missing except for the bottom one. A stringless fishing rod lay on the shelf and several coffee cans that might have been used for bait.

Sid bent to examine the cans, then stopped. "Weird," he muttered.

"What's weird?" Gretchen stepped up behind him.

"I think I recognize this. Isn't this your backpack?"

Gretchen studied it. "Yes. Yes, it is. How'd it get out here?"

Sid bent down and lifted it from the garage floor. "It's empty," he reported. "Oh no. Wait. What *is* this?"

Gretchen stared at it in his hand. A brown glass jar. The size of a mayonnaise jar. "What is it?"

Sid let the backpack fall to the floor. He turned the jar between his hands. A printed label came into view. "Oh, wow," he murmured. His eyes went wide. "Oh, wow."

"What?" Gretchen demanded, grabbing his arm. "Let me see it. What is it?"

He turned the jar so she could read the label:

SULPHURIC ACID.

"This is what they found on Madison's violin," he said. "This is what killed Madison." His hand trembled as he brought the brown jar closer. Then he raised his eyes to Gretchen. "It's half-empty. Gretchen . . . what did you *do*?"

34.

Gretchen uttered a cry. "Huh? You don't think I killed Madison—*do* you?"

Sid didn't answer. His eyes remained on the acid jar trembling in his hand.

"I-I-I . . ." Gretchen stammered. Sid's sudden betrayal made her go speechless.

"Hidden in the garage . . . In your backpack. . . ." Sid murmured, his voice just above a whisper. He kept blinking, as if he was trying to force the bottle out of his sight.

"Well, I didn't put it there!" Gretchen screamed, finding her voice. "Don't be a jerk, Sid. You know Madison was my friend. The only friend I've made here in Shadyside. Why would I kill her? Why?"

He shook his head. "I don't know. I . . . don't understand."

Gretchen pointed a trembling finger at the jar. "Put it down. Put it down, Sid. The police will be looking for fingerprints. Now they'll find your prints all over it."

Sid dropped the jar back into the backpack. He set the backpack down carefully. "I'm sorry, but—"

"I can't believe you thought that acid was mine," Gretchen said, feeling the anger tighten her chest. She crossed her arms in front of her. "Someone put it there."

"But when did you notice your backpack was gone?"

"I . . . I don't know." *Why was he questioning her? Shouldn't he be helping her? Supporting her?*

"But if I killed Madison and had half a bottle of acid left over, I wouldn't put it there," she said. "I wouldn't put it in my backpack and hide it in the front of the garage where anyone could find it. Do you think I'm stupid?"

Sid shook his head but didn't answer. He couldn't hide his confusion. His eyebrows were knitted tightly and his eyes kept darting from side to side, as if his thoughts were overloading him.

"Trust me," Gretchen continued. "If the acid was mine, I would have dumped it in a trash can as far away from my house as you can get." She gave Sid's shoulder a shove. "Think about it. Someone put that here. Someone who wanted it to be found in my garage."

Sid swallowed. "First someone took your backpack? Then they hid it in your garage with the acid in it?"

"You don't think Devra is capable of that?" Gretchen demanded.

"Yeah . . . I guess." He shook his head. "I'm sorry, Gretchen. I didn't mean to accuse you. I was just so shocked. I lost it for a moment."

Gretchen stared at the backpack, gritting her teeth. "Devra put it there. I know she did. She knew no one would believe that I killed Madison. She put it there as a warning, Sid. Don't you see? This is a warning of what she can do."

"But you have no proof—" Sid started.

"I told you," Gretchen interrupted him. "The night before she was killed, Madison said she had something important to tell me. Something she was *desperate* to tell me. Then, before she had a chance, she was murdered."

"I know. I remember. And you think Madison was desperate to tell you something about Devra."

"I'm sure she was, Sid. And I'm sure Devra murdered her to keep her from telling what she found out."

Sid shook his head. "But there's no way to prove it. No way—"

"Yes, there is," Gretchen said. She grabbed his hand and tugged him out of the garage. "We're going to prove it. At least, *almost* prove it. Let's go." She pulled him to the car, which her mother had parked halfway up the drive.

Sid still had his face twisted in confusion. "Where are we going?"

"To Devra's house. And let's hope she isn't home."

35.

Gretchen took Park Drive through town to North Hills, the wealthy section of Shadyside where Devra lived. Sid sat tensely beside her as she lurched through Saturday afternoon traffic.

"She lives on Heather Court," Sid announced. "It's a right turn off Park. You could have taken that shortcut." He pointed out his window.

"I'm new here, remember?" Gretchen snapped. "I don't know the shortcuts. How do you know where Devra lives?"

"I've been to her house," Sid said. "Some kind of school thing. It's a total mansion. I mean, you could fit your house in their ballroom."

"Huh? They have a ballroom?"

He nodded. "They have a pool table in it. And foosball and an awesome air hockey table. It's like an enormous game room."

She stopped at a light, turned, and squinted at him suspiciously. "You know an awful lot about her house."

"I know even more," Sid said. "It's Saturday afternoon, right? Devra has horseback riding lessons every Saturday."

The traffic started to move again. "You and Devra are a lot closer than I thought," Gretchen said, only half-seriously. "How do you know about her lessons?"

"My cousin Ernie works at the stable."

As they entered North Hills, the houses were larger, the front lawns wider and deeper. Tall hedges along the street hid many houses from view.

A team of gardeners was raking the dead leaves off a lawn as they turned onto Heather Court. A group of five or six small kids, shouting and laughing, chased after a soccer ball in the yard next door.

"Do you mind telling me what we're doing?" Sid asked. "Why exactly are we going to Devra's house when we know she isn't there?"

"I hope no one is there," Gretchen said. She slowed the car as the soccer ball bounced into the street. The kids waited at the curb for her to pass before running out to retrieve it.

"It's two blocks down," Sid said. "So? What are we doing?"

"Snooping," Gretchen answered.

Sid stared at her, waiting for her to say more.

"I have an idea," she continued finally. "About the

acid. Devra said she was using acid to remove the paint on the old cabinet she wanted to give her dad. And I think she used that acid to kill Madison. And then she planted it in my garage."

"I *know* that's your theory," Sid said impatiently.

"So what if we sneak into Devra's house, find the cabinet she was working on—and there's no acid anywhere around? Wouldn't that prove that she took the acid and put it in my garage?"

"Not really," Sid said. "Maybe she used the acid and removed the paint. And when she was finished with the acid, she threw it away."

Gretchen shook her head. "People don't just throw away acid. It's too dangerous."

Sid thought about it for a while, scrunching up his face in concentration. "They have servants who could get rid of the acid. Your idea is a bit crazy, Gretchen."

"It's not crazy," Gretchen insisted. She swerved to avoid a large pothole in the street. "Listen to me. When we get there and take a look, there won't be any acid bottle. Maybe it won't *totally* prove the one in my garage was the one Devra used. But it will *almost* prove it."

"What if there *is* an acid bottle there?" Sid said, frowning. "What will that prove?"

"That I'm wrong?" Gretchen replied, slowing at an intersection. "Why are you so eager to prove me wrong? It's like you're defending Devra."

"No way," Sid insisted. "I think Devra is horrible.

Ernie says she is the worst person in the world. She orders everyone around like they're her servants and complains when they're not fast enough for her. Ernie said she isn't even nice to the horses."

Gretchen edged the car into the next block. "Which house is it?"

Sid pointed. "The one with the tall hedge and the lampposts on both sides of the driveway. Park on the street. Don't pull into the driveway."

Gretchen rolled her eyes. "Do you think I'm an idiot? *Of course* I'm not going to pull into the driveway. We don't want to be seen—remember?"

"Okay, okay." Sid swept a hand tensely through his dark hair. "And your plan is?"

"First we have to see if Devra or her father are at home."

"What about servants?" Sid said, eyes on the tall house rising at the top of the tree-dotted lawn.

"Maybe they have Saturday off," Gretchen said. She pulled the car to a stop at the edge of the neighbor's lawn and cut the engine. "We'll start in the garage. Maybe she worked on the cabinet in there."

"And if it isn't there?" Sid demanded.

"We'll have to sneak into the house," Gretchen said, reaching for the car door handle.

Sid didn't move. "We're going to sneak into the house and look for what exactly? No acid bottle?"

Gretchen nodded. "If there's no acid bottle, Devra is a murderer. Trust me. I'm right."

"I . . . don't like this," Sid said, shaking his head.

She gave him a shove. "Let's get going. Get out of the car."

"Gretchen, what do we say if we get caught?"

"We'll think of something."

36.

Gretchen led the way to the driveway. They stopped in the shadow of the tall hedge. Gretchen wrapped her hands around one of the old-fashioned-looking lamp-posts and leaned forward, peering up the wide, gravel driveway.

The house stood at the top of a sloping lawn. A line of tall evergreen trees ran along the far edge of the property. Oak trees dotted the lawn, already winter bare. The grass had been raked. A tall mound of dead leaves leaned against one side of the house.

"The house is dark," Gretchen whispered. "That's a good sign."

Sid didn't reply. He had his hands shoved into his jeans pockets. His eyes glanced all around, revealing his nervousness.

"The garage is attached to the house," Gretchen reported. She shielded her eyes with one hand. "Wow. A three-car garage. The doors are closed." She turned to Sid, who lingered at the curb. "Are you with me or not?"

"I think you're crazy," he replied. "But I'm with you."

She motioned him forward. "If we keep in the shadow of the trees, it will be hard for anyone to see us."

Sid tapped her shoulder. "You don't think Mr. Dalby has a gun—do you?"

She pushed his hand away. "Now *you're* being stupid. He's not going to shoot us. If he sees us, he'll think we're friends of Devra's."

"Friends of Devra's snooping around in the garage."

Gretchen began trotting up the gravel drive, her shoes crunching loudly. "No sign of life, Sid. There's no one home. Let's hurry."

He hesitated another few seconds. Then he followed her, his eyes darting from side to side, his clenched fists still buried deep in his jeans pockets.

A gray squirrel, its jaws bulging with nuts, stood up straight in the center of the lawn and gazed at them as they jogged past. Its tail was raised behind it, and its eyes followed them warily as they made their way to the side of the garage.

Even though it was a short distance, Gretchen found herself breathing hard as she pressed herself against the brick wall at the side. She turned and did a quick survey of the windows of the house. No lights. No movement.

Feeling a little more confident, she slid around to the front of the garage and peered into the window of the first of the three doors. "Only one car in there," she reported to Sid. "At the other end. A convertible. I think it's a Jaguar."

"Sweet," Sid murmured.

Gretchen moved to the window on the middle door and pressed her face against the glass. She cupped her hands around the sides of her head to cut the glare of the sunlight behind them.

"Do you see a cabinet?" Sid stayed by the side wall. His eyes kept darting to the house.

"No. No cabinet," Gretchen reported. "Lots of shelves with gardening tools and supplies and other stuff. All very organized and neat."

"They probably have a garage servant who dusts the garage every day," Sid joked.

"Not funny." She turned to him. "Devra didn't work on the cabinet in here. We're going to have to get into the house."

Sid nodded. His expression went blank.

"They probably have a basement workshop," Gretchen said. "I'll bet that's where Devra worked on the cabinet." Keeping against the wall, she edged toward the entryway down a short passage from the garage.

Sid shook his head. "Maybe someday I'll write a book about two people who broke into a house to see if there was no acid bottle there."

"I didn't know you like to write," Gretchen said.

"I don't," Sid replied. "But I'll have to do *something* while I'm in prison for breaking and entering."

"Sssshh." Gretchen stepped down the five or six concrete steps that led to the door. She peered into the window. "Hey, this door leads right into the basement. We don't even have to go upstairs."

"Awesome," Sid whispered, brightening. "If we're real quiet . . ."

Gretchen tried the door knob. She turned it and pulled, and the door slid open. "Not locked. Come on. We got a break."

Sid took one last look around the backyard and side of the house. Then he slipped through the doorway after Gretchen.

"I don't hear any burglar alarm," Gretchen whispered. "Maybe we're okay."

They found themselves in a small, carpeted room. Gretchen saw a long counter obviously used as a desk, a laptop and printer, a small armchair, and a low vinyl couch. A tall bookshelf filled one wall. A framed photo of the Eiffel Tower in Paris was hung over the desk beside a wall calendar.

"It's like a little office," Gretchen said. She motioned for Sid to follow her as she stepped through a narrow, open doorway.

Gym equipment filled the next room. Gretchen saw a StairMaster machine, a stationary bike, an elliptical machine, a treadmill, several weights stacked on a shelf against the wall. A flatscreen TV was suspended on the wall facing the exercise machines.

"Wow. They've got *everything*," Sid whispered. "And it's just Devra and her dad?"

Gretchen didn't answer. She had her eyes on the low ceiling. She listened for footsteps or any other sounds above them, signs that someone was home.

Silence.

They both crept through the doorway on the far end of the gym. Orange sunlight through windows up at ground level revealed that this was the part that looked like a basement. No carpeting here. A massive furnace took up nearly half the room. Pipes and cables and rolls of insulation material, wooden crates, old furniture covered in bedsheets.

"I knew it. A workshop," Gretchen said, pointing. A long workbench stood against one wall with wooden shelves above it, a huge metal vice attached to one end. As she moved toward it, she saw a large power saw resting on a separate table. Small chunks of wood sat in a puddle of sawdust, littering the floor.

"There it is," Sid whispered, grabbing her shoulder. "You were right. That has to be the cabinet."

Gretchen followed his gaze. There it was, a small wooden cabinet with six drawers across the front. It was about the size of a bed table. Each drawer had a brass knob in its center, newly polished. The top was framed by a carved wooden design that looked a little like ocean waves.

"She removed all the paint," Gretchen said. "Look.

She's already started to stain the cabinet with some kind of dark stain." Her eyes went to the shelves above the workbench. "So where's the acid she used to remove the paint?"

Sid stepped up to the workbench. He gazed at the shelves filled with tools and supplies. A large can of wood stain stood at the edge of the workbench, a paint-brush beside it.

"I don't see it," Gretchen said, turning and searching for another table that might hold the supplies Devra used. "Nope. No acid bottle. I think I was right, Sid. I think the acid she used is in my garage."

"You're wrong," Sid said. He reached onto the high-est shelf and pulled something down. He turned and showed it to her.

Gretchen gasped. An orange bottle, a little larger than the one in her garage. She squinted hard at it. "Is it—?"

"It's an acid bottle," Sid said. "And it's almost empty. You were wrong, Gretchen. This is what Devra used. The acid in your garage—"

"Let me see it." She grabbed the bottle from his hand. She turned it so she could read the label. She raised it closer to her face and read the label out loud. "Muriatic Acid."

She and Sid stared at each other.

"What's Muriatic acid?" Gretchen whispered.

Sid shrugged.

Gretchen fumbled in her pocket and pulled out her

phone. Her fingers trembled as she brought up the Google app and typed in Muriatic Acid.

"It's an acid used to remove paint," she read it to Sid. "It's usually used to remove paint from cars. But it also works on furniture."

Her shoulders slumped. She suddenly felt as if she was deflating, like a balloon emptying out. "Oh, wow."

Sid placed the bottle of acid back on the shelf. "Have we proved anything here?"

Gretchen shook her head. "I don't think so. I . . . I don't know *what* to think, Sid. Now I'm totally confused. The acid in my garage . . . sulfuric acid. . . . That's the acid that killed Madison. And . . . and . . ."

They both heard the car door slam. They froze and listened. The hum of a garage door lowering itself. And then . . . the thud and bump of the basement door being pushed open.

Soft footsteps.

Gretchen gasped. "We're caught."

37.

While Gretchen and Sid were sneaking into the Dalby basement, Devra Dalby was across town, at Shadyside General Hospital. She came to visit her cheerleader friend Stacy. She had come straight from the stables and made quite an image and she walked in wearing her expensive riding outfit.

She arrived to the wail of ambulance sirens and the tense shouts of orderlies in pale green scrubs, who were rushing to the parking lot. The flashing blue-and-red lights reflected in her windshield as she maneuvered her Acura around the cluster of ambulances.

Devra slowed to let a wheeled stretcher go past. She slid down the window. "What happened?"

"Collision on Division Street," a young nurse answered, running beside the stretcher. "Three cars."

The entrance to the main parking lot was blocked, so Devra made her way to the lot in back of the big red-brick building. *Why do they have to block the entire lot?*

Why can't they park the ambulances by the emergency room door?

Devra always felt tense, jumpy, after a horseback riding session. The adrenaline rush stayed with her a long time. Horses, she felt, were smelly and stupid. But the rush of taking them from a trot to a full gallop was *outstanding*.

Mopping perspiration from her forehead with a tissue, she climbed out of the car. *I probably smell like a horse, but Stacy won't care. I'm sure she's bored to tears in there, desperate for visitors.*

The sirens had cut off, but the red-and-blue lights continued to flash. A hush fell over the parking lot as the hospital crew hurried to unload the injured from the ambulances.

Devra turned her head away as she walked. She didn't want to see any injured people. She took a certain pride in avoiding ugly things. Sure, she was squeamish, but wasn't that a good quality? Didn't that mean she was especially sensitive?

She stepped into the crowded reception area of the hospital and fumbled in her bag for her sunglasses. Why did the lighting in hospitals have to be so harsh? Wouldn't it be more comforting to patients to have the lights dim?

The woman in the reception booth was on the phone. Devra snickered. The woman was so fat, she nearly filled the whole booth. She ignored Devra, kept her eyes down as she talked.

Devra tapped her fingernails impatiently on the desktop. "Excuse me. I think you're supposed to help people."

The woman lowered her phone and glared at Devra. "I *am* helping someone."

Devra ignored her reply. "I need the room number of Stacy Grande. If it isn't too much trouble."

Muttering under her breath, the woman found the room number for Devra.

After an endless wait for an elevator, Devra found herself at the doorway to Stacy's room. She peeked in and saw that Courtney was already there, seated on a folding chair beside Stacy's bed.

Courtney jumped to her feet. "Devra! You're here!" She motioned with both hands. "Come see how great Stacy looks."

Devra stepped into the room and turned to Stacy in her bed. She didn't look great. She looked pale and thin, her hair a tangled mess, and tubes in both arms, heavy bandages over both arms and her hands.

"Hey," Devra said weakly, feeling her stomach lurch. "Stacy . . . How's it going?"

"Not so bad," Stacy said.

She's always so bright and perky. Even in a hospital bed covered in bandages.

"I'd hug you," Devra said, "But I don't think I can."

Stacy sighed. "The only hugs I get are when the nurses come to lift me out of bed."

"It's a cheerleader reunion," Courtney said, grinning at Devra. "We could have a spirit rally right here."

"Go, Tigers," Stacy said. Her voice was muffled. She didn't appear to Devra to have much strength.

"Someone should bring you some blusher or something," Devra blurted out.

Stacy blinked. "Am I *that* pale?"

Courtney laughed. "Devra, you're always so tactful." She pulled a folding chair to the other side of Stacy's bed and motioned for Devra to sit down.

"I can't stay long," Devra said. "I just came from the stable, and I'm a smelly mess." She dropped into the chair and gently wrapped a hand around Stacy's bandaged wrist. "So? What's the report?"

"I've got full movement in my hands," Stacy answered. "That's the good news. And the bad news? My chest is taking a long time to heal. The burn wounds are still pretty bad."

"Before you came we were just talking about how she's lucky in one way," Courtney said.

Devra squinted at Stacy. "Lucky?"

"Yes. The flames didn't reach my face. My face isn't burned or scarred at all."

Devra nodded. "You're right. That part is lucky." She leaned closer to Stacy. "I just feel so bad. Guilty."

Stacy blinked. "Guilty?"

"Well . . . I was supposed to take that fire baton,"

Devra said. "If I didn't suddenly have that stomach cramp, it would have been me. Not you."

"Well you can't feel guilty about *that*," Courtney chimed in. "You had no way of knowing."

Devra suddenly felt eager to change the subject. She had said what she came to say. Now she'd really like to get out of there. The hospital smell was making her nauseous. And she really didn't want to think about what Stacy's arms and chest looked like under all those bandages.

"Are your parents around?" she asked.

Stacy shook her head. "No. They were here this morning. But now they're at a lawyer's."

"Lawyers?"

"They're going to sue the school," Stacy said. "The lawyer thinks we can collect damages. If we sue them for negligence, I guess."

Devra shook her head. "Your parents should sue Gretchen Page. She's the one who was negligent."

"What's up with Gretchen?" Stacy asked. "She's the only one on the squad who hasn't come to visit me."

"Probably feels guilty," Courtney said.

"She *is* guilty," Devra said heatedly. "She did this to you, Stacy. Of course, I was supposed to go first. So I guess she wanted to burn *me*."

Stacy gasped. "You can't think it was deliberate, Devra. No way. It was a total accident. I'm sure of it."

"Why are you sure of it?" Devra demanded.

Stacy opened her mouth but didn't reply.

"Gretchen was so desperate to be on the squad," Devra continued. "She felt that I cheated her out of her place. So . . . if she handed me a baton soaked in kerosene, she could accomplish two things. Get rid of me and get her place on the squad."

"That's crazy," Courtney chimed in. "I'm sorry, Devra. I don't like Gretchen, either. But *no one* would try to burn someone up just to get on a cheerleader squad. No way. No way."

"She'd have to be a total psycho," Stacy said.

Devra jumped to her feet. "Well, who says she isn't? Who says she isn't a total psycho? Let's talk about Madison Grossman. Madison tried to be Gretchen's friend. As far as I know, she was Gretchen's only friend. And she ends up with acid burning through her neck and killing her."

Devra was breathless now, her voice high and shrill. She gave her red hair a violent toss behind her shoulders. "You get doused in kerosene and Madison is murdered with acid. You don't think there's a connection? The connection is Gretchen. Do you seriously think I'm just being paranoid?"

"Yes," both girls answered at once.

"Yes, you're being paranoid," Stacy said. "You have no reason to accuse Gretchen . . . no reason at all."

Devra's face was bright red and she was breathing hard, her chest heaving. "I have a real problem with Gretchen Page," she said, lowering her voice to a whisper. "I have to deal with Gretchen. I just haven't figured out how."

38.

Trapped in Devra's basement, Gretchen and Sid froze in panic. They heard the basement door click shut and the soft thud of approaching footsteps.

Gretchen turned to Sid. They both stood still, their bodies locked tight, waiting for their brains to unfreeze.

Nowhere to hide.

Sid dropped to his knees and squeezed under the worktable. But he was still in plain sight. Gretchen looked one way, then the other. The basement became a blur of grays and dark browns in her eyes.

The footsteps grew louder. Heavier.

This was stupid. We shouldn't be here. I didn't even prove anything about the acid.

Finally she dove behind Devra's wooden cabinet and dropped to her knees. She knew she was only half-hidden. But there was nowhere else. . . .

And then there he was, entering from the gym

doorway. A tall man in a dark suit, white shirt open at the collar. Gretchen could see him so clearly . . . *too* clearly. It meant he could see her.

If he turned to the left, he would see both her and Sid.

Her nose suddenly itched. *Oh no. Don't sneeze. This isn't a sitcom. This isn't a comedy. This is serious trouble. Don't sneeze.*

The man carried a black briefcase in one hand. He took long strides across the concrete basement floor. He had wavy dark hair, balding in front. A short mustache. Dark eyes behind owlish glasses.

He's so close to me now. He could almost reach out and touch me.

Devra's dad. It has to be Mr. Dalby.

He had been walking quickly toward the stairs that led to the first floor. But now he stopped.

Gretchen's heart stopped, too.

He senses something. Why did he stop? He knows someone is here. He can feel *it.*

Her panic was almost too much to bear. She almost let out a frightened scream.

We're caught. Caught. And no way to explain why we are here.

She had been holding her breath, struggling to hold back her sneeze. But now her chest felt about to burst.

And then a voice from the gym doorway. "Dad? Are you home? I saw your car."

Mr. Dalby spun around as Devra came walking into the basement. "I just got home," he said. "Where've you been?"

"It's Saturday, Dad. What do I do every Saturday?"

"Oh. Right. You were at the stable."

"Then I went to visit Stacy at the hospital."

He slid an arm around her shoulder, and they began to walk side by side to the stairs. Past Gretchen and Sid. Past them without seeing them.

"How is Stacy doing?" Mr. Dalby asked.

"She looks terrible" Devra said. "But everyone tells her she's doing really well."

"Such a tragedy," her dad murmured. "A tragedy."

"I guess she'll be okay eventually," Devra said. "She'll just have to cover up her arms for the rest of her life. And forget about wearing a bikini."

They disappeared up the stairs.

Gretchen and Sid didn't move. They didn't speak.

The upstairs door closed with a soft click. They could hear footsteps on the ceiling above them. They still didn't move.

Finally, Gretchen pulled herself upright behind the cabinet. "A close one," she whispered. Her whole body shuddered. Her skin tingled with lingering fear.

Sid scrambled out from under the workbench. "We're not out of here yet," he whispered.

Gretchen motioned for him to follow her. They both began to tiptoe toward the door to the garage. They were almost to the gym when a voice shouted, "HEY—WAIT!"

39.

A low cry escaped Gretchen's throat. She felt her knees start to fold. Sid grabbed her arm, his eyes wide with fright.

"Wait—" Devra's voice from the top of the stairs. "Dad, I left all my riding gear in the car. I'll be right back." She started down the steps.

Now we're trapped, Gretchen thought. *Now we're definitely doomed.*

"Get it later," Gretchen heard Mr. Dalby shout. "Come here. I want to show you something."

Gretchen held her breath until Devra had vanished from the stairway. "I guess that's what you call a close one," she whispered to Sid. She and Sid lurched out of the house and, keeping in the shadows as best they could, made their way, still shaking, still breathless, to her car.

"Did you pack any bug spray?" Mrs. Page asked, eyeing Gretchen's travel bag.

Gretchen rolled her eyes. "Mom, it's almost November, remember? I don't think bugs are going to be a problem."

"Spiders live into the winter," her mom said. "Especially in those camp cabins. They're probably infested with spiders."

"Well, thanks for giving me something to worry about once again," Gretchen said sarcastically. "I promise I won't go barefoot, okay?" She lifted the bag and started to the front door. The bag was heavier than she thought.

"Aren't you going to mention snakes?" Gretchen said. "The cabins are probably infested with snakes, too. There are probably snakes in every bed."

"You're so funny," Mrs. Page said, frowning. "Why do you get so much pleasure out of making fun of me?"

"Because it's so easy?"

"Any time I show a little concern, Gretchen, you ridicule me. Shouldn't you think about that?"

Gretchen set the bag down. "You don't show concern, Mom. You just try to create anxiety. You either try to put me down, or you tell me why I shouldn't do something I want to do. Shouldn't you think about *that*?"

Mrs. Page shook her head hard, as if shaking off Gretchen's words. "I don't understand why you have a cheerleader retreat in the middle of the school year. Especially with all the horrible things that have happened."

"I guess it's kind of for healing," Gretchen answered.

"Coach Walker thought we should keep the retreat, and spend some time together. Time to talk about things and just . . . get our heads together. And, I guess we'll concentrate on some new routines."

Mrs. Page didn't seem to hear her. "Did you remember to pack a hat?"

"Yes, Mom."

"I know it's not summer, but the sun is still strong. And with your fair skin—"

"I probably won't be able to call," Gretchen said. "Coach Walker warned us that there's practically no cell service in the woods, and the camp doesn't have WiFi."

"What if I need to reach you?"

Gretchen shrugged. "It's only four days."

"But . . . what if there's an emergency? I'm sure the school has made a plan for communicating in case there's some kind of emergency in the woods."

Gretchen uttered a disgusted groan. "See? There you go again. Worrying about nothing. Creating anxiety."

She suddenly pictured Devra.

Maybe I should be worried. Maybe Devra does have a plan for me, a plan to create an emergency.

A shiver of fear ran down her body. She hoped her mother couldn't see it. She never wanted her mother to see her being the tiniest bit fearful. That would give her mom too big a victory.

A horn honked out at the street.

"I've got to go," Gretchen said. "That's the bus that's

taking us to the campground." She set down her bag to open the front door.

Mrs. Page stepped up behind her. "Don't I at least get a hug? I won't see you for four days."

Gretchen turned and obediently hugged her mother. She felt a stab of emotion. Her mother was a difficult person. No. An impossible person. But Gretchen realized she still loved her. She still needed her.

"Have a good time, dear," Mrs. Page said, forcing a smile.

"I'll try," Gretchen said. And she carried her bag out the front door.

Mrs. Page carried her coffee mug into the den and sat down on the couch. *The Today Show* was on the TV, and they were showing a wildfire somewhere in California. She had the sound turned low. The TV was just a background blur to her thoughts.

The coffee was strong and bitter, the way she liked it. She found herself thinking about her ex-husband, Gretchen's father. She could never have strong coffee when he was around. It gave him heartburn, he said. *Now I can make it as strong as I like.* One of the advantages of being divorced.

Of course, one of the *disadvantages* was having to deal on her own with a teenage daughter. Gretchen had become so sarcastic and bitter. The move to Shadyside had given her a fresh start, a chance to make new friends and start her life all over again. Why was she so angry all the time?

And why does she take it out on me?

Yes, there had been some tragedies at the school. One girl burned so badly in a horrible accident. And another girl murdered in front of the whole school.

Did that explain Gretchen's attitude?

Gretchen's mom swept her hair back over her nightgown. *Time to get dressed.* The TV show had moved on to a scene of damaged buildings and crying people somewhere in the Middle East. The news was just unbearable these days.

She set down her coffee cup and clicked off the TV. Then she made her way upstairs, thinking about how Gretchen never liked the outdoors. *She even hated the day camp we sent her to.*

She stepped into Gretchen's room and gasped. Hurricane Gretchen had struck! The room looked as if it had been turned upside and everything from the closets and shelves and drawers flung everywhere.

The bedspread lay in a heap on the floor. Jeans and T-shirts littered the carpet. Her backpack lay open in a corner with notebooks and papers spilling out of it. A dresser drawer overflowing with black tights sat on the bed next to a pile of sweaters and sweatshirts.

I really don't believe this. She thinks of me as her servant. I'm just here to clean up after her.

Mrs. Page uttered a gasp when she spotted the phone

on top of the pile of sweaters. She picked it up and pushed it on. "Oh, wow," she murmured out loud. "Gretchen is *not* going to be happy. She left her phone behind."

And then . . . she couldn't help herself. She prided herself at not being a snoop. She had to keep watch on Gretchen. Had to act as a responsible parent. More than that, a caring parent. But she never wanted to be a snoop.

But here it was. And here she was, scanning through Gretchen's emails. Nothing interesting . . . nothing interesting at all.

But then Mrs. Page checked out the phone log. She glanced through the recent calls. Squinted hard at the calls Gretchen had made *because she didn't want to see what she was seeing on the screen.*

She didn't want to see these calls. She wanted them to vanish. This was the *last* thing she wanted to see.

And then, she couldn't help herself. She felt the tears run down her cheeks. And she started to murmur in a trembling whisper: "Oh no . . . Oh, please . . . Oh, no."

40.

She knew she had to act, but her brain wouldn't cooperate. The room spun. *I'm not even dressed. I haven't brushed my hair.*

Her first instinct was to drive to school, maybe catch the bus before it left for the woods or wherever it was going. But no. By the time she got dressed . . .

She spun away from Gretchen's room. She strode unsteadily into her room and picked up the phone on the bed table.

How do I reach the school? I don't know the number? Is there still Information, or has the Internet ended that?

She pushed 411 with a trembling finger. One ring . . . two . . .

She brushed the tears off her cheeks. "Can you connect me with Shadyside High School? It's kind of an emergency."

She was transferred to another operator. Then cut off.

Then heard the phone ringing at the high school on her next try.

"I need to speak to the principal. What's his name? Hernandez?"

"Who's calling, please?"

"It's Eleanor Page. I'm Gretchen Page's mother. I really need to speak to the principal."

"Can I put you on hold? I need to see if he's in his office."

"Okay. Okay. But, please—"

A *click*. Then silence.

She tapped her fingers on the bed table. Wrapped the phone cord around her wrist as she waited. And waited.

Finally, a man's voice. "Hello? This is Victor Hernandez."

"The principal?" Her voice came out hoarse. She coughed and cleared her throat. "Mr. Hernandez?" She shut her eyes, trying to steady herself, slow herself down, get her thoughts in order.

"Yes. Can I help you?"

"This is Gretchen Page's mother."

"Oh, yes. Hello, Mrs. Page. How are you?"

"Has the bus taking the cheerleaders to the retreat . . . has it l-left?" she stammered. "I really hope—"

"Yes. It's on its way to the campgrounds," Hernandez replied. "Coach Walker reported everyone is onboard. Do you need to speak to your daughter? Did she forget to bring something?"

"N-no, I don't need to speak to Gretchen. I need to speak to *you*."

"Well . . . if there's a problem . . ."

"I'll be right there," Mrs. Page said. "I'll be right there. I have to see you right away."

Gretchen pawed through her clothing. Some shirts toppled out of the bag and fell over the seat beside her. She reached the bottom of the bag, her hand grappling at the smooth leather.

"Gretchen—what are you doing?" Shannon stood in the bus aisle, leaning over Gretchen. She picked up a sweatshirt that had fallen into the aisle and handed it to her. "Did you lose something?"

Gretchen let out a growl. "Yeah. My phone. I think I left it at home." She started furiously stuffing her clothes back into the travel bag.

The bus hit a bump and several girls cried out. The bag jumped in Gretchen's lap.

"Maybe your mom can FedEx it to you," Shannon suggested.

"I can picture it. I know where I left it," Gretchen said. She slapped her forehead. "How could I be so dumb?"

Coach Walker edged up beside Shannon. "Don't worry about it, Gretchen," she said, eyeing the tangle of clothes on the seat. "I told you girls your phones will probably be worthless at the camp. There is no service up there. No cells for miles."

Gretchen gritted her teeth. "I just hate being forgetful."

Shannon helped her shove all her belongings back into the bag, and she hoisted it back onto the overhead rack. Flat, gray farmland whirred past outside the bus window. The fields were bare. The low clouds that appeared to be following the bus shut out any sunlight and made it look like the middle of winter outside.

Shannon motioned to the back of the bus. "Check out Sid. The only guy on this trip. He gets his own cabin. And he has all six of us to flirt with him. Is he a happy dude or what?"

Gretchen turned and followed Shannon's gaze. No. Actually Sid didn't look happy at all. He was in the very backseat, squeezed next to Devra. They were both talking at once, gesturing with their hands.

Squinting down the bus aisle into the gray light, it took Gretchen a while to realize they were shouting at each other, their expressions cold and angry.

Holding onto the seatback in front of her, Gretchen kept her eyes on them, watched their angry gestures. She couldn't hear what they were saying over the roar and rumble of the bus, but she could see they were practically spitting their words at each other.

Ducking her head so they wouldn't see her watching them, she was suddenly filled with confusion and surprise.

What on earth are Sid and Devra fighting about?

41.

Mrs. Page emptied out her pocketbook into the plastic tray and shoved the tray at the security guard, a lanky black woman wearing a loose-fitting blue uniform and a Chicago Cubs cap over her hair. A plastic name badge said her name was Audrey.

"In my day, we didn't have to go through a metal detector to get into school," Mrs. Page said.

"It's a different world, ma'am," Audrey replied.

Mrs. Page gazed down the long empty hall, yellow tile walls, gray metal lockers lining both sides. She heard a steady thumping sound and saw a boy two-thirds of the way to the end slowly dribbling a basketball on the floor as he walked. A maroon-and-white banner strung from the ceiling read: TIGERS ROAR.

"Do I have to remove my watch?" she asked the guard.

Audrey shook her head. "No. You can go right through. Just sign in." She shoved a long clipboard toward Mrs. Page.

She scribbled her name on the sign-in sheet. Audrey studied the signature. "Oh. Are you Gretchen's mother? She's the cheerleader, right? Very nice girl. Always says good morning."

"I'm kind of in a hurry," Mrs. Page, shoving her stuff back into her pocketbook. "I've never been here. Which way is the principal's office?"

Audrey pointed. "Make a left, then a right."

Mrs. Page turned and started to hurry away.

"Your top is buttoned crooked," Audrey called after her.

"Huh?" She lowered her gaze to the front of her pale green blouse. She saw immediately that the two sides didn't meet. She had the buttons in the wrong button holes. No time to fix it.

A few seconds later, she burst into the principal's office. The secretary behind the front desk looked up from a folder she had been reading. "Can I help you?"

"I need to see Mr. Hernandez right away." Mrs. Page saw the door to the inner office and strode toward it without waiting for the woman's reply.

"He has someone in there—"

She lurched into the doorway. Hernandez, behind the desk, was tall and broad, nearly bursting out of a gray suit, shirt unbuttoned, dark-framed glasses over his eyes.

He looks more like a gym teacher than a principal, she thought.

Two students, both blond, a boy and a girl, sat in chairs facing the desk.

All three of them looked up in surprise as Mrs. Page stepped in.

"I need to talk to you right away." She couldn't keep her voice from trembling. One hand went to her throat as if to be as dramatic as possible.

He squinted at her. "Are you Gretchen's mother?"

She nodded.

He turned to the two kids. "Let's continue our talk after lunch. Can you come back sixth period?"

They both nodded and scurried out without a word.

Hernandez motioned to a seat, but Mrs. Page remained standing. "You look upset. Is there a problem?"

She nodded. "I-I don't know where to start," she stammered. She changed her mind and slid into one of the chairs."

"It's about Gretchen?"

"Yes. Of course." She clasped her hands tightly in her lap. "I thought she was doing well. I thought she was okay. . . ." Her voice trailed off.

Hernandez removed his glasses. Pinched the brim of his nose. Replaced the glasses. Waited for her to continue, not taking his eyes off hers.

"She got on the bus for the retreat," Mrs. Page finally continued. "I went up to her room and I saw that she left her phone behind. I . . . I couldn't resist. I looked through it."

Hernandez leaned forward over the desktop. "You looked at her emails? Her Facebook?"

"Her phone calls," Gretchen mother replied. "I looked through her call log. I haven't done it for a long while. I . . . thought she was okay. But . . ."

She sucked in a deep breath. "But . . . I found all these calls. Gretchen was making calls almost every day . . . to a girl named Polly Brown."

Behind his glasses, Hernandez' eyes narrowed in concentration. "What's wrong with *that*, Mrs. Page?"

"Polly Brown has been dead for two years. Gretchen . . . Gretchen killed her."

PART THREE

42.

Hernandez uttered a sharp gasp. "Killed her?"

Mrs. Page grabbed her throat again. "I . . . shouldn't have said that. Gretchen was *responsible* for Polly's death. I mean, she didn't kill her deliberately. Polly was her best friend. They were inseparable. Closer than sisters. I—I—"

Gretchen's mother started to choke. Shaking her head, she held her throat and coughed.

"Miss Rangell," Hernandez shouted. "Please bring Mrs. Page a bottle of water."

Gretchen's mother heard scurrying in the outer office. She forced herself to swallow. Her throat suddenly felt dry as cotton. The secretary appeared with the bottle of water. Mrs. Page took several long sips.

"Better. Thank you." She smiled at the secretary, who disappeared back to the outer office.

Her smile faded as she turned back to the principal. "Gretchen and Polly were on their way to a basketball game. This was back in Savanna Mills. Gretchen was driving. She'd only had her license a few weeks, but she was a good driver, I think. Confident. Not nervous . . . like me."

She took another sip of water. "They were just a few blocks from the high school. I guess Gretchen was distracted. She was thinking about her cheerleading routines. She was the star . . . the best cheerleader at Savanna Mills. But . . ."

She stifled a sob. "Gretchen didn't see the van. She should have swerved or stopped or something. But she didn't see it. It . . . it . . ."

"Take your time," Hernandez said softly, his big hands spread over the desktop.

"It was a horrible head-on collision. Polly was reaching for something on the floor. She had her seatbelt open. She . . . she flew right through the windshield. She died before she landed. She didn't have a chance."

"Oh my goodness," Hernandez murmured, shaking his head. He lowered his eyes. "How horrible."

"Yes. Horrible," Mrs. Page repeated in a whisper.

Silence for a long moment.

Mrs. Page was the first to break the silence. "Gretchen was lost after that. I mean really lost. We . . . we couldn't get through to her. . . . Her father and I . . . we tried everything. We took her to all the best doctors. But . . ."

Another long pause.

"But we couldn't reach her. Couldn't get through to her. She was lost. Just lost. In her own world. No touch with reality." She raised her eyes to Hernandez. "She wouldn't talk to anyone. For weeks, she wouldn't get out of bed. She wouldn't eat. She . . . just tried to vanish from the world."

Hernandez swallowed. "Take your time, Mrs. Page. Tell me what happened next."

"The doctors brought her around," Gretchen's mother replied. "They found the right meds. They found the right approach. They brought her back. My marriage had broken up by then. The stress was just too much for her father and me. We couldn't handle it, and we divorced."

Hernandez shook his head. He lowered his gaze to the desktop.

"But when Gretchen started coming around, her father and I were overjoyed. We had our daughter back. And she . . . she seemed like her old self in every way."

Mrs. Rangell poked her head into the office. "Mr. Mulrooney from the State Education Board is on line one?"

Hernandez waved a hand. "Tell Anthony I'll have to call him back." He turned back to Mrs. Page. "And now you're worried—?"

"When Gretchen starts to call Polly, it means she's losing it again. Backing away from the real world.

Something starts to bother her . . . something starts to eat at her . . . and she starts to sink back. . . ."

"What do you think caused the problem?" Hernandez asked.

"I . . . I think maybe the cheerleading. I tried to discourage her. I tried to convince her to wait. To take it slow. It meant so much to her. But I shouldn't have let her join. I should have stopped her. I'm afraid she may be going back to her old pattern . . . to what she did back in Savanna Mills."

Hernandez leaned forward over the desk. "Her old pattern?"

"Back home, she picked out one girl. One girl on the cheerleading squad. And then Gretchen made herself look like a victim."

Hernandez squinted hard. "I don't understand."

"She made it look as if the girl was persecuting her. Harassing her. Doing terrible things to embarrass her. Gretchen tried to turn everyone against that girl, even though the girl wasn't doing *anything* to her. Gretchen did it all to *herself.*"

"Oh no," Hernandez muttered. "Gretchen may be doing that again. Devra Dalby, one of the cheerleaders . . ."

"That's what I was afraid of," Mrs. Page said. "When I saw she was making calls to her dead friend, I thought maybe she could be starting the pattern all over again."

Hernandez swept a hand back through his dark hair.

"You should have told the school about your daughter's history," he said. "We don't have any of this in our records, and we really should know about it all."

Mrs. Page lowered her eyes but didn't reply. "I haven't told you the worst of it. I haven't told you about the knife."

Hernandez blinked. His mouth opened slightly. He waited for her to continue.

"When Gretchen was acting most paranoid . . . when she was accusing this girl at school of trying to harm her . . . we found a knife. Hidden at the bottom of her backpack. A hunting knife. Very long and very sharp."

She shuddered. "That was the low point. That was when I was most frightened. Of course, we took the knife away. And she never used it. . . . But we couldn't get Gretchen to talk about it. I tried. The doctors tried. She never said a word."

"Oh my God," Hernandez muttered. "So . . ." He took a breath. "So you think your daughter might be dangerous right now?"

Mrs. Page bit her lip. "I . . . I . . ."

Hernandez was breathing hard. "We've had one girl badly burned and another girl murdered in a most hideous and shocking way. A lot of tragedy for this school. A lot of sadness. Too much sadness for one school." His eyes were suddenly watery. They locked on hers. "You don't think Gretchen—?"

The unfinished question hung in the air.

Then, Mrs. Page spoke in a voice just above a whisper. "I think we have to get Gretchen away from those other cheerleaders as fast as we can."

43.

Gretchen never thought it would come to this.

Sure, there was tension on the bus that brought them to this campgrounds in the woods. More than tension. A long argument between Devra and Sid that soon became a screaming fight.

Coach Walker had to go to the back of the bus and break it up. She demanded to know what the problem was. But, of course, neither of them would speak up. Devra just stared back at Coach Walker, her face tight with disgust.

Sid sat beside Devra, his cheeks bright red and glistening with sweat. He kept his eyes lowered and wouldn't say a word.

Shaking her head, hands clenched into tight fists, Coach Walker returned to her seat at the front of the bus.

The tension between Sid and Devra simmered, but the shouting had stopped.

Gretchen kept twisting in her seat, taking peeks at

them. *What did Devra do to get Sid steamed like that?* She wondered. *He looks ready to explode.*

Sid had slid across the seat, away from Devra. He had his arms crossed tightly in front of him, his face still red. He stared out the window at the passing farm fields.

Devra pushed her earphones into her ears and fiddled with her phone. She blew a strand of red hair off her face and settled back in the seat. She appeared a lot calmer than Sid. And now they both ignored one another as if nothing had happened.

Shannon leaned across the bus aisle and said something to Gretchen. But Gretchen didn't hear her. She was thinking hard about the argument—the fight—in the back of the bus, struggling to guess what could have sparked it.

Was it about me?

And then the bus had come to a stop outside the rustic camp mess hall that looked like a big log cabin. Their bags were being unloaded, and Coach Walker, clipboard in hand, was assigning them to their cabins. One for Walker. One for Sid. Three girls each in the two small cabins on the other side of the mess hall.

Gretchen was put in a cabin with Shannon and Becka.

Did Coach Walker deliberately separate me from Devra?

Not enough time to unpack. They had to rush to their first squad meeting in the mess hall. Coach Walker always insisted on promptness.

The girls wore black tights or jeans and sweatshirts

and still hugged themselves for warmth. There was no heat in the big hall, and no one had started a fire yet in the enormous fireplace against the back wall.

And then the trouble ignited again. The screams and accusations.

And this time it got really bad.

Really bad.

Gretchen covered her ears and ran screaming from the mess hall. The afternoon sun sent shifting patterns on the grass, filtering through the tall trees. Shadows moved at her feet as she ran.

Ran breathlessly to her cabin. Her bag still propped on her bed, only half-unpacked.

Gretchen knew what she had to do.

Yes, her mind was spinning, flying, pictures danced and disappeared, the cabin now a dark swirl of grays and blacks.

But she knew what she had to do.

She had to put an end to it.

She could hear the cries from the mess hall.

She had to hurry.

With a choked cry, Gretchen dug her hand deep into her travel bag . . . slid it under the clothes . . . under her cosmetics bag.

She wrapped her fingers around the knife she had hidden there, lifted it out, the long blade dull in the dim cabin light.

I'm ready.

44.

Mrs. Page struggled to tighten her seatbelt as Mr. Hernandez swerved, guiding his Subaru SUV through traffic in the Old Village. "These streets are too narrow," he said, groaning. "They were too narrow when the town was built. And now they're ridiculous."

He roared the SUV onto the sidewalk to edge it around a slow-moving garbage truck. Mrs. Page bounced against the passenger seat.

"I'm so sorry," she said. "So sorry I didn't let the school know about Gretchen's problems. But she was doing so well. Her therapist felt that getting away to a new place was the right thing to do."

Hernandez nodded, peering through his sunglasses at the line of traffic in front of them. "I don't know if we'd have done anything differently," he said. "Maybe kept a closer eye on her. Listened to her complaints about Devra Dalby a little more seriously . . ."

"How far are we from the camp?" she asked.

"Only about forty-five minutes. If traffic starts moving. We should be okay once we get past town."

They rode in silence for a while. The sun slid over the windshield, forcing Mrs. Page to shield her eyes.

"I'm sorry, but I need to ask," Hernandez said, frowning. "And there's no gentle way to ask it. Do you think Gretchen could have killed Madison Grossman? Wasn't Madison her friend?"

Mrs. Page pressed her hands together, fingers tightly entwined, almost as if praying. "I don't know. I really don't. I . . . I don't think my daughter is a murderer. She is a troubled girl. I mean . . . I can't picture her . . . I just can't imagine—" Her words broke off with a sob.

"Can you think of any reason at all she would have for murdering Madison Grossman?"

Mrs. Page shook her head. "No. No reason. Madison was her only new friend since moving here. At least, I *think* she was. You have to understand, Mr. Hernandez, Gretchen is very private. She doesn't confide in me." And then she added, as if an afterthought: "Oh. I think there was a boy, too."

Hernandez' eyes widened. "A boy?"

"Yes. I met him. Nice looking. Gretchen seemed to like him. I just got a vibe, a feeling. She didn't say they were going together or anything. He came to help her clean out the garage last Saturday."

"You don't remember his name?"

She shook her head. "I'm sorry. I don't. I was so

shocked that she seemed to have a boyfriend. . . ." Her voice trailed off again.

Hernandez hit the brake, nearly hitting the SUV in front of them. "Can you describe him?"

Mrs. Page thought for a while. "Well, he had one of those very trendy haircuts. Awful. You know. Buzzed very short on the sides and long on the top. Brown hair. And . . . I remember he had very big ears. He was nice looking, except for the big ears."

"Sounds like Sid Viviano," Hernandez said. "He's the equipment manager for the cheerleader squad."

"Yeah. Maybe," she said. "That would make sense, I guess."

"But everyone in school knows that Sid and Stacy Grande are a couple. Have been for a long time."

Mrs. Page didn't answer. She took a shuddering breath. "I thought I was paying close attention to Gretchen. She accused me of paying *too much* attention. But . . . I guess I didn't do my job. I should have been more responsible. I should have watched her even more closely."

They drove in silence for a while. The traffic eased as they left Shadyside. The afternoon sun began to dip, lowering itself over the flat gray and brown farms that ringed the town.

Mrs. Page kept her eyes shut. Hernandez knew she wasn't asleep. Was she praying?

He wondered if she had told him everything about Gretchen. He imagined there were big chunks of the story she had left out. He kept thinking about the knife they found in Gretchen's backpack. Thinking about it caused a hard rock to form in the pit of his stomach.

Dread made his entire body feel heavy as he swung the SUV into the dirt driveway to the campgrounds. Tall trees reached their limbs over the narrow drive, sending shadows over them, deepening as they followed the drive to the camp.

Mrs. Page's eyes snapped open. Her face locked in a wide-eyed expression of fear and anxiety. Spotty sunlight dappled the roofs of the line of small wooden cabins, abandoned this time of year.

The car sank into a deep hole in the dirt, then bounced back up, causing Mrs. Page to cry out.

Hernandez slowed the car as they passed two cabins with lights on, the pale light seeping from the small dirt-smeared windows. And then they could see at the end of the row of cabins a large two-story building that must be the mess hall.

A sudden movement along the path caught Mrs. Page's eye. She saw a girl running toward the mess hall entrance. And she gasped. "Is that Gretchen?"

Hernandez stopped the car as the girl neared the building door.

Yes. Yes. It was definitely Gretchen. Her blond hair flying behind her, gleaming dully in the late afternoon sun.

Yes it was Gretchen. And yes, that was a knife in her hand. A knife raised as if ready to attack.

"No. Oh no," Mrs. Page moaned.

She and Hernandez reached for the door handles, intending to leap out of the car and stop her.

Too late.

Gretchen vanished into the mess hall.

And instantly, they heard screams, shrill and frightened. High screams of terror ringing through the open windows. And the horrified shout of Coach Walker: "Stop! No—please! STOP!"

45.

Over the screams of the girls in the mess hall, Gretchen could hear the rapid thump of blood pulsing in her ears and feel the drumbeat of her heart in her chest. Fighting against her panic, she shoved open the mess hall door with her shoulder and burst into the long room.

She blinked. In her panic, her eyes were playing tricks on her. The room was suddenly bathed in red. Blood red. Everyone at the long table in the center of the room shimmering red, as if soaked in blood.

Blinking hard, she forced the real colors back, and as the blanket of red faded, she lurched toward them all, her eyes darting from one to the other. Their screams grew more shrill and desperate as she raised the knife. Waved it in front of her. Made sure that Sid saw the long blade.

Sid saw her. His eyes were wide with surprise.

He stood behind Devra with one arm around her chest, gripping her hard, holding her defenseless against him. And a knife in his other hand pressed against Devra's pale throat.

Devra's eyes rolled crazily. Her hair was wild about her face. She couldn't scream. The knife blade was too tight against her skin.

"Drop it, Sid!" Gretchen screamed in a trembling shrill voice she'd never heard before. "Drop the knife! Let Devra go—*now*!"

The other cheerleaders had jumped up from the table and backed away. They huddled against the wall.

Coach Walker stood frozen at the other end of the table, her arms stretched out helplessly, as if pleading with Sid, her face stuck in an open-mouthed expression of pain and shock.

Gretchen saw her mother burst into the room, followed by Principal Hernandez. *How did they know there was trouble?* They both froze at the door and didn't come any closer.

Gretchen took a step closer to Sid and Devra, waving the knife in her trembling hand. Her heart was beating so hard, she thought her chest might explode.

"Drop it, Sid," she repeated. "I'm serious. Let Devra go. I'll cut you. I'm not afraid. I'll cut you."

Sid pressed his knife blade against Devra's throat. "It was supposed to be Devra," he shouted, his voice ringing with anger. "It was supposed to be Devra—not Stacy. Devra was supposed to burn."

Gretchen gasped. "It was *you*, Sid? You deliberately poured the kerosene on the baton?"

"It was supposed to be Devra!" he screamed. "Not Stacy. I didn't want to burn Stacy. Devra was supposed to burn!" His voice cracked. He tightened his grip around Devra, who slumped as if defeated, sank against him, stopped struggling to escape.

Sid slid the blade against Devra's throat. Girls screamed as a thin trickle of bright blood appeared on her neck.

Devra let out a whispered moan. "Oh, please . . . It hurts. . . ."

"Don't do it! Don't cut her, Sid!" Gretchen cried. She took another step closer, gripping the knife handle so tightly her hand throbbed with pain.

I've got to keep him talking, Gretchen thought. *It's the only way. If I can keep him talking, maybe I can stop him from killing her.*

"Why, Sid? Why does Devra have to die?"

"She knows! She knows!" The words exploded from his mouth.

Blood trickled down Devra's neck. Sid kept the blade pressed against her skin.

Against the wall, Shannon and Ana were sobbing, their faces covered by their hands.

"I did everything . . . everything to ruin Devra. To make everyone hate her. I . . . I had to ruin her . . . the way she ruined my family."

Gretchen kept the knife poised. "What do you mean, Sid? What are you saying?"

"I . . . I did everything," Sid repeated. His eyes were glassy, seemed far away. He was in his own world now. Talking more to himself than to Gretchen and the others. "I stole her phone and sent those threatening text messages to you. I put the drain cleaner in your water bottle and stuffed the cockroaches in your new uniform. I . . . I put on Devra's perfume and attacked you in the gym. I had to ruin Devra. I had to show Devra I could be in charge. I had to pay her back. I wanted *everyone* to hate Devra as much as I do."

"But, why, Sid? Why?"

"She knows! She *knows!*" he screamed, eyes wild, face bright red now. "Devra and I . . . I thought we had a connection. We were going out. Stacy didn't know anything. Devra and I . . . I thought we had a good thing. I really did. I thought we had something real. And then . . ."

His jaw tightened. A low growl escaped his throat. He pressed the blade tighter against Devra's neck.

"Don't kill her! Sid—you don't want to kill her!" Coach Walker shouted, finally finding her voice.

"Why shouldn't I?" He spit the words at her. "She killed my family. She ruined my life. I thought Devra and I were close—really close—but then . . . then . . . My dad, he worked at Dalby's. In the shoe department.

He was a good salesman. And he was a loyal worker. He always talked about what a good department store it was and how he enjoyed his job."

He stopped, his chest heaving. He took a deep breath, as if it was too much for him to tell. His eyes were wild. They wouldn't rest on any spot. Large drops of sweat rolled down his forehead and cheeks.

"Devra had my dad fired," he finally continued his story, lowering his voice to nearly a whisper. "She reported him to the manager. She said he was rude to a customer, and she had him fired. We were going out, Devra and I. I thought we were serious. I thought it was a real thing. And she had my dad fired. Don't you see? I didn't mean *anything* to her. Nothing at all."

He jerked Devra hard, spinning her to the side.

"It broke my dad," he said, his voice cracking again. "My dad was never the same. And neither was my family. She ruined my family. Ruined everything. She was supposed to burn. Not Stacy. Not Stacy. Devra was supposed to burn."

"No!" Gretchen screamed. "Sid—don't!"

I've got to keep him talking. It's the only chance.

"What about Madison?" Gretchen cried. "Sid—what about Madison? Do you know who killed Madison?"

He blinked. "Who killed Madison? I did. I did, of course."

Gretchen gasped. Loud sobs rang out beneath the

low rafters. Gretchen's whole body tingled. The knife trembled in her hand. It wasn't the answer she had expected.

She liked Sid so much. And now she was learning she didn't know him at all. He was a murderer. A murderer. She trusted him. She opened herself to him. And he was a murderer.

"Why, Sid? Why did you kill her?"

"She had a video on her phone. She didn't even know she had it. But she found it. A video at the football game. It showed me wiping kerosene on the fire baton. It showed me. So clearly. Madison had the video. And she said she was taking it to Hernandez."

He nodded to the principal. Hernandez and Mrs. Page still hadn't moved. They stood frozen at the mess hall doorway.

A sob escaped Gretchen's throat. She nearly dropped the knife. "Oh my God, Sid. I don't believe . . . I just can't believe you killed Madison."

He sneered at her. "What choice did I have?" He jerked Devra hard again. "Was I supposed to let her show the video to Hernandez? To the police? Enough talk. Devra has to die now. *She* was supposed to burn—not Stacy. Not Stacy!"

His eyes rolled crazily in his head. Spit flew from his mouth with every word. "It was supposed to be Devra! Devra—not Stacy!"

"Let me go!" Devra found her voice. Her plea came out in a high-pitched shriek. "Let me go! Let me go!"

She made a sick gagging sound as Sid slowly slid the blade across her neck.

46.

Against the wall, girls screamed. Courtney dropped to her knees. Becka and Shannon hugged one another. Ana kept her hands covering her face.

Devra uttered a long groan. Sid loosened his hold on her, the knife still raised, and she sank to her knees.

Gretchen felt a surge of energy. The room went red again. Before she realized it, she was diving forward, stumbling, almost staggering toward Sid. She let out an angry roar, a cry like a hurt animal.

All that betrayal . . . all of the cruel jokes Sid had played on her . . . the cockroaches . . . the threatening texts . . . the acid in her garage . . . his lies . . . all the while, pretending to care about her.

Later, Gretchen would think about how she had been used, how he had entrapped her in his insane desire for revenge.

But now, she felt only fury, a fury that made the room go blood red, that pushed her forward, that forced her to scream like an enraged beast. She tossed away her knife, lowered her shoulder, and barreled into Sid.

He saw her coming, but he didn't react fast enough. She drove her elbow into his midsection, and the knife dropped from his hand. He groaned and tried to back away from her. But Gretchen drove a fist hard under his chin.

She heard a cracking sound—the sound of his neck breaking? His head snapped back. His eyes went wide, his mouth dropping open in pain and shock. He fell backward, fell hard, smashing the back of his head against the wooden table edge as he went down.

Sid crumpled to the floor, his legs splayed at an odd angle, his head tilted, eyes shut. Gretchen stood over him, every muscle tensed, breathing noisily, expecting him to climb to his feet.

But he didn't move.

She turned and saw that Devra had crawled to Coach Walker. Walker had wrapped a dish towel around Devra's throat. "She'll be okay," Walker shouted to everyone. "The cut isn't deep."

The other cheerleaders gathered around Devra and Coach Walker. They all began talking at once.

Principal Hernandez was down on his knees, shaking Sid gently, trying to wake him. "He's breathing. Can anyone call 911?" he demanded. "Does anyone have cell service?"

Gretchen's mom rushed forward and wrapped

Gretchen in a hug. Tears had swollen her cheeks and Gretchen could feel her fluttering heartbeats as they hugged.

"You're okay," Mrs. Page kept repeating. "You're okay. You're okay."

Gretchen swung away from her mother and hurried over to Coach Walker, who wrapped a fresh towel over Devra's cut. "You're not in any trouble, Devra," the coach assured her. "The bleeding has almost stopped. There might be a tiny scar. . . ."

Gretchen knelt beside Devra. "I'm so sorry," she said. "Really. I'm so sorry."

Devra blinked. "Sorry?"

"For acting like such a jerk," Gretchen said. "For accusing you of everything. For blaming you for all the terrible things that happened. All the horrible things that Sid did. I'm so sorry."

Devra narrowed her eyes at Gretchen. She shook her head. "I can't believe you're apologizing. You just saved my life!"

Gretchen stared at her, her mind spinning. "Hey, I *did*—didn't I?"

Despite the horror, both girls broke out laughing.

"A surprise party?" Gretchen said into the phone. "When?" She listened to Courtney's answer. "Ana is having a Sweet 17 party?"

"She was away for her sixteenth," Courtney explained.

"She says she was cheated. So she's doing it this year. Only she doesn't know it. We're going to throw a surprise party for her."

"Awesome," Gretchen said. "Can't wait. How are you going to surprise her?"

Before Courtney could answer, Mrs. Page entered Gretchen's room. "Who are you talking to?" she demanded.

"Got to go," Gretchen told Courtney. "My mom is here." She clicked off the call. "That was Courtney," she told her mother.

Mrs. Page couldn't hide her relief. "Nice. Sorry to interrupt." She squinted hard at Gretchen. "You feel okay? No problems from . . . from what happened?"

Gretchen raised her fist and squeezed it. "My hand still hurts from punching Sid."

"Otherwise you're okay?" her mother demanded. "I talked to Dr. Knoller. She said you seemed fine when she talked with you this morning. But she said it would be understandable if you felt a little in shock, or if you felt emotional or stressed about what you went through."

Gretchen sighed. "Please, Mom. Give it a rest. I'm okay. Really. Physically and mentally. Please believe me."

"You don't have to snap at me," Mrs. Page said. "I'm just trying to show some concern. That's all." She started to the door. "Would you like eggs for lunch?"

"That would be nice," Gretchen said. "Thanks."

She listened to her mother's footsteps going downstairs. For a long moment, she sat against the headboard of her bed, staring at the morning sunlight out the twin bedroom windows. A bright fall day. And she felt bright, too. She felt light as air, as if her problems had been solved, as if all her worries were in the past.

She heard a *ping*. From her phone. At first, she didn't recognize the sound. Then she remembered: a text message.

She picked up the phone and glanced at the screen.

And read the message:

YOU KILLED ME, GRETCHEN. BUT I'M NOT GOING AWAY. BFF. Polly

Dan Nelken

R. L. Stine is one of the bestselling children's authors in history. His Goosebumps series and Fear Street series for young people have over 400 million books in print and have been translated into thirty-five languages. R.L.'s anthology TV series, *R. L. Stine's The Haunting Hour,* has won three Emmy Awards for Outstanding Children's Series. Goosebumps was the basis for the feature film starring Jack Black as Stine himself. R. L. Stine lives in New York City with his wife, Jane. Visit his website at www.rlstine.com.